LIZZIE

A NOVEL

LIZZIE

A NOVEL

DIANE FANNING

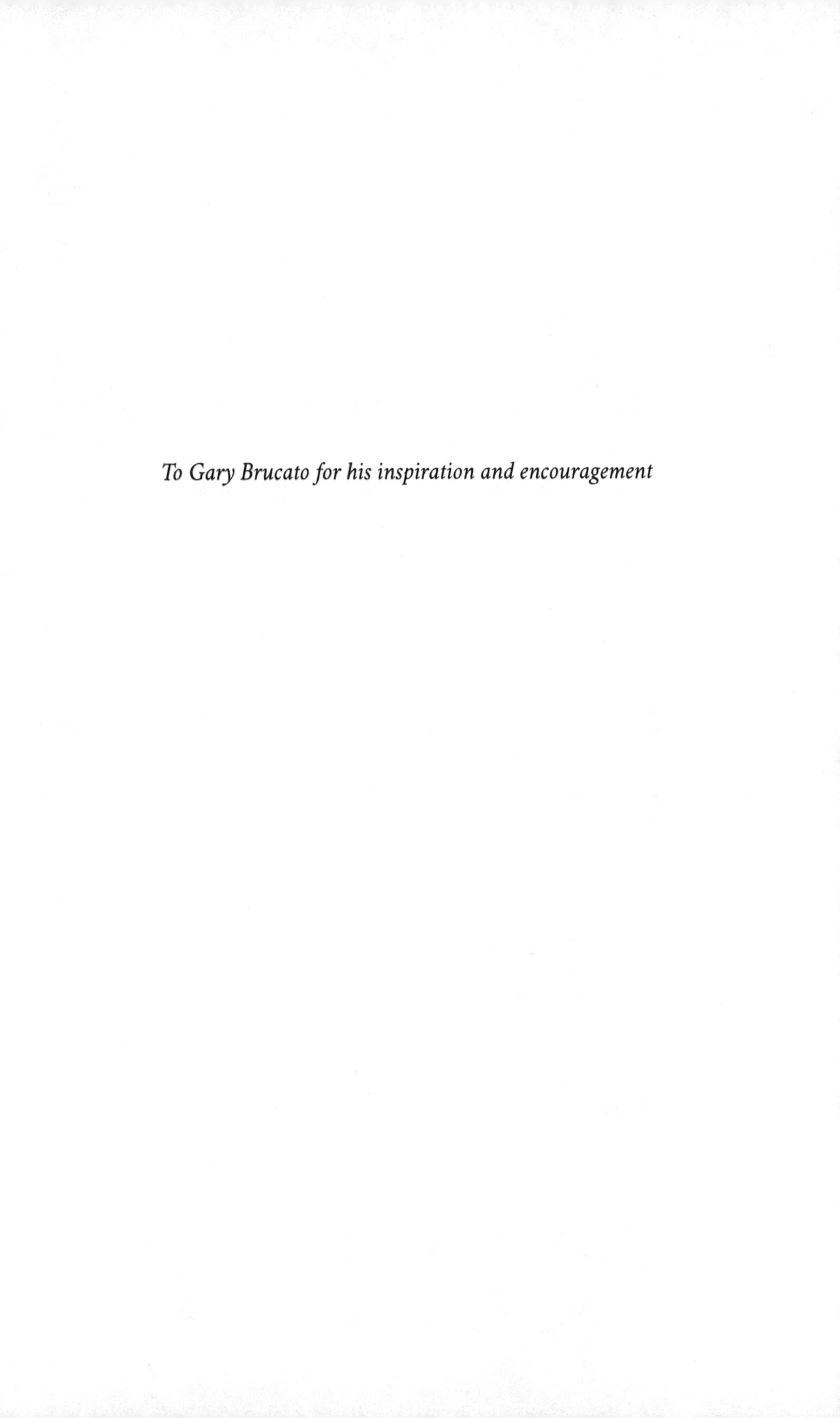

To Gary Brucato for his inspiration and encouragement

Praise for Lizzie

"I once playfully challenged Ms. Fanning, a prolific true crime author with a detective's turn of mind, to write a fictional account of the trial of Lizzie Borden for a ferocious double domestic murder. She responded with *Lizzie*, masterfully blending historical details, intriguing suppositions and thrilling prose to breathe new life into the most infamous cold case in American history."—Gary Brucato, Ph.D., Visiting Scholar, Boston College and Co-author of *The New Evil: Understanding the Emergence of Modern Violent Crime*

"Master of true crime Diane Fanning reimagines in fictional form a case that continues to haunt us, Lizzie Borden. Part true crime and part storytelling, she ably explores the shifting relationship between sisters at the center of a scandalous double homicide."—Dr. Katherine Ramsland, award-winning author of *Confession of a Serial Killer* and *The Serial Killer's Apprentice*

Prologue

Fall River boomed after the Civil War with the explosive addition of many cotton mills with their massive, native granite factories employing thousands. Before long, the town was the world's largest producer of cotton cloth. Growth did not stop there. Soon, iron mills, printing factories, and more were added to the industrial landscape. All were served by Fall River's own railroad line founded by Nathaniel Borden, connecting them directly to Boston.

Despite the surge of wealth into Fall River, it still maintained some of its rural flavor. Downtown—which the locals called downstreet—clung to its old-fashioned storefronts and the rutted, horse-dung littered streets that ran beside them. Everyone knew the shopkeepers' names, and most were personally greeted when they entered their establishments.

Housewives continued to make their own bread for the family but eagerly awaited the arrival of bakery carts to add pies and other sweet treats to the table. They did not need to keep a constant watch but only listen for the sound of the approaching bells attached to the springs on the undercarriage of the delivery vans.

The Quequechan River, running through the downstreet area, had suffered greatly from industrialization. Factories and private privies dumped their waste in its waters, creating a vile stench that grew in intensity every summer. Still, boys regularly swam in the contaminated waters, oblivious to the risks they took.

Grocery shops abounded in the center of town, but in most cases, the variety was limited to one selection of each item. Brown and white sugar and even crackers were stored in bulk containers and sold by the pound. Most households bought flour by the barrel, which stood in every kitchen where abysmal poverty did not rule. Most of these shops had only one scale that they used to weigh everything from cod and mutton to cornmeal and salt. The weighing pan was seldom, if ever, cleaned. With the exception of beets, turnips, and potatoes, fresh produce was not stocked.

Wealthy, prominent citizens thrived in Fall River. They were reluctant, however, to share their riches with the less fortunate. Their employees led desperate lives, struggling to feed their families and keep a roof over their heads that, if they were lucky, did not leak and did not have rickety walls that served as tunnels for the harsh winter winds. Most lived in company housing where the lack of creature comforts left them in a constant struggle for survival. Heaven forbid they had to cope with the serious illness of a family member.

Fall River, though, was not an anomaly in its time. Its social structure was reflected in many cities and towns across the country, where the working poor carried the weight of the wealthy until the strain broke their backs.

Chapter One

Andrew Jackson Borden was born in Fall River, Massachusetts, in 1822 to Abraham and Phoebe, who named him after the man who was a celebrated hero of the War of 1812 and soon to be the seventh president of the United States. Although Andrew's father was a gardener and a laborer, Andrew possessed great ambition. There was no fortune waiting for him upon his parents' demise, but he was determined to carry his modest branch of the Borden family into the prominence that others had bestowed upon the name. His hard work, sharp business acumen, and conservative risk assessment talents drove him and his family from penury to riches.

August 4, 1892, began as an ordinary day for Andrew Jackson Borden. As was his habit, he left his home at 92 Second Street that morning, greeted by the faint odor of horse manure that flowed down every street in town. He walked his bustling street, passing by four homes, a restaurant, stables, a photography studio, a liquor store, a wholesale produce business, a carriage trimmer, a plumbing company, and a machine shop. Turning left and down one block further, he reached Main Street. He had multiple business interests on the Borden Block there that he checked every weekday. He cut a tall figure, neatly clothed in a dark suit with wide lapels, a high-collared white shirt with a black bowtie. He was well known and readily recognized the moment he came into sight.

Even in the morning, the heat and humidity sat heavy on the shoulders of Fall River and beat hard down on Andrew's head. Within a block, the smell of horse waste was overwhelmed by the stench of the river stinging

Andrew's nostrils with every breath. The horses pulling carriages and wagons appeared wilted, their straw hats drooping down on their heads, their tails hung limp with barely enough energy to shoo away flies.

Andrew's first stop was the Union Savings Bank, where he was president. The doors were propped open in the vain hope of teasing a breeze into the building. Abraham Hart, the treasurer, greeted him. "Good morning, Mr. Borden."

"Good morning to you, Mr. Hart. Business running smoothly?"

"Without a doubt, Mr. Borden," he said with a furrowed brow. "Are you feeling well today?"

"I'm a bit under the weather. Probably something I ate. It will pass."

The two men spent a couple of minutes flipping through the pages of the bank's ledger before walking over to the other bank in the building, The National Union Bank, where Andrew was a stockholder and depositor. After a few encouraging words with a colored man seeking a loan, Andrew made a brief stop at B.M.C. Safe Deposit & Trust Company, where he was a director.

Crossing the street, he entered another building he owned at 6 North Main. The lower floor housed a Hatters and Gent's Furnishings shop operated by Jonathan Clegg. Inside felt like an oven despite the fans moving the air as briskly as they could. A subtle trace of the river's odor slipped into the warp and weave of the garments on display. "Do you think I'll be able to move to the new address next week, Mr. Borden?" Clegg asked.

"I don't see why not, Mr. Clegg. I will stop by there on my way home and make sure the changes are moving along in a timely manner."

Leaving the shop, Andrew walked to the new location, past City Hall and down South Main, stopping near Spring Street. Two men were working on the outside of the building, lowering the front windowsills to nearly sidewalk level for the display of goods on offer. He went straight inside and looked around the first floor before climbing the steps to check on the second. Andrew swayed in the increased heat on the higher level and hurried back down the stairs.

He walked away from the building. Realizing he'd failed to greet the workers, he turned around in the middle of the street. As he approached the two carpenters, Joseph Shortsleeves and James Mather, the men stopped their work. Shortsleeves said, "Good morning, Mr. Borden."

"A good morning to both of you," he said and crossed back over the street to head home. His steps grew heavier with every block. At one time, he strode down the street in a blur, now, he always moved at a statelier pace, but today's weather slowed him down even more. The driving force of this once energetic man had faded as he aged. Now as he neared seventy, he tired quickly and needed a nap every day. His once dark, full beard and thick, long hair had turned snowy white. Andrew trimmed both with a fastidiousness that befitted a man of his prominence.

Arriving at 92 Second Street, Andrew paused in a shady spot to admire his home. He was quite proud of his accomplishments. From street fishmonger to undertaker to the owner of mills, a bank, city houses, and farms, he had risen further up the ladder of success than he once thought possible. The two-family house that he'd bought at a steal and renovated for his family made Andrew's heart swell with his love of life. In 1871, he purchased the stately Greek Revival house adorned with two-story columns on each corner of the front façade and smaller ones by the front entrance.

Before Andrew's wife and daughters moved into the house, he removed all the chimneys and installed steam heat. He tore down the wall between the two bedrooms on the first floor and created a dining room. The parlor and the kitchen spaces remained the same. Upstairs, he tore out the second kitchen, transformed the space into a bedroom for himself and his wife, and turned the former parlor into a guest bedroom. The existing two bedrooms were occupied by his two adult daughters, Emma and Lizzie.

When he finished his renovation, the front stairs led up to the front half of the second floor. The guest room there was currently occupied by his first wife's brother and good friend, John Morse. The back stairs in the kitchen led to the marital bedroom and another flight to the third-floor attic where the live-in servant spent her nights.

At first, they had no running water, but as soon as Fall River ran lines up the street, Andrew refurbished the home again. He put a flush toilet in the cellar and ran water into the kitchen. He even installed pipes in the barn. Andrew's only disappointment was the lack of electricity since it was still not available in that neighborhood.

His second wife, Abby, had pressured him to put in gas lines for the lights, but Andrew was too nervous about the frequency of fire and explosions caused by gas in homes to run the risk. They still used kerosene lamps at night, and every woman in the house complained about the oily, acrid smell.

He wished that was his family's only complaint. He had not foreseen the consequences of giving a piece of real estate to his wife, Abby, five years ago. His two adult daughters, Emma and Lizzie, surprised him with their hearty objections that he bestowed real estate upon her, but gave nothing to the two of them. Even though he rectified the situation by presenting the two with an equally valuable property, a current of animosity continued to flow between the women of his household, making him wonder if the previous warmth he perceived among them was nothing but pretense.

Abby told him his daughters were spoiled and ungrateful. His daughters insisted that Abby was greedy and had married him only for his money. In his presence, at least, they never openly confronted each other with their animosity, but he could feel it churning beneath the surface every day.

The other problem with his daughters was their dissatisfaction with the home he had made for them. He was proud of what he had created here but he knew his daughters—particularly his youngest Lizzie—were not happy with the house or the neighborhood. Lizzie blamed their residence for the fact that neither she nor Emma had ever been married. Again and again, she told him, "We are living beneath our station. We should be up on the hill, in a grand house where suitors would call and prominent women would visit us for tea, where party invitations and social outings would fill our days. We don't belong here hemmed in by immigrants and crowded by commercial establishments."

Perhaps he should make their dream come true now—he could certainly afford it. *But was it too late?* He wondered. *Quite probably for Emma, at 43 years of age, she was no man's ideal mate. Likely, my oldest daughter will remain a spinster. But Lizzie? At 32, she was too old for the traditional marriage market, but like my second wife, she could find a widower with a couple of children in need of a female presence in the home.*

Andrew sighed. *Shouldering the responsibility for the well-being of three grown women is a perilous burden—the pitfalls are many, and the rewards are few.* He opened the gate and walked to the side door in the back, but it was locked tight. He retraced his steps and approached the front door. He slid in the key and turned, but it would not open. He banged on the door, muttered under his breath, and kept attempting to achieve the impossible with a key that failed to function. Finally, after a struggle, the door was opened from the inside by the family servant, Bridget Sullivan.

He complained about both doors being locked in the middle of the day before placing his key on the mantle and walking into the kitchen expecting to see his wife. When Abby was not there, he went up the rear stairs certain he would find her in their bedroom. When he returned to the sitting room, his daughter Lizzie came down the other front staircase and joined him. "Was there any mail, Father?"

"Yes, Lizzie. But none for you today. Where is Mrs. Borden? I did not see her in my room or in the kitchen."

"A boy delivered a note from a sick friend, and Mrs. Borden rushed to help the woman."

"Who?"

"I don't know, Father. I did not see the note. You looked exhausted. You need to take a rest."

Andrew muttered in agreement and laid back on the elegant mahogany-framed couch. Lizzie bent over him, helped him get comfortable, with one foot rested on the flowery-carpeted floor and the other balanced on the sofa with its sole pointing outward. Lizzie left the sitting room, passing through the dining room and into the kitchen.

Chapter Two

Abby Durfee Grey was a 37-year-old spinster when widower Andrew surprised her with a wedding proposal. She knew that the main reason he wanted to marry was to have someone around who could care for his home and his two daughters, Emma, 14, and Lizzie, 4. Nonetheless, she gladly accepted his proposal—he was born with a distinguished surname, and his ambition was already making its mark in Fall River. She suspected his fortune would grow with every coming year. Although Andrew and his daughters still lived in his father's house with other relatives, Andrew offered her the possibility of becoming the mistress of her own home in the near future—something she had begun to despair would never happen.

At the time of her marriage, Abby was short—just five foot tall—and already rather overweight. In the ensuing years, her weight had ballooned to 250 pounds. The only thing worrying Abby on August 4, 1892, was the precariousness of her financial security. Now that Andrew was nearing the end of his seventh decade, she was concerned that she would be left homeless and penniless when he died. She did not trust her two stepdaughters—she believed they would want to claim as much of their father's fortune as possible and push her out of the house as soon as they could.

That was why she was delighted when John Morse arrived for a visit the night before. John was the brother of Andrew's first wife, and the two men were confidants and advisors to each other. After an exchange of letters, Andrew clearly understood Abby's point of view and regarded his two nieces as immature and irresponsible with money. John promised Abby he would push Andrew to write a will.

John and Abby's plan included a large endowment for Abby's widowhood. The house, all the other real estate and business interests would become the property of Abby Borden. Andrew's daughters, Emma and Lizzie, would each receive a lump sum of $25,000.

The two co-conspirators strolled around the backyard discussing the details without suspecting that Lizzie, never known to be an early riser, stood just by the side door listening to every word. "Will that make me appear greedy, Mr. Morse?"

"Of course not, Mrs. Borden. Andrew gives both girls an allowance of $4 a week now. They'd have to live 120 more years to spend $25,000 and, of course, they will still live under your roof and not have to worry about food or shelter—unless a miracle happens and one of them wed. That amount is more than generous."

Back inside the house, she carried the coffee tray out to the sitting room and served John, thanking him again for his willingness to speak with Andrew on her behalf. Before Abby could return to the kitchen, Andrew arrived downstairs and joined John in the sitting room. Abby said, "I'll bring the breakfast into the dining room right away, gentlemen."

Abby set the table and invited them to dine. Apart from a few pleasantries, she sat quietly, listening to the two men talk about taking a trip out to Swansea the next day to look over Andrew's farm. John said that he might have a few ideas for making the rural property more profitable for Andrew.

After a second cup of coffee, John left out the back door to go to Weybosset Street to visit the home of his niece and nephew. Abby bid him farewell and added, "Make sure you come back for the noon meal." John nodded his head in agreement.

Andrew emptied slop pails, brushed his teeth in the kitchen sink, and left for work. Lizzie came back down at her usual time and went into the kitchen to get some breakfast. Abby sent Bridget out to wash the windows and flicked the feather duster around the dining room and living room. Abby went up to the guest room to tidy up after John and put fresh pillow slips on the bed.

Only two people were known to be inside the house—Abby and Lizzie.

Chapter Three

Bridget Sullivan was, as always, the first person in the household to rise on the morning of August 4, 1892. She was twenty-five years old with dark hair, deep-set eyes, and a broad mouth that never knew a smile.

She awoke at quarter past six with a dull headache and left her tiny, hot room clutching her chamber pot and descended two floors. She went out the back door to a spot in the far backyard past the heavy-laden pear trees and the dusty leaves of the grape arbor and dumped the contents. She swished it out in the barn faucet and reentered the house. After placing the pot back under her bed, she returned to the kitchen. She had hoped she would feel better after getting a breath of fresh air, but if anything, she felt worse.

The heat of last night's dinner still hung heavy in the kitchen, making her stomach churn. She raked the cold ashes from the previous day and scrubbed the range top with a stiff brush.

Going down to the cellar, she appreciated the cooler temperature even though it was damp and musty. She picked up kindling to revitalize the fire in the cook stove. Upstairs, she added a screw of paper to the dying embers and placed the twigs on top. When that was lit, she went back down the steps to retrieve a full coal hod. Climbing stairs and preparing a meal while feeling headachey and nauseous was an onerous task.

She'd been in the United States just seven years, driven here by the abject poverty in County Cork, Ireland. She'd held several other positions before settling with the Borden family two and a half years ago. She knew the workload in this household was much lighter than in others. She was not expected to clean any of the bedrooms or dump any chamber pots other than her own. Nonetheless, she had threatened to leave on several occasions because of the disharmony between Andrew's daughters and their stepmother. To induce her stay, Abby agreed to take on some of the maid's responsibilities and offered a pay raise as well. Still, she wondered if it would be worth a cut in salary and an increased workload to be out of the house and away from the undercurrent of hostility in the home.

Mrs. Borden came down the back stairs into the kitchen. "Good morning, Maggie. What is that sour look on your face?"

That was another strange thing about being a domestic in this new country. Bridget knew she had to respond to whatever name the family chose to use for her. In this household, the previous servant was named "Maggie," and that is what the Bordens chose to call her. She never dared correct them. "I'm not feeling very well this morning, ma'am."

"Neither am I, but you don't see me making faces. The moment Mr. Borden comes downstairs, I will carry the food into the dining room. Neither Mr. Borden nor Mr. Morse need to start their day looking at your dreary countenance."

At Mrs. Borden's instructions, Bridget prepared a hot mutton broth from the previous night's meat. Once she had the pot boiling, she turned her attention to the side dishes. Coffee was next. A couple of months ago, Emma had come home from a trip to Boston with one of the new filter plungers from France. Bridget didn't quite get all the fuss about the coffee made in the fancy invention, but she had to admit that it required a lot less tending than the percolator.

She heard footsteps coming down the front stairs and was certain that it must be the visitor, John Morse—Miss Emma was out of town, visiting friends in Fairhaven—and Miss Lizzie never rose this early. She unlocked the back door and retrieved the morning milk delivery. Then she put out a pitcher of water for the iceman.

Mr. Morse and Mrs. Borden walked through the kitchen and out into the backyard. Much to her surprise, Miss Lizzie followed them, stopping at the door. The youngest daughter appeared to be eavesdropping on her mother and uncle but that was none of Bridgett's business.

She ignored all three of them as she mixed up cornmeal, salt, butter, and milk and poured it into melted fat from the kitchen grease pot. She browned one side of the johnny cake, flipped it, browned the other side, stacked one after the other on a plate sitting on the stovetop to stay warm, and covered it all with a cloth to remain moist.

As she pulled out platters and filled one with the browning bananas and the other with slices of bread and cookies, Miss Lizzie raced past her without a word. Moments later, Mr. Morse and Mrs. Borden entered the back door. The gentleman went out into the sitting room, and Mrs. Borden gathered up the coffee service and followed him. Bridget dashed out the back door and into the yard to vomit. *All I want to do,* she thought, *is crawl back into bed and sleep the day away.*

Bridget had made a johnny cake for herself, but now she looked at it, and the thought of taking a bite made her stomach somersault. She began cleaning up the kitchen. When the bell rang, indicating they were through with the meal, Bridget retrieved the dirty dishes and cleaned them.

A short time later, Mr. Morse and Mr. Borden entered the kitchen, and Mr. Morse left by the back door. Mr. Borden emptied his slop buckets and brushed his teeth before leaving for work. Miss Lizzie came down to the dining room just after 8:30.

"What do you want for breakfast, Miss Lizzie?" Bridget asked.

"I don't really want anything, but I suppose I should have something. I'll have coffee and cookies. I'll get them myself."

Bridget rushed outside and vomited again. When she returned to the house, she got no sympathy, just curt instructions from Mrs. Borden. "I need you to wash the windows on the first floor, inside and out." Bridget went to the cellar to gather a bucket and brushes, then out to the barn for the ladder.

While the servant washed the windows, Miss Lizzie stepped out the side door and told Bridget she was locking the rear entrance. Bridget assumed that the youngest daughter did not want her to draw water from the kitchen faucet to perform the chore and use the one at the barn, and she did so until it was time to wash the inside of the windows.

Lizzie let Bridget back in the house and re-locked the door. Bridget was washing the interior windows in the dining room at quarter till eleven when she heard a commotion at the front door and hurried to see what was happening. The front door was double-locked and bolted—unusual for that time of day. She struggled to release the bolt, uttering "Oh, Pshaw!" in her frustration, causing Lizzie to laugh on the landing of the front staircase. That startled Bridget, but she brushed it off as meaningless. Later, she would spend a lot of time wondering about its significance.

Bridget returned to the windows in the dining area, and a short while later, Miss Lizzie joined her and set up the ironing board to press her handkerchiefs. "There's a sale of ginghams down the street, Maggie, at Sargent's Yard Goods Store. They are selling it for just eight cents a yard. Why don't you go there and get a bargain before they are all gone."

"I know all my dresses are looking worse for wear, but today, Miss Lizzie, I am feeling so tired and so sick, I think I must lie down for a bit instead."

"In your room in the attic?" Lizzie asked.

What a peculiar question, Bridget thought. *Where else would I rest?* "Yes, Miss Lizzie. If you need nothing else, I'll go up right now and take a break before the noon meal. I'll try to get down to Sergeant's after that."

"Of course, Maggie."

Lizzie followed Bridget into the kitchen and listened while the woman climbed the two sets of stairs.

Chapter Four

L izzie looked down at the body of her father, stretched out on the lounge, both of his feet had slipped down to the floor. She folded his coat and placed it under his head. Blood still flowed on the couch, on his clothing—it seemed to be everywhere—his face a mangled monstrosity of wounds with one eyeball split in two.

She went through the dining room, into the kitchen, and up to the foot of the back stairs and shouted. "Maggie, come down."

With a clatter of footsteps, Bridget rushed down, asking, "What is the matter?"

"Quickly, quickly! I need you to go for Dr. Bowen."

"What?"

"It's Father. Go now."

Bridget turned toward the front of the house and made a step in that direction.

"No, no, Maggie. Don't go into the sitting room. Go out the side door. Go get somebody and return as fast as you can. I cannot bear to stay in this house alone any longer than necessary."

Bridget paused for a moment as more color drained from her already pale face. Then she was gone, racing out the side door and across the street to Dr. Bowen's house. Lizzie felt panic grabbing at her chest. She was all alone in a house with two dead bodies. She struggled to calm her breath and think with clarity. The fading taste of the pears she ate still lazed about her tongue.

In a few minutes, Bridget burst back in the door. "Miss Lizzie, Miss

Lizzie, Mrs. Bowen said the doctor is not in but she is expecting him at any moment. She'll send him over as soon as he arrives. Where were you? Didn't I leave the screen door hooked?"

"I was out in the back yard and heard a groan. I went in, and the screen door was wide open. Maggie, do you know where Alice Russell lives?"

"Yes."

"Go and get her. And hurry. I just can't bear to be alone here."

Bridget grabbed her hat and shawl hanging by the door and raced toward Second and Borden Street, only to learn Alice no longer lived there. She followed directions down Borden to the little cottage shop next to the bakery. Miss Russell was standing at the screen door when she walked up. Bridget quickly explained the problem and then hurried back to the house.

Seeing Bridget leaving for the second time that morning, the next-door neighbor, Mrs. Adelaide Churchill, peered into the Borden windows to see what was afoot. She noticed Lizzie going to and fro, wringing her hands. She knew something must be wrong. When she spotted Lizzie standing by the screen door, she raised her window and asked, "Lizzie, what is the matter?"

With satisfaction, Lizzie recognized the gossip-hungry expression on Mrs. Churchill's face. *She was perfect for spreading my version of the story,* Lizzie thought. "Oh, Mrs. Churchill, is not the weather just awful? So hot. So humid. It's hard to think. But do come over. Somebody has killed Father."

Lizzie sat down on the lower step of the back stairs just before Adelaide entered the door. Her neighbor's tawny curls were pulled back in a bun, framing a plain face and prominent ears. Adelaide crossed the room and placed a hand on Lizzie's arm. "Oh, Lizzie, that cannot be true. Where is your father?"

"In the sitting room," Lizzie said.

Adelaide disappeared through the closed dining room door. She returned to the kitchen; her face was ashen. Her jaw went up and down as if she were trying to form words, but no sound issued from her mouth. When she recovered from her shock, she asked, "Where were you when this happened,

Miss Borden?"

Lizzie suspected that Adelaide might be the first, but she would not be the only person to point a questioning finger at her. "Out in the barn."

"Where?"

"The barn—in back of the house."

A disapproving look replaced the shock in Adelaide's eyes. "Whatever for?"

Lizzie bristled at the thought of justifying her actions to anyone and almost did not respond. Reluctantly, she said, "Oh, I went looking for weights for my fishing trip next weekend at Dr. Benjamin Harding's cottage in Marion."

Adelaide stared at her for a moment, trying to comprehend her overly detailed response. "Where is your mother?"

"I do not know. She received a note to go see someone who was sick. She went to see them. I thought I heard her come in."

Adelaide knew if Abby were home, she would have hurried downstairs after hearing all the noise. In her absence, Adelaide took charge. She crossed the street to the stable, seeking help. There, John Cunningham telephoned the police at 11:15. In unfortunate timing, most of the police officers were on their annual picnic at Rocky Point Amusement Park in Warwick, Rhode Island, leaving a short staff at the station. Marshall Hilliard sent the only man he could locate, Officer George Allen.

When Adelaide returned, she asked if Lizzie had found Abby. Lizzie said, "I don't know, but that she is dead, too. Father must have an enemy because we all have been sick, and we think the milk had been poisoned. I must have a doctor."

Adelaide left immediately to find another physician to come to the house. Dr. Kelly lived in the house next door, but he was Irish. Dr. Chagnon lived just behind the Borden home on Third Street, but he was French Canadian. Worst of all, both were Catholic—the bias against that religion was at a fever pitch in Fall River. Adelaide dismissed them both and hurried further afield to locate an acceptable Protestant physician.

No sooner had she left than Dr. Bowen arrived. "Lizzie, what is the matter?"

"Father has been killed."

"Did you see anybody?"

"I have not."

"Where is your father?"

"In the sitting room."

* * *

When Dr. Seabury Bowen's wife informed him of the tragic death of his neighbor, he assumed heart disease was the culprit. He entered the sitting room and found Andrew lying toward his left side on an old-style mahogany sofa. He recoiled at the first sight of the mutilated face of his patient and friend. The still-dripping blood brought him back to the duty at hand.

He checked for a pulse on his wrist and neck. Finding none, he pulled a stethoscope out of his medical bag, hoping beyond reason that he would hear the slightest murmur of a heartbeat. He found no sign of life. Andrew's coat was wedged behind the pillows where his head rested. He thought it odd that Andrew would bunch up his garment that way when he usually was very particular about his clothing. He looked but found no sign of struggle—Andrew's hands were not clenched, no contraction of muscles that would indicate pain. His clothing was not disarranged, and his pockets appeared untouched. No piece of furniture had been overturned. It seemed that the victim had been asleep when the first blow killed him instantly, allowing his body no time to react. He could not have been dead for more than twenty minutes.

He did not believe that the body had moved at all since the first blow landed. The wounds extended from the eye and nose to the area around the left ear. In that small space, Dr. Bowen counted eleven distinct cuts, each of the same approximate depth and general appearance—each cut four and a half inches in length. Any single one of them would have proven fatal. He checked his watch: 11:30.

* * *

While the doctor was engaged in the sitting room, Alice arrived, and, much to Lizzie's annoyance, her friend's first concern was not for her—Alice was more interested in Abby's whereabouts than in Lizzie's well-being. "Where could she have gone? Which friends are close enough to her that she would run out in such a hurry?"

Lizzie swallowed deeply and answered, "The only person I can think would give her that sense of urgency is her younger sister Sarah Whitehead."

When the doctor strode into the kitchen, tears ran down his face from the brutality of the discovery in the sitting room. He paused as all the faces turned towards him. "Oh! He is murdered! Murdered!" he said. "Lizzie, where were you?"

"In the barn, looking for some iron." As she answered, her neighbor and her friend fluttered around her, patting her forehead with a damp cloth and waving a fan in her direction. Lizzie was the only one present who bore any semblance of calm.

When Dr. Bowen asked for sheets to cover Andrew's body, Bridget said, "They are in Mrs. Borden's room, but Mr. Borden usually leaves the key to their room on the mantlepiece in the sitting room. I don't want to go in there, sir. Could you please get it for me, Dr. Bowen?"

The doctor nodded and returned with the key. Alice took it from him and volunteered to go upstairs with Bridget. Alice unlocked the bedroom door, and Bridget retrieved the sheets.

After covering Andrew's body, Doctor Bowen stepped toward the side door to leave, but Lizzie stopped him. "Please telegraph Emma, beckoning her to return home. Do not tell her the worst, because one of the ladies where Emma is visiting is old, and it would shock her."

As the doctor departed, Bridget said, "Miss Lizzie, if I knew where Mrs. Borden's sister, Mrs. Whitehead, lived, I could see if Mrs. Borden was there and tell her Mr. Borden was sick. When she gets here, we can tell her the horrible truth."

"I am almost sure I heard her come in and go up the front staircase," Lizzie said. "She must be up there. Why don't you go upstairs to see?"

Wringing her hands, Bridget said, "Wouldn't she have heard the commotion and come down by now? I can't go up there alone, Miss Lizzie."

"I'll go with you," Adelaide said.

The trepidation in the women's ponderous steps was heard by the two waiting in the kitchen. Alice held her breath and clung to Lizzie. Adelaide and Bridget gasped, and Alice echoed the sound into Lizzie's ear. Footsteps thundered down the stairs. Bursting into the kitchen, Adelaide and Bridget's breath was ragged, their eyes darting about like cornered rabbits. Bridget wrapped her arms around Adelaide and sobbed.

"Is there another?" Lizzie asked.

Bridget moved her jaw but could not summon a word. Adelaide managed to find her voice. "Yes, she is up there. At the top of the stairs, we could see under the bed to the other side. Mrs. Borden collapsed on the floor, her body resting on her knees and face. Her head is surrounded by a dark pool of blood."

Alice wrapped an arm around Lizzie's shoulders and encouraged her off the step and into a rocking chair. Adelaide fanned Lizzie with a newspaper. Although Lizzie enjoyed the breeze across her face, she was annoyed to have Adelaide standing that close to her. Alice picked up on her friend's discomfort, sat in the chair next to her, and took charge of the fanning. Lizzie rested her head on Alice's shoulder and closed her eyes.

Dr. Bowen returned to the house with his wife Phoebe, entering the kitchen through the side door. "You need to go upstairs now, Doctor," Adelaide said.

The doctor climbed the stairs with dread. Walking into the guest room, he saw the horrifying site of Abby face down on the floor between the bed and dressing table, with her hands under her body. He reached down and felt for her pulse but found nothing. The large pool of blood beneath her body confirmed that she, too, was murdered.

Her head was hacked with eleven distinct cuts that seemed to be the same size as those he found on Andrew's body. All but two or three of the blows came from the rear, but two or three were struck from the front, cutting off nearly two square inches of flesh from the side of her head. Again, there was no sign of struggle—not a chair misplaced, not a towel disturbed on the nearby rack.

* * *

Downstairs, the doctor's wife, her pale hair pulled on top of her head and her startling blue eyes wide with shock, asked, "What can I do to help?"

"Please wet the corner of a towel and come wipe Lizzie's face," Alice said. As Phoebe ministered to Lizzie, Alice suggested, "Why don't we all move into the dining room? It will be cooler in there away from the stove." They opened the dining room door and closed it behind them. "Come, Lizzie, sit on the lounge and put your feet up. You need to rest after your shock."

A few minutes later, a man in a dark blue uniform with a billed cap burst through the kitchen door. "I am sorry, ladies, to intrude, but the front door was locked. I am Officer George Allen."

The policeman drifted out into the sitting room. He returned with his jaw dropped low. "The blood," he said. "It's seeping through the sheet. Are you sure he's dead?"

"Yes," Adelaide answered. "Dr. Bowen told us so."

Shaking his head, Allen said, "There is a crowd gathering in the street. A painter was outside, and I left him to guard the front of the house. I need to search through every room to make sure no one is hiding anywhere."

Allen opened closet doors, moved furniture, and covered every inch of the first floor. Then he left to report his findings at the station house. All the women thought it odd that he did not bother to check the second floor for any intruders.

Much to Lizzie's dismay, more officers swarmed the house in no time. One asked, "Miss Borden, where were you when your father was killed?"

"I was in the barn."

"Are there any Portuguese working at the farm over the river for your father?"

Of course, they would want to blame a foreigner, Lizzie thought. "Mr. Eddy and Mr. Johnson. Mr. Eddy has been sick."

"Has Mr. Eddy or Mr. Johnson been in town this morning or here at the house?"

"No sir," Lizzie insisted. "Neither Mr. Eddy nor Mr. Johnson would hurt my father."

"Did you hear any screams or outcries?"

"No, sir. I heard some sort of peculiar noise."

"Can you describe the noise?"

"No, not very well. Something like scraping."

The officer left the dining room, and Lizzie reclined again on the lounge with Alice wiping her face with cool cloths and Adelaide fluttering about the room in a near panic. She was reluctant to remain in the Borden's house but was too fearful to go outside and return home. Phoebe remained in the kitchen with the distressed Bridget.

The Bristol County Medical Examiner, William Dolan, poked his high forehead and full, dark mustache into the dining room. He studied the women and then withdrew into the sitting room.

Noting the deep downward creases by his mouth, Alice asked, "Does he ever smile?"

"His preoccupation with the dead might make any levity impossible," Lizzie said.

Officer Allen returned with additional officers. Now, there were seven uniformed men in the house. The invasion felt like a military action in the confines of the modest house. The men gathered near the sitting room and had a whispered conference with Dr. Dolan.

Officer Michael Mullaly left the group and approached Lizzie, who sat up when he entered the room. "Miss Borden, what was your father in the habit of carrying in the line of money or jewelry every day?"

"A silver watch, an old pocketbook with some money, and he wore a gold ring on his little finger."

"Are there any hatchets in the house?"

"Oh, yes," Lizzie said. "They are everywhere." The expression on her face turned sour as bile rose in her throat with the belated realization that she should have denied any knowledge of such implements in her home.

Bridget spoke up, pulling the officer's attention away from Lizzie. "I'll be glad to escort you down into the basement to show you where the axes and such are kept."

Chapter Five

John Morse, the brother of Emma and Lizzie's mother, was six-foot tall, with a gray beard and hair, an aquiline nose, and piercing blue eyes. After twenty years spent out west near Hastings Mill, Iowa, where he owned a prosperous cattle business, he sold the business and returned to Massachusetts, settling in South Dartmouth more than two years ago. The morning of August 4, 1892, he left the Borden home before nine o'clock. His first stop was the post office, where he wrote a postal card and sent it west.

He walked more than a mile in the rising heat to the home of his niece and nephew on Weybosset Street. The young man was not at home, but he conversed with his niece, Anna, for more than an hour. When he left, he walked down to Pleasant Street and caught a ride in a horse-drawn carriage, disembarking at the corner of Second Street and walking the rest of the way to the Borden home.

He noticed a lot of noisy people out in the street in front of the house but thought nothing of it. Most days, Second Street bustled with traffic and pedestrians. He slipped down the side yard to the back and stopped at the pear tree in the middle of the yard. He picked two or three pieces of fruit and ate most of one before going inside.

When he entered the kitchen, he knew right away that something was amiss. The room was crowded. Dr. Bowen was there, as well as a couple of police officers. "Is someone sick? Is someone dead?" John asked.

All eyes turned towards him. Dr. Bowen placed a hand on John's forearm. "Andrew and Abby are both dead."

"Both of them? How is that possible?"

"I am sorry to tell you that they have been brutally murdered. Andrew in the sitting room…"

"There must be a mistake," John said as he ran out of the kitchen. When he saw his former brother-in-law lying on the sofa covered with a blood-stained sheet. He did not believe the sight before his eyes. He lifted a corner of the linen, and his heart sank when he recognized Andrew. Dr. Bowen accompanied him up the stairs. John stopped at the point where he could see the body of Abby in a drying pool of blood.

John rushed back into the dining room where Lizzie sat on the lounge accompanied by Adelaide and Alice. "For God's sake, Lizzie, how did this happen?"

"I do not know, Uncle John. I do not know."

John froze in place for a moment, then shook his head. "Something must be done. The person responsible must be arrested," he said as he returned to the kitchen.

In the dining room, the three women listened to John's raised voice as he questioned the police officers. Above their heads, they heard pounding footsteps as other policemen went from room to room, searching for any items of significance. Most hoped answers would soon be forthcoming, and the intrusion into the home would end.

Dr. Bowen entered the dining room and looked closely at the only surviving family member of that morning's tragedy. "Alice, take Lizzie up to her room to rest. And Lizzie, you go upstairs and stay there." The worry on his face stopped any objections before they could start. Adelaide took her leave to return home as Lizzie left the dining room.

* * *

Alice cupped Lizzie's elbow and led her into the parlor and out into the main entry to avoid crossing through the sitting room. She steeled herself to mount the stairs, but after she got Lizzie halfway up, she saw there was no reason for unease—the guest room door was shut tight.

At the door to her room, Lizzie said, "When it is necessary for an undertaker, I want Winward."

Alice was taken aback that her friend could think of practical matters in a time like this and was surprised at Lizzie's willingness to hire the highest-priced man in the business. She knew Andrew would be appalled at the wasteful spending. She wordlessly nodded her head and pulled Lizzie's door shut.

Lizzie heard the door latch click and was grateful to finally be alone. She hadn't imagined that two deaths could bring such chaos and tumult to her home. She wanted them all gone and wished they would take her pounding headache with them.

Her solitude was cut short by a knock on the door. Dr. Bowen entered and found his patient leaning forward, holding her head in her hands. "Do you have a headache?"

"I have throbbing pain wrapping all around my skull."

The doctor pulled out the blue bottle of effervescent bromo caffeine, a common remedy for headaches and mental strain. After giving her a dose, he said, "Lie down, Lizzie, and try to get some sleep."

Lizzie stretched out and tried to drift off, reveling in the easing of her pain, but she could not sleep. The commotion in the house and the turmoil in her thoughts kept her mind jumping too fast to slip into peace. No father, no husband, and still men were controlling her life. She desired her freedom more than her life. She wanted to run away—run for as long as she could—go as far away as possible. Find a place where no one knew her name. She knew it was a foolish dream. She could never survive on her own—she had little education, no skills, and never once worked to buy her food. Hopelessness engulfed her as she slipped into a dreamless sleep.

After a while, she heard a small tap on her door and saw it swing open halfway. Alice peered in and seeing Lizzie's eyes open, she said, "I just came by to check up on you. Are you feeling any better?"

"My headache is gone, but I cannot sleep and still feel out of sorts. Will you sit with me and keep me company?"

Alice took a seat on the sofa, and Lizzie sat beside her. The two women chatted about inconsequential things beyond the horrors of the house. Bridget knocked on the doorframe a bit later and showed in the Reverend Mr. Buck, the city missionary at Central Congregational Church into the room. He was perfect for his role—he looked like an Old Testament prophet with his full, white beard and his wavy white hair. Alice relinquished her seat, and the Reverend sat next to Lizzie.

He read encouraging and comforting verses of scripture to Lizzie and offered homilies to lift up her soul. Lizzie felt a calm come over her as if this man was a direct conduit to immortal life.

The peaceful interlude did not last. A balding man with a walrus moustache poked his head into the room. "I'm Assistant Marshal John Fleet. Do you know who committed the murders, or had you seen anyone around the premises whom you would suspect?"

"I only saw Maggie and Mr. John Morse, who stayed the night in the room where Mrs. Borden was found dead. But they could not know anything about this."

Fleet, a man of suspicious nature, squinted his eyes in disbelief. "Who is this Mr. Morse?"

"He is my uncle."

"Do you think Mr. Morse had anything to do with the killing of your parents?"

"No. I do not think that he had because he left the house this morning before nine o'clock and did not return until after the murders."

Fleet leaned in towards her as if daring her to lie. "Where were you when the murders were committed?"

"I was up in the barn."

Pointing an index finger at her face, he asked, "What do you mean by up in the barn?"

"I mean that I was on the second story," Lizzie said, forcing a blank countenance and erect posture.

"Where was Bridget Sullivan at this time?"

"She had gone upstairs to make her bed."

"Do you think she had anything to do with the killing?"

"No. Maggie had gone upstairs before Father rested on the lounge. And when I returned to the house, she was still in her room."

"How long were you in the barn and away from the house?"

"About half an hour."

"Did you see anyone while in the barn going in or leaving the house?"

"No, I did not."

"Do you know anything further about these murders?"

"I know nothing further than my father came in about 10:30 or 10:45. I was in the dining room, ironing handkerchiefs and left that task to greet him. He seemed very tired and weak. I encouraged him to lie down on the lounge in the sitting room and rest."

"Did you return to your ironing?"

"No. I'd planned to do so but then remembered I needed to go out to the barn. I went out and up to the top floor. I was gone for about half an hour. When I came back inside, I found Father dead where I left him. I called Mag—uh, Bridget to come downstairs because someone had killed Father. I sent her to get Dr. Bowen."

"Have you any idea who could have done this?"

"No. I do not know that my father had trouble with anyone."

Alice interrupted. "Lizzie, tell him all you know about the man who came to the house."

"Well, about two weeks ago, a man came. They had some talk about Father's vacant shop on South Main Street. Their voices grew louder. The man sounded angry. I heard Father say, 'You cannot have the store for that kind of business.'"

"Who was that man?"

"I do not know. I did not see him and could not hear all that he said. I do know that he came here that morning at about nine o'clock. When their conversation ended, I heard Father say, 'You have stayed long enough, and I would thank you to go.' I heard the door shut and assumed the man went away."

"Did your mother receive a note?" he asked.

Before answering, Lizzie corrected his false assumption. "Abby is not my mother. She is my stepmother, but yes, she did receive a note."

"Did you see it?"

"No."

"Do you know who brought it?"

"I do not know, but I thought it was a boy."

"What did your mother do with the note?"

Lizzie opened her mouth to correct him again but saw Alice give a quick shake of her head. "I do not know but, in all probability, she burned it in the kitchen stove."

When both Marshall and the Reverend left the room, Lizzie's headache was threatening to return. She removed her Bengaline silk skirt and navy-blue blouse for something more comfortable—a pink and white wrap—and went downstairs.

Lizzie realized the error of returning to the throng almost immediately. The Assistant Marshall spotted her change of clothing and said, "Miss Borden, you changed your clothing?"

"It is my home, sir. I did not know I needed your permission here." She turned away from him, but before returning upstairs, she noticed that the bodies of Andrew and Abby had been moved into the dining room and placed on undertaker's boards. She turned to the medical examiner and said, "Doctor Dolan?"

"Yes, Miss Borden."

"What is happening now?"

"We will be performing the autopsy in here," he said.

Lizzie paled. "But—"

"I imagine you would not know, Miss Borden, but that is standard procedure with a murder in one's home. I don't think you will want to pass through this room until we have completed the procedure."

Lizzie turned away abruptly, her skirt making a tight swirl as she retreated to her bedroom. Sergeant Phillip Harrington followed her and asked for the clothing she had been wearing.

Lizzie glared at the man who was years younger than her. "I will not turn over my personal items to a boy I do not know."

To Lizzie's dismay, her haughty tone did not send him on his way. He exasperated Lizzie by asking her many of the same questions she just heard from Fleet. The sergeant was equally disturbed by Lizzie's behavior and her calm and collected manner. He sought out Fleet to share his concerns.

Chapter Six

Bridget was descending the stairs when she heard voices in the kitchen and paused to listen. A man who sounded like the first policeman to arrive at the house said, "I don't like that girl."

"What is that?" the Marshall asked.

"I don't like that girl. Under the circumstances, she does not act in a manner to suit me; it is strange, to say the least."

"I was out in the barn, and what she said makes no sense. I want your men to give that place a complete going over. Every nook and corner must be looked into, and the hay turned over."

Nodding, the policeman said, "If any girl can show you or me, or anybody else, what could interest her up here for twenty minutes, I would like to have her do it."

"I know. It's incredible."

Bridget waited until the men had left the kitchen before coming all the way down. She knew they must be talking about Miss Lizzie. *Did they think she did it? Can they be right? Either way, I don't think I can bear spending another night in this house.*

* * *

Dr. Bowen went upstairs to check on his patient, closing the door behind him when he entered. Seeing the pained expression on Lizzie's face, he asked, "Has your headache returned?"

Lizzie mutely nodded her head.

"You really must avoid going downstairs again until the police and medical examiner are out of here. I'm sure your maid can bring you anything you need."

"I feel lost, Dr. Bowen. Lost in my own home."

"I know. It is a trying day. But you need to avoid the chaos as much as you can."

A sharp rap on the door startled them both. Dr. Bowen cracked it open. "May I help you, Marshall Fleet?"

"We need to search this bedroom."

"I'll see Miss Lizzie. Just wait a moment," he said and shut the door. "The police want to search your bedroom."

"Must I see all these people now? It seems as if I cannot think a moment longer, my head pains me so."

"I'll explain and see what they say." He stepped out into the hallway. "My patient is not doing well. She wants to know if it is absolutely necessary for you to search this room."

"Yes," Fleet said. "I've got to do my duty as an officer and cannot leave the premises until I have searched the whole of the house."

Dr. Bowen slipped back into the room. "I believe you should let them search your room now, Lizzie. The assistant Marshall said that he will not leave until he does. I think it would be best to get it over with and get them out of your home."

"Very well, Dr. Bowen. I am sure you are right. Let them in."

As soon as the door opened, I asked, "How long will it take you?"

"It won't take me that long, Miss, but I have to search it thoroughly."

"I do hope you finish soon I am under a doctor's care. All this uproar will make me sick. You won't find anything since I always keep my door locked. No one else could enter my room or even throw anything in here."

Lizzie turned to leave the room, but Fleet stopped her. "You say, Miss Borden, that you went out to the barn this morning and remained out for a half an hour."

"No, sir. I did not."

"What do you say then?"

"I say that I went out in the barn and was out there from twenty minutes to half an hour.

"You told me this morning, or you told me when I saw you before, that you were in there half an hour."

Lizzie jutted out her chin and straightened her spine. "Well, I do not say so now I was there from twenty minutes to half an hour."

"What do you make it now, twenty minutes?"

Lizzie's eyes widened, and her nostrils flared. Through gritted teeth, she said, "No. From twenty minutes to half an hour."

Lizzie stood guard at the bedroom door, suspecting the first cut into one of the bodies had begun as a whiff of slaughterhouse rose from the lower floor, making her nose twitch. She tried to ignore the stench as she watched the men open her bureau drawers and ruffle their hairy hands through her undergarments. She observed them tearing her bedclothes apart, searching among the linens and under the pillows. She felt violated. There was one place she prayed that they would not look—and they did not. Her prayers were answered.

* * *

The searchers went into Emma's bedroom, and Lizzie breathed a sigh of relief. The feeling, however, was short-lived. Fleet barged in on her again, going straight to the door that connected her room to Andrew and Abby's room. "Where is the key to this door?"

"That is Father's room. You cannot get in that door. It is always locked."

"I should like to get in there some way or another."

"The only way is to get in there is by going round to the back stairs and going up that way."

Fleet narrowed his eyes, suspecting the credibility of every word from Lizzie's mouth. He started to leave but stopped again and pointed to another door. "What door is this?"

"A clothespress. I have a key that will open it."

Fleet's shoulders slouched. "I wish you would produce it. I want to know

31

what is in there."

"Well, there's nothing in there but clothing," she said, knowing full that he wanted her to unlock the door but not wanting to give an inch without a direct order.

"I want to see," Fleet said. "I want to look in there."

Lizzie unlocked the door and stepped out of his way, feeling sullied as if Fleet were touching her as he ran his hands through all the dresses hanging neatly on hooks. Nonetheless, she was grateful he was not pulling them out one by one and throwing them on the floor. The way his fingers twitched, she felt certain that he would have if she had not been standing there watching him.

Chapter Seven

Emma Lenore Borden was ten years older than her sister Lizzie. After their biological mother died, the day-to-day responsibility of caring for her two-year-old sister landed on her shoulders. Their interactions developed more like a mother-daughter bond than a relationship between siblings.

On August 4, 1892, she was about 15 miles away from the family home on Green Street in Fairhaven, visiting Helen and Rebecca Brownell. When the telegram sent by Dr. Bowen arrived at that house, Emma was reading in the parlor. She heard a knock on the front door before hearing Helen call out. "Emma, you have a telegram.

Emma rushed into the entrance, where one look at the solemn expression on her friend's face informed her it was not good news. "What is it, Helen?"

Helen handed the paper to Emma, who grew alarmed the moment she realized it was from Dr. Bowen. "Oh dear, Helen! Dr. Bowen wants me to return home immediately. It must be Father's health is failing. Oh my!"

"I'm so sorry, Emma. There's a train leaving for Falls River shortly, but we have enough time to make it there if you pack quickly," Helen said.

Emma's eyes darted around the room. She felt frozen in place. "Come, Emma." Helen grasped her elbow and led her to the guest room, where they gathered Emma's belongings.

"I know Dr. Bowen would not have asked me to return home immediately unless Father's illness threatened his very life. I cannot fathom living without him. I am so sorry to be rushing out on you like this."

"Do not give it a thought, Emma. Come now, let's get to the station and put you on that train. I will pray it is all a false alarm. Please let me know as soon as you can."

"Thank you, Helen."

Helen sat with her on the bench, waiting for the train's arrival. Beside her, Emma sat upright and rigid as if the slightest slouch could doom her father's life. Boarding the train, she settled into a plush seat in a secluded spot away from other passengers. She resumed her upright posture with her feet side-by-side on the floor and her hands embracing each other in her lap.

Although it was a sunny day, the world outside looked drab and forbidding. Listening to the clack of the train speeding over the tracks, she made contradictory wishes that the miles would fly faster and that she would never arrive to face the bad news. From time to time, she had to shake her hands to relieve the numbness caused by the tightness of the fingers wrapped around each other.

Upon arrival in Fall River, Emma hired a carriage to take her home. Coming down Second Street, she heard the murmurs of a large crowd of people. She grew alarmed, realizing they were all standing in the street in front of her house, and a line of police officers were keeping them out of the yard. Before facing all those people, she wanted to know what happened.

Exiting the conveyance, she crossed the street to Dr. Bowen's house. The Bowen's maid, Molly, answered her knock on the door. "Is Dr. Bowen here?"

"No, Miss Borden, he is not. I believe he is—"

"Miss Emma," Dr. Bowen's twelve-year-old daughter Florence interrupted. "What is happening at your home?"

"I do not know. I just arrived from Fairhaven. Your father sent me a telegram, but it did not explain. Is your mother here?"

"No. I believe she is over at your house, too."

"What's happened?" Emma said, grabbing Florence's hands. "Please tell me?"

"I do not know. Mother told me to stay over here and not go outside."

"Oh dear, how shall I get through that crowd?"

"I will help you, Miss Borden," Molly said. "Let me have your case. I will walk up to the front gate and loudly demand entrance to bring it inside. That should distract enough of the crowd that you can slip up the side and into the rear door."

"And put Mother's old shawl across your shoulders and over your head. It will help disguise you," Florence suggested.

Emma looked across the street at the murmuring horde. She was not certain that it would work, but she nodded her head in assent because she could think of nothing else. She watched as Molly shouldered through the mass of people, some of whom shouted at her as she pushed them aside. As she spoke loudly to the policeman by the gate, Emma saw most heads turning in Molly's direction. She scurried across the street and heard someone shout out her name as she approached the police officer at the side door.

"Please, sir, I am Emma Borden. This is my home." Emma looked back over her shoulder and saw the crowd turning and moving in her direction. "Please, sir, let me in before they catch up with me."

"I'll have to check—"

"There is no time, sir."

The screen door slammed into the officer's back. Dr. Bowen's arm reached out and pulled Emma inside. In the kitchen, she was greeted by sighs, pats, and expressions of regret from Bridget, Phoebe, and Alice.

"Why?" she said. "What has happened? What is wrong?"

Dr. Bowen slid his arm under her elbow. "Come, Miss Emma. Let us go into the parlor. It is cooler there."

"Dr. Bowen, is it Father? Did he have a stroke? Did he take ill from something he ate?"

"Sit down, Miss Emma," Dr. Bowen said.

"But—"

"Sit, please."

Emma complied, and Dr. Bowen sat next to her and took her hands in his. "Miss Emma, your father is gone."

"Gone? What happened? Couldn't you save him?"

"Emma, your father did not take sick. Your father was murdered in his home."

Emma bolted to her feet and pushed Dr. Bowen's hands away. "No. I do not believe it. It is impossible. I want to see him immediately."

The doctor rose, put an arm around her shoulders, and eased her back down on the lounge. "Miss Emma, it breaks my heart to tell you, but you do not want to see him until the mortician has time to clean him up."

"Abby, I must see to Abby," Emma said as she started to rise again.

Dr. Bowen gently lowered her back down. "Miss Emma, your stepmother was murdered, too."

Disbelief, shock, and horror danced across Emma's face. "Oh no, my sister? My little Lizzie? Is she gone, too?"

"No. Miss Lizzie is alive and well but quite distressed, as is to be expected."

John strode into the parlor. "Emma, you're home." He turned to Dr. Bowen and asked, "Does she know?"

"Yes, Uncle John, I know. How is Lizzie?"

"Dr. Bowen, have you told her the worst about Lizzie?" John asked.

"No, I have not." Dr. Bowen shook his head.

"What? What is it? What is wrong with Lizzie?" Emma asked.

Dr. Bowen sighed. "Judging by their behavior, I fear that the police believe Miss Lizzie to be responsible for the murders."

"No! No! That cannot be true. They cannot believe that," Emma protested.

"I worried about the same thing, Emma," John said.

"Does Lizzie know?"

Both John and Dr. Bowen shook their heads. Dr. Bowen said, "I did not think it would be in the best interest of her health to be aware of that at this time, Miss Emma."

"Where is she?"

"She is resting in her room," John said.

"I am watching her closely and giving her the medications she needs," Dr. Bowen added. "I suggest that you have some nourishment and retire to your room soon after."

"I am not hungry, doctor. I'll have a cup of tea, then go upstairs."

The crowded and oppressive environment was getting to everyone in the household. At Phoebe's suggestion, Bridget decided to vacate the premises and spend the night with Molly at the Bowen home. Alice slept in Andrew and Abby's bedroom, and John in the guest room where Abby met her death. A police officer was posted at the side door, and more than one at the front of the house.

No one at 92 Second Street slept well that night. Emma cried herself to sleep and jerked awake several times, clutching her bedclothes in fear. John's sleep was disturbed by every little noise outside the house, keenly aware that with Andrew's death, he was the only male family member in the house and that came with the responsibility of keeping everyone under its roof safe until morning. Lizzie's peace was torn to shreds as she was haunted by repetitious, dark dreams of Mrs. Borden pounding on her door and her father crying at the foot of the bed.

Chapter Eight

Phoebe accompanied Bridget over to the Bowen home and called for her maid when she entered the front door. "Molly, Bridget will sleep in your room tonight. You know where to find spare blankets to make a pallet on the floor."

"But, Mother," Florence interrupted, "Wouldn't Bridget be more comfortable in our guest room?"

"I think not, Florence. It is not appropriate. She would not be able to relax in such an unfamiliar setting. She'll be more at ease in Molly's room, which is much like her own."

"It's in the attic and horribly hot, Mother. I don't know how you even expect Molly to sleep there in the summer."

"That is quite enough, young lady. Please go to your room."

"But I haven't had any supper," Florence whined.

"Molly will call you when supper is prepared. Now, go."

In the kitchen, Molly and Bridget worked together, preparing the family meal. "That Florence seems to be a very sweet girl," Bridget said.

"That she is," Molly said. "She'll probably be just like her mother when she grows up, though. Don't take me wrong. Mrs. Bowen is a good and fair mistress, but she wants everything and everyone in their place, and that includes me."

* * *

When Lizzie awoke the next morning, she thought for a moment that yesterday had been nothing but a bad dream. The enormity of that day's events confirmed reality and turned her stomach into a hard, cold pit. She was grateful when she stood in front of her washstand and saw that a pitcher of water was waiting for her. She did not remember bringing one up yesterday, but someone did.

She poured water into the basin noticing that it was a lukewarm, pleasant temperature thanks to the heat that remained in the house from the preceding day. She picked up a clean flannel and dipped it into the water, wringing before applying a generous amount of lavender soap. Reaching under her nightgown, she applied the lather to her armpits and under her breasts.

She rinsed out the cloth and wiped down the soapy areas. She continued this process all over her body, uncovering one piece at a time while remaining in her full, loose night attire. Halfway through, when the water appeared murky, she dumped it into her slop bucket and refilled the basin.

After dressing, she came downstairs Friday morning with her slop bucket and disposed of its contents in the toilet in the basement. Back upstairs, Emma was in the kitchen. She had already started the fire in the stove and had the coffee pot heating on a burner. "What do you want for breakfast, Lizzie?"

"Where is Maggie?"

"She spent the night with Dr. Bowen's maid. I don't know that she will ever be back."

"What will we do? Who will take care of the house?"

"That's the least of our worries right now, Lizzie. The two of us will manage today. After the funeral, we will worry about domestic matters. Bridget may change her mind, or we may have to find someone else. We'll have to wait and see. Now, what can I get you for breakfast?"

"I'll just have a couple of cookies with my coffee. I'm too weary to consume anything more."

Emma put cookies on a plate, poured two cups, and placed it all on a tray. She took two steps towards the dining room before remembering that it was occupied by the undertakers preparing the bodies for burial. "Let's go in the parlor, Lizzie."

Sitting down, Emma asked, "Lizzie, where were you when Father and Abby were murdered?"

Lizzie pursed her lips, and her eyes narrowed to slits. "You, too, Emma?"

"Lizzie, I am sure others have asked you, but I mean no ill will. I do not know how you survived and, in that moment when I thought I'd lost you, I nearly crumbled into dust."

Lizzie cast a sidelong glance in her sister's direction. "Maybe *you* will believe me. I needed lead. I had a broken window screen needing repair. I went out to the barn to look for it." The moment the words left her mouth, Lizzie wished she could swallow them whole. She had told others she needed sinkers for a fishing trip. *No matter*, she told herself. *Surely, confusion is a sign of grief.* "I answered you, Emma, now please leave me in peace. I've answered so many questions from so many people; I am sure to get another headache if you continue."

Emma picked up the tray and carried it into the kitchen but returned in just a few minutes. "Lizzie, we need to publish a reward announcement. It would be best to have it published tomorrow."

"Whatever for?"

"To find whoever is responsible for this tragedy in our home."

"Pray tell, sister, what will that accomplish? Will it bring Father back to us?"

"No, Lizzie, but if we do not announce a reward, people will wonder why, and they will gossip, and rumors will grow until no one in town will even look at us."

"We're Bordens, Emma. People will always pay attention to us."

"That is true, sister. But what kind of attention? A delay could raise suspicions that we were responsible for the loss of Abby's and Father's lives."

"I can understand that reasoning and see why you find the timing important, Emma. But why do we need to spend our money? Father has many friends and business associates who owe a lot to them. They should post the reward."

"And perhaps they may, Lizzie. But we must be the first, and we must offer the most."

"Our financial security is finally insured. We know what our future now holds. We will be able to have comfort until our dying day. Why should we throw any of that away?"

"No matter how or when Father died, he would have provided for us."

"I would have thought so, too, Emma, until I overheard Mrs. Borden and Uncle John whispering about the will. They wanted to get Father to change it. Abby wanted the whole estate to be under her control. The plan was that we would receive a pittance, and we would be dependent on that woman once Father died."

Emma's eyes went wide and wild. She darted around the room, looking through doorways to see if anyone could have overheard Lizzie. She stood in front of her younger sister and said, "Lizzie, you must not say anything like that ever again. People will read the wrong meaning into your words. Of course, we want to post a reward. We want the killers captured. We want them tried for murder. Period. Say nothing else about the reward except that we hope to award it to the person who brings the answers to us."

Lizzie leaned forward and whispered, "Eventually, someone will be arrested—not necessarily the guilty party. They will be charged and buffaloed into a guilty verdict, and the town will be satisfied. No one cares who did it. They only care that someone is punished. I only hope that it is not someone I know."

"Oh, hush, Lizzie, please. Do not draw any more attention to yourself. Rumors against you are already in the street and in the newspaper."

"The newspaper? Really? Father has not even been laid to rest yet. What did you read?"

"A druggist somewhere has claimed that you tried to purchase prussic acid from him the day before the murders."

"That is ridiculous, Emma. Clearly, Father and Mrs. Borden were not poisoned."

"I know, Lizzie. Nonetheless, a vacuum gives rise to rumors. People in fear readily succumb to deceit. We must take a public stand now. And I think a reward is the strongest statement we could make."

Lizzie stared at the floor and sighed. "Very well, Emma. What do you think is the appropriate amount for the reward?"

"I think $5000 would entice anyone with information to come forward."

"$5000 for *any* information?"

"Oh no! That would set us up for paying multiple rewards, and that will never do."

"That's the first practical thing that you've said this morning."

"Here's what I have written for the announcement so far: 'To anyone who may secure the arrest and conviction of the person or persons who occasioned the death of Mr. Andrew J. Borden and wife.' Does that sound right to you?"

"Yes, it does, Emma. But $5000? Does it need to be that much?"

"We cannot afford to be stingy. Half the town seems to believe we have inherited a massive fortune. Although not paltry, the amount is far less than suggested by many gossips. We do not want to appear greedy."

"It galls me, sister. However, you have convinced me. Please proceed with the publication of the announcement. And let us pray that no poor but innocent wretch gets swept up and hanged by his neck until he dies."

Chapter Nine

In Fall River, the latest news, and its counterpart, unadulterated gossip, flowed like water through rapids. Before long, the prussic acid story in the newspaper brought multiple visitors to the Borden door. First was the Reverend Mr. Buck. He automatically assumed the story was false and desired only to commiserate with Lizzie. "My dear child, you must feel wounded to the quick with that treacherous story in the newspaper."

"I don't even know that pharmacist. I was home sick all day when he claims I called on his establishment," Lizzie insisted.

"Hush, hush. You do not need to defend yourself to me. I know of your good works and your good heart. I only come to extend my sympathy for what you are suffering from people who want to attack you when you are vulnerable. I defend you to everyone I encounter with lies on their lips."

Mrs. Mary Anna Holmes, with her basset eyes and broad mouth, was missing the smile that usually lit up her face. She arrived with her lawyer husband, Charles Jarvis Holmes, whose abundant sideburns swept down below his chin. He was a prominent businessman in banking and mill management and a long-time friend of Andrew. He'd served in the Massachusetts legislature as both a representative and as a senator and for years, has been a senior deacon at the Central Congregational Church.

Because of their prestige in the community, their supportive attitudes buoyed the sisters. "Lizzie and Emma, if there is anything we can do for you to help you through this difficult time, please let us know."

"Mary Anna, I swear," Lizzie said, "I have never purchased prussic acid and I do not use it to clean anything. They can search the house from rafters to cellar floor they will not find any—not even an empty bottle."

"There, there, Lizzie," Mary Anna said. "I will pray for God to rescue you from under this cloud of suspicion. Mr. Holmes and I have no doubts about your character."

After their departure, Emma noticed the strain in Lizzie's face and said, "Sister dear, I think you should go to your room and rest for a while. I can handle everything down here for now."

"Thank you, Emma. The headache keeps creeping back. Rest might chase it away."

Alone, Emma faced the next visitor with dread—Mr. Hiram Harrington, the brother-in-law of Andrew and Abby Borden. He entered their home with his walrus moustache twitching in his jowly face. The cruel sparkle in his eyes illuminated much of his history with the family. Andrew had despised him, and the feeling was mutual.

Emma smiled, though it pained her. "Uncle Hiram, what is the reason for your call?"

"I wanted to find out exactly what happened. People on the street are telling me that Lizzie killed her parents. Do you feel safe staying under the same roof with her?"

"I have no fear of my sister, sir. I am frightened that whoever brutally murdered Father and Abby will return and kill us both as well."

"I imagine the police are guarding your house not to keep the guilty party away but to keep the guilty killer inside. Am I right?"

"Sir, my father did not desire you to enter our home. And now I feel the same. Please take your leave."

"I want to see Lizzie before I go."

Submerged anger flashed in Emma's eyes as she fought to keep her voice under control. "Lizzie has been sedated by her doctor and is in no condition to spend any time with you. Please leave our home and do not return until we have recovered from our grief."

"Hah! You've always protected your nasty little sister. Maybe it's because you are just like her. Maybe the two of you planned these killings together. I wouldn't be surprised."

A deep-rose tint colored Emma's cheek. "If you do not depart at once, I will summon one of the police officers to escort you outside."

Hiram laughed at her but left the house just the same.

Emma grabbed her skirts and raced up the stairs to her sister's room. "You won't believe who was just here. Our loathsome Uncle Hiram."

"Whatever for? Did he come to gloat over Father's death?"

"Probably. The visit was unpleasant, and I told him not to return until we had time to recover from our grief."

"You should have told him not to return ever."

"That would be so rude, Lizzie. I couldn't do that," Emma said. With a grin, she added, "But it would have been rather fun to see the expression on his face, wouldn't it?"

"Indeed," Lizzie answered just as knocks landed on the front door again.

"I'll go see who it is. You stay up here and rest." Emma pulled the door shut behind her and rushed down to the first floor.

"Mr. Borden," Emma said. She was even more astonished at his arrival than she had been at Hiram's. James Cook Borden was at the pinnacle of Fall River Society, the best and the brightest of the Borden elite. Emma didn't believe he'd ever darkened their modest door before. "And to what do we owe this honor, sir?"

"I came to express my deepest sympathies for the loss of your parents. Also, to inform you, that as your father's cousin, I have been asked and have accepted the invitation to serve as one of your father's pallbearers."

"Thank you very much, sir. It has been a difficult two days, but I appreciate your willingness to help see Father off to his final resting place."

Jerome bid Emma good day, but as Emma watched him settle into his carriage. She wondered if he came out of sympathy or if he only desired to protect the Borden family name.

* * *

Emma found her Uncle John in the parlor. "I am worried."

"You have reason to be," he said.

"Do you really think Dr. Bowen is right that the police suspect Lizzie?"

"I do not know, but at times, I felt certain they do."

"Uncle John, I won't sleep tonight, not knowing the answer."

"I'll send one of Marshall Hilliard's men down to the station to request that he call on us. We can ask him directly."

Emma cringed. "I am loathe to hear his answer."

"Not knowing is worse. If we know where they are headed, we can be better prepared."

Emma nodded, and John opened the front door and talked to an officer.

"Done. Now we await an answer."

Emma sighed. "Uncle John, do you think Lizzie is capable of—" she choked on her words.

"Hush, Emma. No, I do not. I do not believe that my dear departed sister could have given birth to a child who would be capable of that."

Emma's eyes searched his face, and he wrapped her in his arms and held her tight. They parted when they heard a knock on the door.

When John opened it, Marshall Hilliard said, "You wanted to see me."

"Yes, please come in."

The three stepped into the parlor, but no one took a seat. "Marshall," John began, "we have questions, and we hope we can trust you to give us honest answers."

"If I can, I will."

"Do you believe that someone in this house committed those murders?"

Hilliard looked at John's face, then Emma's. He cleared his throat before he began speaking. "Yes, I do."

"Can you tell us whom you suspect?"

Hilliard looked down at the floor and scuffed his toe across the carpet. "I don't think I could tell you outright at this time."

"Do you suspect me?" John asked.

Without looking up, Hilliard shook his head.

"Miss Emma?"

Hilliard's head moved side to side again.

"Bridget Sullivan?"

After a long pause and without lifting his head, he said, "She may have been involved."

"I sincerely doubt that, sir," Emma objected.

"Hush, Emma," John said. "Marshall Hilliard, do you suspect our Miss Lizzie?"

Hilliard raised his head and looked John in the eye, without saying a word. His gaze shifted to Emma. Still, he said not a word.

"And where, pray tell, do you think Lizzie would have gotten the knowledge to commit such a gruesome crime and to cover her tracks so exceedingly well? Do you think she learned that barbarism by teaching Sunday School to the Chinese?" John said.

Marshall stared at him but uttered not a word.

"That's it then?" John glared back at him.

"No, no," Emma said, shaking her head. "You are wrong. You are making a foolish mistake. Someone out there killed Father and Abby, and they will get away with it because you are focused on my sister."

"I am sorry, Miss Emma. I can only look where the arrow points. Good evening. And to you, Mr. Morse." The Marshall turned on his heel and left the house.

"How will we tell Lizzie?" Emma asked.

"We won't. Not now. Let's get through the funeral tomorrow first."

Emma nodded. "I'll make some tea."

* * *

After darkness had fallen and the undertakers had departed the home, Alice Russell rapped quietly on Lizzie's bedroom door. "Lizzie, are you awake?"

"Yes, Alice. The door is not locked, please come in."

"Lizzie, I know it will not be easy, but I think you should come down and see your father. He looks at peace."

Lizzie shook her head briskly. "No, I don't think I can."

"I think you must. The last look you had at your father was grotesque and horrific. You must replace that with his face at repose. If not, the nightmare

47

of how he looked will never leave your mind."

Lizzie sighed and allowed Alice to wrap an arm around her shoulder and lead her downstairs to the dining room. Lizzie stood in the doorway and gazed at the sight before her. Floral baskets and wreaths filled the space around where the bodies rested. The caskets were plain, in the European style, made of cedar with oxidized silver handles and draped in black cloth. Lizzie was delighted that Windward used those instead of the vulgar-styled rectangular pine ones. Her father's coffin bore a wreath of ivy. Its vine and tendrils often a chosen decoration because they represented fidelity and the persistence of life in the presence of death. Abby's casket was adorned with a bouquet of white roses, fern and pea blossoms, tied together with a white satin ribbon—the white roses for eternal love, the ferns for sincerity, and the sweet peas as a sign of farewell. The meaning behind that bunch of flowers irritated Lizzie but she said not a word.

Lizzie stood by her father's body. She noted the absence of blood and the undertaker's attempts to calm the little curl that always—even in death—sought to wrap around his ear. The undamaged side of her father's face was turned upward. He appeared to be sleeping and restful. Lizzie's gold ring wrapped around his little finger. "How old Father looks."

Alice squeezed Lizzie tight and murmured, "And may God bless his soul."

He looks so much smaller stuffed into this box."

"Oh, don't call it a box, Lizzie. That sounds so cold and disrespectful. It is a coffin or casket. Surely you know that."

"It's still a box, Alice, no matter what name you give it. And it's awful," Lizzie snapped.

Alice patted her shoulder. "Of course, Lizzie, of course. I'm sorry."

"How much he looks like Grandfather." Lizzie bent down and kissed her father's cold lips. She whispered in his ear, "I did not want you to die, Father. I wish you were still with us. But it was not possible to allow you to live." Lizzie's body shook.

Alice stepped forward and wrapped an arm around her shoulders. "Let's go back upstairs, Lizzie." Lizzie sobbed all the way back to her room.

Lizzie's hands were shaking, and her legs were weak by the time she made it upstairs. Alice was concerned about Lizzie's fragile state and called Dr. Bowen over to see if she was okay. The doctor agreed with Alice's assessment and administered an injection of sulfate of morphine. Lizzie drifted into its peaceful depths and slept for hours.

Chapter Ten

The following day, Saturday, August 6, Lizzie dressed with care, although not according to long-held custom. She began as was expected, removing her nightgown and pulling on her cotton chemise and knickers. She pulled a black stocking onto each leg, then stepped into a corset that raised her bustline, lessened the dimension of her waist, and straightened her posture. The suspender-like appendages clasped the stockings and held them in place. She gave the cords of the corset a tug to make sure the fit was firm, then she topped it all with a cotton petticoat. For her final layer, Lizzie chose a black lace dress with a form-fitting top that covered her arms and bosom and added a loose, flowing skirt. Her dark hat defied tradition by being brightened by small light flowers, and she wore no veil. She could not abide widow's weeds and thought those who wore them looked like refugees from one of Mr. Shakespeare's plays.

Emma wore a less fashionable black dress and a plain dark hat with a long veil hiding her face. "Are those blue flowers on your hat, Lizzie? Where is your veil? Father and Mrs. Borden would not approve of your attire."

"But they are dead, and I am not," Lizzie said, turning her back on her sister and returning to the dining room for a final farewell to her father.

As she gazed down upon his face, Mrs. Holmes approached and said, "He looks wonderfully peaceful."

"Yes, he does," Lizzie said and bent down to kiss his cheek.

Lizzie heard a bustle at the door and realized that Dr. Adams of the First Congregational Church and Reverend Buck of the Central Congregational

Church arrived to perform the services. Lizzie and Emma hurried upstairs. It was not appropriate for either of them to mingle with the mourners. A few minutes before eleven o'clock, the invited shuffled into the house.

Emma and Lizzie heard Alice greeting the guests on their behalf, seventy-five of them in all. "I wonder how many entered our home to show respect and how many are here out of morbid curiosity," Lizzie wondered out loud.

"Oh, Lizzie, simply be grateful they are here," Emma said. "Do not let the gossips twist your thoughts in that manner."

They stood together at the top of the stairs listening to the rustle of black skirts and the clink of jet beads as Dr. Adams delivered the invocation and read a short passage of scripture and The Reverend Mr. Buck offered up a prayer. The visitors all filed outside to join the funeral procession.

"Father will be pleased," Emma said. "It was short and modest as he would have liked."

"Does that really matter, Emma?"

"Of course, it does. We followed his wishes, and now he can rest in peace."

"You really think he knows or cares?"

"Lizzie—" Emma's comment was interrupted by the call for them to come down the stairs.

Lizzie, escorted by Undertaker Winward, was the first family member to emerge from the house. She paused for a moment at the top of the stairs, shocked by the hushing silence of the enormous crowd on Second Street. A burning sun beat down upon the heads before it hid behind the clouds of a temperamental sky. Lizzie straightened her spine. With her head held high, she boarded the carriage. Emma followed her, bent over and hesitant. Descending the steps, her feet faltered, and she would have fallen to the ground but for the quick hand of the escort on her elbow that centered her balance.

From inside the carriage, the sisters watched as the pallbearers carried out Andrew's casket and placed it in the hearse. Lizzie turned her gaze to the crowd on the street when a different group of men brought Abby's coffin down.

The hearse pulled away from the curb, followed by the wagon transporting the undertaker and the pallbearers. Emma and Lizzie's carriage was third in line, followed by all the others. Second Street was lined with people as if for a parade—but the women bowed their heads, and all the men clutched their hats in their hands as Andrew and Abby passed by.

The procession turned up Borden Street to make the traditional passage past the dead man's business in the Andrew J. Borden building on North Main Street. Emma choked out a sob. "It's wrong to see Father's business like this—the lights all out, the windows all shuttered. It makes his death far too real."

Lizzie patted Emma's clenched hands. "I suspect his death will impact us both for quite some time—I doubt if this is even our worst day."

The long line of carriages turned down Cherry Street, then Rock Street, and finally Prospect Street. All along the way, solemn townspeople paused by the roadway in silence. They entered the Oak Grove Cemetery beneath a granite Gothic arch bearing the ominous motto: "The shadows have fallen, and they wait for the day."

Chapter Eleven

Emma and Lizzie waited in the carriage as the ministers, pallbearers, and the other men went down to the grassy plot surrounded by trees. "Emma, let's go down and make sure pine branches are lining Father's grave and bear witness to his lowering into the ground."

"It is not seemly, Lizzie."

"It is not seemly to have one's father murdered in the sitting room, Emma. He is our father. All that keeps us from his side are the rules of men designed to keep us under control."

"Be still, sister. You do not want the shock of seeing the deep pit where they will be entombed. Besides, people would talk."

"They are talking already, sister dear, or haven't you noticed?"

"No need to give them more reason, Lizzie. It sounds as if the prayers are over already."

"Who is that?" Lizzie asked, pointing to a shabbily dressed woman approaching the graves.

"I don't know, Lizzie."

"Oh, look, Emma. She's kneeling by Abby's coffin."

The two sisters watched as the woman buried her face in her hands as her shoulders shook. Police approached her and pulled her to her feet, and led her away.

"Who is she?" Lizzie asked again.

"We'll find out, Lizzie," Emma said as the police led the woman past the carriage. "Oh my, I think I recognize her. I can't remember her name, but I believe she is the housekeeper we employed when we first moved to Second

Street."

"Really, are you sure?"

"Nearly. As I recall, she did not want to leave us, but her knuckles were so swollen, she could no longer work. It makes sense that it is her. She thought Abby was a saint."

"Abby? Truly, you jest."

"At the time, many saw her that way because she was willing to raise two motherless children."

"But I didn't need her, Emma. I had you. She was not there for us—she was there for Father's money."

"Hush, Lizzie! Do not speak ill of the dead. What will people say?"

"Forget what they say, Emma. Look at what they are doing. Why are they not burying father?"

The pallbearers walked back toward the entrance and entered a building near the gate. The men stepped back outside but left the coffins inside.

"Why are they putting the caskets in there?"

"I don't know. Look, there's Uncle John," Emma said.

He approached the carriage with a long face. "I regret to inform you that the police are not satisfied. They have insisted on a more thorough autopsy. The bodies will be stored in the holding tomb until the task is complete."

"I thought that was only used when the ground was frozen too hard to bury the deceased," Emma said.

"Normally, yes," John said.

"How dare they!" Lizzie exclaimed. "Do they not need to seek our permission? Do we have no say in the matter?"

"Unfortunately not, Lizzie. I asked but nothing can be done."

Emma tried to calm Lizzie, patting the back of her hand all the way home. This small kindness, however, was not sufficient to quiet her younger sister's flames of anger.

"Father should be allowed to rest in peace, Emma."

"I know, Lizzie, I know."

"They said themselves that the cause of both of their deaths was obvious. Why further desecrate their bodies?"

"I don't know, Lizzie. All I do know is that we are powerless to stop them."

"Yes. Because we are women. Uncle John should have done more."

"Please do not place the blame on him. He said he did all he could. He cared deeply about Father. He could do no less. If you must be angry, put it where it belongs—on the police, on the Marshall, on the medical examiner—but spare Uncle John."

Emma and Lizzie stepped down from the coach and walked to the front door. The coach had barely pulled away when six men—some in uniform—followed us into the house, intent on a thorough search. On this occasion, neither sister objected—Emma was too drained of emotion, and Lizzie was too full of anger to trust herself to speak.

The sisters remained downstairs while above them, the policemen rampaged in the four rooms on the second floor. When Emma tried to speak, Lizzie hushed her. She was intent on listening to every single sound for any indication that they breached her hidey-hole.

When the horde of marauders descended to the first floor, Lizzie and Emma went upstairs. The hook on Lizzie's door latch was pulled loose from the wood. Lizzie entered and found her bed disheveled for the second time that day. She made sure Emma was still in her own room before checking the sanctity of the hiding place beneath the bed. It appeared undisturbed.

Emma walked past Lizzie's door. "I'm going to see if the bed in the guest room needs to be made." Emma gasped. "Lizzie, come look at this. I cannot believe what they have done."

Lizzie rushed into the adjoining room and froze in place. The ticking on the mattress was slashed open. The two sisters pushed the escaped stuffing back inside and, starting at opposite ends, stitched it back together and flipped the mattress to hide the scar. They both went to Lizzie's room and huddled on the couch.

"Emma, I have never felt more helpless and frightened in my life. If only Father was here."

"What kind of people are let loose in our home?"

They winced in each other's arms with every thump and bump echoing down below.

Chapter Twelve

Mr. Andrew Jackson Jennings arrived at the Borden home soon after the arrival of the police. Long a friend and attorney of Andrew Borden, he knew his services would be required. He was a prominent personage in Fall River, having served in both the Massachusetts House of Representatives and the state Senate. Emma and Lizzie heard him talking to Marshall Hilliard but could not understand the words they spoke.

As he walked up the stairs, his nose picked up a whiff of the iron tang of shed blood. He was surprised that the scent lingered so long after the bodies had left the home.

The door to Lizzie's room was open but still Mr. Jennings tapped on the frame before entering. Despite his intimidating mane of a beard, his downturned eyes gave him the look of meekness, but Andrew Borden had assured his daughters that his attorney's docile appearance was overcome by his passionate oratory in the courtroom and the legislature.

"Lizzie," he said, "the Marshall wants the clothing you wore Thursday morning."

"Is that necessary?" Emma asked.

"If Lizzie does not turn them over willingly, the Marshall said he could take them by force and possibly arrest her for impeding an investigation."

Emma rose to her feet and stepped in front of Lizzie. "Perhaps then I should speak to him and remind him that despite what happened here, this is a decent home, and he has violated the peace of it without cause."

"Mr. and Mrs. Borden were murdered here, Emma—that alone gives him cause to do whatever he wishes. I admire your desire to protect your sister but surely you must understand that they are doing their job to find who perpetuated this horror. And nothing you say to him will make any difference."

Emma's shoulders slumped.

"Lizzie, It would be best if you gathered up the clothing, and I will take it down to the Marshall," the attorney said.

Lizzie gathered her blue Bengaline silk skirt, navy blue blouse, and white underskirt, folding each garment before handing the stack to Jennings. "I would like to register my outrage at this violation of privacy, sir."

"I have heard you, Lizzie, and I understand. Before I hand these items over, though, I need to know if there are any stains that look like blood."

Lizzie pulled her underskirt from the pile and unfolded it. Pointing to a small spot, she pointed to it and said, "It is but a fleabite" as her face reddened.

A light blush raced across Jennings' face, assuring her that he understood the common vernacular used for menstrual blood. "Thank you, Miss Borden," was all that he said.

He passed through the doorway and turned back. "I will do everything I can to erase this blemish on your character, Miss Lizzie. Stay strong; this torment won't last forever."

Emma and Lizzie nodded mutely. They back sank down on the sofa, holding hands, silently wrapped in their misery. He went downstairs to hand everything over to Marshall Hilliard.

Jennings was as convinced of Lizzie's innocence as the police appeared to be of her guilt. An able, painstaking, and energetic defender, he set out from the house determined to gather up any rumor, gossip, or fact that would point suspicion away from his client.

He spoke to grocer John St. Laurent. Between half past twelve and one o'clock on the day of the murders, he was driving his wood wagon to New Bedford and stopped in front of Merchants Mill. A ghastly white man about 5'6" tall stopped him and climbed in. He asked to be driven to Westport and shoved $4 into St. Laurent's hand. Then, the stranger took the reins and drove the horse.

St. Laurent told the man that he must stop at his wood yard and get another horse as the one pulling the wagon had already worked hard that day. When they arrived, St. Laurent's wife was troubled by the stranger's agitation and sense of urgency. She insisted that her husband not give the man a ride. Feeling some of the same apprehension, St. Laurent returned the man's money and sent him to Arcand's Livery Stable on Flint Street to find a ride.

Mr. Jennings stopped next at that stable. He learned there that the man had asked to borrow a horse but was told they did not lend horses to strangers. Jennings could find no one else who had seen the man since that encounter.

Next on Jennings' list was John Donnelly, who had gone into the barn in the immediate aftermath of the discovery of Andrew's body. "What did you see there, sir?" Jennings asked.

"I went inside hoping I might find the man who committed this horrible crime or maybe even find a weapon. I found neither, but I did notice something interesting—the perfect outline of a man impressed into the hay in two different places."

"What did you take that to mean?"

"I thought that the murderer had slept here waiting for his opportunity to attack."

"Couldn't it have been Mr. Borden resting in his own barn?"

"Oh, no, Mr. Jennings. Whoever this man was, he was a great deal shorter than the dearly departed Mr. Borden."

Jennings heard the rumor of a bloody axe wrapped in a similarly stained cloth sitting on a shelf in the house of the farm near the Borden's place in South Somerset the day after the murder. The lawyer found the source of the story, painter, and paperhanger Peleg Brightman, to learn more details.

"Mr. Brightman, did you see anything unusual when you went out to that farm on Friday morning?"

"Yes, I did. There was a man who was walking toward the path I was using. He stopped dead in his tracks and looked like he wanted to run."

"Did he?"

"Nah. But when I got a little closer, the man walked away as quickly as he could, looking back over his shoulder as if he was fearful that I would follow him."

"How did you find the axe?"

"I was replacing glass in the window, and I saw something odd sitting on a shelf. I looked at it a bit closer and saw it was an axe wrapped in a cloth—both smeared with blood.

"Did you report it to the police?"

"I did not want to. Didn't think much of it until my employer told me about the Borden murders and urged me to report it to the police. When I did, they wanted me to go out there with them and show them where to find it."

"Who went with you?"

"One of the officers was named Harrington, I believe. The other was Medley."

"How did you find the place?"

"We drove across the river and turned down the road leading to Brayton's point. We stopped to open a gate, crossed the bars, and then went through another gate. We went over a sand hill, around the frog pond, and there was Joseph Silva's cottage. There was another carriage following us with two fellers in it who said they were reporters."

"Was Mr. Silva there?"

"Yeah, him and his wife and sister and a bunch of youngsters playing in the yard. I took them to the axe, but it had been wiped off, and the worn knickers were hanging on a nail. So, one of the officers asked Joseph whose axe it was. He admitted it was his. Then they picked up the cloth, asked who it belonged to. His wife snatched it from their hands."

"Did they try to stop her?"

"Nope. They said they was sorry, but they hadn't seen the buttons and assumed it belonged to her husband. Then they asked her how come there was blood on it?

"And she says: 'we wanted a chicken for dinner last Thursday and Joseph keeps these old knickers to put the chicken in to keep the blood off the feathers when he chops the heads off. It's a first-rate idea, she says, cause he can kill two at a time, thataway. You just stick one through this opening and another through the other. I thought it was pretty clever, but those policemen were a bit disappointed."

"Was there any connection between the Borden family and that farmhouse?" Jennings asked.

"Oh, yeah. Those people in that house knew Andrew Borden quite well, I think."

After talking to these men, Jennings was even more baffled that the police were so focused on Miss Lizzie. Marshall Hilliard told him that he would not have placed any weight on the pharmacist's claims of an attempted purchase of Prussic Acid if not for Dr. Bowen's reports of poisoning.

The lawyer stopped at Dr. Bowen's home, hoping to get to the bottom of the matter. "The police told me that you reported an attempted poisoning at the Borden house before the murders. Is that true?"

"Yes. Sometimes I wish I had not mentioned it, but I did," Dr. Bowen said with a sigh. "On Wednesday morning, Mrs. Borden was talking to my wife. She said, 'I am afraid my husband and I were poisoned last night. We ate our supper as usual with nothing on the table out of the ordinary. That night, we both got terribly sick with vomiting and stomach pains. We did not send for the doctor last night, but I thought I should see him this morning.'"

"Did you examine her?"

"I talked to her about the symptoms but did not reach any conclusion about the cause of their discomfort the night before. When the weather is this warm, there are many things that could cause their distress. Soured milk, a rotted piece of meat, this time of year, my patients suffer lots of stomach distress. A short time after talking to her, I went over to check on Mr. Borden. 'How are you, Andrew? Do you think anything had poisoned you?' Andrew laughed and said, 'No, I've not been poisoned. There's not very much the matter with me at all.' We talked about inconsequential things for a bit after that, and that was the last time that I spoke with him."

"What do you think of Mrs. Borden's concerns about poisoning?" Jennings asked.

"Personally, I do not take any stock in that theory. I see nothing sufficiently strong to indicate it. It is a very serious matter to make reflections and insinuations of a woman of unstained character as some papers are doing in their reports of this case. I have known Lizzie Borden for many years and have seen her frequently since the tragedy. I believe her absolutely innocent of even a guilty knowledge of the crime."

"What about the stories of great conflict in the family?"

"I will not say there may not have been occasional family differences between Mr. Borden and the girls. It is a matter I was in a position to know little about, but so far as I ever observed, the inter-family relations were cordial."

"Thank you, Dr. Bowen. If you think of anything else I should know, please contact me."

"Of course, I want this persecution of Miss Lizzie to come to an end as much as you do."

Chapter Thirteen

A knock on the front door brought them downstairs. Their uncle reached the door before the sisters did. Two men stood in the entry: Mayor John Coughlin, appearing sanctimonious with his immaculate dress, tightly manicured beard and mustache, receding hairline, and pursed mouth, crossed the threshold first.

He was followed by Marshall Rufus Hilliard and his chaotic mustache that poked out in all directions like a worn flat broom. Emma approached the men with a tear-stained face and shaking hands. "Please, please, I beg of you, do everything in your power to relieve us from the grip of this merciless suspense and bring the guilty to justice."

"Miss Emma," the mayor bristled, "I am insulted that you felt you had to ask." The harsh tone of his voice made Emma recoil and take a few steps backward.

John snapped at the man, "I hope you are aware that this is a house in the throes of mourning and will conduct yourselves accordingly."

The mayor ignored him and turned to Lizzie. "When did you last see your mother?"

"I don't think I saw her after 9 o'clock. She went upstairs to put shams on the pillows."

The mayor asked the same question many times, using different words until he, too, seemed to grow tired of his queries. "You went out to the barn for twenty minutes to find lead for fishing, you say?"

"Twenty minutes to half an hour."

"Did you have a difficult time finding the lead?"

"I don't know, but that I did, or perhaps something else engaged my attention. I do not recall. Much has happened since then."

"The barn is just a short distance from the house, is it not?"

"Perhaps twenty feet from the back door."

"And still, you could not hear anyone killing your father with that axe, Miss Lizzie?"

Lizzie shook her head. "No. I heard nothing of the sort."

"The noise must have resembled that made by a person chopping meat?"

Emma gasped and staggered backwards. John, fearing Emma would faint ,rushed to her side and wrapped a supportive arm around her. "Gentlemen, please—"

Coughlin turned to the doorway that led to the staircase in the front hall. "This door must have been opened when you returned from the barn."

"I do not believe it was," Lizzie insisted.

"You do not believe it? What does that mean? Have you forgotten? Or are you trying to fashion a statement to point us in another direction?" the mayor asked.

"Gentlemen, what is the purpose of this call?" Lizzie asked.

"I would like to request that all members of the family remain in the house for a few days," the mayor said. "There is a great deal of excitement in town, and it would be better for all concerned if you remain here and not go out in the street. If people out on the street annoy you, send words to the City Marshall or me, and we will see that the crowd is dispersed."

"How are we going to get our mail from the post office?" John asked.

"It would be better to send someone to get your mail."

"What?" Lizzie asked. "Is there anybody suspected in this house?"

"Perhaps Mr. Morse could answer that," the mayor said.

"I want to know the truth. Now," Lizzie insisted.

The mayor looked her straight in the eye. "Well, I regret very much to say, Miss Borden, but you are suspected."

Emma said, "We have tried to keep it from you as long as we could."

Lizzie's jaw dropped. *I was a suspect? They told the rest of the family. Why couldn't they have held off until a day or two or three after the funeral? The lack of respect was not something I would ever forget.* "Well, I am ready to go at any time."

Lizzie looked out the windows and saw the crowd milling in front of the house, staring as if they could see through walls. It was another image she would never forget, even as she withdrew behind the curtains. She listened to the murmurs of dozens of conversations in front of her house and to the squad of police officers constantly shouting at those gathered to get out of the street. There were, however, far too many people to be contained on the sidewalk.

Lizzie went upstairs to repair the hook on her bedroom door. Alice followed her and stared at Lizzie with a question written in her eyes. "Yes, Alice," Lizzie asked.

Alice blushed and shook her head. "Nothing. Nothing at all." She turned and went downstairs.

Lizzie knew Alice long enough to realize that she was lying. She went to the window and twitched at the curtain in time to hear the gruff voice of Dr. Bowen pushing his way through the multitudes. Emma let him in, and he went straight to Lizzie's room to administer another injection.

Chapter Fourteen

Sunday morning, Lizzie checked the lock on her bedroom door before lying down on the floor on her stomach. Pulling with her hands and pushing her toes against the floral carpet, she wiggled under the bed. Lifting the loose board, she pulled out a wad of blue from its hiding place. Nestled beneath it were the items she stole from her father's bedroom the year before. Twenty to thirty dollars in gold, a few Globe Street railway tickets, a red leather pocketbook, Mrs. Borden's watch and chain, her lady's chain with a slide and a tassel attached, and a few other pieces of her jewelry. Beneath it all was a hatchet wrapped in a rag. It would have to wait for later for disposal.

Carefully, she slid the loose board into place and blew hard to distribute the dust across its surface. She made sure the blood stains on the dress were folded into the center of the bundle and not visible from the outside. She believed if she burned the dress in plain sight of others, it would not be suspicious. She took a deep breath and left her bedroom to go to the kitchen.

Emma and Alice were tidying up after their breakfast. Lizzie went to the cookstove and, using a steel handle, lifted the lid. She held up the folded-up dress. "This old thing is covered with paint."

Alice said, "I'm heading upstairs to make my bed."

"What are you going to do?" Emma asked Lizzie.

"I'm going to burn it up."

Lizzie took care not to reveal the stains as she ripped it into pieces and jammed it into the flames.

"Father would have wanted you to make rags with that," Emma said. "Burning it is just wasteful.

"Bother father's frugality. We do not live under his roof any longer. Besides, what good would it do as a rag, hardened with all this dried paint?

"You had better burn it then," Emma said.

* * *

Despite the medical examiner's request that the bloodied clothing worn by Abby and Andrew be preserved, John had a man dig a hole in the backyard under the supervision of Officer Chace. A foot down, the digging came to a halt when the blade of the shovel hit a bone. Chace rushed to the house. "Mr. Morris, before we go any further, I need an explanation of the bones we found."

John went out to the hole with the officer, hoping it was all much ado about nothing. He instructed the man to brush away dirt with his hands. As the bones were revealed, it became obvious that they were not human. "Looks like a dog's body, Officer," John said.

Chace took a long look down in the hole, then nodded his head. "You are right. Please proceed."

Another foot deeper, and John sent the man to get the soiled garments from the basement. When he returned with his burden, Chace said, "Set them down here. I need to make an inventory before we cover it all up."

One by one, each article of clothing was noted and dropped into the hole. Bundled in the garments, they uncovered a piece of Abby's skull displaying a clean cut that went all the way through the bone. Clumps of Abby's hair were added to the burial site.

Emma came into the yard and asked, "Uncle John, I still see locks of hair and other bloodied items on the cellar floor, could you please see that every trace of the tragedy is removed." The workman went inside and retrieved the remnants of Abby's hair, the two sheets that had covered the bodies, and the chunk of bloodied carpet removed from the guest room. For a while, Emma remained in the back yard, her face wiped of all emotion as she stared out past the house to the curious crowd that gathered on the sidewalk in front of the house all day.

* * *

Police Officer Desmond and mason Charles Bryant disrupted the fragile peace of the Borden home that afternoon. The officer supervised while the mason opened and examined every closed-up fireplace in the house. Lizzie was furious, Emma distraught. John argued with them about the expense of repairing the house after they left. While the mason worked, another group of police officers spent most of their time in the basement, turning over stacks of wood and stomping up and down the stairs.

When they left, Lizzie was flustered. John tried to soothe her and Emma by reading an article from the newspaper. "Look, Lizzie, the Reverend Mister Buck spoke of you to the newspaper: "Aside from her Christian character, her actions at the time of the murder count with me as indicating ignorance of the crime. I called on her less than one hour after the discovery of her father's body. I asked her if there was anyone she suspected, and she replied in tears that she did not know of a person in the world who could have a motive for murdering her father. She highly endorsed the character of a Swede farmhand in Mr. Borden's employ and said he was above suspicion. A guilty person takes every opportunity to throw suspicion on the innocent. Lizzie Borden did not do that."

When Emma finished reading, she said, "Now, who could suspect you of responsibility when a man of God rises to your defense."

"Thank you, Emma. I cannot forget, though, that the desire of man often does not heed the will of God."

* * *

Mr. Jennings arrived at the house with a stranger. Emma let them inside and asked, "What can we do for you, Mr. Jennings?"

"Please gather Miss Lizzie and Mr. Morse and join us in the parlor, Miss

Emma." When all were standing together, Mr. Jennings said, "I have with me today, Mr. Orinton Hanscom. He is a private detective—a Pinkerton man from Boston. Mr. Hanscom, this is Miss Emma, Miss Lizzie, and Mr. Morse, the girls' uncle."

John stepped forward and shook Mr. Hanscom's hand. "Shall we be seated?"

Emma, Lizzie, and Uncle John sat in a row on the sofa, and the other two men sat opposite them in a pair of chairs. "Mr. Hanscom," Jennings said, "please tell them what you have learned."

"I have found nothing conclusive pointing to a suspect. However, I have heard a disturbing rumor. According to gossips, Miss Lizzie and Mr. Morse had concocted the murder and hired someone to do it."

Lizzie rose to her feet, her face red with rage. "That is outrageous and blatantly untrue, sir. Who started that vicious rumor?

Hanscom said, "As best as I can tell, the original source was George B. Fish. Do you know him?

"Yes, yes," Lizzie said. "He is the worthless husband of Abby's sister Priscilla. I am surprised anyone took him seriously."

"It is but a rumor," Jennings said, "but it demonstrates that we are on shaky ground. The main suspect of the police remains you, Miss Lizzie."

Lizzie slid down on the sofa. "You must clear Uncle John's name, Mr. Jennings."

"The Marshall is convinced that Mr. Morse was not present at the house when the murders occurred, Miss Lizzie. That does not stop the lips of the rumormongers, though, and we will have to deal with them in the courtroom," Jennings said. "Did any of you see a ghastly white man with a black mustache and wild eyes anywhere on the morning Andrew and Abby were killed?"

The sisters mumbled "no" as they shook their heads. John asked, "Is it a significant lead? Was a man like that near this home?"

"Apparently, he had been seen by a passing doctor and by Officer Hyde. Neither I nor Mr. Hanscom can confirm that. With your permission, my detective will examine the sitting room and the guest bedroom."

"Of course," John said.

"After he had left, Mr. Jennings said, "There will be an inquest, Miss Lizzie, and you will need to testify."

Lizzie's hand flew to her throat. "I cannot. I cannot."

"You must," Mr. Jennings said. "But do not be fearful. An inquest is a normal part of the process, and you have nothing to fear if you speak the truth. Hopefully, the information they gather from the hearing will lead to another suspect, and the police will leave you at peace."

Lizzie did not appear comforted by the lawyer's reassurances. Only she knew how much she could damage herself by telling the truth.

Chapter Fifteen

When escorting the two men out of the house, Emma noticed stains on the door frame of the sitting room. Once she bid them farewell, she returned there and examined them. *That's blood. My father's blood.*

She grabbed a rag and wet it in the kitchen sink. She applied it to the wood and scrubbed. Alice came down the front stairs. "What are you doing, Emma?"

"I am wiping away my father's blood. The police should have done that, but they did not."

"Are you sure it is allowed?"

"Alice, it is my father's blood. Do you think I could bear knowing it was there?"

Lizzie said, "Leave Emma alone, Alice. If the police think it is wrong, they will accuse me anyway. Let Emma do what she wants; she'll remain blameless."

"You certainly sound bitter, Lizzie," Alice said.

"And who could blame her?" Emma interjected.

"Well, it's none of my affair, I suppose," Alice said. "I came down to tell you that I told Mr. Hanscom a falsehood."

"About what?" Emma asked.

"He asked me if all the dresses were there that were there on the day of the tragedy and I said, 'Yes.' I'll talk to you later. I have a carriage waiting."

Emma and Lizzie looked at each other for a long moment. Emma broke the silence. "She must be talking about the dress you burned in the stove."

"Yes, but she didn't object when I did it," Lizzie said.

"Why did she lie to him?" Emma wondered.

Lizzie rose and paced the room. "That way, she can keep holding it over our heads, threatening to weave it into some dark purpose."

"Oh, that doesn't sound like Alice."

Lizzie crossed the room again. "Then why would she tell us that she spoke a falsehood? Why didn't she simply correct it?"

"I don't know, Lizzie, but if she has a desire to hurt us, we can disarm her."

"How?" Lizzie asked.

"If we tell her to admit the truth to Mr. Hanscom, then we will not appear as if we had encouraged her to be dishonest."

"That does make sense, sister, but what if she reveals some other harmless thing in a bad light."

"She won't do that, Lizzie, she's been our friend for years."

"Your friend, Emma. She was friendly to me only because I am your sister. I fear she will betray me."

"When she returns then, I will tell her to speak to the detective, and we will see how she reacts."

"'False face must hide what the false heart doth know,'" Lizzie said.

"Shakespeare does not have answers for every occasion, sister."

* * *

"I saw your Maggie at the dry goods store," Alice said as she entered the house.

"Did you speak to her?" Emma asked.

"No. Whatever would I have to say to her? She was looking at some fabric. Is she still staying at Dr. Bowen's house?"

"I don't know, but probably so."

"I'm surprised she hasn't been arrested."

"Arrested?" Emma exclaimed. "Whatever for?"

"They always blame the servants, don't they? They usually carry grudges,"

Alice said.

"Maggie didn't," Lizzie said. "You ought not to repeat that to anyone else. That's how rumors are started. You don't want to be responsible for her having a noose around her neck because of your idle gossip."

"I'm going upstairs." Alice turned away from the sisters.

"Wait, Alice," Emma implored.

Alice turned back around. "What, Emma?"

"You need to tell Mr. Hanscom that you told him a falsehood. And tell him that I told you to do so."

Alice looked first at Emma, then at Lizzie, her eyelids beating a fast tattoo on her cheeks. Without saying a word, she turned and went out the front door. A half-hour later, she returned. "I spoke to Mr. Hanscom."

"I am glad to hear it," Emma said.

Alice turned to Lizzie. "If I were you, Lizzie, I wouldn't have let anyone see me burn that dress."

"I am certainly not going to worry about my sister telling tales. What did Mr. Hanscom say?" Lizzie replied.

"I am afraid that the burning of the dress was the worst thing you could have done, Lizzie," Alice said.

The red heat rose in Lizzie's face. *Is she warning me? Will she betray me? No. She wants to remain friends with Emma. But why would she say that?* "Oh, what made you let me do it then? Why did you let me burn the dress?"

Alice went upstairs without making a response.

* * *

Lizzie was delighted at the sight of Mrs. Mary Brigham. Beneath her modest nose, her smile spread as wide as her face. Lizzie clasped her hands as she invited her into the parlor. Emma went into the kitchen to prepare tea.

"Lizzie, dear, how are you? I cannot imagine the horror of the last few days. Did you know there are still policemen outside of your house?"

"Yes, they refuse to allow us a moment of peace. And we are not allowed to leave the house."

"No! That is outrageous. Should I ask Mr. Brigham to speak to the mayor about this?"

"That would do no good, Mary. The mayor was here, and he is in accordance with the Marshall. Enough of gloomy things. I have been cooped up and know nothing of our friends' comings and goings. Please enlighten me," Lizzie said.

"Did you hear about Isabella Bates?"

"No, not a word."

"She's been in Fall River all summer at her grandmother's house on Belmont. None of us knew but she'd run away from home because she did not want to marry the man her father selected for her. Her grandmother has been denying that Isabella was with her, but the father found out. He sent men to seize her and place her in the Boston Lunatic Asylum."

"No! Just because she did not want to marry?" Lizzie asked with panic written across her face.

"Precisely. But I can hardly blame her. The man her father selected was 67 years old. It was part of a business deal between two gentlemen," Mary said.

"How could a father do that?" Emma asked.

"Really, Emma," Lizzie said, "men have been doing that to unwanted daughters and wives for quite some time. We are lucky we escaped that fate."

"Father would never," Emma objected.

"It would be comfortable to think so, sister, but he did have that power over us. We will never really know if he would have been capable of putting us away."

A heavy-fisted pounding sounded on the front door. Emma hurried to answer it. When she saw Marshall Hilliard and a handful of policemen standing outside the door, she wanted to slam it shut, but before she could stammer an objection, the Marshall pushed past her and into the parlor.

He stopped in front of Lizzie. "Lizzie Borden, you will come with us. I come bearing a subpoena to appear before Judge Josiah Blaisdell of the

Second District Court to be questioned in the deaths of Andrew Borden and Abby Borden."

Lizzie rose, swaying a bit as she stood. She turned to Emma. "My mind still feels a bit cloudy from the injection last evening. I will strive to do my best and quickly so I can return to you."

Mary noticed the trembling in Lizzie's hands and said, "I will go with you, Lizzie." Turning toward the Marshall and glaring into his eyes, she added, "Surely no one can object to a lady having an escort by her side."

Hilliard returned her glare. He had no patience for women who thought they could stand up to a man—particularly not those women who live on the hill with the family and wealth to look down on him. He wanted to tell her to sit down and be quiet, but he did not dare. He shook his head and turned to the door.

"Marshall, you need to wait for a moment," Mary said. "Miss Borden is a patient of Dr. Bowen. I must inform him of where she is going."

"I can't wait—"

"Yes, you can. I'll just be a minute."

When she returned from seeing Dr. Bowen, she nodded at the window, and Lizzie stepped out of the house. Neither of the two women displayed any sign of dismay as they stepped into a hack accompanied by Marshall Hilliard and Officer Harrington. Before they could move, a crowd, buzzing like hornets, surrounded the carriage despite the grueling heat. As the horses drew down the street, people milled along the route and stared at its passage. The distance from the Borden house to Central Police Station was short and walkable, but to Lizzie, it felt as if it would never end.

They pulled up in front of the large granite building on Court Square. When they disembarked, the crowds pressed in on the police force holding them back. Mary linked arms with Lizzie and led her past journalists, shouting questions, hoping for a quote. One voice yelled, "Murderer!" nearly stopping Lizzie where she stood. Mary's persistent pull was all that kept her moving.

Just inside the entrance, the Marshall pulled Lizzie aside to tell her that police were going to her house to search for the prescription Dr. Bowen gave the whole family when they were ill a week before the murders. Lizzie maintained her calm demeanor, but inside, she was seething.

"What was that about?" Mary asked.

"They are violating the sanctity of my home again with another unnecessary search. I fear they will never leave me in peace, Mary."

Mary grabbed Lizzie's hand and held it tight. "This, too, shall pass, my dear friend. Lean on me whenever you need."

Mary walked inside the building with Lizzie, but when they reached the Clerk's Office, Marshall Hilliard stopped them. "Mrs. Brigham, you may go no further. The judge has forbidden anyone to get within hearing distance of the inquest except for the called witnesses. You must wait out here."

"For how long?" Mary asked.

"I cannot say. District Attorney Knowlton and Judge Blaisdell will make that determination. It has naught to do with me."

Mary squeezed Lizzie's hand. "Even though I am not by your side, you are not alone. I will wait for you on the bench just down the hall, no matter how long it takes."

Lizzie forced a smile and nodded her head as her eyes swelled with unspent tears. Marshall escorted Lizzie to the courtroom. As she walked through the door, she looked for any familiar faces. She saw Judge Blaisdell, Dr. Dolan, Detective Seaver, and District Attorney Knowlton. She tapped Hilliard's arm, "Where, sir, is my attorney?"

"Who?"

"Mr. Jennings, Mr. Andrew Jennings, where is he?"

"He is in my office. He cannot be present at this proceeding. You have not been arrested."

"But—"

"Please take a seat. The judge is waiting."

Lizzie eased down to await her call to the stand. Looking around the room, she saw a forest of mustaches, beards, sideburns, uniforms, and suits—not another woman present. *Only those who wish to control me and hold me down are present here. Will it be thus for every woman to the end of time?* She struggled to maintain a stern exterior that gave no indication of the rising dread that rose higher with every passing minute.

Chapter Sixteen

Emma stood motionless by the window, watching the marshall take her sister away. Fearful, angry, and frustrated, she tried to think of something—anything she could do. She wrote a message to Mr. Jennings.

The Marshall took my sister from our home. They want her to testify
at the inquest now. I am certain she would be well-served by your
presence at her side. Please hurry.

Emma Lenore Borden

She sealed it in an envelope and stepped on the porch to find a boy to deliver it. She saw Jimmy running a stick across a picket fence across the street. "Jimmy! Jimmy! Can you deliver a letter for me?"

"Sure, Miss Emma," he said as he ran over to her house. "Where does it need to go?"

"To Mr. Andrew Jennings, on the southeast corner of June and French Street. You know where that is?"

Jimmy nodded.

"Now, Jimmy, do not place this envelope in anyone else's hands. Mr. Andrew Jennings and no one else, you understand?"

"Yes, ma'am."

She placed the envelope into one grubby hand and a few coins into the other. "Jimmy, the quicker you return with an answer, the more I'll give you when you get here."

"I'm the fastest boy in Fall River. I won't let you down." He ran as fast as he could up Second Street. Emma watched him until he was out of sight.

By the time he reached the Victorian home of Mr. Jennings, he was out of breath. And, as it happened, out of luck. He ran up the stone steps to the porch only to learn that Mr. Jennings had gone to the Central Police Station for an inquest.

Jimmy sped back down the hill to North Main. He raced inside with perspiration dripping from his forehead. "I have a message for Mr. Jennings. I was told he is in the inquest."

"Then it will have to wait."

"It can't," Jimmy protested. "It's urgent," the desperate young man insisted, imagining his reward diminishing with every passing minute.

"Give it to me, then. I'll see that he gets it," an officer said.

"No, sir, Jimmy said as he clutched the note to his chest. "With all due respect, sir. I was instructed to place it in Mr. Jennings's hands and only his hands."

A few of the men tried to shoo him away but one officer who delivered messages when he was a child took pity on the boy. "You wait right here. I'll go check with the Marshall." He went up the stairs to Hilliard's office, but instead of his superior, he found Andrew Jennings at the desk. "Sir, there is a boy downstairs with a message for you."

"Who is it from?"

"He did not say, sir. But he did say it was urgent."

Jennings followed the officer down to the main floor, where the sweaty little boy was still trying to catch his breath. "You have a message for me?"

Jimmy handed over the envelope now limp and damp from the heat and perspiration. "Miss Emma wants an answer, sir."

"And she shall have it, lad."

Jennings borrowed a piece of paper and a pen from a nearby office and scrawled a response.

I know your sister is here. She is before the judge, answering questions at this moment. I have not seen her, but I will not leave the police station until I have done so. The judge refused my admittance into the hearing room, but I am gleaning all the information I can from others

here. Be strong—your father would want it so.
Andrew Jackson Jennings

He placed the note in the same envelope, scratching out his name and adding Emma's. He slipped a coin into Jimmy's hand. "You hurry back now. No tomfoolery along the way. It is important that Miss Emma get this message right away."

Jimmy bobbed his head and ran off again—past a pack of boys calling his name, past the sweet shop where he wanted to spend a coin or two, all the way to 92 Second Street. Emma opened the door when his first step hit the porch. "Did you find him?"

"Yes, ma'am. He sent an answer."

Emma fumbled with the envelope and pulled out the response with shaking hands. Jimmy watched as her eyes moved back and forth across the page. When she reached the end, she pressed a palm to her forehead. "Oh dear, oh dear, oh dear." She shook her head and looked down at the expectant but red face of Jimmy. "You look as if you are about to combust before my eyes. Come in and rest for a moment. I'll get you a cool glass of milk and some cookies."

"Thank you, ma'am, but—"

"Silly boy, that is not your reward. I'll fetch that for you, too. You went to Mr. Jennings's home first, I assume."

"Yes, ma'am. The housekeeper sent me to the police station."

"You were very quick. I will remember to always look for you before anyone else."

Jimmy sat at the kitchen table and downed half a glass before touching the three cookies. He gobbled them up in record time and washed them down with the rest of the milk. He left the Borden house with a grin on his face and a pocket full of coins.

Emma sat down to try to read her book while she awaited her sister's return. She'd only turned the page once when there was a knock on the door. She opened it to Marshall Hilliard and State Detective George Seaver, who were accompanied by two men carrying carpentry toolboxes. "What do you want here, now, gentlemen?"

"We need to gather bloodstain evidence, Miss Borden."

"As many times as you have been through this house, and evidence still remains?"

"Yes. Some of it is on floorboards and wooden trim. That is why I brought two carpenters to cut it all out."

"You are cutting into our floor? Our doors? Our trim?"

"It is necessary."

Emma stepped back and allowed them all inside. She was shocked by all that she had missed. She would have cleaned it all if she had known.

"Miss Borden," the Marshall called out. "Come over here, please."

Emma stepped over to where he stood by the door that led between the sitting room and dining room.

"There was blood on this door jamb and along the mopboard. It is not there now."

Emma blanched but did not give an inch. "No sir, I do not see any blood there."

"Did Lizzie clean it off?"

"No, she did not."

"You haven't been with her every minute of the day, could she have done it when you were not aware."

"No, sir. I am certain that Lizzie did not clean the blood off that trim."

"How can you be so certain, Miss Borden?"

"Because I cleaned the blood off."

"You did what?"

Emma straightened her spine and jutted out her chin. "I washed the blood clean on Sunday."

"How dare you?"

"How do I dare not, sir? It was my father's blood. I could not bear the sight of it any longer."

"I will speak to the District Attorney about this."

"Certainly, sir. Be sure to tell him that you did not bother to try to collect that evidence until four days after my father's murder."

Marshall glared at Emma, and she returned his steely stare. They broke eye contact only when one of the carpenters said, "We've gotten it all down here. Should we go upstairs now?"

"Yes," Marshall said. "I will go with you."

Emma stepped into the dining room and sat on the lounge as she listened to the sounds of men upstairs, tromping, sawing, shifting furniture around. She struggled against slipping into a slough of despond, clinging tightly to her success and standing up to the Marshall. She vowed she would never relent until they left her Lizzie alone.

A half-hour later, she heard footsteps pounding down the stairs. The Marshall stuck his head into the dining room. "We are leaving now, Miss Borden."

"At last, Mr. Hilliard. I will pray you have no further reason to return."

Chapter Seventeen

With a skirt to her ankles, sleeves to her wrists, and a neckline that embraced her throat, Lizzie walked to the witness chair, trying to ignore the stifling heat that made her head swirl and her knees weaken. She faced District Attorney Hosea Knowlton, a blustery man with a full beard, a jutting chin, and large ears. He asked her full name. "Lizzie Andrew Borden," she said.

"Is it Lizzie or Elizabeth?"

She stared at him wondering if he were playing a game or thought her too stupid to know that she needed to use her full legal name in any court of law. "Lizzie."

"You were so christened?"

"I was so christened," she said, reminding herself that it was far too early to allow her irritation to mount.

Knowlton's rudeness offended Lizzie when he asked for her age. When he asked if her mother was still living, she wanted to say, *for heaven's sake, if she were, none of us would be here now.* Instead, she said, "She died when I was only two and a half years old, and no, I do not remember her."

The District Attorney asked multiple questions about her father and stepmother and then turned to the finances of the couple for which she claimed ignorance. He peppered Lizzie with questions about her relationship with her stepmother. Then he asked, "Were your father and mother happily united?"

Lizzie paused, confused about how to answer. "I do not know, but that they were."

"Why did you hesitate?" he pressed.

Knowlton continued in this vein, leaving Lizzie perplexed. *How should I know what goes on between Father and Abby when they are alone? And what did that have to do with their deaths? They obviously did not kill each other.*

Lizzie knew she was on dangerous ground when his questions turned to the dress she had worn that day. It was a relief when he switched to inquiries about her Uncle John. Still, she felt her ire rising with every word that crossed his lips.

She felt as if the District Attorney who questioned her every answer was treating her with great disrespect but kept answering his questions as best as she could. From time to time, her fingernails pressed into her palms when she worried about the answer she'd given and feared she contradicted herself.

She forced her fists to unclench, stretched her fingers, and checked her hands for any blood but only found deep indentations. When he confronted her about whether she had been upstairs or downstairs when Father returned from downstreet, she shook her head and tried to appear forlorn. *He thinks women's heads are full of feathers—I'll take advantage of his bias.* "I do not know what I have said. I have answered so many questions, and I am so confused. I am telling you just as nearly as I know how. I think I was downstairs in the kitchen."

Through the next series of queries, Lizzie continued to play to Knowlton's prejudice toward women until the judge tired of it all. "It is getting late. We will continue this inquest tomorrow. Proceedings are now dismissed." He banged his gavel, making a sharp retort. Relief coursed through Lizzie's body. She rose to meet Mary in the hall.

* * *

While Lizzie sat on the stand, Medical Examiner Dolan drove up in a buggy to 92 Second Street. He sent a man to fetch the laborer who had dug the hole to bury the bloodied clothing. He made a transit of the house, speaking to each police officer. "My presence here is not to be known to anyone.

Under no circumstances do I want my actions observed. Use all vigilance to prevent anyone coming into the yard and keep all passers-by moving past the house. Do not let them stop and stare."

John walked out of the back door. "What is going on here?"

"I'm sorry, sir," the officer said, "No one is permitted back here at this time."

"Why not?"

"I cannot say, sir. But you must go back inside, or I will have to arrest you."

John glared at him and stomped into the house.

The hole-digger uncovered his previous day's work and spread the items out in the grass for Dolan to examine. Dolan selected what he wanted: he cut a large section out of Andrew's coat and shirt, the waist of the dress Abby had worn, and cut off a sizable piece of carpet. He obtained a large cardboard shoe box, placed all the items inside, and left the yard. What remained was buried again.

A while later, Dolan returned carrying the shoe box wrapped in manila paper and ordered that it be buried in the yard, four feet deep. Throughout the whole time, Dolan offered no explanation for the purpose of the excavation.

* * *

At 5 o'clock, Bridget Sullivan, released on her own recognizance with stern warnings not to talk about any of her testimony, left the police station escorted by Officer Patrick Dougherty. They passed through Court Square. Dressed in a green gown with a hat to match, she walked with jerky movements and constantly looked over her shoulder, but no one recognized her and did not approach her with questions.

From there, Bridgett and the officer went to 92 Second Street and rang the bell. A surprised Emma opened the door. "Oh, Maggie, you are back. I am so pleased."

"My name is Bridget, if you please. And no, Miss Emma, I have not returned to this household to stay. I just came to get my belongings if you will allow."

"Of course, of course." Emma was chagrined that Maggie felt it necessary to bring an officer with her to enter the house but did not question her. She opened the door wide. "Please come in."

Bridget went into the kitchen and up the back stairs with the policeman. When they returned, the officer carried a bundle. Emma was saddened by the small size of it. "Is that everything, Mag—Bridget? If you need a trunk, we can get one for you."

"No, that is everything."

"You are always welcome to return."

Thank you, Miss Emma," Bridget said and walked out without another word. The officer escorted her to 95 Division Street, where she spent the night with her cousin, Patrick Harrington.

* * *

A dazed Lizzie met Mary in the lower hallway, and together, they went to the carriage, relieved to discover that much of the crowd had dissipated. On the ride home, Mary said, "How are you doing, my dear?"

"Right now, I am delighted that this day is over."

"I will not ask you any questions about your testimony because I doubt you want to relive it. But I am here always whenever you want to talk."

"Thank you, Mary. You are a true friend."

"I do need to get back home, though. They will all wonder what happened to me."

"Shall I send for a carriage?" Lizzie asked.

"You have had enough to contend with today. I will walk across the street to the stable. No need for you to trouble yourself further."

Entering her home, Lizzie was confronted by a barrage of questions from Uncle John and Emma.

"What did he ask you?"

What did you say?"

"Did anyone accuse you of murder?"

"Was Mr. Jennings there?"

Lizzie raised her hands, palms out. "I felt a lot of hostility from Mr. Knowlton, but I remained calm throughout. What have you heard happened today?"

"I heard that Maggie testified," Emma said. "People are saying that when she left the inquest, she was crying as she came down the stairs."

"Surely, no one thinks she is responsible," Lizzie said. "She has nothing to gain from the deaths of Father and Abby."

"I imagine if she felt any hostility from the District Attorney, it would drive the poor girl to tears. Not everyone can retain composure in the face of adversity as you do, Lizzie," Emma said. "But she has left us. She came by for her things this afternoon."

"Did you ask her to stay? What will we do without her, Emma?"

"I think she wanted to be away from the house altogether, Lizzie. She did not feel safe here—a policeman accompanied her."

Uncle John added a new wrinkle. "Apparently, they are not looking at her with any more rigor than they are looking at many others. I was walking through Main Street and down to the banks when I realized I was being followed by an officer. When I confronted him, he produced a statement from that man G.E. Fish from Hartford who claimed that he knew that you and I, Lizzie, concocted the plot and hired someone to commit the murders. I told the officer that he knew as well as I what little grounds there were for such an absurd charge. I told him it was highly unreasonable, but I would say no more.

"How could Abby's brother-in-law file a report with the police? A rumor whispered on the street is one thing, but this is entirely different. It is an outrage," Emma said. "It is careless and without merit."

"That never stopped a gossip, Emma," Lizzie said.

"But this was not just gossip, sister. We knew of the rumor, but we did not know he gave a report to the police. Could he possibly bear a grudge against you, Uncle John?"

"If he does, I know not why. I do not know the man."

"I, for one, know that I did not plot with you to murder Father and Mrs. Borden. No such question has been asked of me, and if it is, I will proclaim your innocence loud and clear. I truly dread returning to the inquest tomorrow."

"You spent the afternoon answering their questions, and still they are not done?" Emma said.

"No," Lizzie sighed. "The inquest resumes at 10 o'clock tomorrow morning. I understand, though, that I will not be the only witness."

"Who else will appear?"

"I do not know. They keep me in the dark. And I do not know what else they can possibly ask me." Lizzie pled fatigue from the day's proceedings and retired to her room. In truth, the family's questions and concerns wearied her as much as the inquest itself.

Chapter Eighteen

arshall Hilliard arrived at the Borden house the next morning and transported Lizzie back to the inquest. This time, she went alone. She held her head up high and stared straight ahead as she walked into the Central Police Station. She summoned her dignity as she eased into the witness chair.

Much to Lizzie's annoyance, Mr. Knowlton embarked on a repetition of yesterday's queries. She repeated her answers from the day before, with each one fraying away at her patience.

When he finished, he went over the same ground again, making Lizzie repeat herself time after time. She suspected he was leading into a specific line of inquiry but was not certain where he was going until he asked, "So, it would have been extremely difficult for anybody to have gone through the kitchen and dining room and front hall without you seeing them?"

"They could have gone from the kitchen into the sitting room while I was in the dining room, if there was anybody to go."

After pushing Lizzie through a series of repetitious questions again, the District Attorney said, "Miss Borden, I am trying in good faith to get all the doings of that morning of yourself and Miss Sullivan. I have not succeeded in doing it. Do you desire to give me information or not?"

Lizzie shouted, "I don't know it!" When she saw the delighted twinkle in his eyes, she regretted her loss of patience. She struggled to push down her anger and frustration and wipe the evidence of emotion from her face.

"When you saw your father, where was he?"

"On the sofa."

"What was his position?"

"Lying down."

"Describe anything you noticed at the time."

Lizzie swallowed as she fought against the resurrection of that image in her mind. "I did not notice anything else. I was so frightened and horrified. I ran to the foot of the stairs and called Maggie."

"Did you notice he had been cut?"

Please stop, Lizzie thought. "Yes, that is what made me afraid."

"Did you make any search for your mother?"

Lizzie wanted to say: *My mother died when I was a small child.* She bit that back and answered, "No, sir."

"Why not?"

At the tip of her tongue were the deadly words: *because I did not care.* Instead of uttering that damning statement, she said, "I thought she was out of the house. I thought she had gone out. I called Maggie to go to Dr. Bowen's."

"You made no effort to find your mother at all?"

"No, sir."

"Who did you send Maggie for?"

"I said, 'Go for Dr. Bowen as soon as you can. I think father is hurt.'"

"Did you know that he was dead?"

"No, sir."

"You saw him."

"Yes, sir."

"You went into the room."

"No, sir. I opened the door and rushed back."

"You saw his face?"

Please stop. Please stop. Please stop. Her fingernails dug into her palms as she fought off the scream that rose in her throat. Through clenched teeth, she answered, "No, I did not see his face because he was all covered with blood."

"You saw his face covered with blood?"

"Yes, sir."

"Did you see his eyeball hanging out?"

"No, sir," she said. *But I will loathe you until you die, Hosea Knowlton.*

"Nothing of that kind?"

"No, sir." Lizzie threw a hand over her face and moved her shoulders in a sobbing motion. *Better that the judge thinks I am distraught than to see my countenance and know I am filled with rage. I never wanted to envision my father's condition again. I could not go on living with that horrid image in my head. I really wished my father was still alive.* When Lizzie had cleared her face clean of all emotion, she dropped her hand and raised it to face Knowlton's torture again.

When the District Attorney moved to questions about axes and hatchets, all Lizzie could think of was her anger at her Father for killing the pigeons after she had built a new cote for them. "Father killed some pigeons in the barn last May or June. I thought he had wrung their necks, but some of the pigeons he brought to the kitchen were missing their heads. He may have used an axe or hatchet on them." The image of the little birds' bodies pulsed in Lizzie's head, forcing her to fight the urge to scream yet again.

"Can you tell me anything else that you did that you have not told me during your absence from the house?"

"No, sir."

In response to Knowlton's implication that the arrival of attorney Andrew Jennings soon after her parents' deaths had a sinister meaning, Lizzie said. "Emma sent for him, not I."

His raised eyebrows gave a clear indication of his lack of belief in her statement. "Now, tell me once more, if you please, the particulars of that trouble you had with your mother four or five years ago."

Lizzie sighed. "Her father's house on Ferry Street was for sale—"

The District Attorney interrupted. "Who's father's house?"

Lizzie gritted her teeth, recognizing the deliberate obtuseness of his question. She forced her jaw to relax as she answered. "Mrs. Borden's father's house. She had a stepmother and a half-sister, Mrs. Borden did, and this house was left to the stepmother and half-sister, if I understand right, and the house was for sale. The stepmother wanted to sell it, and

Father bought out her share. Father did not inform Emma nor I that he had done so, but we found out from someone else. I told Father that since he bought it for her and put it in her name, he ought to give something to Emma and I.

"I told Mrs. Borden so. She said that did not care anything for the house herself. She wanted it so her half-sister could have a home since she married a man who was not doing the best he could, and she wanted her sister to have a home. So, Father gave Emma and I Grandfather's old house. That was all the trouble we ever had."

After another series of questions, Lizzie was finally released for the day from the stuffy, hot courtroom. Outside, she turned to Marshall Hilliard. "May we pause for a moment on the sidewalk to breathe in some fresh air."

She was surprised and grateful when he agreed. The interlude did not last long. People on the street were moving toward them, and Hilliard rushed her into the carriage and escorted her to her front door. Much to her dismay, he pushed his way inside. "Miss Borden, would you be kind enough to hand me the articles you spoke about at the inquest."

"Certainly," she said, "I will get them right away." She retrieved the black stockings and shoes from her room and handed them to the Marshall with a forced smile. Shutting the front door, she turned to face her uncle and her sister.

"I was called to testify," Uncle John said.

"So was I," Emma added.

"And Dr. Bowen took the stand as well. As best as I could gather, he delivered a straight-forward recounting of his visit to the house a few days before the murders and everything he did that morning," Uncle John said.

"Who else was there today?" Lizzie asked.

"Your neighbor, Mrs. Churchill."

"Of course. She must have been thrilled. She is the nosiest woman and the biggest gossip in Fall River. I imagine taking the stand was the highlight of her life."

Emma placed a hand on Lizzie's arm. "Really, Lizzie, must you be so harsh? Mrs. Churchill is a kind, Christian woman who came to our home to assist in any way she could."

"Emma, you see the best in everyone—even when no best is there. I assure you, Mrs. Churchill does nothing that does not benefit herself. Uncle John, anyone else there?"

"A Mr. Hiram Harrington."

"He and father have not been friendly for years. Whatever would he have to contribute?" Lizzie asked.

"I believe there was interest in him by some parties as a suspect in the murders. He testified that he knew nothing about them and that he was far away from Fall River on the day that occurred."

"I don't think Father ever believed a word that man said, and I won't either. I hope the judge did not take his statement at face value."

Emma said, "Oh, Lizzie, do not distress yourself. The inquest will be over soon. Perhaps you should go rest for a while. I'll prepare supper on my own."

Lizzie took her leave and went upstairs. She wanted a short nap, but sleep would not come. Emma and Uncle John had done their best to comfort her, but they did not possess the disturbing knowledge that Lizzie held tight to her chest.

Chapter Nineteen

Lizzie entered the Central Police Station for the third time that week. Bile rose in her throat when she looked across the room and saw Mr. Knowlton. She wished the floor would open up beneath him and swallow him whole.

She forced a placid look on her face, hoping she successfully hid her disdain and annoyance. She folded her hands in her lap and tried to imagine snow outside of the windows to fight the oppressive heat.

"Is there anything in your previous testimony you would like to correct?" Knowlton asked.

The question rang in her head like a church bell at noon. She knew he wanted to catch her in a lie, but she refused to fall into his trap. "No, sir."

"Did you buy a dress pattern in New Bedford?"

"A dress pattern?" she asked. *What does this have to do with anything in this proceeding?* Senseless as the question may have seemed to her, she continued answering numerous questions about the pattern before Knowlton jumped to a new subject entirely.

"Your attention has already been called to the circumstances of going into the drug store of Smith's on the corner of Columbus and Main Streets, by the same officer on the day before the tragedy, has it not?"

"I don't know whether some officer asked me but somebody has spoken of it to me. I don't know who that was."

"Did that take place?"

"It did not. I was home all day Wednesday and did not go out until evening."

"Miss Borden, of course, you appreciate the anxiety that everybody has to find the author of this tragedy. I now ask you if you can furnish any other fact—or even suspicion, that will assist officers in this matter."

Lizzie related the times she'd seen shadowy figures around the house at night but admitted she never told any police officer about them. She struggled to hang on to her equilibrium when Knowlton made another sudden change of topic.

"When was the reward made for the detection of the criminals?"

"I think it was made Friday."

"Who suggested that?"

"We suggested it ourselves and asked Mr. Buck if he did not think it was a good plan."

"Whose suggestion was it, yours or Emma's?"

"I do not remember. I think it was mine."

With that lie, Lizzie was released from the stand and told she would not need to return. She felt light-headed, and only the force of her will got her up from the seat and out of the hearing room. Once she was out of sight of the judge, she wobbled and grabbed at the wall to keep from falling. A police officer took her to Police Matron Reagan's room. The presence of a desk and the absence of family photographs made the space appear much like an austere version of a sitting room found in any home. The carving on the mantlepiece was elegant and detailed oak decorated with a cityscape above the fireplace.

"You look as if you might swoon," the Matron said. "Lie down on the couch until you recover." The matron stood over her, looking down with deep-set eyes, heavily arched eyebrows, and a patrician nose. Lizzie wondered if she gazed at everyone with that intimidating, superior stare.

Emma and Mary Brigham rushed into the room and fluttered around Lizzie like ladies-in-waiting. Emma plumped the pillow behind her head and Mary held Lizzie's hand and stroked the back of it.

"They said I do not have to return to the hearing again," Lizzie said.

"Wonderful," Emma said. "You'll be able to come home soon."

"In a short while, Lizzie, you will be able to look back and take pride in the fact that you survived this ordeal," Mary echoed.

The two women tried to distract Lizzie with town news and gossip but still, time rolled on at an aggravating slow pace. Even the clock hanging on the wall seemed to tick only in long-delayed intervals.

The hearing ended at four o'clock, but Lizzie maintained vigil in the Matron's room, waiting for her dismissal. She did not really absorb anything that her friend and sister said. Their voices were like rumbles of thunder from far away. She sat rigid on the sofa with her hands clenched tightly in her lap.

Mr. Jennings, who had received a visit from the Marshall and the Mayor informing him of Lizzie's imminent arrest, hurried into the room. He assured the women that it all would be over soon. Lizzie thought she noticed insincerity in his words but still held on to hope until 6 o'clock when she turned to her sister. "Emma, they are not going to allow me to go home."

"Nonsense, Lizzie," Emma said. "We just need to wait for the district attorney to release you."

Mary added, "They should be here shortly."

Lizzie looked at Mr. Jennings, but he looked away from her before she could catch his eye. She knew in that instant that her ordeal was far from over and still she waited. She wanted to pace and scream and stomp on anyone in her way. She knew, however, that if she lost control for even a moment, she would never be able to corral her emotions again. She clenched her hands tighter.

At seven o'clock, the dreaded and longed-for visitors arrived. Marshall Hilliard entered the room, followed by District Attorney Knowlton. Lizzie rose to her feet. Emma and Mary clustered behind her. The marshall pulled a paper from his pocket. "I have here an order for your arrest. I shall read it if you so desire, but you have the right to waive the reading."

Lizzie did not know which choice was the wisest one. She turned to Mr. Jennings, and he said, "Waive the reading."

Lizzie searched Jennings' face, seeking understanding, but he remained somber and unreadable. "You need not read it," she echoed. She held tight to her calm façade.

Emma crumbled with the news, dropping down to the sofa, wailing. "It is not fair. It is not right. It is so cruel. We have lost our parents, and now you will take my sister away from me, too." Tears streamed down her face.

Although Mary was more in control of her emotions, she still was distressed. She rushed to Lizzie, who hugged her and patted her back. "Everything will be fine, Mary. God will watch over me."

Lizzie knelt beside her sister. "Hush, Emma, hush. Mr. Jennings will work all of this out. I will come home to you, just not today. You and Mary must leave now. I don't want you to see them taking me away."

"But—"

"Please, Emma."

Emma nodded, rose, and clutched Mary's hand as they walked away, trying and failing to look strong for Lizzie. Mr. Jennings patted Lizzie on the shoulder. "I will work for your vindication every day, Miss Lizzie. I will do whatever it takes to get you back home where you belong."

Lizzie, feeling a lump rising in her throat, simply nodded in response.

The Marshall stood stiff as streetlamp and spoke in a stilted, emotionless voice. "You are now in custody on suspicion of murder. You will be transferred to the Bristol County Jail in Taunton tomorrow. Tonight, you will remain in the custody of the matron."

The matron searched Lizzie looking for any hidden items. Lizzie stood rigid, staring at a wall, imagining her visit to the Louvre in Paris. When the matron finished, and the two of them were alone, Lizzie's control dissolved. She sobbed with enough violence that it caused her to vomit. Even when her stomach was empty, the painful retching continued.

Matron sent for Dr. Bowen, who gave Lizzie another injection. "Matron, I do not think it in my patient's best interest to spend the night in a cell."

Matron delivered her iciest glare to the doctor, but he did not waver. She made up the sofa in her room. Lizzie drifted off into a drug-induced sleep, wondering why her good deeds had not saved her from this fate.

Chapter Twenty

On the morning of August 12, 1892, Emma, Jennings, and the Reverend Mr. Buck brought a carriage to the police station to give Lizzie a ride to the train depot. Emma was proud of her sister as she walked towards them with her head held high, her posture perfectly straight. She had taken care with her dress, donning her dark blue street gown and her cherry-trimmed hat with a short veil. Flanked by the Marshall and the Mayor, she gave no indication that she was intimidated by their presence.

They passed a few onlookers on the way to the depot, but the short ride was uneventful. Lizzie disembarked from the carriage and stumbled. She was rescued from falling by the Marshall and the Reverend.

Mr. Jennings waited on the platform as the others boarded the train. Lizzie sat down beside a window, trying to regain her composure after her near fall. Emma sat beside her and reached across to pull down the shade to conceal her sister from prying eyes.

Unlike the relative serenity in Fall River, the Taunton train station was a madhouse. Lizzie's eyes scanned the boisterous gawkers who shouted and reached out to touch her as she descended and walked to the carriage.

"Don't worry, Lizzie," the reverend said, "it is only a short ride to the jail."

It took far longer than anticipated. Carriages and wagons blocked their way as the riders struggled for a glimpse of Lizzie. Crowds of people stood in the streets, causing the driver to stop several times to clear the way. Others ran alongside the carriage, slapping it with their open hands. Lizzie was appalled—*if they are this excitable when I have not yet gone to trial, how much worse they will be if I am judged to be guilty.*

Lizzie and Emma had expected to pull up to a forbidding fortress with massive gray walls and dusty dirt grounds. Instead, the building was a pleasant sight with its ivy-covered walls surrounded by shade trees and flower beds. It looked more like a private school or sanitarium.

The sisters were even more surprised to find two of their family friends waiting to greet them, Sheriff Wright, once the Marshall of Fall River, and his wife and prison matron, Mary. Although initially cheered, Lizzie braced herself for a hostile welcome when she recalled the matron had a very close relationship with Abby.

Mary, with her broad forehead, kindly face, and nimbus of silver hair, approached Lizzie with tears glittering behind her gold glasses. She clasped Lizzie's hands between her own. "Oh, Lizzie, Lizzie. I do not believe you are guilty. I have known you too long to think such a thing is possible."

Mary ushered Lizzie inside, leaving Emma standing in front of the building, drowning in her helplessness to alter the situation. Lizzie held her head high as she walked past the five cells containing other prisoners who were all beneath her station.

"Miss Lizzie," Mary said as she led her into a room with a bathtub, "I know this is naturally abhorrent to you, but rules are rules. Please disrobe while I prepare your bath."

"Right here?" Lizzie asked.

Mary nodded her head.

"With you in the room?"

"I am sorry, my dear, but it must be done. Every incoming prisoner must be bathed."

A horrified Lizzie removed her outer garments, one at a time, folding each piece carefully on a chair. She saw two drab, shapeless prison dresses hanging on hooks and felt nauseous at the thought of having to don one of those vermin-ridden sacks after her bath. Down to her undergarments, her fingers froze and refused to do her bidding.

"Come now, Miss Lizzie, I do not want to have to forcibly remove your clothing," Mary said. "Please do so yourself."

Lizzie nodded her head, stepped out of her petticoat, and removed her chemise. Loosening her corset, she blushed a brilliant red as she removed it and then pulled down her bloomers. Mary held up a large towel between them, and Lizzie slid down into the tub.

Mary continued to hold up the towel and turned her head toward the far wall. "Be quick, Lizzie. I cannot hold this up for much longer."

Lizzie lathered, wiped, and rinsed. "I'm ready now, Mrs. Wright."

"Step out, and I'll wrap the towel around you."

Lizzie stood and stared with dread at the prison garb hanging on the wall. She felt her gorge rising and despaired that she would be further humiliated by vomiting in front of Mrs. Wright.

"Oh, Miss Lizzie, do not worry about those dresses over there. You will be allowed to wear your own clothing while you are here. I told Emma to bring another outfit for you when she comes to visit."

Lizzie's knees buckled with relief as she donned her undergarments and her dress and hat. Still, she could not silence the inner quaver that caused her to feel unsteady and frightened of what the future might bring.

Mary escorted her to her cell down cleanly swept halls into her new residence—a small cell less than ten feet deep and eight feet across. One small, grated window allowed a modicum of light to filter into the room. The walls bore a new coat of snowy whitewash, erasing Lizzie's expectation of filthy surroundings.

"Now, Miss Lizzie, I know this is not what you are used to and I am sorry for that. But I did bring you one of my own pillows to replace the flattened standard one in the jail. And most women do not get a rocking chair and stool like the ones I had brought to your cell."

"Thank you, Mrs. Wright." Once the matron left, Lizzie absorbed her surroundings and although she was being treated better than most, it still was far beneath her accustomed standards of quality. Self-pity engulfed her thoughts. *I never envisioned this outcome. I only saw what I could gain.*

* * *

Lizzie fell into the predictable pattern of jail life. Bread and coffee at seven o'clock each morning. Lunch at 11:30, consisting of a monotonous menu repeated week after week: corned beef twice, corned beef hash made from leftovers for two days, soup twice, and codfish and potatoes rounding out the week. At 5:30 each evening, all the prisoners were served tea and bread. On occasion, Lizzie ordered food from the outside world. Taunton Inn delivered meals in six-layer tins—a luxury not many could afford.

Lizzie was flooded with correspondence—lots of letters and cards from friends along with missives from far-flung parts of the country. Most of the latter were from members of the Temperance Union and the Christian Endeavor Society expressing sympathy over her plight. All of them were a comfort. She only regretted that some were anonymous and she could not communicate her appreciation to the senders.

When Emma visited Lizzie, Mrs. Wright allowed the sisters to stroll up and down the hallway while they talked. On the first visit, Emma's fingers rubbed the opposing palm without ceasing. Lizzie wondered if the jail itself made her nervous and tried to ignore the fidgeting. After a short time, though, she felt compelled to ask Emma what was troubling her.

"I don't know how to begin. I need your permission to do something. If you say no, I will not do it."

"My permission? For heaven's sake, Emma, look where I am. You do not need my permission to do anything."

"Yes, I do, Lizzie, for my own peace of mind, if nothing else."

"What is it, Emma?"

"I was thinking I might pack up Abby's personal effects and send them to her half-sister."

"That makes perfect sense to me. We do not need reminders of her in our home. Why do you hesitate?"

"It is difficult acting on my own. I am used to Father telling me what should be done in important matters such as these. I thought about asking Mr. Jennings, but I don't want to distract his attention from your defense."

"Of course, you can do it, Emma. You need to accept that you are an independent woman now. You can make your own decisions. You do not need the approval of any man. Get one of Father's men to fetch one of the trunks down from the attic. Don't do it yourself—the trunks are too heavy and, besides, neither you nor Maggie should be going into the attic while it is still hot outside. The attic will be ablaze. Maggie can help you pack the trunks. Maggie did come back, did she not?"

"No, she did not, Lizzie. I have not found a replacement yet. I followed up on a few recommendations, but they were all reluctant to move into our home."

"Someone must be found. You cannot continue on all alone, particularly not right now. Offer more money than the typical householders offer for domestics. Emphasize the light duty involved—no need to make up bedrooms and the like. If a housekeeper you do like is still hesitant, offer two half-days off instead of one."

"I will do that and make the benefits clear to all prospects. But, Lizzie, I would do without a housekeeper all the rest of my life if it meant having you at home with me."

"There, there, Emma." Lizzie patted the back of her sister's hand. "Place your faith in Mr. Jennings. He will get me home as soon as he can. Let's talk of happier things. Come back to my room, and I'll show you all the uplifting notes I have received." Lizzie pulled out many pieces of correspondence, including the sympathetic missive from Mary Livermore.

Emma pulled that one out of the stack. "Lizzie, you know who she is, don't you?"

"Of course, she's an important suffragist, but I can't say that I know her."

"You met her once when you were quite small. She was a close friend of our mother."

"Did mother share Mary's beliefs about women?"

"Certainly. Our mother was involved in the movement, much to Father's dismay. I think we both picked up bits and pieces of her philosophy."

"Surely not I, I was so young."

"Yes, Lizzie, but you had a fertile, impressionable mind. That's probably why you balked against Father's control so fiercely."

"For all the good it did me. I am offended by the sentiment that women's lot in life should be learning how to best serve the egos and interests of males."

Chapter Twenty-One

The courts did not wait long to schedule a preliminary hearing. For that, Lizzie had to travel back to Fall River on August 22. The authorities told the reporters that she would be moved in the afternoon, then secreted her out of the jail in the morning to the Taunton train depot. The ruse ensured that no crowds were gathered shouting questions and blocking their route.

Lizzie was accompanied by Marshall Hilliard, Detective Seaver, and the ever-faithful Reverend Buck. Lizzie forgot her anxiety at the upcoming hearing as she reveled in the delicious pleasure of stepping outside beyond the jail walls to breathe fresh air. In the carriage, she ignored the men escorting her and imagined taking a leisurely drive with her friends.

The Taunton station, too, was devoid of onlookers, much to everyone's relief, making the journey back to Fall River uneventful. The peace continued at the Fall River depot. At the police station, however, they were greeted by loud multitudes of men and women lined up for blocks, waiting patiently as if their long-suffering presence could expand the size of the 300-seat courtroom to contain them all.

Once the carriage halted, the word of the occupants spread through those gathered with ever-noisier shouts and whispers. The three men flanked Lizzie, pushing her through the unruly crowd. Lizzie ignored the mayhem as best she could, grateful for the short distance from the road to the front steps. She was led into the Matron's Quarters, where she greeted the warmth of Emma and Marianna Holmes as they all sat down for lunch.

After the tense experience out front, however, Lizzie was eager to get started on the proceedings in hopes of a quick ending to the ongoing nightmare. District Attorney Knowlton had other ideas. He requested and received a three-day continuance to await the results of the examination of her clothing and the analysis of Andrew and Abby's stomach contents. Three days—seventy-two hours—for Lizzie to wait, fret and worry.

Jennings, however, made more productive use of the delay. The realization that his lack of criminal trial experience was a handicap, he searched around, looking for someone who would counteract that deficit. He went to meet with Melvin O. Adams, attorney, and president of the Boston, Revere Beach, and Lynn Railroad.

Adams served as an assistant district attorney in Suffolk County and was now in private practice. "Mr. Jennings, it seems uncommon strange to me that for many years, Andrew Borden had been your client, and now you want to lead a vigorous defense for the accused killer."

"I knew the whole family and the loving relations they had one for another to find the whole idea of Miss Lizzie's guilt preposterous. She is a thirty-two-year-old woman against whom suspicions of anything evil has never rested before. To my client, she was a gentle and loving daughter who would have shrunk from torturing a fly or killing a mouse. She has been a prominent worker in the church and in the temperance cause. Everyone considered her an earnest Christian woman of noble character who moved in the best society in Fall River."

"But she was the only person in the house when it happened."

"She was not inside the house, Mr. Adams. She was outside in the barn when her father's murder occurred. Besides, everything points to the murders having been committed by a long-handled axe. Lizzie Borden could not have wielded such a weapon. Not even if she had been maddened by rage or inflamed by insanity. She could not have swung the instrument around to inflict such deep and sharply defined cuts. No soft-handed, gentle-minded, timorous woman could have done that."

"What about the poison purchase I have read about?"

"You know, as well as I, that poisons are no strange thing to be found on the dressing table of a woman. What woman does not have arsenic to beautify her complexion and brighten her eyes? And who knows what poisonous substances they have for cleaning furs and feathers and such. But really, until the chemists find prussic acid in the bodies of the victims, Why is it even relevant?"

"It is an uncomfortable coincidence, Mr. Jennings."

"Nothing more than that. Miss Borden was as sick as her parents from some mysterious cause—most likely spoiled milk. If she had poisoned it, wouldn't she refuse to imbibe it?"

"I've heard of money as a motive. It's been mentioned in many newspaper reports."

"Mr. Adams, despite the horrid gossip in Fall River. Andrew Borden was not a parsimonious man with his family. He paid for Miss Lizzie's grand tour of Europe. He gave both sisters a generous allowance, paid for new clothing twice a year and when they needed additional funds for a special purchase, his purse was always opened to them."

"You've given me a lot to think about, Mr. Jennings. I will give it some thought this evening. I should have an answer for you tomorrow. I know you believe Miss Borden to be innocent but what do you think of your chances for success in her defense?"

"Far better with you by my side than with me battling alone. I need someone with your experience."

"Very well. Until tomorrow."

Chapter Twenty-Two

Andrew Jennings arrived in Matron Reagan's quarters with a man Lizzie did not know. He had the rigid posture of a former military man with dark, wavy hair parted in the middle, deep-set eyes, and a magnificent bush of a mustache that curled up at each end. Jennings introduced him as Melvin O. Adams.

"Mr. Adams agreed to assist me in your case, Lizzie. I have but little experience in criminal law. My new co-counsel, however, has served as an assistant district attorney in Suffolk County. He is now in private practice and willing to stand by my side in your defense."

Lizzie smiled at her new ally but feared his motives. *Does he believe as firmly in my innocence as Mr. Jennings?* "I trust your judgment completely, Mr. Jennings. If you feel I need Mr. Adams, I will not argue with you."

"Good. You are about to face a difficult and trying preliminary hearing, but no matter how distressed or oppressed you feel, bear in mind that this ordeal will be very helpful to your defense. We will learn what evidence the prosecution thinks they have to obtain a guilty verdict, and our awareness will help us be prepared to defend against it. Do you understand?"

"To some degree. I just do not understand why Mr. Knowlton wants to do this when it will be of use to the defense."

"Unlike the inquest, this hearing will be open to the public. I am certain Mr. Knowlton wants to strengthen his case in the minds of prospective jurors before they come to trial. I think his theories are full of holes and we will be able to march through them with ease."

"Again, Mr. Jennings, I trust you, and I put my life in your hands."

The lawyer was pleased he gave his client hope, but at the same time, he staggered under the heavy burden of responsibility to make that optimistic assessment a reality. He knew failure to gain acquittal for the most innocent defendant was a gamble that often brought him to the edge of despair.

* * *

Lizzie's hearing, scheduled to commence at ten o'clock that morning, was delayed by an overly long session of ordinary court. Mr. Jennings went into the back of the courtroom to find out the reason. While he was gone, Lizzie and the others could hear outbursts of tittering coming from the proceeding.

Mr. Jennings was laughing when he returned to the Matron's Quarters. "The judge is hearing arguments from a man who had purchased more hogsheads of beer than the law allows for those without a license to sell it. The man insists that he had no plans to sell any of it. He brought it to celebrate the ascension of William Gladstone as the Prime Minister of England. When the judge asked why what happened on the other side of the Atlantic mattered to him, the man placed his hand on his heart and said, 'Like all Irish-born everywhere across the world, I left a wee bit of my heart in the homeland. Mr. Gladstone has long fought for my country to possess home rule and be free of the yoke of their oppressors in London.'"

Everyone in the room chuckled at the story but Lizzie. She saw no humor in the delay—the waiting it caused aggravated her nerves and turned her thoughts to endless worry.

Fifteen minutes later, Jennings and Adams entered the courtroom. A court officer shouted, "Make way for the witnesses." Lizzie's tension drew taut as a new clothesline. Still, she waited as the cacophony in the courtroom swelled. Abruptly, the room went quiet. She turned to a nearby officer. "Excuse me, officer. What has happened out there?"

"The District Attorney has arrived." Lizzie paled; her fear of Knowlton intensified at this display of his power.

The officer nodded at Emma, who walked into the courtroom with Mr.

Holmes. Mary Brigham and Marianna Holmes followed them. Lizzie's turn at last. Leaning on the arm of the Reverend Mr. Buck, she stepped through the doorway into a cyclone of pure madness as whispers raised to muffled shouts. She felt as if she were approaching the center ring of a circus.

Looking outside, she saw more chaos as a large crowd gathered, and the droning of loud voices struggling to be heard by their neighbors rose even higher. Inside, newspaper reporters jostled for seats, with every single body raising the heat to unbearable heights, and it was only morning. She cringed at the thought of how stifling it would be by afternoon.

One by one, every pair of eyes in the room turned toward Lizzie. People rose to their feet as if she were a bride approaching the altar. Lizzie felt as if she were on stage where she was at a disadvantage since no one had given her a script.

Reverend Buck escorted her to her seat next to Emma, who squeezed her hand and then stared straight ahead as the first witness, Medical Examiner Doctor Dolan, stepped up to testify. Both sisters dreaded hearing the words he had to say—they knew they would be devoid of emotion, absent of humanity, and as cold as the tomb. His talk of oozing blood and the indentations in the skulls made them exchange wincing expressions.

The way Mr. Knowlton and Dr. Dolan recounted every spot and smear of blood was ghoulish. Lizzie whispered, "Father is dead. What else matters?"

Emma patted the back of her hand. "Sssh, Lizzie."

Mr. Jennings and Mr. Adams both leaped to their feet, startling the sisters to the point of lifting them up from their seats for a moment. Lizzie's two lawyers simultaneously objected that Dr. Dolan was testifying beyond his area of expertise. The wrangling between the defense, the prosecution, and the judge went on for quite some time.

When the medical examiner switched his attention away from Andrew and drilled down on Abby's body, Lizzie relaxed and allowed her mind to drift. Emma, however, remained rigid and intense as one gory detail after another escaped from Dolan's lips.

Knowlton turned his questioning to the axes and hatchets found in the Borden home. Dr. Dolan asserted that one of the hatchets appeared to have been scraped, and all of the implements had spots that looked like blood. Lizzie leaned toward Emma and said, "Bah! He's making it up as he goes along."

"How do you know?" Emma asked.

"The murder weapon was not found in the cellar."

Emma leaned back in her seat and grabbed Lizzie's arm. "How do you know that, sister?"

"Hush!" Lizzie hissed.

Both Lizzie and Emma leaned forward in their seats when Mr. Adams rose to cross-examine Dr. Dolan. The lawyer was like a woodpecker, hammering on the witness with the same intensity employed by Knowlton on Lizzie during the inquest.

Emma and Lizzie exchanged eyebrow raises as they enjoyed the battle waged against the doctor. Soon, though, the pleasure turned to discomfort where the topics grew macabre, focusing on blood and wounds.

Judge Blaisdell interrupted to pepper Dolan with questions of his own, wanting to know why his final report had not been presented to the court. Mr. Adams followed up that line of questioning by inquiring about the minutes and notes the doctor was supposed to preserve. The doctor claimed ignorance of their whereabouts.

Lizzie and Emma bowed their heads to hide a chuckle when Adams shredded his responses, making him appear to know nothing about body temperatures. Dolan again detailed Abby's wounds. Lizzie, knowing her father's would be next, visibly retreated into a shell. Her face lengthened downward, and her eyes grew dull and lifeless. It was obvious to her attorneys that she was no longer paying any attention to the proceedings.

At the rap of the gavel, Lizzie shook her head and returned her attention to the present. Dr. Dolan stepped down after testifying for 7 hours. Lizzie was escorted back to the Matron's chamber, where Mr. Jennings and Mr. Adams waited.

"Miss Borden," Mr. Adams said, "you must pay more attention to the proceedings. You can be a great help to us by pointing out any false testimony or witnesses with a grudge against you or your family. We need your assistance."

Lizzie sighed. "It has been a most difficult day, Mr. Adams."

"Yes, it has, Lizzie," Mr. Jennings said. "I'm sure Mr. Adams understands your horror over the graphic testimony presented today. But he is right. We need to know all your thoughts on the words spoken on the stand. We need you to focus on that."

Lizzie nodded. She knew they were correct to admonish her, but if anyone else offered up the same gruesome details, she did not know if she could pay attention and maintain a quiet dignity at the same time. She knew, at this moment, she wanted her father back more than anything.

Chapter Twenty-Three

The next day of the hearing, Lizzie soon grew weary of the testimony. Knowlton called a tedious string of witnesses who did or did not see other people near the Borden home or in the yard on the morning of the murders. He followed that with several witnesses who had seen Andrew downstreet that day.

After that, the man Lizzie most dreaded, Dr. Dolan, returned to the stand. Lizzie's mind drifted to more pleasant places, like the memories of being in Marion, standing on the banks of the river, tossing her line into the water. Raised voices jerked her back to the present, where Knowlton and Dolan were arguing about the relative dampness of our cellar.

Dr. Dolan insisted: "I do not think this is a very sensible question—a more or less damp cellar."

Mr. Knowlton snapped back: "I beg your pardon, Mr. Witness, if you wish to criticize my question—"

"I think that is a foolish question."

Lizzie and Emma lowered their heads to keep their amusement out of sight. The entertainment ended with neither side getting any satisfaction when the district attorney asked if the doctor had removed anything from the bodies before burial."

"Yes sir, I removed the skulls—the heads."

Emma gasped. Other observers joined her as reporters shuffled papers to take notes. Lizzie gripped the arms of her chair. She looked at her sister, whose tears flowed as her head slumped onto the palm of her hands. Everything, everywhere, swirled before Lizzie's eyes. She shut them, hoping to make it stop. *Father was buried without his head? What a horrid desecration. How could they?"*

Both the daughters of Andrew Borden remained stunned when the court recessed at midday. They gathered in the Matron's chamber for lunch. Emma could hardly swallow a bite. "Headless, Lizzie, headless! Father and Abby are in their graves without their heads! How can they rest in peace?"

Lizzie clasped Emma's hands between her own. "Emma, I promise you, as soon as this is over, we will have Father's skull buried with the rest of his body. I promise."

"But their heads are detached! Will they have to go through eternity with their heads cradled in their arms?"

"No, Emma, God is more merciful than that. He will make Father whole in heaven."

"Are you sure?"

"As sure as we can be of anything beyond our mortal coil. Now, eat a bite or two. We'll need to be back in court soon, and you'll need your strength to get through the day."

* * *

When the hearing resumed, the sisters were relieved to see new witnesses called to the stand. First, the carpenters Joseph Shortsleeves and James Mather, who had spoken to Andrew that morning, followed by their Uncle John.

John spoke of Abby's concern that the family had been poisoned by baker's bread or milk that made her, Andrew, and Lizzie sick Tuesday night. On Wednesday, Andrew was still feeling unwell and declined a planned trip out to Swansea that day.

Knowlton moved from there to the cellar door. John insisted it had been open that morning. The prosecutor refused to believe him and then cast suspicions on Lizzie for cleaning the blood spots from the parlor door to cover up her crime. John rushed to Lizzie's defense, insisting that Emma had used a cloth to do that one morning.

The final witness that day was Bridget Sullivan. She mounted the stand, her eyes as wide and wandering as a terrified pony. Looking around the courtroom, she was overwhelmed by her awareness that she was the lowliest person in the room. As an immigrant and a domestic, she had learned not to expect any favors—in fact, she did not have any notion that she might even be treated fairly.

Knowlton sensed her fear, but it only reinforced in his mind the belief that she was hiding something. Because of that, he hammered her with intense questions and demonstrations of disbelief. The sisters felt very sorry for her ordeal and filled with gratitude when she denied knowing about the burning of any dress and claimed she did not remember what Lizzie wore on the day of the murders. They had feared that her anxiety would make her agree to anything that the district attorney wanted.

When Bridget was released from the stand, she felt only dread as soon as she was told she needed to return the next day for further questioning. Her slumped figure stumbled as she stepped down and shuffled to the exit.

Once outside, some of her tension ebbed. She fought through the overflow crowds as people yelled at her to get her attention as she tried to escape. Finally, she reached a friend's home, where she collapsed and spent the whole night worrying about what she would face on the morrow.

Lizzie was the only witness on Saturday. She looked drained before the first question was asked. Knowlton repeated all the questions that distressed her the day before and she answered with unshed tears welling in her eyes. Finally, at noon, court was dismissed for the day.

Lizzie returned to the Matron's chamber and welcomed the Reverend Mr. Buck. "Thank you for coming to see me. Your presence is such a comfort."

"I brought you a book, Miss Lizzie, to help you pass the time of your solitude." He handed her *Pendennis* by William Makepeace Thackery.

"Thank you. I so enjoyed his previous book, *Vanity Fair*. I feel certain this one will take my mind away from my troubles."

"That is my ardent wish. Come sit down and let us share some scripture and follow it with a prayer. I had in mind words of comfort from Matthew, chapter 8."

"If you don't mind, Mr. Buck, I believe I would receive more comfort from the 59th Psalm."

Buck flipped open his Bible. He glanced at the requested passage and turned to Lizzie with questioning eyes. She nodded, and he began.

> *"Deliver me from my enemies, O my God; defend me from those who rise up against me. Deliver me from the workers of iniquity and save me from bloody men. For, lo, they lie in wait for my soul; the mighty are gathered against me, not for my transgressions nor for my sin, O Lord."*

The reverend continued to the end, referencing her enemies as dogs. When he finished, he said, "Do not let your heart be embittered by the darkness of this Psalm, Miss Lizzie. Do not forget that all things work together for good for those who love God. Now, let us pray."

After he left, Lizzie sat down to read *Pendennis*. To her great dismay, she kept re-reading the same page, her mind too distracted to focus on the words she read.

* * *

Just two and a half days of testimony resulted in a flood of letters in Hosea Knowlton's office. Many letters arrived from other professionals around the country giving him tips on how to investigate the crime. Some expressed opinions about the evidence gathered. Others provided theories on who did it or how they did it—some suggesting that the murder weapon could have been a flat iron. A bevy of mediums and seers contacted him with urgent news from their visions and conversations with the dead. Some wrote pages of vitriol about the character of Lizzie Borden and the desire to pull her out of the courtroom and hang her forthwith.

Quite a few made it clear that his political future was in serious peril if he did not get a conviction of the defendant.

"Elizabeth Borden should be <u>hung twice</u>. She committed <u>Two</u> murders and <u>chopped up</u> her poor Father and his wife in <u>cold</u> blood. She is a wicked wretch, a vile <u>cruel</u> murderer. She is the child of the Devil. DO not let her off. She will 'chop up' someone else if you let her off. Do your Duty and Hang her twice. Elizabeth Borden committed Two murders; the Jezebel Mrs. Serratt was hung—she did not commit murder, only harbored the Lincoln murderer."

One letter, however, stood out from the rest. It was a confession that threw doubts into the stew of his firm conviction of Lizzie's guilt.

"You are fooling your time away trying to place the Deed of the Borden Family upon young Lady Miss Lizzie Borden as I can Satisfy you if you Could only get hold of me that she is not guilty the Peddler Robesky speaks the truth I did purchase several articles of him, and took his advice and walked to New Bedford then took the train for Boston Where I have been ever since. Will ever hang me for the deed, for I Shall Blow My Brains out, but before I do, I shall Clear Miss Borden in some way."

The writer detailed what transpired during and after the crime, where they could find evidence, and wrapped up his missive:

"please try to convince all people that poor Lizzie is <u>Innocent</u> for God Knows she is and so do I Murder will out, but I will kill Myself before any of you get hold of me. Poor girl poor girl She is all I care for. I have a good mind to give Myself up, but I know I will Clear the Girl before she will suffer more than she does not. I live at North Street ever since. Whiskey done the deed, not me."

Knowlton knew that most probably the letter was a prank or the work of a deranged person. Still, he knew it had to be investigated if only to extinguish that flicker of doubt that kept him awake at night.

Chapter Twenty-Four

Although the idea of returning to the courtroom on Monday filled Lizzie with dread, facing a Sunday with nothing but emptiness felt even worse. The window to the street was open in the Matron's Chamber, allowing Lizzie to eavesdrop on the pedestrians below. She was amazed by the great number of people who walked by discussing her fate.

She expected a high level of interest from newspapermen and policemen, but ordinary people all had something to say, too. One person was convinced of her guilt and looked forward to her hanging. Another would argue for her innocence by citing her work in the church and her quiet spinster life. A third type was adamant that no well-brought-up woman of means would be capable of committing such an act.

After a while, the theories about the murders grew boring, and she tried to read a book, then some journals, but to no avail. Concentrating was impossible. She was pacing around the room when the welcome distraction of visitors disrupted the day.

Seeing Mr. and Mrs. Charles Holmes thrilled Lizzie. Charles was the leading banker in Fall River. He and his wife Marianna were close family friends. Lizzie went to school with their daughters, Annie and Mary. The family attended the same church as she did, the Central Congregational. Lizzie had served with Marianna on the Women's Board at the Hospital of the Good Samaritan for more than two years.

Marianna sat next to Lizzie and reached out to hold both hands in her own. "Oh, Lizzie, it saddens my heart to see you in this place. Annie and May send their greetings. I spoke with Charles," she said, nodding at her husband, "and he says there is nothing we can do."

"Regretfully, Miss Lizzie, we can do no more than let this dreadful persecution run its course. At the end of this hearing, your ordeal may come to an end. It is an eventuality we pray for every day."

"But, Mr. Holmes, without a proper trial, will my name ever be cleared?"

"Sadly, some people are too stubborn to let go of their mistaken beliefs even when the judge rules that there is no cause for the state to pursue you any longer."

Lizzie rose to her feet, her brow furrowed, her hands rubbing each other with vigor. "Where would that leave me, Mr. Holmes? What if Mr. Knowlton is one of those stubborn men?"

Charles sighed. "If the judge dismisses the case, you will go home. However, the district attorney could be stubborn enough to push forward with further investigation and possibly another arrest warrant."

"Oh, no, I could not face this all over again."

"Miss Lizzie, calm yourself. I am certain that further investigation will only uncover additional information that will point away from you. I do not think it will come to that."

Marianna patted the sofa. "Come sit down here and rest with me, Lizzie. Let's talk of happier days."

After a deep sigh, Lizzie returned to her seat. "Tell me, what is new among our friends at the hospital?"

"You remember Miss Collins? Lettie?"

"Lettie Collins, of course I do."

"She is engaged to be married."

"Anyone I would know?"

"Not likely, Lizzie. His family is from Boston. The couple will live with his parents until he finishes medical school."

"Why the unseemly rush?"

"You know what the gossips say, Lizzie. But just because they say it does not make it true."

"I, for one, cannot imagine that Lettie Collins could have done something like that," Lizzie said.

"Nor can I," Marianna agreed.

After a half an hour of gossip, the Holmes departed. Lizzie was left with her anxious thoughts about the outcome of the hearing. She did not know which result would be the best for her, but she knew she desperately wanted to go home. She was not left alone with her worries for long. Emma and her Uncle John walked in carrying food that Emma prepared.

"I'm just going to stay a minute, Lizzie," John said. "I wanted to remind you that you need to maintain your calm next week at the hearing. You've done a lovely job up until now, and I hope you have the fortitude to remain serene as this ugly business moves forward. Enjoy your meal, ladies."

"Thank you, Uncle John. Sometimes, it is difficult not to disrupt the proceedings when someone tells a lie or twists the truth, but I do my best to appear above it all even as I am quaking inside."

Emma laid out the plates and utensils, and the two sisters set down to their meal. "This is very good, Emma," Lizzie said. "If I close my eyes, I can imagine you and I sitting in the grand dining room of a ship on an Atlantic crossing."

"Would that we could be there now, Lizzie."

"I wish you would have come on the European Tour with us, Emma. Or at least, travelled with your friends. The beauty I saw in those ancient cities left memories I will cherish all my life."

"Perhaps the two of us could go there together, Lizzie. I'm certain we could afford it."

Lizzie beamed. "And we would not need to ask anyone for the money. It is ours. We are women of independent means, no longer ruled by a man." Her smile drooped. "Well, we will be as soon as these men around me tire of making my life miserable."

"Surely, this, too, will pass, sister. Keep your faith in God, and he will see you through. And, of course, I will always be here. Just remember, these men are only doing their job."

"A job that should earn them a place in the deepest pits of hell."

* * *

Lizzie spent another fitful night ruminating over her fate. She rose Monday morning, already weary of the ordeal she would face in the day ahead.

That morning's hearing began with Mrs. Adelaide Churchill stepping forward to testify. She started answering inquiries about the blue and white one-piece cotton dress Lizzie was wearing when Adelaide went over to the Borden house.

Lizzie shook her head and passed a note to her attorneys that Adelaide was mistaken. "When she arrived, I was wearing my blue Bengaline silk skirt and my navy blue blouse." Lizzie did not know if Adelaide had peered into our windows and seen that dress earlier that morning or if she was just confused about what she saw.

On cross-examination, Mrs. Churchill was adamant that she saw no blood on Lizzie's clothing or in her hair. She also related that Bridget had said: "Mrs. Borden had a note to go see someone that was sick. She was dusting the sitting room, and she hurried off. She did not tell me where she was going. She usually does."

Mrs. Churchill was followed by Alice who confirmed the absence of blood on Lizzie's person and, to Emma and Lizzie's great relief, she, too, did not mention the burning of the dress.

To many court observers, the third witness, Lucy Collet, offered nothing of any use. She testified that she saw no one crossing through Dr. Chagnon's yard next to Bordens. And she may not have been able to see anyone coming by the barn if they did not make a noise.

In the afternoon, Mr. Knowlton paraded three drug clerks and a medical student before the court. Lizzie swore to her attorneys the men were lying when they said she went into Smith's drug store and requested Prussic acid to clean her sealskin on the Wednesday before the murders. Lizzie maintained her insistence to Mr. Jennings that she did not leave the house Wednesday before 6 o'clock that evening.

Lizzie bit her lips and fiddled with her hands, despairing that no one would believe her. She knew four men would always be more credible than one woman. In fact, she thought, it would only take one man, because that is the lot of women, held too long under the masculine heel.

Mr. Jennings made one of the men look foolish when he was unable to identify any other woman who came into the store that day, nor could he remember any of their purchases. He also insisted he did not talk to anyone before the inquest and could not explain how his story made it into the newspaper before that. He said he was certain of his identification because the police took him to the Borden house, and he listened outside to Lizzie's voice. He described it as tremulous, just as it was when I spoke in his shop.

"Tremulous?" Lizzie hissed at Emma behind her fan. "I am not that old."

Emma patted the back of her sister's hand and shook her head.

* * *

The first witness on Tuesday was the distinguished Harvard chemist and Cambridge expert, Professor Edward Stickney Wood. His elegant bearing and careful grooming of his hair and mustache made it obvious that he was a man of credibility and sincerity. When he came to the front of the courtroom, the silence was absolute. Lizzie looked at Emma's flushed face that told her, if she had any doubts, that his testimony could be her death or her salvation.

When he pronounced that there was no sign of prussic acid or any other poisonous irritant in the stomachs of Father or Abby, the atmosphere in the courtroom shifted as if everyone had exhaled a sigh of relief.

Tension built again when Knowlton began a series of questions about the blood evidence. The professor answers were succinct: no blood on the clothing, except for a tiny spot on Lizzie's underskirt, which may or may not be human; no blood on the hatchet or axes, and the hair found on one of them was from a cow or other animal. He also noted that a packet marked as containing hair from one of the deceased was empty of any contents. Lizzie closed her eyes and breathed deeply to absorb that welcome testimony. Emma smiled at her and squeezed her hand.

After a short round of testimony from Police Officer Phillip Harrington, Undertaker Benjamin Windward, and stonecutter John Dennie, the court broke for lunch. Over the meal, Lizzie asked Mr. Jennings, "I know I do not know much about science, but after going through all that dishonest testimony about my attempted prussic acid purchase, why did they bother to test the stomach contents for it?"

"I suppose they believed it possible that you obtained the acid elsewhere?"

"But if the Medical Examiner determined the cause of death to be violence on my father's head, what would that even matter?"

"You must understand, Miss Lizzie, that the prosecutor wants you to look as badly as possible. He wants the court to believe that you are capable of anything. However, I do believe the prussic acid testimony is irrelevant and damaging to your defense; therefore, I will ask the judge to exclude it if there is a trial."

"Will there be a trial, Mr. Jennings?"

"At this time, I do not know. It is all up to the judge whether or not the case should be presented to the jury. I am optimistic that he will not, but I must be prepared for the possibility of a trial."

* * *

The afternoon session began promptly with the court stenographer Annie White and her enormous stack of paper containing Lizzie's testimony at the inquest. Mr. Knowlton entered the large document into evidence and read it in its entirety to the court. Lizzie was flabbergasted—no one, not even her attorney, was allowed in the courtroom during the inquest, and now it was all made public. It felt unfair and a clear demonstration of the district attorney's disdain for her. When Knowlton finished, he rested his case.

Mr. Adams rose to voice the defense's objections. "Before we proceed with this case, I should like his honor's ruling with reference to this: some evidence has been offered of an attempt to buy some prussic acid. Whether true or false, I desire your Honor to rule that out of the record as it does not pertain to this case. The defendant is charged with the homicide of Mr. Andrew J. Borden with an axe, and that alone; therefore, any evidence of any other form of, or attempted form of, killing would not be pertinent to this case. I agree it is negative testimony, but I ask your Honor, before we proceed with our case, that it should be excluded, should be ruled out now."

The judge asked Knowlton, "Does the government rely on that testimony?"

"Yes, sir. It does not follow because a man is charged with committing a crime in some other way that an attempt was made to commit it some other way, for some reason, cannot be shown, I do not care to argue the force or effect of the testimony at present."

"This testimony is absolutely negative in character," Mr. Adams responded. "There is no evidence tending to show that it was even an attempt. I ask your Honor, as a special ruling, to rule out that evidence as not being pertinent to the issue that we are trying. It clearly ought not to encumber the records."

"I think it must stand for now," the judge ruled. "it may be of no great importance or materiality, but I think the evidence must stand as it is. I must decline the ruling that you asked."

Adams shrugged off the defeat and called his first witness, the Borden family doctor, Seabury Bowen. He insisted there was no way to determine in a precise manner when Abby and Andrew died, but he was certain only a short time had passed before he arrived on the scene.

For quite some time, Knowlton attempted to get the doctor to alter his testimony, but Bowen would not be rattled by his conviction. After he stepped down, the court adjourned for the day.

Back in Matron's Quarters, Lizzie turned to Emma and said, "May Judge Blaisdell and Mr. Knowlton rot where they stand."

"Quiet, Lizzie, the Matron can hear you."

"As if that matters at all. They are determined to convict me and have me hang. They do not care if I am innocent or guilty."

"You may be right about the district attorney, but the judge is a wise and good man. He does not bear you ill will."

"Let us see if you still feel the same when this ridiculous proceeding has ended."

Chapter Twenty-Five

The defense started the next day by calling Marshall Hilliard to the stand. Adams had the Marshall confirm that there was no running water on the second floor, making it impossible for Lizzie to clean up in the privacy of her room. Hilliard also admitted that neither Miss Borden had made any attempt to obstruct the thorough search of the home.

Dr. Learned testified that Abby's arms were under her body, not over her head, meaning that someone had moved the body before his arrival. Hack driver John Donnelley told the court about seeing an impression in the hay. "The form of a body on there that had been sleeping there or something." The impression," he added, "was five to six inches deep."

Lizzie's despairing thoughts the night before began to be tempered with hope for her future. She could prayed that the judge was paying attention as Mr. Adams battered against the gate of the prosecution's case.

When Dr. Frank Draper of Boston described Andrew's wounds, Lizzie's awareness slipped to memories of far-away places. She thought of the crossing of the Atlantic with the wind blowing through her hair and the fresh salt tang tingling her nose.

Her attention abruptly went back to the present when Draper contradicted medical examiner Dolan. He insisted that the heat and other conditions upstairs differed from those downstairs, making it impossible to estimate the time between their deaths with any accuracy.

The next witnesses riveted Lizzie. Mrs. Chagnon and her daughter spoke of the suspicious sounds coming from the area of the Borden fence on the night before the murder. Dr. Benjamin Handy reported a frightening-looking person in the Borden yard the morning of the murders. Della Manley confirmed the presence of a man by the house. Dr. Bowen's wife undermined the pharmacy witnesses, assuring the court that Abby told her that Lizzie had not been out of the house once on Wednesday until six o'clock in the evening. The painter Charles Sawyer, who was posted by the back door by a police officer, testified that he had seen Lizzie, but there were no signs of blood on Lizzie's clothing, her hair, or on the hatchet the police left on the kitchen table.

The defense rested. Adelaide Bingham and Emma accompanied Lizzie back to Matron's Quarters. All three women were optimistic about the outcome. Matron Reagan was upbeat as well. The Matron said, "I can tell you one thing you can't do, Miss Borden."

"Tell me what it is, Mrs. Reagan."

"Break an egg, Miss Borden."

"Break an egg?"

"Yes."

"I can break an egg."

"Not the way I would tell you to break it," Matron Reagan said with a smug smile.

"What way is that, Mrs. Reagan?"

"I'll bet you a quarter, you can't do it?"

Lizzie said, "That is too much. I'll wager a quarter."

The matron left the room and returned with an egg. "Miss Emma, move a bit further away from Miss Lizzie. If she breaks the egg the wrong way, it will ruin your dress."

Handing the egg to Lizzie, the matron said, "Hold the egg in mid-air and do not touch it against any surface."

Lizzie held it firmly and studied it. She brought one knuckle up and tapped on it. She did it again, only with more force, nearly knocking it out of her hand. Finally, she admitted, "That is the first thing I undertook to do that I never could. Here is your quarter."

All the women laughed at the Matron's cleverness and sat around sharing funny stories until it was time to bring the day to a close. Although Lizzie's spirits were buoyed by the excellent testimony that day, she would not sleep well that night. The judge would make his ruling tomorrow.

* * *

When the sun rose, Lizzie sat up in her bed, the levity of the previous day now ashes in her mouth. A mantle of dread weighed down upon her shoulders. Her insides crawled as if an industrious anthill had taken possession of her body. She had an ugly brown taste in her mouth and grit lining her eyes, which made her wonder if she cried in her fitful sleep.

She washed her face, brushed her teeth, and attempted to smooth her ragged breath. She pushed one thought to the front of her mind: *Today, this nightmare might be over. Tonight, I may lay my head on my own pillow in my own bed."*

Lizzie wiped the apprehension from her face as she entered the courtroom once again. She took her seat and placed her faith in Mr. Jennings, who would deliver the closing arguments to defend her with forceful passion.

"The murderer of Mr. and Mrs. Andrew Borden is a person with a heart blacker than hell itself." Knowing that many in the courtroom believed she was the object of that sentence, Lizzie's lips twitched, her shoulders heaved. She covered her face with her hands but could not stop the tears welling in her eyes.

When Jennings shifted from emotional to legal arguments, Lizzie bit her lips as hard as she could and wiped her eyes, which felt swollen to twice their normal size. "She is the youngest daughter of an old man, twining herself lovingly around the heart of her father."

Lizzie's tears erupted again, and she could not control her sobs. She was ashamed at her show of emotion but could not stop it. She looked up at Mr. Adams and saw that he, too, was crying.

Mr. Jennings continued, talking of the absence of motive, the failure of the police to find the murder weapon, and the inability of the government to find any blood on any of Miss Borden's clothing. He finished his argument with a plea to the judge: "Don't, Your Honor, put the stigma of guilt on this woman, reared as she has been with a character beyond reproach." The courtroom erupted in exuberant applause. Hope filled Lizzie's heart. *All those people believe in my innocence. Surely, the judge must see it, too.*

Mr. Knowlton stood for his closing argument. "I would rather resign from my position than press this case, but the stern finger of duty pointed and would not shirk. It was not possible for anyone except Lizzie Andrew Borden to have committed this crime. No one else was in the house. No one else held animosity toward either party."

Lizzie turned rigid where she sat. *Most men have no soul. The male of the species has no comprehension of the pain and suffering they inflict on all women who fall under their thumb. Their domineering, controlling, judgmental behavior wounds us and corrupts their hearts.* As he wrapped up, Lizzie prayed that she would never have to hear his voice again.

Filled with foreboding, Lizzie stood before the bar and faced Judge Blaisdell, old friend of her father, as he read his decision. "The long examination is now concluded and there remains but for the magistrate to perform what he believes to be his duty. It would be a pleasure for him to say, 'Lizzie, I judge you probably not guilty, you may go home.'" He paused to wipe tears from his eyes.

What is he saying? Why is he crying? raced through Lizzie's thoughts.

"But," the judge continued, "upon the character of the evidence presented through the witnesses who have been so closely and thoroughly examined, there is but one thing to be done. Suppose, for a single moment, a man was standing there. He was found close by the guest chamber, which, to Mrs. Borden, was a chamber of death. Suppose a man had been found in the vicinity of Mr. Borden, was the first to find the body, and the only account he could give of himself was the unreasonable one that he was out in the barn looking for sinkers; then he was out in the yard; then he was out for something else; would there be any questions in the minds of men what should be done with this man?

"So, there is only one thing to do—painful as it may be—the judgment of the court is that you are probably guilty, and you are ordered committed to await the action of the Superior Court."

Despite the heat of the courtroom, Lizzie felt a chill run across her head and down her spine, leaving her dazed. The noise in the courtroom brought her back to the present—the scurrying of reporters' feet and the groans and protests as they shoved one another to be the first out of the courtroom and into the telegraph office. Above it all, the anguished sobs of Emma tore through the clamor. Lizzie turned toward the open windows, struggling to inhale deeply of the freshness of the air outside, and patted the back of her sister's hand.

When Matron Regan brought Lizzie her supper that evening, she found her bent over, crying bitter tears. Lizzie waved her away and refused the meal. The Matron walked away with the tray, but a few minutes later, Lizzie realized her outburst was childish and foolish. She needed her nourishment. She called for her supper and cleaned her plate even though every bit tasted like sawdust.

Chapter Twenty-Six

Lizzie still felt numb when she rose the next morning to prepare for transport back to Taunton Jail. She donned her blue serge dress, a short black jacket, and a small black bonnet with a blue veil drawn down over her face. Mr. Reverend Buck waited outside the Matron's room to accompany Lizzie downstairs. He took charge of Lizzie's black grip bag. He whispered uplifting passages of scripture to her as they descended and boarded the carriage. Marshall Hilliard and Detective Seaver were her official escorts.

Although she appreciated the minister's presence, she was appalled that she must spend any time with the two men who desired to step on her and grind her into the dirt of the road. She was convinced that they pinned the blame for the deaths on her only because she was a woman and, therefore, more powerless and less fortunate than a man.

The people gathered outside of the train station surged toward the carriage as it pulled up under the portico. Inside the depot, hundreds more pressed against the windows, staring out at the prisoner and her jailers.

"Miss Borden, Reverend Buck, please remain inside the carriage until my men can push back the crowds and make an opening for your passage," Hilliard said.

"Miss Lizzie, would you like me to read your favorite Psalm again," the Reverend asked.

"No, thank you, but no. I could not concentrate."

The two stared out at a medley of angry countenances, curious faces, and tear-filled eyes. Lizzie knew she must know some of the people gathered here, but she was too dazed to recognize a single soul.

When Hilliard invited them to step out, Lizzie could see a clear path ahead, but it soon collapsed inward. People pushed against her, reached out and touched her, growled with ugliness. Lizzie inhaled a feral odor and feared for her safety. She boarded as quickly as she could, praying she would not stumble. If she did, she feared she would be trampled by the crowd.

Lizzie slid into a seat next to a window and pulled down the shade. Reverend Buck sat beside her. Hilliard and Seaver took the pair of seats behind them. As they pulled out of the station, Lizzie eased up the curtain halfway to gaze out at the moving landscape. She wondered how long it would be before she would be able to enjoy a view of the countryside again.

As the train pulled into Taunton Station, Lizzie saw another boisterous crowd up ahead and pulled down the shade. Lizzie disembarked while police officers struggled to provide a protective barrier around her. Once in the carriage, she felt safe for only a moment. People surrounded them and filled the street in front of the carriage, making passage difficult and slow.

At the jail, Mrs. Wright was waiting for Lizzie with a welcoming smile and greeted her like an old friend before escorting her and Mr. Buck inside. Lizzie suffered through the obligatory bath, had a brief conversation with the Reverend before Mrs. Wright led her back to her old cell.

Lizzie looked around the familiar room. She felt comforted, as if she just returned home after a long journey. She remembered Mr. Buck's last words: "You are one step closer to achieving your goal. One obstacle removed to your return to normal life. How could the jury find you guilty at trial when you made the judge cry at your hearing."

* * *

Back to the old routine the next morning, Lizzie grabbed her slop bucket and got in line with the five other female prisoners. She was used to performing this chore but it was a different matter to doing it in a group and going out alone. More people meant more stench. It filled the air like a noxious cloud. She tried to breathe through her mouth to lessen the smell, but being able to taste it on her tongue made it so much worse. She trudged out to the foul-smelling pit and deposited her waste before getting back in line for the return inside.

When she was back in her cell, she vigorously washed her hands, trying to eradicate the smell before her breakfast of bread and coffee arrived at seven o'clock. Soon after, Sheriff Wright visited her. "Miss Borden, you should be aware that now you are going to trial, you need to strictly adhere to the rules."

"Certainly, Mr. Wright."

"And you need to make sure your friends and supporters do so as well. I understand that women from the Christian Endeavor Society have been sending you a box of sweetmeats every week. Those gifts are against jail policy. I will inform them to stop sending the packages. If they do not do so, I will merely send them back. No more boxes will come to you."

"Of course not, Mr. Wright," Lizzie said. As he left, she simmered in a fresh stew of anger. *Those treats meant so much to me. They told me that others were thinking of me and wishing me well. The boxes also included small tokens of regard like a new toothbrush or comb, a pretty postcard, and good wishes and prayers for my release. I have not been convicted—why should I be denied these comforts?*

Lizzie found distraction in a visit from her sister, who arrived trembling all over with excitement. "Look, Lizzie, look at this article in the *New York Times*. Dr. John Abbott of Fall River has come back to town from a trip out west. And listen to what this says: 'He saw the bodies a short time after they were discovered by the daughter and viewed by the police, and that both were warm. There was not the slightest indication that one had been dead over an hour before the other.' You know what that means?"

"No, Emma. What do you think it means?"

"Mr. Knowlton's theories no longer stand up to scrutiny. He said it had to be you because no one would have been able to hide in the house for an extended period. But here it is! Proof that no one had to do that to murder them both."

Lizzie sighed. "It's only one man's opinion, Emma. I am sure, though, if Mr. Abbott is correct, Mr. Knowlton can twist his theory to fit a new puzzle."

"But, Lizzie, there is more news. The lawyer, Mr. Sayles of Providence, who the newspapers reported spoke to you about the distribution of Father's estate after his death, has denied it. He said that he never discussed any matter with you and was not in Fall River during the preliminary hearing."

Lizzie turned away from her sister but said not a word.

"You should be happy about this news," Emma said.

"I'm glad you are, but I cannot get my hopes up. They would only be smashed down once again. When I have returned to my home, I will celebrate with you. Now, however, I must prepare for the worst."

"No, Lizzie, that will not come. You will return home. Justice will prevail."

Lizzie turned away again, afraid of what her face might reveal. *Justice would find me hanging from the nearest tree. Sweet Emma can never see anything but the best in everyone.*

* * *

Mrs. Wright arrived at Lizzie's cell bearing yet another New York Times article. "Lizzie, Lizzie, Lizzie, look! Mrs. Mary Livermore proclaimed your innocence."

"How good of her," Lizzie responded.

"Do you know who she is?"

"Yes, Mrs. Wright. She was a friend of my mother.

"She is much more than that, Lizzie. She is a leading suffragist. She is the champion of women."

"I know that. She is a remarkable woman. But she is tilting at windmills. Men will never allow us the vote."

"Listen, Lizzie, please. She said, 'I believe most firmly that Lizzie Borden is as innocent and as much in the dark as to the crime and how it was done and is as much puzzled about it as I am. It is the work of a maniac. It was the most unwise course in the world for Judge Blaisdell to sit first at the inquest and then at the hearing.' Isn't it wonderful that she is speaking up for you like that?"

"It is Mrs. Wright, but Mrs. Livermore, for all her strength and support, is still only a woman. It is men who control the affairs of this earth. It is men who will judge me at trial. It is men who judge us all and inevitably find us lacking."

"Oh, Lizzie, you are too young to feel so bitter and defeated. I know you have been carrying a heavy burden, but I believe in my heart that your vindication is coming soon."

"If only women served on juries, I might be able to feel your hope and optimism, Mrs. Wright. I will work on being more positive and trust you will continue to sustain me."

Chapter Twenty-Seven

District Attorney Knowlton rejoiced in the outcome of the preliminary hearing but felt at sea about what the future might hold. Although he expected Attorney General Pillsbury to serve as chief prosecutor for Lizzie's trial, but what would his role be? He assumed he would be second to Pillsbury, but he had no assurance of that and felt that he had earned the right to lead the trial on his own.

After congratulating Knowlton on his victory, Pillsbury warned, "In your interactions with journalists, Mr. Knowlton, remember that they can be bribed to slant their stories to our detriment."

"Yes, sir. I am well aware of that and have long been suspicious of the *Boston Herald* and *Globe* reports. They purported to print my argument stenographically, but almost entirely omitted the part of it which dwelt upon the attempt to purchase the poison."

"Be forewarned. They cannot be trusted. Watch with care every word you utter in their presence. You should also know that I have contacted Dr. Edward Cowles of McLean Asylum for the Insane to explore the possibility of insanity playing a role in the Borden murders."

"I do not find insanity to be an excuse for murder."

"Nor do I—except, perhaps, in the case of a raving lunatic who runs around town screaming and attacking with total abandon and no discernible motive."

"That does not describe Lizzie Borden," Knowlton said.

"Indeed, it does not. She is not one of those tragic creatures. She is a cold-blooded murderess and deserves no mercy. But we must explore this possibility in the event that the defense claims she is insane."

"Agreed, sir. When do you suspect the trial will commence?"

"I hope to prolong her suffering as long as possible, Mr. Knowlton. I want her confined for months. It will beat down her spirit and perhaps induce a confession which would save us a lot of bother."

"The defense will object."

"Of course, they will. That is their job. But we may outlast Lizzie Borden yet."

* * *

Knowlton welcomed Jennings into his office and offered him a seat and a cup of coffee. They exchanged brief pleasantries about people with whom they had mutual acquaintance. Tiring of the idle conversation, Knowlton asked, "Why are you here, Mr. Jennings?"

"We have not yet discussed bail for Lizzie Borden."

"No, we have not. There is nothing to discuss. If you apply for it, the state will strongly object."

"On what grounds?"

"The offense charged—murder—it does not get any worse than that."

"It is her first offense."

"Really, Mr. Jennings, you think that is an argument."

"She is an established member of the community. She was born here and lived her all her life."

"I could say the same of many now confined in jail or prison."

"I doubt any of them are property owners."

"But how, pray tell, did she come to own property? You say she is an orphan. I say she killed to gain her wealth."

"We are not talking about a shrewd, devious, greedy businessman, Mr. Knowlton. We are talking about Lizzie Borden, a young woman who is regularly in her pew at church, who performs charitable deeds as a habit—a Sunday School teacher, for heaven's sake."

"No, actually, we are talking about murder—two murders."

"For which she has not been found guilty. The Grand Jury has not even considered her case yet. There is no reason for her continued confinement."

"There is my reason—and that supersedes all else. Lizzie Borden is a cold-blooded axe murderer."

"You think her release would put the public in danger?"

"Probably not, but I cannot risk setting her free. The public will not stand for it."

"Ah, that makes it very simple. It all boils down to your concern about re-election, not your ethical responsibility for justice at all."

"Good day, Mr. Jennings. Request bail from the court if you wish. I will fight you tooth and nail."

* * *

In Boston, Susan Fessenden of the Massachusetts Women's Christian Temperance Union stood up at the meeting of the organization. "Lizzie Borden is being persecuted for one reason and one reason only—she is a woman. We women are easier targets for scapegoating than men. Her upcoming trial is one of the most surprising revelations of the possibilities of gross injustice under the name of the law.

"Lizzie Borden has worked for the Christian Endeavor Society with great energy for many years serving as secretary-treasurer. At the Central Congregational Church, she taught a Sunday School class to the Chinese children of the laundrymen of Falls River. She helped cook the church's annual Christmas dinner for local newsboys. She was active in the Ladies Fruit and Flowers Mission, delivering fruit and flowers to the sick in our hospitals. She was always ready to volunteer for the Women's Christian Temperance Union and the Good Samaritan Charity Hospital. Our sympathy and support overflow to her.

"Yet, despite her sterling character and many good works, Lizzie Borden, a woman who has not been convicted, is being held without bail in Taunton Jail. We find this unacceptable. She is innocent until proven guilty and should be allowed to dwell with her family in the comfort of her home.

"Let us pray that God will show his hand, and she will be exonerated from the least shadow of suspicion, and the heavy cloud enveloping her in its merciless fold will ere long be lifted. While we wait on God, we must implore the governor to allow her some well-deserved freedom until the sitting of the Grand Jury. I have prepared a petition to send to the Governor and hope all of you will sign it.

The petition reads as follows:

> *We, the undersigned, feeling that the probable innocence of Miss Lizzie A. Borden, now confined in the jail at Taunton, on the charge of murdering her father, is at least as great as that of her guilt, and believing likewise that 30 years of virtuous living should count for much in such a doubtful case, do most earnestly beseech your executive authority to the extent of releasing said Lizzie A. Borden on bail—the amount to be set by yourself—until the meeting of the grand jury in November 1892.*

Much to the disappointment of the two thousand who signed the petition, their plan did not work. The governor's executive powers gave him no control over the courts. Even if he was inclined to help Lizzie Borden, his hands were tied.

Mrs. Lucy Stone, a pioneer in the anti-slavery movement, a campaigner for the rights of black men to vote, the first woman in Massachusetts to earn a college degree, the first woman in the United States to retain her maiden name after marriage, and a crusader for women's rights, spoke out for Lizzie, too. "I firmly believe in her innocence and am certain that every testimony brought against her by the government has been refuted."

Lizzie Borden, a non-descript spinster, unknown outside of Fall River, became a national symbol of men's oppression of women. Few who knew her before August 1892 would have ever thought it possible.

* * *

One October afternoon, Lizzie wrote a letter to her friend Annie Lindsey, who lived in Dorchester. Her dread of the future laid bare on the page.

My Dear Annie,

The wind is blowing outside a gale but never a blast inside. Everything as as calm and placid as a summer sea, even to the large white and yellow cat who is lying under the radiator, as sound asleep as if he were dead. He is the quietest boy I ever saw but he is lots of company for me. His name is Daisy.

No, my dear, do not send me a tea kettle. I have no place for it but under the bed. You were awfully kind to think of it, though. I feel awfully blue indeed the skies are nowhere. Do you tell me to keep up courage a <u>little</u> while longer? My counsel gives me no hopes of anything <u>soon</u>, or ever of an <u>acquittal</u>. Your dreams are too rosy, for <u>they</u> must know.

Do be as careful as you can of scarlet fever. As if I need to warn you. Your sister Ella was here last week. Are you to visit the "World's Fair?"

Yours with love, L.A.B.

Chapter Twenty-Eight

The monotony of the days left Lizzie dazed and confused. She searched constantly for diversions. She read Mrs. Wright's journals and books and looked forward to the matron's daily visits and her valiant attempts to lift her spirits. When left to her own devices, her thoughts went to the dark catacombs of her dread. The endless life behind bars, the jerk of the rope when she hanged, standing before God in judgment.

Except for Emma, her most loyal visitor was Elizabeth Johnson, one of Lizzie's companions on the European Tour in 1890. She stopped by to see her every Saturday. Because she had known Mr. and Mrs. Wright since her childhood, Elizabeth was allowed the privilege of spending the day with Lizzie in her cell. She always brought a fresh supply of photos, magazines, and books.

Elizabeth asked interesting questions which stuck with Lizzie for days after she left. "What do you miss the most, Lizzie?"

"I miss teaching Sunday School and attending the Christian Endeavor Society meetings."

"But what about the ordinary things of life that are forbidden to you because of your confinement? What would you like to do right now?"

"I'd like to stroll down Main Street and window shop for whatever caught my eye. I want to greet my friends as we pass one another on the sidewalk, confident that I would see them again. I want to sleep in my own bed. I want to sit in my church in my pew and listen to my minister preach the gospel."

"They do have church services in here, don't they?' Elizabeth asked.

"Yes, I went once. The other women stared at me, though, and whispered behind their hands even during the singing of hymns. It made it hard—nay, impossible—to commune with God in those circumstances."

"I can understand that. You can, however, commune with God, right here, right now. Just close your eyes and imagine yourself in that pew. Listen to the echoes of the songs in your head. You can do this, Lizzie. You can survive and when you finally are allowed to go home, life will taste twice as sweet."

"I know you're right, Elizabeth. I just do not want to be here any longer. I do not understand why they won't just have the trial and be done with it. Every day, I brood and cannot stop. My confinement is affecting my health. The lack of exercise and fresh air is hard on me."

"I know. I understand. I will pray for your peace and comfort, Lizzie. You must fight against your darkest thoughts and remember the good times you have had. For they shall return."

The women embraced, and Lizzie was alone again, trying to understand how anyone could suspect her. She had led an upright life. She helped the poor, ministered to the sick. This was not the payment she expected for her good deeds.

***

Lizzie woke on October 10 expecting another ordinary, monotonous day. After dressing, she emptied her slop bucket and took as much time as possible with her modest breakfast as she could. She was in between books, but she did not feel as if she had the energy to start another. She picked up a magazine and flipped through the pages, paying little heed to the contents.

She was interrupted by a disruption in the hallway and the pounding of feet. Mrs. Wright allowed Mr. Jennings and Mr. Adams into her cell. Concern carved deep lines in their faces.

"What is wrong? Is Emma all right? Has she taken ill?" Lizzie asked. *Did Mr. Knowlton drop dead?*

"Miss Lizzie, your sister is fine," Mr. Jennings said. "We need to ask you some troubling questions."

Mr. Adams added, "There was a story in the *Boston Globe* that could destroy our case if true."

Lizzie rose to her feet and turned her back to them. *They found it. The police found my hidey-hole.*

Jennings placed his hands on her shoulders and gently turned her back around. "You are very pale, Miss Lizzie. Please sit down before you faint."

Lizzie eased into the rocking chair and steadied her breath.

"You are not asking any questions, Miss Borden," Adams said. Do you already know why we are here? Have you seen the newspaper?"

"No. No." Lizzie tried to still the trembling in her hands.

"We just need to ask you a few questions, Miss Lizzie. No need to be distressed," Jennings said.

"Miss Borden, where were you when your father returned home that morning?"

"In the kitchen, Mr. Adams, as I said at the inquest."

"Very good. Do you possess a rubber cap, or is there one in your house that another might use?"

"I, I don't think so," Lizzie stammered. *A rubber cap? Whatever purpose would that serve?*

Four different witnesses were named in the newspaper who claimed that they saw you, in a rubber cap, pulling up the window in the room where Mrs. Borden died at the same time your father was arriving home?"

"It is not possible," Lizzie said. "Who are these people?"

"Do the names John Murphy, Mrs. Gustave Ronal, Peter Mahany, or Augustus Gunning mean anything to you?" Adams asked.

Lizzie furrowed her brow and bent her head in thought. No matter how she tried, she could not grasp the smallest thread of familiarity. "No, no. None of those names sound familiar to me. Are they Fall River folk?"

"Some of them. Now, Miss Borden, let us return to the Wednesday evening before the murders. You stated you were home all day and did not leave the house until 6 o'clock in the late afternoon. Do you still stand by those statements?"

"Yes—yes indeed. I was not feeling well and—"

"Very well. Very well. Do you know Mr. and Mrs. Frederick Chase or their daughter, Mrs. Abigail Manchester?"

Lizzie could not recall those names either. She shook her head. "Should I, Mr. Adams?"

"If the newspaper report is accurate, they were friends of your parents. It was reported that they called at your house the night before Mr. and Mrs. Borden died. The claim is that before they were admitted into the sitting room, they heard you arguing with your father. Is there any truth in that?" Adams asked.

"I did not argue with my father that evening," Lizzie said, jerking to her feet. "No. Uncle John was there. I would not air any differences we had in front of company—even if it were family."

"Miss Borden, is it true that—" Adams began

"Wait, Mr. Adams," Jennings interrupted. "Let us not be too abrupt. Lizzie, what we need to ask you about right now is very delicate. We do not mean to offend you or to question your honor. We simply need to ask you directly to weigh the credibility of this newspaper article."

Adams stepped towards Lizzie and looked her straight in the eye. Lizzie clutched her hands together, and her lips trembled with dread. "Miss Borden, are you with child?"

Lizzie collapsed into her chair, banging against its back. For a few moments, she did not breathe. She moved her jaw up and down, but no words issued forth. She had never felt so insulted, so sullied, so devastated.

"Miss Lizzie, Lizzie, please." Jennings leaned over her and patted the back of her hand. "Please, dear girl, please give us an answer."

She brushed him away and rose back to her feet. She turned her back toward the men as she struggled to gather herself together. When she turned around to face them, she stared at the space above their heads. "That is a lie. A despicable lie. Anyone who said that is a vicious liar. I am as pure as any woman can be." *It would have been preferable if they found the hatchet under my bed. I am ruined now. Absolutely ruined.*

"Miss Borden, I understand your outrage at this falsehood, but I must read to you the conversation that is reported to have been heard by Mr. and Mrs. Chase. I need you to hear these words in case you have any alternative explanation of their meaning."

Lizzie nodded her head but still would not look either man in the face.

Adams pulled a sheet of paper from his pocket. "It is reported that your father said: 'You can make your own choice and do it tonight. Either let us know what his name is, or take the door on Saturday and when you go fishing, fish for some other place to live, as I will never listen to you again. I will know the name of the man who got you into trouble.'

"Further, the newspaper wrote that you replied: 'If I marry this man, will you be satisfied that everything will be kept from the outside world?'"

The heat rose up her neck and into her cheeks. She struggled to speak and finally succeeded. "That conversation never happened. I will never marry any man. I will never put myself in a position where it would be necessary."

"The article continues to state that the visitors entered the sitting room and asked about the quarrel, and your father said: 'I would rather see her dead than have it come out.' What could have these people heard, Miss Borden?" Adams pressed.

She spun around and looked Adams straight in his eye. "Nothing, Mr. Adams. Nothing. I do not know these people. Do you know if they even exist? If they were friends of my father, surely, I would have heard their names and I have not. Go ask my Uncle John. Go out and search Fall River and bring them here to make these shameless statements to my face. Truly, you do not believe these lies, do you, Mr. Adams? Mr. Jennings?

Getting no answer, Lizzie rushed to the door of her cell. "Mrs. Wright!" she shouted. "Mrs. Wright!"

The matron bustled down the hall. "Miss Lizzie, whatever is the matter? Do you need me to escort these gentlemen outside?"

"No, Mrs. Wright. What I need you to do is to explain to them the standard procedure—the one I went through—when a prisoner is admitted or returns from court."

CHAPTER TWENTY-EIGHT

Mrs. Wright blinked her eyes and blushed. "Everything?"

"Yes, Mrs. Wright. Everything. Please."

Mrs. Wright kept her eyes on the floor and stammered as she explained that I undressed in front of her and bathed in a tub. After drying off, she dressed again in the clothes she arrived in, "Most prisoners are given jail dresses to wear after their bath, but we made an exception for Miss Borden." She looked up at Lizzie when she finished.

"And Mrs. Wright, I know this is an indelicate question, but it is an important one: Did you see any indications that I am with child?"

"Oh my heavens. Oh my. Oh dear. Oh no, Miss Borden."

"Did you notice anything in my habits in the time I've been here?"

Mrs. Wright counted on her fingers. "At least three months along you would be now. I know for a fact that you could not be because of the supplies I have provided for you." With that last statement, her face looked as bright as the maple trees out on the grounds,

"I am sorry I have embarrassed you, Mrs. Wright. But a newspaper article has made an accusation. Thank you for your cooperation. Why don't you go lay down a bit to get over the shock?"

Mrs. Wright nodded at Lizzie but would not even glance at Adams or Jennings as she made her way out of the cell and down the hall.

"There, gentlemen, I hope you are satisfied."

Unfortunately, Miss Lizzie," Jennings said, "we need to ask a few more questions but they are not quite so delicate. Mr. Adams, please continue."

"I need to ask you about another conversation—this one overheard by a Mrs. George Sisson. The newspaper reported, according to this woman, that you spoke to Bridget and said, 'Why don't you just say how much money you want to keep quiet?' And Bridget responded, 'I don't know what you mean, but you are not the girl I took you to be.' What do you say to that, Miss Borden?"

Lizzie straightened her shoulders. "Balderdash, Mr. Adams. Unadulterated lies. That conversation did not happen, and as I said, I know no one with that name."

"Furthermore," Adams continued, "that woman's husband said that on the afternoon of the murders, he heard you whispering to Bridget: 'Keep your tongue still and don't talk to these officers, and you can have all the money you want.' Do you call that out as a lie, too?"

Lizzie's outraged eyes flashed at Jennings before returning to Adams. "Yes, yes, and yes. The whole newspaper story sounds manufactured by a rumormonger. And I do not think Mr. and Mrs. George Sisson even exist. Is that the end to the lies in this story?"

"Not quite, Miss Lizzie," Jennings said. I am sorry we need to subject you to this questioning, but better now than in the courtroom. We will do our best to keep it away from there."

Adams continued, "Miss Borden, did you ever go to New York and consult with Lawyer Frank Burroughs about your property rights should your stepmother die before your father?"

"Of course not. I never heard of the man."

"One final question: did you have an argument with your sister while you were staying in the Matron's chamber during the preliminary hearing?"

"Yes, we did have an argument, as I recall."

"Did you accuse Emma of giving you away?"

"No! That is absurd. Did you ask Emma about this?"

"Yes," Adams admitted. "she said it was not true. It was also written in the newspaper that you kicked your sister in the shin several times during the argument. Miss Emma has denied that. What say you, Miss Borden?"

Lizzie sighed, and her shoulders slouched downward. "Emma is protecting me. I have been kicking her in the shin when I was angry since I was a small girl. I know I should not do it. It is an old childish habit. But I did not kick her several times—I only kicked her once, and then I apologized."

"Thank you, Miss Lizzie," Jennings said with a smile. "I am sorry we had to distress you, but we needed to confirm what others already told us. Your statements have been in accord on all but one point—that of kicking your sister. We have a search ongoing for all the people named in this story and thus far, cannot find anyone. When we have completed our research, we will prepare a writ and hand-deliver it in Boston."

Mrs. Wright saw the gentlemen out and then returned with a cup of tea.

"Don't mention this tea to Mr. Wright. He would not be pleased, but I felt you needed it after that ordeal. I know it helped me."

"Thank you, Mrs. Wright." Lizzie sipped on her tea, struggling to repress her fury. *If I am found guilty because of manufactured lies, it would be a miscarriage of justice. How could I bear up under that unfair burden? If my downfall is brought about by true evidence, then so be it.*

Chapter Twenty-Nine

As soon as she read it, Mrs. Wright rushed to Lizzie with the apology published by the *Boston Globe* along with the news that the reporter and the private detective working with the police were subjected to ridicule, shame, and a loss of position. The matron was quite excited about it, but Lizzie knew that some people would continue to cling to the lies and think the worst of her. A desire for revenge kept building inside of her even though she knew she was powerless, and that made her even angrier.

Her sister was angry as well. When she came to visit, however, her ire was directed at a different story. "It is dreadful how reporters are dredging up and publishing any rumor they can find."

"I agree, Emma. What is the latest?"

"Remember last year when the robbery occurred, and Father's money and Abby's watch were stolen?"

"Of course, I do."

"Well, now, Lizzie, they are saying you did it, and the evidence will be presented at trial. They will do anything to besmirch your character."

A lump formed in Lizzie's throat. *Maybe this wasn't a rumor. Maybe they found the loose board under my bed. Maybe they do have the evidence.* Lizzie wondered if this was the moment that she should confess everything to her sister, or, at least, confirm *I did rob Father and Abby. Her ardent support of me is far too valuable to gamble it away.* "Emma, rumors don't matter. People will gossip. They will fabricate. The only thing that counts is the trial. Pray for it to happen soon, and let all your other worries dissipate like fog. They do not matter. Not one little bit. Come, I'll show you the flower boxes Mrs. Wright assigned to my care."

Emma oohed and aahed over the pink, white, and red geraniums and the dark-leaved begonias. "Beautiful, Lizzie, and your care of them is obvious. They look healthy and cheerful."

"They do brighten my days. I keep them watered and make sure the faded blossoms are plucked. While caring for them, I can almost forget I am a prisoner."

"I will thank Matron for her kindness, Lizzie. Knowing she is here watching over you is the only thing that lets me sleep at night."

After her sister left and the sun slowly set, Lizzie was alone in the darkness. It was the most difficult part of her day. Too early for sleep. No light for reading. The rules forbid a candle in the cells. Mrs. Wright was trying to get permission to provide a reading light for her. But so far, nothing. All she could do was sit in the dark all evening long with nothing for company but her thoughts. The grand jury. The trial. The gallows. Father. All in an endless loop. *My only desire was to ensure a future for me and my sister and yet, it feels like that dream will never come true.*

＊ ＊ ＊

Jennings arrived at Lizzie's cell to explain the upcoming grand jury meeting. "The body will convene on November 7 and will consist of twenty-three men from all around the country."

"Men—always men—are set up to judge women. Where is the justice in that?"

"Miss Lizzie, as I have told you before, I did not create the legal processes and cannot alter them. We need to focus on what we can do. Before hearing your case, they will need to clear their docket of other less weighty matters. After that, they will go to your issue."

"Men will never give up their power, will they?"

Jennings closed his eyes and took a deep breath. "Only twelve of these men," he began but then paused at that last word, "only twelve need to vote in favor of a decision."

"Where is the fairness in that? Barely more than half are required to agree in order to tear my life apart?"

"The law is rigid, Miss Lizzie. I have been informed that the district attorney will call forty to fifty witnesses who will testify over two or three days."

"Does it not seem odd to you that a decision-making body decides a person's fate after only one side of the story?"

"It is part of the process, Miss Lizzie. The final decision of your fate is the trial. You and your arguments will be heard there. We will fight valiantly for your freedom."

"I do not deserve to be in this position, Mr. Jennings."

"I have never said that you do. You must have faith that we will prevail."

* * *

November 7 came and went. Lizzie grew more anxious and edgy with every passing day. A week went by, and still, she waited, her nerves shredding every pleasure out of her life. One morning, when her coffee and bread arrived, Lizzie's rage erupted at the thought of another day of not knowing what the grand jury was doing or what they would decide. She grabbed the cup and threw it across the room, where it shattered against the wall.

She was dumbfounded by her actions. She had never done anything like that before—never unmasked her rage when others could see or hear. Mrs. Wright bustled into her cell. "I will get a cloth and bucket to clean this up."

"Give it to me, Mrs. Wright. I must clean up my own mess. I am very sorry for that childish outburst."

"Miss Lizzie, I understand your frustration. I have had moments when I wanted to throw things at the wall—more of them than you know. I think all women do."

After everything was put right again, Mrs. Wright returned with a fresh cup of coffee. "Here you go, dear. Sip on this and calm yourself."

"I don't deserve it, Mrs. Wright."

"I disagree, Miss Lizzie. Please don't deny me the ability to help you through your morning."

* * *

On November 22, Lizzie heard footsteps, looked down the hall, and saw Jennings approaching. He did not look like a man bearing good news. Still, she hoped against logic that she was misreading his expression.

"Miss Lizzie, the grand jury adjourned yesterday without issuing an indictment."

"At first hearing, that sounds like good news, Mr. Jennings, but your face betrays the lie of that assumption.

Jennings exhaled a long and heavy sigh. "No, Lizzie, it is not what I anticipated. They are scheduled to return to their deliberations on December 1."

"I thought they were supposed to dissolve the grand jury today. Why are they delaying this?"

"Exactly the question I put to Mr. Knowlton. I told him it was unfair to keep you in suspense. He refused to tell me why but the newspapers are reporting two different reasons."

"Two? Can they both be correct?"

"Not likely, Miss Lizzie. And it is possible that neither one is. One paper reported that they have got a new lead and the reason for the delay is their need to find evidence to produce one more indictment against you. The other reason is that they have uncovered others involved in a conspiracy with you and need time to prepare those indictments."

Lizzie rose to her feet. "Oh no, not that old story about Uncle John plotting with me again. That is a blatant lie."

"Miss Lizzie, please sit and calm yourself. I have my own theory for the delay. I think it is more than likely that they will serve you with an additional indictment. After all, you have only been charged with your father's death. I have long anticipated a second charge for your stepmother's murder."

"For what purpose, Mr. Jennings? If the grand jury finds me guilty of one, will they not find me guilty of the other? They can only hang me once."

"Do not get distressed. No matter what the grand jury does, if it comes to a trial, I am convinced you will be acquitted."

"I feel like Mr. Knowlton's toy ball to be batted around in whatever direction he chooses."

"Regardless, Miss Lizzie, I will protect you to the best of my ability—I will guard your well-being as well as I have ever done for my son Oliver and my daughter Marion. I owe you safekeeping as much as I do to any member of my family."

"You are a good man, Mr. Jennings. My gratitude to you overflows my heart."

* * *

That afternoon, Emma arrived at Lizzie's cell looking quite distressed. "I talked to Mr. Jennings. I—"

"He came to see me, too, Emma. I don't know why they are dragging this out."

"It is so unfair. It's as if guilty or not, they want to punish you because you were not killed, too."

"I know. You need not fret, Emma. Mrs. Wright is good to me. Men think they can wear us down, but we cannot let them. We need to focus on other things and bide our time."

"Speaking of Mr. Jennings, Mary told me her mother knew him when they were younger. She said he is a splendid dancer. The one time she waltzed with him, she felt as if she were floating on a cloud."

"It's hard to imagine an older, serious man having once had a carefree youth, isn't it?"

Emma smiled and nodded in agreement. "Lizzie, I brought you two new books: *The Private Life* by Henry James and *The Speckled Band* by Arthur Conan Doyle," she said as she pulled them out of the sack.

"Have you read them?"

"Only a few pages of the Henry James book. I thought it was more to your taste than mine. But the Sherlock Holmes book was absolutely fascinating."

"You've always loved a good mystery, Emma."

"Only in books. Real-life mysteries no longer hold any charm for me—not since Father."

"I know. Let's not talk of that now. Let's walk the hallway and consider pleasant things." They traversed their gloomy concourse with silence for a companion. Lizzie felt badly about her sister and wished she could protect her from the consequences of her actions. *She was a mother figure to me for so long and now I feel very maternal towards her. She has seemed vulnerable and frail since Father died. I need to return home to care for her as she did for me when we lost our mother. And yet, what I did, I did as much for her as for me I wonder if she will ever be able to understand that. I wonder if she will ever feel a measure of gratitude.*

Emma and Lizzie broke the quiet spell at the same time, talking over each other before bursting into laughter. "You go ahead, Lizzie," Emma said.

"No, no, after you, Emma."

"All right. I was just thinking about the two of us living together again under the same roof. It will be so pleasant. We can come and go as we please."

"And have whatever we want when we dine. I grew so tired of the mutton Abby always wanted to serve."

"Yes, me, too. We can get recipes from friends."

"Not just any friends, Emma. We need to make sure to ask those who we know serve scrumptious meals.

"And we don't need to buy the cheapest cuts of meat because we won't need to explain our spending to anyone."

Back in her cell, Lizzie watched Emma leave. It had been good to see her smile again. If only the tide would turn and lift all her sister's worries.

* * *

Three days later, Emma returned, beaming with excitement. Normally, she speaks at a slow, even pace, but now she talked so fast that Lizzie had to get her to repeat herself. "The Fall River News reported about the coverage of your case in the Boston newspapers. One wrote, 'the grand jury will not find a bill against Lizzie Borden.' The other proclaimed 'the grand jury will find no-bill in the case of the Commonwealth versus Lizzie Borden.' Oh, Lizzie, you will be home soon."

Lizzie loved her sister's optimism and her ability to grasp onto any thread of hope and cling to it for dear life. Lizzie knew, though, that life has a way of disappointing, but she shared none of her negative thoughts with Emma. *Let her be joyful, if only for a day.*

"But that Marshall Hilliard!" Emma continued. "I don't think he is just biased against you—I think he is hostile to all women. You should have seen what he said to reporters."

"Nothing much would surprise me, Emma, but what did he say?"

"You know a lot of women from the Christian Endeavor Society and the Christian Temperance Society have been chastising those in charge for the conditions you have to endure being imprisoned so long?"

"Yes," Lizzie smiled, "their support has heartened me."

"The Marshall was questioned about those complaints, and he said, 'No short-haired women freaks have written to the press about Lizzie Borden's hardships for two days.' Freaks, Lizzie. He called your supporters freaks. Where is the Christian spirit in that, I ask you?"

"Calm yourself, Emma. He has been convinced of my guilt since the day Father died. You cannot expect a man like him to deliver kindly words about those who believe he is wrong."

"But even the law says you are innocent until proven guilty."

"Yes, Emma, it says that. But look where I am. I have been imprisoned now for more than three months. Is that what you do to someone who is presumed innocent? The words of the law and the reality of life are often in opposition."

"I just want this all to be over. I want you to come home."

Lizzie wrapped her arms around her sister and patted her back. "In time, sweet sister, in time."

* * *

Three days before the grand jury was set to reconvene, John arrived for a visit with Lizzie in a very agitated state. "Has anyone been sent in to examine you for insanity?"

"No. Do you think I am insane?"

"Absolutely not, Lizzie. I wanted to make sure no one had come to see you for that purpose."

"Why do you think they would?"

"Newspapers all over the state are speculating that you committed the murders while you were insane and that the grand jury was suspended to allow time for you to be examined in this regard."

"No one has been there for that purpose. I am not, nor have I ever been insane. I swear it on my mother's grave."

"I know. I have assured everyone, Lizzie, that it is not possible. On your mother's side, there are no incidents of insanity in all history. I sought out one of the older members on your father's side and found you were free from inheriting insanity from the Bordens, as well. This claim is a horrendous insult to both families."

"If I never get out of here, if these rumors don't stop, I am very well go insane, Uncle John."

"Rest assured, Lizzie, you have no queer mental traits, and you possess unusual mental strength. Have no fear. Mr. Jennings has made it clear a number of times that he, too, does not believe you to be insane."

"Do you believe I am innocent of these crimes?" Lizzie could barely breathe as she waited for an answer.

"Of course, I do. I shared my theory when I went to New Bedford. The night before the murders, an enemy of your father got into the house through the open cellar window. He slipped upstairs and hid in the clothes press. When Abby came up to make the bed, he found it necessary to kill her to get her out of the way. Then, he waited for the right moment. After your father came home, when Bridget was outside washing windows, and you went to the barn, he made his move. He killed your father and escaped."

Not only does he believe in my innocence, he has manufactured scenarios to vindicate me. My mother in heaven will be proud of her brother's loyalty. With downcast eyes, I stretched out my hand and said, "Thank you, Uncle John. That is the best explanation of any I have heard. I appreciate your steadfast belief in my innocence."

He tucked a finger under her chin and raised her face to his. "You need not thank me, Lizzie. I wish I could have done something to prevent your current calamity. I owed it to my sister to be more aggressive and protective of you. I am the one who is sorry."

Chapter Thirty

Lizzie spent much of her time reading the books that Emma brought her as she awaited the decision of the grand jury. She found the Henry James book quite delightful, the contrast between the public life and the private life of the writer resonated strongly with her. She felt she had spent her adult life hiding behind a façade, engaging in church work and charitable efforts to better perfect the character that concealed her inner heart. With every page, she felt a kinship with the author.

Arthur Conan Doyle was another experience entirely. She enjoyed the distraction from glum thoughts about the future but did not feel connected to the writer or the characters to the extent she did with Henry James. She had finished the Sherlock Holmes the day before and now shuffled through the stack of books she'd already read looking for one that would be good to peruse again.

A commotion in the hall drew her to the bars of her cell. The thickset Reverend Mr. Jubb, with his almost white hair and beard, was arguing with Mrs. Wright. "My visit is very important. I must see Miss Lizzie right away."

"What about?" Mrs. Wright asked.

"I cannot tell you until I speak to Miss Lizzie. I must tell her first."

"If you insist, Reverend. But I will be standing right here."

"As you wish, madame."

Jubb stepped in front of her door, placing a hand on his chest as he caught his breath. "Miss Lizzie. Oh, Miss Lizzie. I bring dreadful news."

"Emma? Has Emma been hurt? Has she taken ill?"

"Oh, Miss Lizzie, in comparison, that would be good news. The grand jury has returned indictments against you for the murder of your father and stepmother. I ran all the way here from the train depot, praying all the way. Oh, you poor girl! To lose your parents and then this. It is outrageous and insufferable."

"Mr. Jubb," Lizzie said. "Perhaps we should pray together."

"Yes, yes, of course. Mrs. Wright, could I enter her cell and sit by Miss Lizzie's side while we pray?"

Mrs. Wright did not hesitate long enough to answer. She slipped the key into the lock and opened the door. As she refastened it, she looked at the prisoner with a sorrowful smile. "I am so sorry, Miss Lizzie. I will continue to pray for you. Reverend Jubb, just call out when you are ready to leave, and I will return immediately." She turned and walked away, her shoulders rounded and the soles of her shoes scraping the floor.

Inside the cell, the two huddled together and recited the Lord's Prayer. Jubb followed that with a personal prayer. "Please, dear God, lift up your good and faithful servant, Lizzie Borden, bring her strength and courage, and let her return home all the more enlightened for her travails. In Jesus' name, please bless this child of God."

* * *

Her hat askew, her eyes red and wild, Emma arrived at the jail the next day. "Oh, dear sister, I think I know why they returned an indictment against you. I saw it when I read the newspaper this morning."

Mrs. Wright unlocked the door and hovered in the hall, concerned and curious about Emma's disheveled and anxious state. Lizzie was annoyed that the matron lingered and listened. She placed a hand around her sister's waist and led her into the cell. "Emma, Emma, please sit down—here in the rocking chair. You are overwrought. You know you cannot believe everything you read in the newspaper."

Emma did not resist but grasped Lizzie's hand with the intensity of a hawk gripping its prey. "It's horrible, Lizzie. It's betrayal."

Lizzie shook off Emma's hand and sat on the edge of her bed. "Whatever are you talking about, Emma?"

"Someone told the grand jury about the dress."

"What dress?"

"The paint-stained one. The one you burned the day after the funeral."

"Who, Emma?"

"I don't know, Lizzie. It didn't say. The newspaper described the witness as 'an intimate friend.' Was anyone there besides you, me, and Alice Russell?"

"I don't think so. Except there were policemen about all the time."

"We would not call a single one of them an intimate friend."

"No. Perhaps that nosy Adelaide Churchill was spying on us," Lizzie said. "I often saw her peering into our window."

"She could not have seen the stove from her window. And she did not come over Sunday at all. It must have been Maggie."

"She was already gone—"

"But she came by to pick up her things. When was that?"

"I don't know," Emma whined in frustration.

"Anyway, I still trust Maggie. Besides, who would describe our maid as an intimate friend?"

"Who else could it be? We know Alice is a faithful and true friend. You heard her testimony at the preliminary hearing. She didn't say a word about the dress."

"I guess that leaves you, Emma."

Emma flung herself out of the chair and down to her knees on the floor. She placed folded hands upon Lizzie's knees. "I swear to you, Lizzie, it was not me. I swear on the soul of our dearly departed mother."

"Please rise, Emma. You are embarrassing us both." Lizzie shot a stern look at Mrs. Wright, who took the hint and hurried down the hall. "Don't cry. I was only teasing. I didn't mean it. I didn't think for a minute that you would do such a thing."

Emma sniffled as she rose and sat back on the rocker. "Maybe Maggie told a maid in another household who shared it with her mistress."

"I imagine that's possible if the timing of her return was right, but I don't think that it was. Alice is possible, too. She was always more your friend than mine."

"If that is true, how could she do this to me? How could she betray a secret in our household? I told her you only burned it because it was covered with paint stains. But she knew it was fraught with other inaccurate but credible meanings. The grand jury could have thought it of great importance."

"Perhaps Alice did, too," Lizzie said.

"Then why wait so long to tell it?"

"Watch her, Emma. Do not share any confidences with her until we know with certainty. If she is the one who spoke to the grand jury about the burned dress, then she can twist anything you do or say into something malevolent."

"I can't believe it was Alice," Emma objected.

"I am not asking you to believe. I'm just asking you to take care."

* * *

When Jennings visited Lizzie, he slouched as if the weight of the indictment hung heavy on his shoulders. "I know you have been informed that the grand jury issued indictments against you. I want to be certain that you understand the nature of all three."

"Three, Mr. Jennings?" I thought there were two—one for Father and one for Mrs. Borden."

"You are right about those two, Miss Lizzie, but the third indictment is for the act of double murder."

"They can do that? Charge me twice for the same acts?"

"Unfortunately, yes. I know it does not make sense to you—it barely makes sense to me—but it is within the parameters of the law. Your trial is liable to come up at any time, and because of that, I cannot take on any new cases." Jennings often fretted about the twists and turns of the judicial system that placed an onerous burden on those who seek truth and justice. It often felt to him as if those who were charged were assumed to be guilty in contradiction of the nation's purported principles.

"But, Mr. Jennings, surely you must earn a living while you wait to represent me in the courtroom."

"I cannot get your case out of my mind to focus on anything else. I often lay awake half the night thinking about it and arranging matters in my head."

Lizzie was touched by the passion for her predicament that burned in her lawyer's heart. "I have complete faith in you, Mr. Jennings, as Father did before me. I am certain you will leave no stone unturned in your quest for vindication."

To this end, Jennings approached another attorney to help with the case, ex-Governor George D. Robinson. After a round of teaching and five years as a high school principal, Robinson studied law, being admitted to the bar in 1866. In 1873, he was elected to the Massachusetts House of Representatives.

His meteoric rise continued with elections to the state Senate and then to the United States House of Representatives. In 1883, he was nominated to run for Governor, and he was re-elected twice to one-year terms. He was now in private practice once again, and Jennings hoped he would be eager to take on the defense of Lizzie Borden.

"I treasure your belief in me. I will do all in my power. I am currently considering a third member of them."

"Who would that be, Mr. Jennings?"

"I am hoping ex-Governor Robinson will take on your defense with Mr. Adams and I. In addition to his governorship, he has broad experience in the Massachusetts legislature. He graduated from Harvard, and three of his capital cases have ended in the acquittal of his clients." Jennings paused and grinned. "Most delightfully, Miss Lizzie, when he was governor, he appointed the likely judge for your trial to the bench."

"That is delightful, Mr. Jennings!" *And a little bit sneaky, too. Perhaps Mr. Jennings has more iron in his spine than I thought.*

"Do you remember Mr. Henry Trickey, Miss Lizzie?"

"How could I not after he told such terrible lies about me?"

"You will never have to be concerned about him again He fell to his death under a moving railroad train."

"Perhaps they will indict me for his murder as well," Lizzie hissed.

"This is the one positive from your incarceration—you have an ironclad alibi. But do not turn bitter, my dear. Keep your head up. There is another piece of good news about his death. The night before he died, he told an associate that he paid Detective McKinney $300 for information about the case. Now, the detective has admitted that he created the whole story to deceive Mr. Trickey. I have doubts about his statement of motive, though. I think he meant to discredit you by telling the story to a reporter. Nonetheless, his deception has been revealed by his own words, as often is the case."

What of my deception? Lizzie wondered. *Will I be undone by my own words one day?*

Chapter Thirty-One

The week before Christmas, a flood of packages arrived at the jail for Lizzie Borden. Mrs. Wright convinced her husband that he had to lift the rules because of the holidays. He relented, and Lizzie was greatly cheered by the remembrances. She had half-expected she would have been forgotten in the flurry of celebrations.

Emma arrived on Christmas Eve, loaded with presents and disturbing news. " I learned who told the grand jury about the dress burning."

"Alice, I presume," Lizzie said.

Emma sighed. "Yes, you were right. She has not been to visit me all month. And I feel she is arguing for your guilt with many of our other acquaintances."

"I am not surprised, Emma. I would have sworn that Maggie would not betray us, and I believed that you would not either. There was no one else."

Emma hung her head. "I was so certain she was a true friend."

"I am sorry, sister. Alice and Elizabeth Johnston are quite close, aren't they?"

"I believe so."

"That explains Elizabeth's absence. She used to come and see me every Saturday. She has not called on me once all this month and not sent a single Christmas token. I shall miss her friendship—but I guess I can't call it that, can I? She has sided with my betrayer and left me to suffer alone."

"When you are acquitted, Lizzie, they will beg for your forgiveness."

"No, I don't think so. I will be a constant reminder of their wrongheadedness. They will avoid me because no one likes to be reminded of those moments."

"But Christian charity…"

"Bah, Emma. It may be a sincere and true feeling in your breast, but I ceased believing it was a common attribute among others since they locked the door of this cell."

"What about Mrs. Wright? I believed you thought highly of her."

"Oh, yes, like you, she is another exception to common human behavior. She provides what I need and requests everything I want. She has recently managed to get permission for a gas lamp in my cell in the evenings, allowing me to read after dark. And you should have seen her this past week. She has been overjoyed by every package and letter I have received, staying around the cell doors as I open them. You would think she was my mother."

"I must be going to catch the train to Fall River. I won't wish you a Merry Christmas since I know it will be very dull for you tomorrow. But know this, you will be in my heart all day long. I plan to come again the day after."

At times like this, Lizzie thought her imprisonment was harder on Emma than on herself. After all, her sister has done nothing to deserve a punishment of any sort.

* * *

Christmas Day was long and cheerless for Lizzie. She could not help thinking of the holiday in years past when she helped cook and serve the church's yearly dinner for the newsboys. All their little smiling faces and the camaraderie among the volunteers was one of the highlights of her previous life.

Since visitors were never allowed on Sundays, there was nothing to look forward to as the hours crawled along. The other women prisoners were particularly noisy and argumentative that day, making Lizzie's head hurt.

When, at last, the day was over, Emma returned on Monday and brought John with her. After they exchanged greetings, Lizzie asked, "Uncle John, have you heard any news of a trial date?"

"No, and I realize how frustrating it is to you. I know that Attorney

General Pillsbury is supposed to take part in all capital cases, but there is a provision for exceptions. If he is genuinely too ill to appear in court, he can delegate an assistant or the district attorney to prosecute the case. I do not understand why he will not do that."

"Mr. Jennings does not appear to know either," Lizzie said.

"His lack of action is making a laughingstock of Fall River and Massachusetts. The *Baltimore Sun* and the Washington D.C. newspapers are mocking our system of justice. The *Sun* referred to the delay of your trial as the torture of a woman who was indicted on nothing more than flimsy circumstantial evidence."

"I can't argue with that sentiment," Lizzie said.

"I think the prosecutors do not believe that they can prove their case to a jury and are hoping that if they hold you behind bars long enough, you will confess and save them from themselves. But you won't confess to something you did not do, will you, Lizzie?" A desperate urgency draped his features as he gazed at his niece.

Men never seem to understand that some women possess an inner strength that will not succumb to their bullying. "I have no intention of confessing now or ever. There are times when I think I would do anything to end this purgatory-like existence, but I do draw the line at confession—that would only doom me to a hangman's noose. Not only would I lose my life, but it would besmirch the family name, and Emma would have to live with the consequences."

* * *

The New Year brought another mountain of remembrances from family and friends to Lizzie's cell. Mrs. Wright grew ill and could not drop by to cheer her spirits. Her daughter moved in to nurse her. The world outside turned bitter cold, with snow falling with unusual frequency, leading to a spell of despondency for Lizzie. She wrote to her friend Annie Lindsey:

My Dear Annie,

I meant to have written long ago, but my head troubles me so much I write very little. I think soon they can take me up the road to the insane asylum.

We all feel very sober here this week. Mrs. Wright is very ill with pneumonia, both lungs affected. Her daughter is with her and a trained nurse.

A box of nice candy came to me Tuesday and no one but my friend Annie sent it. Thank you very much indeed.

Do you know, I cannot for the life of me see how you and the rest of my friends can be so full of hope over the case. To me, I see nothing but the densest shadows.

It is fine sleighing here; the bells jingle all night long. I must say goodbye for this time.

With much love for my loyal friend
L.A.B.

Soon after writing that letter, Mrs. Wright's daughter needed to return to her home, and Mr. Wright moved Lizzie into his residence to tend to and comfort his wife. One afternoon, as Lizzie watched the snowflakes twisting outside the window of the sick room, her thoughts went to the joy of spring flowers—the riot of pinks, yellows, blue, and lilac that burst out each year and caused the grateful to forget the drab, bare branches of winter.

Those thoughts gave birth to a new plan of action for Lizzie—a good deed to make the recipients simultaneously pleased and uneasy. She arranged for a bouquet of flowers to be delivered to Matron Reagan. She hoped that if she returned to that woman's care, she might think twice before spying on her again. She sent a boutonniere to Assistant Marshall Fleet to give him pause the next time he embraces a rumor in his quest for her execution.

* * *

New, distressing news came to Lizzie, prompting her to send an urgent request for a visit to Jennings. He hurried to his client's side on January 31,

CHAPTER THIRTY-ONE

1893. "What is so catastrophic, Miss Lizzie?"

"Someone is writing a book about my case—a Mr. Edwin Porter. How can he write a book when I have not been found guilty? He will have to fill it with rumors and conjectures and the foul assaults of others. And what of the conclusions he will reach?"

"Be calm, Miss Lizzie. I will make our position clear. We cannot stop him from publishing a book, but we can legally constrain its contents. When I return to my office, I will send Mr. Porter and his publisher a notice that they will be held responsible for any false or colored descriptions in the book. They will also be forbidden from printing any photographs or likenesses of you, your father, your sister, your Uncle John, or any member of your defense team. We will protect you as best as we can."

The legal team's biggest pressing problem was locating and pinning down Attorney General Pillsbury to get him to step up with a trial or appoint someone to take his place. He was a hard man to find. Reports placed him in Washington D.C., Florida, Cuba, and a vague location out west, all while he was supposedly too sick to perform in the courtroom. Every day, the delay appeared more contrived and fueled the credibility of the hoping-for-a-confession theory.

Chapter Thirty-Two

In April, Kate Curley arrived at Taunton Jail. Many imprisoned there already knew her well—it was far from her first visit behind bars. She made it her mission to harass Lizzie Borden.

Walking out to empty slops, she spoke loudly to the woman closest to her. "That's Lizzie Borden," she pointed, "It is dangerous having murderers living around decent people like us who just made a simple mistake."

Passing by Lizzie's cell, she said, "Watch out for that one. She is an axe murderer. If she ever gets her hand on a hatchet, she will kill us in our sleep."

Every time Lizzie was near, Kate made similar comments, further isolating Lizzie from the other prisoners. She never said anything directly to her until one day in late April.

Kate sidled up to Lizzie on the way to empty their pails. "I know you think you are better than us but just you wait. You fill your slop bucket just like us. And one day, when no one is looking, I will bring you down. You think you better, but you're worse, murderer." Kate walked faster, putting another woman between her and Lizzie.

"Kate, stop dodging around. Keep your place in line," Mrs. Wright said.

"Yes, Mrs. Wright. I'm sorry. Won't happen again."

Returning to her cell, Lizzie was frightened, despondent, and helpless. Fortunately, in a stack of newspapers and magazines brought to her cell was a Boston newspaper. She opened it up and saw her name in an article about Reverend Hinnman of the Fourth Presbyterian Church in Boston. In the pulpit, he compared the punishment of Lizzie Borden with that of an ex-banker who stole funds and violated the public trust. "That man's sentence was a one thousand dollar fine and sixty days in jail, while Lizzie Borden has been held in jail for 8 months without being found guilty of any crime. If Lizzie Borden be found guilty of the fearful crime charged, then let her suffer the penalty of her crime, but let not the punishment precede the trial."

Lizzie decided not to tell her sister about Kate, but she shared the story from Boston with her on the next visit. "Oh, Emma, if only I could have a few days or weeks at home with you before this trial, wouldn't that be heavenly?"

"Yes, it would." Emma's reaction was more subdued than usual because her mind was preoccupied with far more pedestrian concerns. "Finally, at last, I found a housekeeper willing to set foot in our home."

"What is the matter with all the help, Emma? Do they all believe in ghosts?"

"I don't know, sister, but I realize that most of them are a superstitious lot, particularly the Catholic ones from Ireland."

"It seems to me that if they were strongly committed to their religion, they would not fear ghosts or goblins."

"Be that as it may, Lizzie, we have a new Maggie in our household. Sadly, she is quite old and moves very slowly. I don't think her sight is the best, either. I must follow behind her to clean the spots she missed."

"What about her cooking? Is that passable?"

"Quite adequate. I won't go hungry. And her cakes are exceptional. Her angel cake is so light, it nearly floats off the plate."

"Makes my mouth water thinking about it."

"I'll be sure to bring you a slice the next time she makes one," Emma promised. "Speaking of Maggie, our last one is now working for the keeper of the New Bedford House of Correction. If the trial is moved there, you may see her about."

"I hope not. I would not know what to say. I fear she blames me for turning her life upside down. What of Uncle John?"

"He is in Iowa now. I am supposed to let him know as soon as I can about the trial date. You haven't heard, have you?"

"One would think that I, as the main player in their tragic play, would be the first to know if a firm date had been set. I have heard rumors, but I don't know if they are to be believed."

"Let me know when you do," Emma said. "Mrs. Livermore paid me a visit. She said that the officials have done all they could to ruin our lives, and because of that, she does not expect a trial until fall. She thinks the Attorney General's illness is a ruse. Even if it is true, she said, 'If his health can interfere with speedy justice, what would happen if he died? Would Lizzie have to spend the rest of her life in jail?'"

Lizzie shuddered. "Please ask Mrs. Livermore to come see me."

"I will write her a note as soon as I return home. And I will pray that she is wrong about the trial."

The next day, an official decision was announced. The trial will take place in New Bedford on June 5, 1893. Lizzie had hoped it would happen in Taunton, where she could continue with Mrs. Wright, stay in the cell that had become home, and deal with the known but bleak routine of that institution.

* * *

On May 1, Emma returned for her regular Monday visit and brought a guest, Mrs. Livermore. "Lizzie, I know you have had solitude for contemplation, do you now have any idea who could have committed these murders?"

Lizzie shook her head, and Emma filled the gap. "Father had no enemies, and Mrs. Borden never made an enemy in her life. She was always just and kind and regardful of others' feelings."

"But you said you never cared for her," Mrs. Livermore responded.

"Yes, but that was very different. I could never help comparing her with my own dear mother, and always felt she occupied a place that belonged to my mother. If I had known her except as a stepmother, I know I should have loved her."

"I never felt that way," Lizzie said, "for I know no other mother and she was a true mother to me always."

Emma added, "I know that whenever Lizzie wanted anything from her father, and he seemed reluctant to grant it, Mrs. Borden always interceded and secured for Lizzie what she wanted."

Lizzie summoned tears appropriate for the occasion. "But there were not many things that I asked of Father that he did not grant. He was very giving for a man."

"You do not like men, Lizzie?"

"I do not like that they think they can control my life and the lives of all the women they encounter. Why am I here right now? Men. Why has my trial been delayed? Men. I know women can be just as bossy as men, but they do not really have the power over any of us that men do. They hold us back to make themselves look superior."

"There is much truth in what you say, Lizzie. But remember, there are men out there who are helping you and others that would if they could. Do not condemn the whole sex for the manipulations of a few."

"There is where we will have to disagree, Mrs. Livermore. I think those who believe women are equally endowed by their creator are the few—not the many."

"I need to go now and catch my train, Lizzie, but I promise we will continue this conversation. I am very interested in your point of view."

"Thank you for coming, Mrs. Livermore. Your support of me in my time of need will never be forgotten."

Chapter Thirty-Three

The news of Lizzie's May 8 arraignment was concealed from the public, the press, and Lizzie herself. That morning, Sheriff Wright hopped on the earliest train to travel to New Bedford. He moved around the town making sure he was seen by townspeople and reporters as he rambled about without any sense of purpose. He then took the train back to Taunton, hoping he left the impression that there was nothing special about that day.

Returning to the jail, he told his wife to prepare Lizzie for travel. Lizzie donned the same blue dress and short black jacket she wore to the preliminary hearing and topped it with a turban-like hat. As the two women emerged to await the carriage, Emma arrived for her usual Monday visit bearing a box of chocolates.

Mrs. Wright informed Emma of the plans for her sister's day and granted her permission to ride in the carriage with her and Sheriff Wright to the train station. Emma hesitated to say anything of a personal nature in front of the sheriff but did comfort her younger sister. "Lizzie, I will be praying for you all day. I hope your trip is uneventful, and you will be back here soon."

The station had only its ordinary bustle; no one paid much attention to the arrival from the jail. Emma boarded a train to Fall River and Lizzie took a later one to New Bedford with the Wrights by her side. Much to everyone's relief, no crowd gathered at the train station at the end of their journey. Only a few seemed to have noticed the presence of the area's most infamous prisoner.

In the carriage, Sheriff Wright pulled down all the blinds to keep Lizzie out of sight of the passers-by as they rolled through town. The ruse had paid off, a couple of reporters and a handful of the curious were all that greeted Lizzie at the courthouse.

Walking down the hallway, half a dozen men leaned against the walls, staring at the prisoner. Lizzie shrank from their gaze, then straightened her posture and wiped her face of all expression.

Mr. Jennings joined the party from Taunton in the District Attorney's office. While the lawyers discussed the upcoming arraignment, Mrs. Wright sat next to Lizzie and held her hand. "Have you ever been in this courthouse before?"

"No, I have had no reason to go here."

"I would think not. They have shined the brass, polished the wood, and put in new flooring since the last time I was here. I wonder if they did all that for your trial. I imagine they are expecting a lot of outsiders from newspapers and such."

"I hope they all stay away. I just want this all over and done."

Mrs. Wright patted the back of Lizzie's hand. "I know, my dear, I am confident justice will prevail. It's exciting, though, that they saw fit to give you a renewed backdrop. In the spectator section, the floor used to be covered with straw matting. Now, it's velvet carpet—even the clerk's pen is covered with it. I've never seen this court as clean as it is now."

At 5:15, it was time to move into the chamber. Sheriff Wright was the first to cross the threshold, then Mrs. Wright. Lizzie hesitated at the doorway, fearing she would swoon. She leaned against the door frame, took a deep breath and stepped inside to take her place at the dock. The heat rose to flush her face as she moved her eyes around the courtroom,

The clerk called the court into session and then said, "Lizzie Andrew Borden, stand up."

Lizzie rose to her feet despite the wobbling in her knees. She prayed she would not collapse.

The clerk spoke again. "Could you please raise your hand?"

She stretched her tremulous hand upwards to the level of her face.

"Harken unto the indictment found against you by the grand inquest of the county of Bristol. You may drop your hand."

The clerk cleared his throat and began reading the first indictment. "Lizzie Andrew Borden of Fall River in the county of Bristol, on the fourth day of August in the year eighteen hundred and ninety-two, in and upon on Andrew Jackson Borden, feloniously, willfully and of her malice aforethought, an assault did make with a certain weapon, to wit, a sharp cutting instrument, did strike, cut, beat and bruise upon the head of him, ten mortal wounds, of which said mortal wounds the said Andrew Jackson Borden then and there instantly died. The jurors say that Lizzie Andrew Borden did kill and murder against the peace of the Commonwealth."

After a pause, the clerk asked, "Lizzie Andrew Borden, what say you to the first count of the indictment?"

In a clear, bold voice, Lizzie said, "I am not guilty."

The clerk then read the second indictment. It was the same as the first, with the substitution of Abby Durfee Gray Burden in place of Andrew's name. Again, Lizzie said, "I am not guilty."

The third one followed, charging Lizzie with the murder of her father and stepmother. One more time, she said, "I am not guilty."

At 5:30, the judge gaveled the court to its conclusion. Twenty minutes later, Lizzie was on a train back to Taunton and her jail cell.

Chapter Thirty-Four

Lizzie woke the next morning with a dreadful cough, a sore throat, a runny nose, and an unrelenting chill. Mrs. Wright called for a doctor who said it was a bad case of bronchitis and pneumonia. Mrs. Wright moved Lizzie to her house, where a physician called on her two or three times a day.

While Lizzie was still in bed, Mary Livermore paid another visit. She came bearing bad news about one of Lizzie's most valiant supporters in Boston, Miss Clydesdale, had passed away from consumption.

To hide her violent emotional reaction to the woman's death, Lizzie threw a sheet over her head and shook all over. *Was her death an omen? Does this mean my lawyers will fail to set me free?* She stifled the sounds of her sobs and calmed herself before lowering the sheet. "Oh, Mrs. Livermore, I think sometimes I shall collapse entirely, but I will not show these people who have tortured me how much I have suffered. What hurts me most is the malignant feeling that has been shown. Is my character of 30 years to count for nothing—nothing?"

"My dear, you have many, many supporters, and many prayers have been sent up on your behalf."

"But women, Mrs. Livermore, mostly women. The men seem to rejoice in my suffering and want to prolong it as long as possible."

"Not all, men, Lizzie. Most men do not see their actions in a negative light. They think they are protecting others who cannot protect themselves."

"I don't mean to contradict, but most men want to control women just as they do cattle. We are no more significant to them than that."

"After you are free, Lizzie, I think you should get involved in suffrage. We have many male supporters who are working to gain the right to vote for women."

"Not enough, I am sure. Men will not give up any measure of control of elections. They will never give us that right. We would have to take it by force. But, alas, we are the weaker sex and not trained in the art of war. Look at the history of mankind. Until women are willing to take up arms and remove the power of men by force, it is a useless cause."

"Right now, everything looks darker than it did just a year ago. Since Grover Cleveland's election as president, I fear women will not get the vote in my lifetime. All he wants to do is roll back everything President Benjamin Harrison has done—most particularly, he wants to end protection of voting rights."

"As I have been saying, Mrs. Livermore, men will never give the right to vote to women."

"Lizzie, someday, we will prevail."

"I wish I could agree with you, but men are our enemies."

"Once you are free, you will be grateful to the jurymen who found you not guilty. Promise me, in that light, you will reconsider getting involved."

Two days later, Lizzie finally met the third member of her legal team, Ex-governor Robinson. He had a high, broad forehead, an ample paintbrush of a mustache, deep-set eyes, prominent ears, and the manner of the school principal he once was.

He sat down and looked at Lizzie as if he could read her heart. She felt as if he were searching for some proof or disproof of guilt in her face. She tried to appear at ease and answer his questions without hesitation. It was a difficult task. So many had stared at her, twisted her words, and criticized every move she made.

He encouraged her to talk and said very little as he listened intently to her cries of distress as she pled her innocence. He placed a firm hand on her arm. "It's going to be all right, little girl."

At that moment, Lizzie knew he was the perfect man to shelter her from the coming storm and lead her into the sunshine once again. A part of her flinched at being treated like a child, but she knew she needed someone more like a father than an attorney to rescue her.

"I do not want you to come into the courtroom wearing widow-weeds or heavy veils of any sort. Just wear black without any distracting ornaments or colors. You want to look somber and humble. The same holds for all the time before you come to trial. I know with the warmer weather, dark dresses will be even more uncomfortable, but just think of me stuffed into a suit with a vest and a bowtie clenched around my neck like a garrot."

"Is there hope for me, Mr. Robinson?"

"All the hope the heavens can hold, my child. I am confident I can deliver an acquittal. And if God is just, I will. Aside from the verdict of not guilty, what else do you want, Miss Borden?"

"All I want, sir, is to go home."

"We will do our best to see that you do."

* * *

On May 17, Mrs. Livermore arrived at Taunton Jail. Mrs. Wright greeted her with exuberance. "So pleased to see you again, Mrs. Livermore. I am a great admirer of all that you do. Your visits are very uplifting for Miss Borden. Please come inside my house. I will bring Lizzie to you."

Hurrying down the hall of the jail, Mrs. Wright unlocked Lizzie's cell. "Come, dear. You have a special visitor. Mrs. Livermore is in my sitting room waiting for you."

Lizzie was quite pleased to have two amazingly different supporters—one who was remarkably intelligent and worldly and the other relatively uneducated and unsophisticated. If women in different walks of life, like those two, believe totally in my innocence, how could I possibly be convicted?

Once inside the Wright's home, Mrs. Wright prepared tea, and the three women sat down to talk. "I am delighted, Miss Borden, to see a smile on your face," Mrs. Livermore said. "You sounded very bitter during my last visit."

175

"I was still getting over my illness. Mrs. Wright took such good care of me that I have been restored physically and spiritually."

"Honestly, Mrs. Livermore, she was a delightful patient. It made my job quite easy."

"I imagine you will miss her when she is gone."

"I try not to think about that. I know it will not be many days until she has to leave for her trial in New Bedford. I don't have a high opinion of the Ashe Jail. It does not ever seem to be up to my standards in cleanliness."

"Then we shall pray that her stay there is as short as possible."

"And that she does not have to return to my care after the trial. Although, Miss Borden, I do hope you will visit me."

"How could I not, Mrs. Wright? You have shown me remarkable kindness."

* * *

Mr. Jennings paid another pre-trial visit to inform Lizzie that Attorney General Pillsbury had withdrawn from the case. "The lawyers now opposing us are not quite as formidable—Mr. Hosea Knowlton, whom we encountered in the preliminary hearing, and District Attorney W.H. Moody of Essex County."

"Knowlton?" Lizzie asked. "I had so thought I would not have to see him again. He is a horrible man."

"Even so, Miss Lizzie, he is a lesser court presence than Pillsbury. It is a move in your best interests. We are also looking into another murder investigation that has not been solved in more than a year. Do you remember the name David Belanger?"

"No, I cannot say that I do."

"He used to have a remnant shop on Pleasant Street in Fall River. He moved his shop to Main Street in Lowell. He was found dead on the floor of his shop."

"Pray, what does that have to do with me?"

"The case has startling things in common with yours, and they still have no viable suspect. Mr. Belanger was killed with what is assumed to be a butcher's cleaver. The blows were perfectly accurate, so much so that he cleanly sliced on the edge of the victim's linen collar. The slashing appeared to by done by a practiced hand. Remarkably, all traces were concealed, and there were no drippings from the murder weapon found as the killer was in retreat."

"Are you thinking it could be the same person as killed Father?"

"Possibly. If we can work up a strong connection, we will use it at trial to raise reasonable doubt about your guilt."

Or else, Lizzie thought, *Knowlton will use it to charge me with that crime as well.* Lizzie was convinced that Mr. Jennings held a firm belief in her innocence. She was not as sure of Mr. Adams. Mr. Robinson was confident he could obtain an acquittal—and that was all that mattered to Lizzie.

"One more thing, Miss Lizzie, I regret to inform you that Mr. Robinson has banned any visitors for the week before your trial, except your attorneys, of course, and your sister, Emma. I know even though it is just a week, it will be difficult to not to feel abandoned—because you are not. You are innocent, and we will prove it."

Despite the new restriction, Lizzie was in a positive frame of mind just two weeks before her trial. Bolstering hope and confidence, Lizzie won a contest with the Boston Journal—the prize, a set of ten Thackery novels. She was one of five lucky winners. She considered it a very good omen for what lay ahead.

* * *

The arrival of June filled Lizzie with both excitement and dread. Soon, she hoped she would return home and be able to walk around the neighborhood, visit with friends, and stop in a shop whenever the urge struck. She fought to banish all thoughts of the alternative.

Chapter Thirty-Five

Mr. Jennings rushed down to Lizzie's cell so quickly he had to pause to catch his breath before he could talk. "Miss Lizzie, a horrible thing has happened, but it might be the best thing ever for your case in court.

Lizzie inspected his appearance, fearing that the stress of her case may have caused him to take leave of his senses. No mismatched shoes, no rumpled clothes, not a single hair out of place, just that crazed look in his eyes. "What in heaven's name are you talking about, Mr. Jennings?"

"When I returned from Boston, where I conferred with Mr. Robinson about your trial, I learned that there has been another axe murder. Right here in Fall River. Bertha Manchester was in her kitchen making gingerbread when someone forced their way into her home in broad daylight. He picked up the axe from the wood box and struck her once. When she fell to the floor, he struck her again. He took a gold watch and a small amount of money but left behind an obvious jewelry box with some valuable contents. I am convinced whoever killed Miss Manchester also murdered your father and stepmother."

"But can you prove it?" Lizzie asked.

Mr. Jennings stroked his chin. "No. No. Not yet. But still, the many similarities provide you with a foundation of reasonable doubt and that is all the jury needs to acquit. Frankly, it is all anyone wanted to talk to me about when I returned to Fall River. A Boston Globe reporter approached me and asked me about the Bertha Manchester killing, and I said, "Well, are they going to say Lizzie Borden did this also?""

Lizzie laughed at his audacity, then pulled up short at the reality. "For the first time in ten months, I can honestly say that I am glad I am behind bars. If I were out on a bail bond, Mr. Knowlton would be pointing the finger at me."

"Yes. It is a blessing—a small one—but a blessing indeed."

"Do you know when I'll be moved to New Bedford?"

"No," Mr. Jennings said. "They always keep that a mystery. They are concerned that letting the accused know the time of their moving from one facility to the next could allow escape plans to be put in place. I am sure, though, that it will be any day now. Perhaps even by the time I leave you."

* * *

Two days later, the time had come. Lizzie donned a dress of blue serge in a shade so dark, it appeared to be black. She wore a black toque on her head and carried a long black fan to cover her face when needed. Before leaving her room, she snatched up a magazine and the bouquet of pansies that Aunt Carrie sent her. Sheriff Wright escorted her in a closed carriage to Taunton Station to catch the 10:31 train to New Bedford.

Once again, there were no crowds, only one policeman and one reporter waited at the station to observe the departure. Lizzie and the Sheriff disembarked the carriage at the end of the platform. Lizzie slipped inside the station to the Ladies' Room, where Emma and a friend were waiting with best wishes and hugs. The sheriff and his prisoner entered the rear car and settled in for the short ride.

In New Bedford, a large crowd had amassed for her arrival in that town. The sheriff and his charge were rushed to an awaiting cab. Lizzie took the rear seat and pulled down the curtains to shut out the gaze of the pesky curiosity seekers who had surrounded the carriage.

They rode to Ashe jail, an ominous three-story brick structure massive enough to cover nearly a square block. Lizzie lifted the curtain and the sheriff pointed out Keeper Josiah Hunt, a man with a bushy mustache and sharp nose, waiting near the stoop of his residence. Lizzie looked up at the second floor of the building and saw Bridget with another woman observing the arrival of the cab. A group of newspapermen and other citizens surrounded the gate to the jail. Lizzie drew back in the carriage, hoping they had not seen her.

Keeper Hunt rushed toward them to disengage the big iron bolt and open the great gates. He slammed it shut as soon as they passed through. A chill coursed through Lizzie's body, and a veil of darkness passed before her eyes. The heavy clank of the gate sounded like judgment. Its echo sounded like the rolling arrival of doom.

Inside, she was not stopped to answer the formal questions of the clerk as she had done in Taunton. She was escorted straight to an ordinary cell in the women's apartments, a room smaller than what she occupied at Taunton. For furniture, she had a simple iron cot and a frayed, worn chair.

The floor was marked with stains and diestrus accumulated beside the walls, especially in the corners. She had an expanded appreciation for Mrs. Wright and the pride she had taken in the cleanliness of the halls and cells. The gloominess of the room wrapped arms of despair around her shoulders and drove her spirits low.

She tried to shake it off the next day when Mr. Jennings arrived. She did not want to dampen his confidence with her fears.

Jennings looked around Lizzie's cell with a pursed mouth. "I am sorry that you could not remain in Taunton for the trial, but I expect Mr. Knowlton thought New Bedford was a larger platform for his performance."

"Performance?"

"Make no mistake, Miss Lizzie, the courtroom is as much theatrics as the stage—the consequences are what makes the difference. I need you to know what to expect with the trial. The prosecution is going to be harsh with you. Do not let them overpower you. They will present evidence about the burning of the dress, the mysterious robbery in your home on June 24, two years ago, the strained relations between you and your father and your stepmother, the finding of the hatchet—"

"They found the hatchet?"

"They believe they have. They plan to present it at trial."

"Where did they find it?" Lizzie asked as she stuffed down her rising apprehension.

"I do not know, Miss Lizzie. We will find out at trial."

"Tell me, Mr. Jennings, did they find any of the items that were stolen two years ago?" She held her breath as she waited for an answer.

"If they have, they have not spoken to me of it."

Lizzie's stomach felt squeezed in an iron vise. She knew if they found her special hiding place under the floorboards, all would be lost.

"They have two more points to make in their case. They will say that all leads they followed led to failure except for those that led to you, and they will say that no one had an opportunity to commit the crime except for you."

Lizzie nodded as her fear rose and her focus intensified.

"On our part, we will offer an explanation rather than an outright denial. We will tell the jury that although your relations with your stepmother were strained five years ago, they were pleasant and harmonious at the time of her death. We will argue that much of what the prosecution presented is inadmissible evidence and exaggerated hearsay. We will tell them that the police have presented no conclusive evidence that you are responsible for these crimes. We will also show there was an abundant opportunity for another to enter your home and leave undetected. Do you understand all of that? Do you have any questions?"

"Yes, Mr. Jennings, I do understand. But, no, I do not have any questions."

"The first thing that will happen is jury selection. One hundred and fifty men have been summoned for jury duty—thirty from Taunton, forty-five from New Bedford, and seventy-five from smaller cities and towns in the county."

"Are any from Fall River?"

"I don't know right now, but I should get that information tomorrow. Fall River citizens could be a boon or a disaster, depending on the attention they pay to groundless rumors. After the jurors are seated, gossip becomes less of a problem. Jurors are not allowed to have written or verbal communications with anyone outside of their panel. They must sleep in the same room, go to church together, go everywhere together. If say, on a Sunday, they want to get out to the country, they must hire a horsecar, barge, or boat which will hold them all. If they want to walk anywhere, they need to do it as a chain gang. They cannot be separated until the verdict is read in court."

"Could they resent me for their imprisonment? What if someone does not like their fellow jurors, could he disagree with them because of his animosity to the others?"

"That is a risk, Miss Lizzie, but the bigger problem is that they might be influenced by outsiders or even bribed by the prosecution."

"That happens?"

"I have known it to."

"I suppose that means I cannot buy any jury members either."

Mr. Jennings rose to his feet, and all color drained from his cheeks. "Miss Borden!"

Lizzie laughed. "I am just making a silly joke, Mr. Jennings. I have not seriously entertained such a course of action."

"Of course, you haven't," he replied, but uneasiness still gathered in his eyes. "The last thing you need to know is that we have three judges presiding over the court: Judge Albert Mason, Judge Justin Dewey, and Judge Caleb Blodgett. All three are known for their independence and impartiality. On the prosecution side, we will be facing District Attorney Knowlton as before and know what to expect from him. But he will be assisted by the District Attorney of Essex County, Mr. W.H. Moody. He's more of a wild card. I am not sure we will be able to manage him well. Right now, though, it looks very good for us. If you need nothing else, I will see you next in the courtroom."

"Thank you, Mr. Jennings." Lizzie did not mention it to Jennings, but she thought it odd that he always referred to "us" when, in reality, if they lost the case, they will go home to their families, but she would rot in prison or die in the hangman's noose. There would be no "us" on the scaffold.

Chapter Thirty-Six

Getting ready for her appearance in court, Lizzie felt that she had been on trial for ten long months. She had spent nearly a year having to declare her innocence to all who visited, to the jailer, to the jailer's wife—it had been so tiring. The only time she felt a reprieve was when she was lost in a book, and some days, she could not push her cares away long enough to concentrate on the pages.

She dressed carefully that morning in a form-fitting black brocade dress with stylish leg-of-mutton sleeves. She wore a black lace hat with blue rosettes and a tiny blue feather breaking the monotony. She wanted to appear as feminine as possible on this day, although part of her resented the fact that pretending to be a helpless woman was an act forced upon her to gain her freedom.

The Reverend Mr. Jubb, her friend and counselor, visited her that morning. He brought words of comfort, and his faith in Lizzie's lack of guilt was so complete that she never had to repeat her protestations of innocence. He kept her company until Deputy Sheriff Kirby arrived with a carriage to take her to court.

They approached the building on the road behind the courthouse, where the horse shed was a bustle of activity. When Lizzie asked about the commotion, Kirby said, "The building has been converted into headquarters for the telegraph operators. We put in a floor and created three small rooms. One for Western Union, another for the Postal Telegraph-Cable company and the third is being shared by the Evening Standard and the Associated Press. They're just setting up and testing equipment now, but I imagine the hum of instruments and the pounding of keys will be heard down the block when something happens that the reporters deem important. Frankly, I don't understand what the fuss is all about."

Lizzie found the front of the building far more pleasing and less forbidding than the exterior of the jail. The Greek Revival cupola with its shiny bell was showcased by four tall Corinthian columns in the front. Surrounded by a neat lawn, the walk was lined on both sides by beds of tulips.

Kirby said, "Unfortunately, every last reporter is standing out here between you and the courthouse, along with a mob of the curious. It will be a difficult journey until we get inside. But they have nothing better to do, since they are not allowed in the building today."

"Why not?"

"All the jurors called have taken up every seat. There's not room for any of these gadflies or nosy parkers."

Seeing much of the crowd moving toward their carriage, Kirby leaned out of the cab and said, "Take us to the back. We'll disembark there. And be quick about it so we can get inside before they gather there."

Lizzie felt a flutter of excitement in her chest as the sheriff led her up to the second floor and brought her to the door of the chamber which was much smaller than she would have thought from judging the grandeur of the exterior. Four windows provided abundant light but also allowed the sunshine to heat up the space more and more as the day went on.

Mr. Jubb took her arm to escort her to the hard wooden bench near the front of the courtroom. When Lizzie first spotted Mr. Jennings, he was barely recognizable. He had shaved off his sideburns and his beard, leaving his moustache as the sole hirsute adornment. As she passed by her legal team, Mr. Adams stepped forward and bowed. She nodded her head in acknowledgement but dared not meet his eyes, fearing what she would see in the depths. She suspected none of her attorneys were as confident as their reassurances to her.

The bell in the cupola rang, startling Lizzie. Unbeknownst to her, the gongs signaled the start of the court's day. It would also ring when a verdict was reached. It was nearly half past eleven when the three judges entered the chambers. Lizzie stood with the rest of the courtroom to watch their procession to the bench. Chief Justice Mason entered first with his remarkable mutton chops on his otherwise placid face. Justice Blodgett followed with his long face with heavy, puffed eyelids and swollen bags under his eyes. For some reason, he had a smile on his face as if amused by the courtroom and all who were in it. Arriving last was Judge Dewey, a tiny, spry man with a smile that never wavered. He wore a pince-nez and bore an ever-moving palm fan in one hand.

All remained standing while the clerk read out an alphabetical list of the juror's names. Of the 148 summoned, only three did not respond. That accomplished, Reverend Julien of New Bedford said the obligatory prayer for divine enlightenment, and everyone took their seat.

The tedious day was made even worse by the heat from the outside and the tightly crammed bodies inside. Perspiration dotted nearly every forehead. Lizzie wiped her face with a handkerchief and kept her fan in perpetual motion, moving the air as best she could.

To add to the tedium, Judge Mason asked every potential juror the same questions, lulling Lizzie into somnolence. She startled to alertness every time he asked, "Have you any opinions that would preclude you from finding a defendant guilty of an offense punishable by death?"

For Lizzie, the sight of those who were dismissed for their unwillingness to sentence her to die sent daggers of pain into her body. She could not believe that those who believed in God's commandment to not kill were inferior to those who chose to ignore it.

She remained in constant struggle to remain alert enough to stand and declare, "I challenge" to any man the prosecution approved, but her lawyers found unacceptable. A cow in a nearby field helped her with the uncanny timing of his baleful mooing that often punctuated a response from a respective juror. The noisy cow caused a fleeting smile on her face from time to time.

Finally, at 5 o'clock, the clerk swore in the last juror. All the newspapers reported beforehand that it would be impossible to seat a jury on the first day; however, the court only needed to question a total of forty men before the job was done.

The judge gave the chosen a thirty-minute recess to make arrangements for the mandatory seclusion. When they returned, the judge appointed a man from North Attleborough to serve as foreman.

After court was dismissed, Jennings lingered with Lizzie. "I think we have done well with our jury. We have six farmers, three mechanics, two manufacturers and that one real estate man who is now the foreman. I do think they will be quite fair."

"But Mr. Jennings, does not the constitution entitle me to a jury of my peers?"

"Yes, but surely you cannot object to the working class?"

"Of course not. But it seems to me, a jury of my peers would need to be comprised of women—and not a one of them are."

"Miss Lizzie, I do understand, but women are not allowed to be members of the jury."

"Not for any factual reason, sir, just because men desired nothing more than to keep us in our place. So instead of a jury of my peers, I face a coven of righteous, hairy faces."

"Miss Lizzie…" Jennings pleaded.

"Never mind, Mr. Jennings. The world is not fair to women. It often forces us into desperate situations. I know it is not personally your fault—but it is the imperative of your gender."

"Miss Lizzie…" he began again.

"Good day, Mr. Jennings." Lizzie rose and walked over to Sheriff Wright, who led her back to her cell.

Jennings shook his head. He'd often heard the same complaints from his wife even though he tried very hard to treat her as his equal. When he was most honest with himself, he knew what Lizzie and his spouse said was true. He believed he was, by far, not the worst offender but knew he was often a reflection of his male-dominated society.

Chapter Thirty-Seven

The next morning, Sheriff Wright arrived in the courtroom before anyone else. He personally numbered each seat in the press box and gave tickets to select newspaper reporters—twelve from Fall River and New Bedford, five to Boston's most prominent papers, four to the Associated Press, and one each to journalists from Attleborough and Taunton.

Before court was called into session, the bell in the courthouse tower signaled the start of the court's day, making Lizzie and many other observers flinch and jump in their seats. Like all the other rituals of the court, it wore on Lizzie's already frazzled nerves. The indictments were read again as if some in the courtroom were unaware of why they were there that day. Mr. Moody delivered the opening statement for the prosecution.

"Upon the fourth day of August of the last year, an old man and woman, husband and wife, each without a known enemy in the world, in their own home, upon a frequented street in the most populous city in this County, under the light of day and in the midst of its activities, were, first one, then, after an interval of an hour, another, severally killed by unlawful human agency. Today, a woman of good social position, of hitherto unquestioned character, a member of a Christian church and active in good works, the own daughter of one the victims, is at the bar of this Court, accused by the Grand Jury of this County of these crimes."

Lizzie was surprised that the prosecution even mentioned her character and good deeds. Moody made a lengthy description of the Borden's home that was so convoluted that she could not understand how any member of the jury could follow his steps—she herself got lost at moments in his explanation.

She felt many of the details about the evening before and the morning of the murders were unnecessary, as if he were trying to stuff the jurors' brains so full of minutiae that they could not discern the lack of evidence in the state's case. After that, he turned to the disgusting topics of stomach and intestine contents and the stickiness of blood. The former seemed to be irrelevant, considering the cause of death.

When Moody spoke about the burned dress, Lizzie comforted herself with the knowledge that he did not have a single shred of it in his possession, and the only witness could not say whether it was covered with paint or spattered with blood. All they had was a theory.

To Lizzie's relief, Moody never mentioned finding a hatchet hidden under her bed. Her hidey-hole remained sacrosanct, the murder weapon undiscovered. Moody made a final plea to the jury to choose a guilty verdict. Lizzie had to acknowledge that he was eloquent in his speech, even though each word felt like a dagger to her heart.

"We shall prove that this prisoner made contradictory statements about her whereabouts and, above all, gave a statement vitally different upon the manner in which she discovered the homicides. We shall prove beyond all reasonable doubt that this death of Mrs. Borden was a prior death. Then, we shall ask you to say whether any reasonable hypothesis except that of the guilt of this prisoner can account for the sad occurrences that happened on the morning of August 4. If your minds, considering all these circumstances, are led irresistibly to the conclusion of her guilt, we ask you in your verdict to declare the truth and make true deliverance of the great issue which has been committed to your keeping."

Lizzie swayed in her seat. The heat in the courtroom seemed to rise to an alarming level as he spoke. She heard a ringing in her ears. She felt faint, and then she felt nothing. The acrid scent of smelling salts drew her back to the present. The Reverend Mr. Jubb leaned over the rail, patting her hand. Jennings urged her to sip from a glass of water.

Chapter Thirty-Eight

Mrs. Livermore joined Lizzie during the lunch recess. Lizzie expected she came to distract her—to question about the social and industrial life she saw in Europe on her tour. Mrs. Livermore, however, had other things on her mind. "Lizzie, they say you are stolid and insensible to the horror of your position."

"Let them talk. I fainted because it was beyond my control. However, I was raised to be genteel, to always avoid emotional outbursts, and now, they expect me to weep and wail. Besides, do you think I would allow any of my feelings to be shown to these men who have hounded me for so long and with such bitter hate? I would die first."

"I do understand that feeling, my dear. Think, however, of the jurors. They are not the ones who have been harassing you. You want them to know you have heart; you have feelings, you are not the monster the prosecution wants them to believe.

"Mrs. Livermore, I appreciate your concern. I really do. But now, in this time of my greatest distress, I do not think I can escape the disciplines that I spent all my whole life learning."

"It is what society expects, but I am not sure that it is in your best interest."

"Men make the rules, and we follow them only to discover that they change them without warning. But heaven forbid if we should break one of their rules before it suits them," Lizzie complained.

"The world is not fair, Lizzie. But we must always work to make tomorrow better than today."

The two women returned to the abominable heat of the courtroom to listen to the testimony of an engineer who laid out the Borden home and its surroundings. His time on the stand was interrupted by Knowlton requesting that the jury take a tour of the house and yard. Lizzie was offered the option of joining them, but she declined. She felt a crowd of staring, gawking strangers would only add to her sense of distress of not being there to sleep in her own bed.

* * *

To everyone's delight, the second day's trial opened to much cooler temperatures. Even so, the heat built in the overcrowded chamber as the day progressed. When John Morris took the stand, Lizzie marveled that at his age, her uncle was still quite a handsome man—a bit like Abraham Lincoln but a more attractive version.

Lizzie soon grew bored with its testimony since it was identical to that he provided at the preliminary hearing. He was followed by six additional witnesses who also had nothing new to offer.

Lizzie was roused to full attention, though, when Bridget Sullivan's name was called. She barely recognized her former maid in her new finery—a fashionable, new burgundy dress with black trim, a black hat adorned with matching plume and veil, and a new pair of kid gloves. Lizzie thought that Bridget never looked so lovely as she was when she took the stand. If the maid was nervous being surrounded by so many strangers, she did not give any outward signs of it. She did not alter the story she offered at the earlier hearing, much to Lizzie's relief.

* * *

The third day of the trial began with testimony from neighbor and physician, Dr. Seabury Bowen. During direct, he reiterated the day he had arrived at the Borden home to find Andrew dead. "Mrs. Borden appeared to have been killed by the same weapon. It was very fortunate that Lizzie was out of the house when the killer struck downstairs."

In a moment of comic relief, District Attorney Moody pulled out a blue dress held in evidence. He tried to get it right side up but fumbled, could not find the waistline, and was not able to hang it correctly. Knowlton came to his rescue, apologizing for his bachelor colleague with a laugh.

Moody asked, "Dr. Bowen, what is the style of this dress?"

"I don't pretend to describe a woman's dress, and I never did so."

"Was Miss Borden wearing this dress when you arrived at the Borden house?"

"I don't know whether this is the dress she had on that morning or not. I could not even tell you what my wife was wearing this morning."

On cross-examination, Dr. Bowen explained that he had given Lizzie Borden a double dose of morphine to calm her nerves and allay her mental stress. He emphasized that the medication would have affected the defendant's memory and her view of things when she was being questioned by police.

The levity Lizzie felt from that interlude soon dissipated when Alice Russell stepped up to the stand. Her jaw stiffened, her chest grew rigid, and her fingernails dug into her skin. She kept her eyes on Alice's treasonous face throughout the length of her appearance.

When Alice entered, she looked all around the courtroom but never in Lizzie's direction. She testified about the burning of the dress, looking at her questioners, at the ceiling, at the floor—everywhere but at Lizzie.

Lizzie, however, was more unsettled than she would admit even to herself. She noticed she had been rubbing her shoes against the rung of the chair. She made her feet stop, but then they resumed their actions while her attention was elsewhere. She heard a small plink, though, and when she looked down, she realized that she had rubbed one of her buttons loose. Emma leaned over and picked it up.

On cross-examination, Mr. Robinson backed Alice into a corner, forcing her to admit that she never saw Lizzie put the dress into the stove. He made her testimony sound like conjecture wrapped around a nugget of malice. Lizzie could not understand, though, what she had done to Alice to create that virulent dislike.

Lizzie struggled to suppress any outward expressions of delight when Robinson questioned Assistant Marshall John Fleet. He squirmed through the lawyer's highlighting of his many discrepancies in previous testimony, focusing on his denial that he had observed the broken handle of the hatchet.

Officer Mullaly told the jurors that he found a box containing the missing piece of the handle. "Assistant Marshall Fleet took it out of the box and returned it. I have no idea where that missing piece of the handle or box is now. I haven't seen it since it was found in the basement."

After the officer stepped down, Knowlton told the court that he did not have possession of the hatchet handle and had never had it. Robinson asked that Fleet return to the chamber where again, the assistant Marshall insisted he had never seen the piece of handle.

Knowlton called Annie White, the stenographer who took down the testimony during the inquest. Without hesitation, Robinson requested a suspension of the witness to hear testimony without the jury present to enable the judges to rule on its admissibility. The request was granted.

A series of police officials and officers testified next, resurrecting Lizzie's ire at the violation of her home during the search. She was still fuming when the day ended. As soon as it was, Emma took Lizzie's shoes and hurried off to find someone who could refasten the button.

Marianne Holmes kept Lizzie company while she waited to be transported back to the jail. "How are you holding up, Lizzie?"

"Not well at all, Marianne. So many witnesses with nothing new to say except that they want me hung."

"Oh, now, dear, no one said that."

"Not openly, but I know they were thinking it. All those policemen talking about the search of my home. You could say I have no right to be irate at a bunch of men stomping into my room and defiling my dresses, but what about Emma? They tore apart her bed, mauled her garments, and violated her privacy. She was not even in the same town when the crime occurred."

"I know, Lizzie. I have spoken to Emma many times and know what a great tribulation this has been for both of you. Rest assured, though, your sister is not focused on what she had to endure, but with what you are facing daily."

"And what of Maggie? A simple servant whose belongings are few—she did not deserve that treatment. I told them it was not possible for her to have committed those murders. Why could they not leave her meagre possessions alone?"

"Yes, it's all very unseemly, but recall that state policeman's testimony. He did a complete search of the clothes closet, and yet he could not remember the color of any of the dresses. They may have pawed through your belongings, but they were not paying close attention."

Emma returned with a smile on her face. "Here are your shoes. The woman not only fixed the one that fell off, but she reinforced the buttons on both shoes and told me to check them every day at the end of court to be sure none had worked loose. She said that she whole-heartedly believed in your innocence and did not want to see you hobbling out of the courtroom in just one shoe."

"Oh, Emma, thank you. And if you see the woman again, please express my gratitude. How can I ever repay you for your kindness and dedication to me?"

"You would do the same if the shoe was on the other foot," Emma said.

The three women laughed. As Lizzie was led away to the jail, she wondered if she would follow her sister's example. Or would she shun her?

Chapter Thirty-Nine

Sunday, Jennings visited Lizzie in jail. "I want you to understand how important tomorrow's court hearings are. We do not want your testimony at the inquest to be admitted as evidence in court. It could mean the difference between a finding of guilt and an acquittal."

"Why? I did not confess—I denied any guilt."

"Yes, Miss Lizzie, you did. However, there were minor contradictions in your testimony that Mr. Knowlton would use to rip you to shreds. Mr. Robinson will argue that you were suffering from grief and shock and were heavily medicated by Dr. Bowen. All of that created a situation in which no one could be expected to be lucid and consistent in their testimony.

"The biggest point we will drive home, however, is that you were, for all intents and purposes, under arrest from the day your parents died until you were whisked off to jail. You were under close observation and control by the police every moment of every day—the city marshal himself escorted you to the inquest.

"When you asked for your attorney to accompany you, your request should have been granted. Unbeknownst to any of us at the time, Marshall Fleet had your arrest warrant in his pocket throughout the duration of your testimony—from beginning to end. He had the authority to arrest you before you spoke a word, and yet, he kept that to himself and did not warn you that you were not obligated to testify."

"Is that legal, Mr. Jennings?"

A slow smile crossed my lawyer's face. "We think not Lizzie. Everyone has the right not to testify against themselves. The police and Mr. Knowlton denied you that right and blocked your right to counsel as well. For that reason, we believe the judges will not allow your inquest testimony to be entered at trial."

"Thank you, Mr. Jennings, for that explanation and for your tireless work on my behalf. Please extend my gratitude to the others on the legal team."

When he left, Lizzie sat in her chair and stared at the wall. *I thought I had done well at the hearing. I never made an incriminating statement. I never showed anger. I tried to be as honest as I could about all the peripheral details. I do not understand why that was not enough.*

For a while, she tried reading *Great Expectations*. Charles Dickens had long been a marvelous diversion for her. Today, each sentence dissipated into a mental fog the moment she finished reading it. Her anxiety about tomorrow's outcome did not allow any room for comprehension. It twisted like a knot in her gut that did not unravel all night long.

The next morning, the heaviness of oppression settled in Lizzie's chest and worsened when she realized that a breezeless, scorching day had dawned. Vases of flowers lining the judges' bench looked fresh and bright in defiance of the heat. She looked over at Jennings and Adams. Both of their faces were flushed and wrinkled with apprehension. When she caught Robinson's eyes, he was leaning back in his chair, looking relaxed and satisfied. He nodded at Lizzie and turned to face front, appearing as cool and collected as a well-fed cat.

The judges filed into their seats, and the jury was seated, but before they could get comfortable, the chief judge sent them out. Lizzie wondered if the panel was annoyed at being excluded. Lizzie left the chamber for the adjoining room where she could avoid the stares but still hear all the words being spoken.

As Moody argued for the inclusion of the inquest testimony, Lizzie's anger and the color in her cheeks rose with every sentence. Robinson argued to exclude with an eloquence that eradicated her anger and filled her with hope. At 11:15, the judges retired to consider their decision.

The court was in session again at 12:35. Lizzie returned to her seat. Judge Mason delivered the full decision. Lizzie listened as his voice turned into an unintelligible drone in her ears. She was convinced that he would rule for the prosecution. He surprised her at the end when he pronounced: "The evidence at the inquest is excluded."

For a moment, Lizzie was certain she misheard, but when Jennings erupted with a spontaneous "By golly," she knew it was true. She bent forward and held a fan in front of her face to hide her flowing tears. The muscles of her shoulders heaved up and down, but she was powerless to still them.

Testimony continued after lunch recess, but it was the third witness that jarred Lizzie. Dr. Dolan's discussion of crushed skull bones, feces, and undigested food churned in her stomach and made her head spin. When he pulled out and waved a blood-covered handkerchief, Lizzie was undone. She covered her face again and struggled to maintain control.

On cross examination, Adams asked, "Did you get the permission of Miss Emma Borden or Miss Lizzie Borden before you removed the heads of Mr. and Mrs. Borden?"

Dolan's face betrayed his loathing of the attorney. "No, I did not. It was not necessary."

Gasps echoed in the courtroom.

"Did you get permission from any family member?"

"No, I did not."

The audience, as a whole, exhaled.

"Did you ever inform Miss Emma Borden or Miss Lizzie Borden that you had severed their parents' head from their bodies?"

"No, I did not."

Adams turned to the jurors, eyebrows raised as he sought their full attention before lowering his chin and shaking his head. The jurors' faces curdled with distaste as they stared at Dolan.

Dr. Edward Wood from Boston took the stand. "I tested the hatchet and axe presented as evidence. I found no blood on either one. Two of the stains on Miss Borden's skirt that police also thought were blood were not. And the stained piece of door frame I was given to test for blood only had tobacco juice or some kind of soup on it."

On cross-examination, Adams shocked every woman in the audience—and probably many of the men—when he asked, "Could the tiny spot on Miss Borden's underskirt be the result of menstrual flow?"

"Yes, it could, and most likely it was."

Dr. Frank Draper's testimony involved gruesome descriptions of the injuries to the bodies and the demonstration of how the axe fit into the plaster cast of Andrew's head.

Lizzie and her sister were invited to leave the courtroom and sit on a bench out in the hall. "Emma, is this not rather ironic?"

"What, Lizzie?"

"I am considered too delicate to hear the doctor's testimony about the axe splitting an imaginary skull, yet they think I am indelicate enough to plunge that same weapon into my living father ten or eleven times?"

"None of what they have done to you makes any sense, but I am grateful, nonetheless, that we do not have to observe that testimony. But, yes, excluding you from this moment makes a mockery of the reason for the trial.

The court went into lunch recess; the sheriff transported Lizzie back to the jail for her meal. When she returned, the carriage horse startled as she disembarked, throwing her towards the stone steps. Fortunately, an elderly white-haired attendant was quicker than his age would imply. He grabbed Lizzie and set her upright before she collided with the hard surface.

Draper continued his testimony. The sisters were admitted to the courtroom for his cross-examination, which in itself was a brutal assault on the memories of their father. At day's end, Lizzie was relieved to go back to her cell.

On the ride there, she thought about Mary Livermore, her stalwart supporter who had attended the trial more days than not. She composed a letter to her to clear her head of negative thoughts.

One thing that hurts me inexpressively, and causes me to weep when I am alone, is the malignancy that is directed against me. I have never knowingly harmed another human being. I have done much good to many persons who now desert me.

In my own home, there have been hands stretched out against me that I have loaded with favors in the past, and there is no one so humble that does not dare condemn me before a word has been said to prove me innocent.

***

Lizzie woke at dawn on Wednesday, June 14, with an intense longing for home. The cell looked alien when she opened her eyes. For a moment, she could not remember where she had gone to bed.

Outside matched her melancholy mood with the falling rain and suffocating dampness that magnified the heat in the air. Lizzie hoped that the nasty weather would keep observers in the courtroom to a minimum. Unfortunately, the crowd gathered at the door sporting a bouquet of umbrellas appeared to be as large as ever.

Marshall Hilliard and Mayor Coughlin repeated their testimony from the preliminary hearing. The next witness, cloak maker Hannah Gifford, surprised Lizzie. "When I referred to Mrs. Borden as Lizzie's mother last year, Miss Lizzie said, "Don't say that to me, for she is a mean, good-for-nothing thing.'"

Lizzie turned to Emma and whispered behind her fan, "I have never called her a 'thing.' How dare a person in my hire make a disparaging and dishonest comment about me."

Moody then wanted Annie Borden to testify about comments Lizzie made on their return trip from Europe, three years earlier. Mr. Robinson objected, and the jurors were sent out of the courtroom. Judge Mason ruled in favor of the defense since nothing in Annie's testimony contained specific statements regarding Lizzie's feelings towards her father or stepmother.

A series of nine witnesses, whose only testimony involved not seeing anything unusual at the Borden house that morning, churned in and out of the witness stand. These empty vessels of meaningless words made Lizzie believe, more than ever, that the prosecutors were doing all they could to make the trial drag and consume more days than justice required.

The final witness of the morning was Mrs. Hannah Reagan, the matron at the Fall River police station. She told the court that Emma and I argued, and Lizzie accused her sister of giving her away.

On cross-examination, Robinson made her pay the price for her testimony. The attorney produced a document. "Do you remember signing this document when the Reverend Mr. Buck brought it to you?"

"I do remember signing something, but I don't remember what it said."

"I'd be glad to refresh your memory by reading it back to you." Robinson snapped the paper straight and read: "This is to certify that my attention has been called to a report said to have been made by me in regard to a quarrel between Lizzie and her sister Emma, in which Lizzie said to Emma, 'You have given me away,' etc., and that I expressly and positively deny any such conversation took place, and I further deny that I ever heard anything that could be construed as a quarrel between the two sisters."

That afternoon, Dr. Dolan was recalled and asked about blood spots again and Bridget Sullivan was made to repeat her testimony about the blood-stained handkerchief and the screen door lock. She looked worn from all the attention and the humid, stuffy environment—even the plume in her hat drooped from the experience.

The jurors were sent from the room again, and Knowlton argued for and Robinson against the inclusion of the prussic acid purchase and the ability of Dr. Dolan to return to the stand after sitting in the chamber listening to court proceedings since he last testified.

A weary Lizzie left for the day, notably worse for wear. She dreaded what the morrow would bring.

Chapter Forty

The next day, to cheer herself up and appear more positive than she felt, Lizzie came to the courtroom with a large bunch of pink and white flowers surrounded by the lovely green of maidenhair fern. She hoped that, at the least, the cheerful bouquet would confuse her enemies.

Outside of the presence of the jury, the judges dismissed further testimony by Dr. Dolan, and after hearing the furrier discuss the cleaning of furs, they found all the prussic acid testimony inadmissible. The prosecution then submitted evidentiary objects and rested its case.

After a short break, Jennings delivered emotional opening arguments for the defense case. Lizzie felt the impact of his words and hid her face with her fan to keep her sentiments from public view. Jennings spoke about Lizzie's character and her charitable and church activities and explained the difference between direct and circumstantial evidence. "There is no evidence tying Miss Borden directly to the crime."

As he spoke, Lizzie listened to the barely audible noises of the courtroom: the gentle whoosh of fans moving air, the sound of a nib scratching Jennings' words on paper, the quiet brush of shoe leather rubbing against the floor. These sounds of silence rumbled beneath the lawyer's eloquent words.

He ended his comments with a flourish. "Without spending further time, we shall ask you to say in view of the presumptions in favor of human nature, in view of the feelings which exist between a father and a daughter who stands here, from the fact that there is no blood, no a spot on her hands, her head, her dress, or any part of her, no connection with any weapon whatever shown by any direct evidence; with an opportunity for others to do the deed; with herself in the barn when it was done—we shall ask you to say whether the government has satisfied you beyond a reasonable doubt that she did not kill not only her stepmother, Abby Durfee Borden, but her loved and loving father, Andrew Jackson Borden, on the fourth day of August last."

The defense called a parade of witnesses who heard loud noises or saw suspicious individuals in the vicinity of the Borden home on the night before or the day of the murders. The painter testified that Lizzie was close to him and his work when he was painting the house, making it possible for her to get wet paint on her clothing. Others spoke of what they observed on the scene in the immediate aftermath of the murders.

Even though the witnesses were all testifying on her behalf, she grew weary of it all. *The ordeal has gone on long enough. Stop calling witnesses. Let the jury decide.* For her, the unknowing had grown worse than the possibility of conviction—even the terror of hanging. She just wanted to know what tomorrow, next week, next month held for her. *Even knowing I will die is less of a burden than knowing nothing.*

When the chief judge adjourned for the day, Lizzie's impatience dragged her thoughts to ruminating about the next day in court. She paced in her cell until her feet ached. The evening was eternal. Sleep was elusive. She prayed that tomorrow would be the last she would see of the courtroom.

When the next day arrived, she could not concentrate there either. She shut out the nattering and the hostility of Knowlton, cross-examining the defense witnesses. She riveted her attention, however, the moment the defense called Emma to testify.

Knowlton objected often. As the lawyers argued their points, Emma sat straight and still, gazing out at her sister, keeping her breath smooth and even. When she spoke, her soft voice was steady and rang with the purity of a harpsichord.

Jennings asked, "Miss Emma, did your father wear a ring on his finger?"

"Yes, he did. It was the only article of jewelry he wore. My sister Lizzie gave it to him ten or fifteen years ago. Before that, she wore it every day.

After she gave it to him, Father wore the ring always. It was on his finger when he was buried."

Jennings asked about Emma's recollection of the dresses in the house spawning a lengthy argument with the prosecution. Finally, Emma was allowed to answer. "There were somewhere between seventeen and eighteen dresses in the clothes press. All belonged to my sister and I except for one that was Mrs. Borden's."

"How many of the dresses were blue?"

"Ten, two belonged to me, and eight to my sister."

Another lawyer-to-lawyer squabble erupted at that answer delaying Emma's testimony again. When it resumed, Jennings asked, "Did you or your sister cooperate with the officers in their search of your home?"

"Yes. We told them to come as often as they pleased and to search as thoroughly as they could. We both went into the attic to assist them in opening a trunk."

"What can you tell us about Miss Lizzie's Bedford cord dress?"

"I was in the room with my sister and the dressmaker when it was made with an inexpensive fabric in a simple style. Two weeks after that, Father had painters in the house, and my sister got paint on it along the front, on one side toward the bottom, and some on the right side of the skirt."

"Did you see that dress again?"

"Yes, I saw Lizzie wearing it around the house on one occasion. Then, the Saturday after the deaths, I needed to hang a dress in the clothes press, but all the nails were taken. I noticed the damaged Bedford cord hanging there and took it down to use that nail. I said to my sister, 'You haven't destroyed that old dress yet, why don't you?"

"What happened to that dress on Sunday morning?"

"I was washing dishes, and I heard my sister's voice. I turned around and saw she was standing at the foot of the stove—between the stove and the dining room door—with that dress hanging over her arm." She said, 'I think I should burn this old dress.' I told her, 'I would if I were you' and turned back to the dishes."

"Did she do anything to prevent others from hearing or seeing her?"

"No, the windows and the curtains were wide open, as was the door, and there were officers all about the yard."

Before lunch recess, Knowlton began his cross-examination by badgering Emma about the relationship between her sister and Mrs. Borden. Emma stood against the barrage, never faltering from her insistence that all was cordial.

* * *

During the break, Lizzie spoke with Mrs. Livermore who said, "There has been a decided change in public opinion. There are hosts of people everywhere crying out for your deliverance."

"But what people say on the street and in their parlors cannot reach the twelve men sitting judgment on me. Do you think they will be just and true?"

"My dear, I cannot doubt it. They look like honest men who will deliver a righteous judgment. Oh, if you could only be judged by the three men behind the bench instead. I am certain they would set you free."

"Mrs. Livermore, I do not want you to further witness Emma's nervous discomfort. If Mr. Knowlton presses her on cross-examination, she may be forced to reveal her negative feelings toward Mrs. Borden. She may have to admit that she saw her as a usurper. Emma spent far more years with our mother than I, and I feel she was influenced by our mother's horrific experiences with her stepmother. I do not want you to judge her too harshly."

"I would not do so, Lizzie. But if you feel more comfortable, I will not return to the courtroom for the afternoon session."

* * *

Emma walked up for the rest of her cross-examination and put an end to Lizzie's fears. Knowlton tried to make her alter her testimony about the Bedford cord dress, but Emma stood firm. Lizzie gained new respect for her sister that afternoon.

The dressmaker, Phoebe Bowen, and Mrs. Brigham all reinforced Emma's testimony. Knowlton then recalled Marshall Hilliard, Officer Mullaly, and stenographer Annie White to rebut the testimony of the defense witnesses. Then Lizzie breathed a sigh of relief upon hearing, "The evidence is closed on both sides."

Judge Mason quickly squashed her pleasure when he announced there would be no court on Saturday and the trial would resume on Monday, June 19th, at 9 o'clock. Lizzie now had two full days to agonize over her fate, to live in a fog of the unknown. She feared she would go mad.

Chapter Forty-One

Sensing his client's dismay, Jennings arranged a surprise for Lizzie after the end of court that day. He secured permission for her to spend a half hour with friends from Fall River before she returned to her cell in the jail. They lifted her spirits in the moment, but the weekend wait loomed large in her mind.

A cloudy sky and dreary rain heralded the arrival of dawn on Saturday, drowning Lizzie's hopes again. At times, it pounded on the glass as if it could shatter it. When it stilled to a light drizzle, the dripping from the eaves sounded like a roar. Lizzie felt as if nature was preparing her for her doom. Mrs. Livermore walked in and disrupted her melancholy. "How is your health, Lizzie?"

"It seems I have not slept an hour since the trial began. I feel that I must be awake, that my enemies would hang me if they could, even though they know I am innocent. I am very tired, all the time."

"You must try to get some rest, Lizzie. You'll need it for next week."

"When they first told me they suspected me of murdering my poor father, I was struck with horror. They say I was defiant, but I only felt as if some horrible menace had been directed against me. After I was arrested and heard the dreadful things people said, I was overcome and felt a cloud of despair settling down over me. But, when I came to know the men defending me, I did not feel I could be condemned, and I never lost faith in the result since the day Governor Robinson saw me in the jail—even though I have had to fight my thoughts to maintain that belief. The governor has made me feel that he is so strong and good that no injustice can prevail while he stands in the way. Mr. Jennings has fought for me as if his own life and not mine were at peril."

"Hope springs eternal from an innocent heart, my Lizzie. Do not despair. We are all praying for you."

Lizzie bid her friend farewell, wishing her heart was as innocent as Mrs. Livermore and Emma believed it to be.

The rain still pounded the walls outside of Lizzie's cell when Robinson dropped by that afternoon. Lizzie asked, "Will we finish on Monday?"

"I do not know, Miss Borden. I have quite a lot to say to the jury, and I will take the time I need to do it. I need to cover every piece of circumstantial evidence the state presented and show why it is irrelevant. I must speak of your sterling character and your good deeds. I must tell them about your close relationship with your father. Then, the prosecutors have the final word. I do not know how detailed they will be. Most of the time, though, the commonwealth likes to use up as much time making their points as the defense did making theirs."

"What are my chances, Governor Robinson? Will I go home or go to my death?"

"I am not a gambling man, Miss Borden, so I will not say with certainty what the outcome will be. However, if the law is followed to the letter, you will come home free next week."

"How long will it take the jury to reach a verdict?"

"There is no way to know. And do not put any stock in the myths of the courthouse. The length of time they spend reaching their decision does not reflect their ultimate verdict. Some say a short time means the state has won, but I've seen it go either way. And do not waste your time studying the faces of the jurors when they come back in court. Some will try to hide their true feelings. Others will be striving to look serious. You cannot judge the outcome by appearances."

As Robinson talked about his optimism in her acquittal, Lizzie wondered if he truly believed that would happen or if he were trying to convince himself. It was a valiant effort, but Lizzie's doubts continued to circle through her thoughts.

***

Sunday, Lizzie listened to the church bells ring. They used to lift her spirits. Now, they reminded her of the bell that sounded on the courthouse at the start of every trial day. Later that afternoon, she heard the strains of music wafting through the air. Matron told her there was a concert in Riverside Park. Her heart ached thinking about how long it had been since she strolled through any park or sat in front of a bandstand. The afternoon moved slowly, but the night stretched on forever. She dreaded the resumption of court as much as she was eager for it to get started.

In the morning, she climbed into the carriage and felt as if she were heading for her execution. She feared she would not be able to hold herself together all day but knew that she must. She held her head up high as she entered the courtroom with a black folding fan in her hands. She sat down in court with Emma by her side.

Governor Robinson began his closing argument at 9:10 that morning. Once he started, Lizzie pulled her fan to her face. She did not want anyone to see any signs of the despondency or fear she was feeling. When Robinson spoke of the ring Lizzie had given to her father, she felt Emma tense beside her and saw silent tears roll down her face. Lizzie was undone. Her tears flowed, and the heat rose from her neck into her cheeks, setting her face afire. She was relieved when Judge Mason interrupted Robinson for recess at 11 o'clock.

Mrs. Livermore arrived at the courthouse at 11:30 bearing a huge bundle of field daisies bringing a smile to Lizzie's face. "Oh my Lizzie," she said, "your eyes are red, your lips are swollen, have you been weeping?"

"I am ashamed to say it, but I was, Mrs. Livermore. Governor Robinson brought up memories of Father that are still painful to recall."

"My dear, it will be all over soon. Only time stands between you and your home. Clutch your faith close to your heart."

After the break was over, Robinson went on the attack on every piece of evidence that the prosecutors used to point to Lizzie's guilt. He tore each one down with vigor and mocked them as they fell. Lizzie's emotions remained close to the surface, and the fan near her face. She studied the jurors but could not find a clue to their thoughts. *Were they believing Governor Robinson? If they did, would they be swayed the other way by Mr. Knowlton's words?* She shuddered at the thought.

A short recess followed Robinson's plea to find Lizzie not guilty. Then Knowlton rose to speak of the defendant's guilt. Lizzie's loathing of her sworn enemy steeled her heart from any show of emotion. She dropped her fan and watched him as intently as a cat stared at its prey. From time to time, Lizzie suppressed chuckles as Mrs. Livermore muttered her disapproval of Knowlton's statements. She seemed particularly affronted when the prosecutor spoke of women and crime.

"It is hard," he said, "to believe a woman can be guilty of such a crime. But women are human. If they lack man's strength and vigor, they possess more cunning. If they love more devotedly than men, they hate more cordially. History records the fact that some of the most dastardly and fiendish crimes were committed by women. We must face this case then as men, not gallants. The crime was done for a purpose. It was done out of hatred. It was done by whom? In this sacred presence, there is no room for any vestige of prejudice. Sex is not a protection against crime."

Lizzie cheered when she noticed that the courtroom was more restless when the prosecutor spoke than it had been for her lawyer's arguments. Papers rustled and crinkled, benches creaked as bodies shifted weight from one side to another, seeking comfort, coughs erupted, and throats cleared as he droned through his summation.

At 5 o'clock that afternoon, Mr. Knowlton was still talking. The defense had hoped the case would go to the jury this afternoon. Lizzie would have to spend yet another lonely night desperate to return home as she remained in the shadow of the gallows.

Chapter Forty-Two

In the morning, Knowlton continued to paint as dark a portrait of the accused as anyone could conceive. Lizzie felt jolts of fear as he made repeated arguments for her death. Finally, he finished, and court was adjourned until 1:45 that afternoon.

Chef Justice Mason opened the proceedings and said, "Lizzie Andrew Borden, it is now your privilege to say any word you wish."

Lizzie rose to her feet and spoke clearly and forcefully. "I am innocent. I leave it all to my counsel."

Judge Dewey stood in the bench closest to the jury, and the panel of men moved into standing positions in response. The judge read the charge in a conversational tone of voice as if he were talking to a friend over at the corner market.

At 24 minutes past 3, the jury was dismissed to consider the verdict away from prying eyes. The judges approved several items of evidence for delivery into the deliberation room and retired to their private chambers.

Annie Holmes slipped into a seat by Lizzie. "Lizzie, you won't believe who is sitting with the journalists."

"Who, Annie?"

"See that stern-looking, short-haired woman?" Annie pointed behind the shield of her hand.

"Yes."

"She is Mrs. Marilla Ricker, a lawyer from the District of Columbia. She just told a reporter that she believes an acquittal will be delivered within an hour and a half."

"I certainly hope she is right," Lizzie said. "Her name sounds familiar to me, but I do not know why."

"Mother told me about her when we were just children. She stirred up a ruckus in Dover, New Hampshire, when she tried to vote. She was the first woman to attempt that. She is also the first woman admitted to the New Hampshire bar, but she had to go through the courts to make it happen."

"A woman lawyer? Amazing. I am delighted to have Miss Ricker on my side."

As the minutes continued to creep by, Lizzie felt ants crawling across her scalp. She tried to ignore them, but then felt the ants again going up and down her legs. She bent over to brush at them but felt nothing there. Little ant footsteps marched across her face. She reached up to knock them off but realized that no one else appeared to be aware of them—they were just figments of her fear. She sat as quietly as she could, fighting the urge to jump up and run, to do something to escape her torment.

An hour after they departed the courtroom, the jurors filed back into their seats. The crier called out each name, and they responded. Lizzie was told to stand. She tottered to her feet and felt the floor quaver beneath her feet. She pressed her lips tightly together to steady herself.

The clerk asked, "Gentlemen of the jury, have you agreed upon your verdict?"

Lizzie held her breath.

The foreman said, "We have."

Lizzie feared looking at them and just stared straight ahead.

"Lizzie Andrew Borden, hold up your right hand."

She lifted it up, hoping the trembling she felt was not visible.

"Mr. Foreman, look upon the prisoner. Prisoner, look upon the foreman."

Lizzie slowly turned her head, tightening her jaw.

"What say you, Mr. Foreman?"

"Not guilty."

Applause erupted, and cheers broke out in the courtroom. Officers shouted and milled about, attempting to hush the exuberant crowd. Jennings, with tears quivering on his eyelashes, grabbed Mr. Adams' hand.

His voice cracked as he spoke. "Thank God."

Lizzie fell to her knees, resting her forehead on the railing to keep from collapsing altogether. She hoped she had heard correctly. She worried her ears had played a wicked trick on her.

Deputy Kirby grabbed Lizzie around the waist and helped her to her feet. She glanced at her attorneys and saw grins on their faces and dropped down into her seat. She stole a glance over to the commonwealth's table. Knowlton's face was expressionless, but Moody stared at her with a look that would sour the sweetest confections.

The clerk spoke again. "Gentlemen of the jury, you, upon your oaths, do say that Lizzie Andrew Borden, the prisoner at the board, is not guilty?"

"We do."

"So say you, Mr. Foreman; so say all of you, gentlemen."

"We do."

Robinson ducked under the railing and threw an arm around Lizzie, pulling her close, resting her face on his cheek. Lizzie thought she could not feel a greater intensity of emotion, felt it surge again. She wiped away the tears that fell unbidden on her cheeks.

After thanking the jurors for their service, Judge Mason adjourned the court. Emma embraced her sister, whispering, "You're free, you're free" into her ear.

Mr. Holmes was the first to press Lizzie's hand. A weeping Reverend Mr. Buck stepped forward and held her hand tightly. Lizzie was too overcome to speak. She spotted Mr. Adams and reached out her hand to him. He grasped both sides and squeezed. Lizzie looked for Emma but when she saw her, the sisters were separated by a crowd too dense to navigate.

Lizzie looked up and saw the jurors gathered in a bunch at the bench. She nodded, and they marched single file to shake her hand. She smiled and thanked each one of them as she held their hands in hers.

Robinson put a hand around her shoulders and guided her past correspondents, telegraph operators, and typists, who gave her three lusty cheers. Lizzie still worried, still waited for someone to proclaim "Wait a minute, we made a mistake."

The governor led her to a nearby antechamber where they were joined by Mr. Adams. Mr. Jennings manned the door, allowing only close friends inside. Lizzie smiled when she saw *Herald* reporter Julius Ralph, who was always kind to her in everything he wrote. "How are you, Miss Lizzie?" he asked.

"Oh, I am so glad to see you again. I'm not very well, but I am the happiest girl in the whole world."

Lizzie could barely believe it. She did it. She convinced them all.

Chapter Forty-Three

Lizzie, Emma, John, Mr. and Mrs. Holmes, and Governor Robinson walked through the halls of the courthouse toward the rear entrance. A court official stopped them. "There is a boisterous crowd waiting for you just outside. Wait a moment until we can disperse them."

He sent two policemen outside who shouted at the gathered masses. "Miss Lizzie Borden is not here. She left the building through the front entrance."

Little Abram Lee, the colored man who drove Lizzie from the courthouse to jail every day, drove his wagon away from the front of the courthouse and down the street as if he were headed to the jail.

The combined tactics caused the crowd to disperse and Lizzie and her party to proceed to an awaiting barouche. John embraced both of his nieces and bid them farewell as they boarded the carriage. Before they could depart, hundreds of well-wishers engulfed their carriage, stretching their arms out to Lizzie's window. For ten full minutes, Lizzie reached out and shook hands with everyone who got close enough. As they pulled away, three cheers filled the air for Lizzie and another three for Governor Robinson. Lizzie waved her white handkerchief at the crowd until they were out of sight.

The driver, Deputy Kirby, stopped first at Ashe jail to retrieve Lizzie's belongings. Governor Robinson disembarked there to find transportation home. The other four passengers continued to Fall River.

The scenery from the barouche seemed much more intimate to Lizzie than her view from the train. Her new freedom imbued everything with more vibrancy and color. Soft, undulating hills stretched out as far as her eyes could see, filling her with a peace that had been elusive for so long. Even the jostling of the carriage crossing railroad tracks could not disrupt her pleasure. At the five-mile mark, when the last weather-beaten wooden house was behind them, the deputy pulled over to the side of the road and opened the carriage doors.

Lizzie stared in wonder at the glorious reddening of the western skyline and inhaled the aroma of the fresh greenery in the forest that swelled out to the road. While the horses grazed and the passengers took in the bucolic scene, Deputy Kirby entertained them. "Did you hear about Abe Duncan and the last snowstorm? He went out to his barn to feed his cattle, and when he came back outside, he ran into a black bear. Instead of backing right up into the barn, he made a run for his farmhouse. Of course, the chase was on, right up to the back door. Old Abe jerked it open, but before he could close it, the bear swatted it wide open.

"Abe ran through the kitchen, into the dining room, around to the living room and back to the kitchen and the open back door. He wiggled around it, hoping with the door in the way, the bear would waste enough time to let him get back to the barn. Instead, that bear reared up on his hind legs behind that door, and when his front paws hit it, the door slammed shut. The bear was caught inside the house, and old Abe was stuck outside.

"When he and his neighbors finally managed to get the bear back outside, Mrs. Duncan got her first look at what was left of her house. The bear tore that place apart looking for food and when he found it, he was quite a messy eater. I think, for a few days, poor old Abe was more scared of Mrs. Duncan than he'd ever been of the bear."

Lizzie understood the bear. She knew the destructive anger that tore through her and filled her with a desire to destroy everything in sight. She knew how the bear felt in his confinement and cheered him for getting his revenge.

Moving on to their destination, Lizzie felt giddy with her unfettered freedom to be outdoors. No bars on the windows, no hostile stares aimed her way, just a ride in the country with friends. It was such an ordinary thing, but now it felt extraordinary.

As they ascended the last hill of their journey, Lizzie saw Fall River stretched out at her feet. Plumes of smoke rose from chimneys as if welcoming her home. The sunset that evening was prolonged and glorious, as if it, too, were celebrating her release.

The carriage pulled up to the brightly lit Holmes house on Pine Street, where Lizzie and Emma planned on visiting with a few friends before heading home. The front door flew open before the horses came to a full stop. Their uniformed maid rushed out, her apron flapping. "Mr. Holmes, I've been told that there is a mob of people gathered at the Borden house on Second Street. So many of them that the police were called to keep the street clear."

"Oh dear," Emma sighed.

Annie Holmes patted the sisters' arms. "Don't worry. You two can stay with us tonight. You will be more than welcome. You know you won't get any rest with all that hubbub at your house."

"Thank you so much, Annie," Emma said, looking up and down the street. "Seems to be quite a few reporters gathered here as well. Lizzie, when you step out of the carriage, head straight for the front door. Do not wait for us. Just get inside and out of sight as quickly as you can."

Lizzie walked into a sea of happy faces inside—about twenty of them in all—the most jubilant group she had ever seen outside of a holiday celebration. Doctor and Mrs. Bowen rushed toward her, as did Mr. Reverend Jubb's daughters. Lizzie reached out both hands to her lawyer Mr. Jennings. It was difficult to tell whose smile was broader.

A bevy of reporters rushed to the front door, shouting Lizzie's name. Mr. Holmes. "Good evening, gentlemen. I understand your interest in Miss Borden, but she will not be available for an interview tonight."

"How is she doing?" a journalist shouted.

"Miss Borden is doing quite well. On the ride home, she was in high spirits.

"What did Miss Borden have to say about the trial?" another voice shouted.

"By common consent, we did not speak about it on the ride home Miss Borden's thoughts are looking to her future."

"What are her future plans?"

"I do not know, but I see no reason why she will not return to her home and live there in peace."

"What about you, Mr. Holmes? What do you think about the trial?"

"I am highly gratified with the results," Holmes said.

"Do you have any bitterness toward the police or the prosecutor?"

"Considering the outcome, I have no harsh words to say. They were simply doing their jobs to the best of their ability. Now, gentlemen, if you would please leave us in peace."

With a lot of grumbling, the reporters exited the entry of the house but after shutting the door, Holmes turned around and realized a United Press reporter was still lurking in a corner. "Excuse me, sir. Could I just ask Miss Borden one question?"

Holmes turned to Lizzie, who nodded in agreement.

The reporter asked, "How are you feeling tonight, Miss Borden?"

"I am the happiest person in the world," she said.

"Are you returning home tonight?"

Mr. Holmes stepped between Lizzie and the journalist. "Sir, you said one question, and that is asked."

"Well, can you answer it?"

"I invited Miss Borden and her sister to stay here for the night since the crowds around their home are bound to be annoying." Holmes reached over and opened the door. "If you please, sir."

The reporter looked over at Lizzie, hoping for a reprieve, but she turned her back on him. Lizzie sat a bit apart from all her friends, keeping still and soaking in their bonhomie. Some passed around clippings from newspapers about the trial, but everyone honored Lizzie's request to not ask her questions about it.

A rap on the door drove Mr. Holmes to his feet. "I hope it's not those reporters again." When he returned, he handed a telegram to Lizzie. "For you, from Mary Livermore."

Lizzie read out loud. "Thank God, Lizzie, that you were acquitted. Everybody is rejoicing, and the wires all over the country are freighted with the good news. I kiss you with all my heart." Lizzie pressed the message to her chest. *What a wonderful woman. I am certain, no matter what the future holds, she will remain by my side as I rebuild my life.*

Chapter Forty-Four

Lizzie and Emma slipped quietly toward home the next morning, apprehensive about what they would find there. They were prepared to turn around and go back to the Holmes residence if the clamor was still present. Their carriage passed many people walking on the sidewalk and travelling on the road, but no one stared or pointed. To their great relief, as they pulled up to the house not a single person idled there.

Minutes after entering the house, however, everything changed. "Emma, come look!" Lizzie cried.

Emma pulled back a curtain and gasped. "Did someone send out a town crier to announce our arrival?"

A crowd milled on the sidewalk and spilled into the street. The only saving grace was that no one was rude enough to come through the gate. For the rest of the day, Lizzie and Emma stayed upstairs or ventured into the kitchen or dining room, avoiding the front of the house. Neither one of them had any desire to speak about the tribulations of the past year. They just kept busy performing mundane household chores.

The sisters met up in the kitchen to fix a pot of tea. Emma said, "I was thinking of moving into Father's room, Lizzie."

"Really, I was hoping we would move to a house on the hill in the near future."

"Even if we do, it will take some time to find the right home, and for now, I do not want to spend much time, if any, out in public."

"That's probably wise," Lizzie agreed.

"Anyway, Lizzie, I've been thinking about changing rooms for months, but I wanted to get your blessing before I did so, and I certainly did not want to burden you with it before now."

"I see no problem, Emma. You clearly have the smallest and darkest bedroom. I think you deserve more space and windows. Do you want to start now? I'll be glad to help."

"We have to clear out Father's and the rest of Abby's belongings first."

"We can do it right now."

The sisters went up the back stairs and hauled an empty trunk down from the attic. They filled it with Abby's clothing and personal effects. "We can send it down to her sister's house when we get a chance," Emma said.

Lizzie readily agreed. She wanted nothing of her stepmother's anywhere in the house. "Do you know if there is anything else of hers in any other room?"

"I don't think so. I already sent one trunk down there, and since then, the housekeeper and I have placed any stray items we found back in this room."

The sisters spent much more time with their father's possessions. They each selected items they wanted to keep in remembrance of him and set aside items for his special friends like their Uncle John. After that, they sorted what remained into two piles—one of clothing to donate to the church for the poor and the other that was only fit for the rag pickers. As they worked, they exchanged sorrowful glances and numerous sighs, thinking about their memories of him.

When they retired for the night, mobs of people still circled in front of the house, but thankfully, they had all departed by the time the two women woke the next morning. They hoped their lives had finally returned to normal, but then, the postman arrived. Normally, the family had to retrieve their mail from the post office, but the volume of their correspondence was such that they needed to clear it out of the way to have enough work space to sort the rest of the mail.

A crateful of hundreds of letters was left in the front hall. Emma and Lizzie each took a side and carried it to the dining room table. Lizzie reached for a letter, but Emma stopped her hand. "Let me look at them first,

Lizzie. Please."

"Why?"

"In your absence, I received some very ugly letters. Let me sort through them and remove the objectionable ones. It is too soon after your ordeal to be exposed to that kind of thing."

Lizzie complied with Emma's request but still was quite curious. What could those letters possibly say that she hadn't heard before? "Emma, the courts have already reached a decision. Why would anyone want to write a scurrilous letter now?"

"You'd be surprised, sister, at how many people seem to have nothing better to do with their lives. Oh, read this one." Emma handed Lizzie a letter. "Oh, and this one. And—oh my—it seems that most of these are from members of the Christian Endeavor Society and the Women's Temperance Union from all over the country. Here's one from Maine and another from North Dakota. They are all praising God for your deliverance. Many want you to come speak to their groups."

"Oh, I couldn't do that. No. Absolutely not. I will not stand before strangers and live through this past year again and again."

"I don't blame you, sister. I would not welcome that kind of attention either. Still, it is wonderful that they are interested in you and support you. You must send them very kind letters turning down their offers."

* * *

For the second night in a row, Lizzie woke repeatedly in the night, startled by loud noises in the house. She lay awake for a long time, afraid to breathe, before realizing the sounds were the mere stuff of dreams. When she woke for the final time, she knew she must convince Emma that they needed to get out of that house as soon as possible.

Lizzie brought the subject up at breakfast and was delighted to discover that Emma was as eager to leave as she was. They cleaned the kitchen, dressed in their best afternoon frocks, and walked up the street to the office of their father's business manager, Charles Clark Cook. He was a natural choice since he had handled all real estate transactions for the family and managed the properties on the Borden block ever since the new A.J. Borden building opened downstreet.

The sisters were aware of the many stares that came their way and saw several people whispering to each other behind their hands as they approached. They felt as conspicuous as a mouse on the communion altar.

Mr. Cook greeted them with a warm smile beneath his fulsome mustache. The sisters thought the ends curled up with such extravagance that he looked a bit silly. He was a good and trusted friend of the family, though, and they did not hold his brushy splendor against him.

"We want to buy a house," Emma said.

"On the hill. In the area around French Street," Lizzie added.

"I have one that might be perfect for you ladies. Would you like to look at it now?"

Emma and Lizzie smiled at one another, then turned their smiles on Mr. Cook. "Yes, we would," they said in unison.

They all rode in Mr. Cook's carriage up the hill to High Street to the Butterworth Mansion. Lizzie looked at the two-and-a-half-story Queen Anne-style home. "I do admire the steep roof, larges gables, and expansive porch. But it doesn't have that adorable corner tower with its charming conical roof that I would expect to see in a Queen Anne."

"Come inside. I think you will see the interior rooms more than make up for that deficiency." He opened the door and ushered them inside. "I am quite fond of the main staircase—the intricate newel post, the turned spindles—it is quite a work of art."

"Emma, look at this fireplace. The wood carving is exquisite."

"And the wood is all walnut. The mantle itself is marbleized slate," Cook said.

"It is lovely," Emma said. "But is that the only source of heat?"

"Oh, no," Mr. Cook said, "there is a boiler in the cellar and an abundant bin for coal. I imagine you would not have to order more than once for the whole winter."

Lizzie found much to like in the Butterworth home, and in her eagerness to leave Second Street, she was ready to purchase even though it did not match her ideal. Emma, on the other hand, balked at the house's history. "Just last year, the same year Father died, Mr. Butterworth's body was found hanging in a tree in the nearby wood."

"But, Emma, you should not dismiss this home for superstitious fears. After all, it was suicide, not homicide."

"Still—" Emma said.

"He died away from the house, not inside it," Lizzie argued.

"Please do not insist on this residence. I know I would not feel a moment's peace in a home so shrouded with tragedy."

Lizzie sighed but conceded. "Thank you, Mr. Cook, for allowing us to see this house. But, frankly, its macabre history would surely engender more gossip about my sister and myself. We will have to keep looking."

* * *

Walking back home from Mr. Cook's office, Emma and Lizzie approached their home and saw a large number of people milling about the front of the house. They crossed the street and knocked on Dr. Bowen's door. Phoebe invited them in for tea, which they accepted with relief and gratitude.

As the doctor's wife poured steaming liquid into their cups, she said, "I truly thought the interest would die down in the aftermath of your acquittal, Lizzie. Have you two considered renting out your house and going away for a year or more? You could stay away until it suited you to return."

"Absolutely not, Phoebe," Lizzie snapped. "I will not have that riffraff drive me from my place of birth. I have been a citizen of Fall River all my life, and I have every right to be here."

"Of course you do, Lizzie. But at what cost to your peace of mind?"

"Phoebe," Emma interjected, "although we do not wish to leave our hometown, we do not want to live in that house where the ghastly crime took place. The cries of their souls still reverberate from the walls. We looked at another house just this afternoon."

"Thirteen-year-old Florence suggested, "Why don't you just tear that house down to the ground and be done with it."

Lizzie shuddered. "Father would roll over in his grave if we destroyed his real estate investment."

An hour after their arrival, Emma looked out the front window. "It appears as if no one is loitering in front of our house now. Perhaps it is a good time to go home. Thank you so much, Phoebe."

"You can take refuge in our home any time. If the doctor and I are not home, I will tell the housekeeper to let you come inside."

Over dinner that evening, Emma brought up the Butterworth mansion. "I've reconsidered, Lizzie. I think I have been short-sighted and foolish. Perhaps we should get Mr. Cook to make an offer on the house. With its dark history, we should be able to get a good price—one that would make Father proud."

"Are you sure, Emma?"

"Yes, but only if it is for far less than they are asking. The home is lovely, and we do need to leave this place. I believe I could come to terms with its past since, as you said, Mr. Butterworth's death did not occur within its walls."

"I'll go see Mr. Cook on Monday morning and get his help in deciding on an opening bid and defining our final offer amount."

"Thank you, Lizzie. I have been desperate to leave this dreadful house for so long."

Chapter Forty-Five

The owner of the Butterworth house and the Borden sisters exchanged offers and counter-offers, but the estate would not go as low as the Borden's upper limit. Mr. Cook vowed to find them another option before the summer's end.

A week after the viewing, Mr. Holmes and his daughter Annie called on the women late in the morning. Mr. Holmes looked apoplectic. "Miss Lizzie, Miss Emma, this is an outrage. There are strangers in your front yard and your back yard. They are walking around your barn and examining your fences. Have you sent for the police?"

"Oh, Mr. Holmes," Lizzie said, "the police run them off when they block the street, but they just return. Some say a good number of them lately are coming from Boston where the Christian Endeavor Society and the Knights Templar conventions are in session."

"Then you need to get away. This is not a fit way for two women to live."

"I will not run from my home and live in exile, Mr. Holmes."

"Of course not, Miss Lizzie, and you should not have to do so. I'm merely suggesting you take a break from this hubbub."

Annie smiled and interjected, "I've already written to my Uncle William in Newport. He has a lovely home and a massive library. He has horses stabled nearby as well. We could ride, read and relax to our hearts' content. I asked him for a week's stay for you, Emma and me. And he agreed. Please say you will come."

Lizzie turned to Emma, who said, "It would be nice to have a peaceful spell out in the country."

"You're right," Lizzie agreed. We cannot allow those people to prevent us from getting some enjoyment out of life, can we? Annie, when do we depart?"

"I was thinking next Friday morning would be ideal. We could catch the morning train, and Uncle could send someone to meet us at the station."

Another delightful visitor arrived that afternoon, Mary Livermore. Lizzie often wondered if the woman's suffragist sensibilities made her likely to understand the reasons if she told her the whole truth. She decided it was too much of a gamble. Mary viewed her incarceration and trial as another act of the tyranny of men. The small risk of alienating her was far too great to take.

"Have you been as overrun with letters as I have?" Mrs. Livermore asked.

"We've been getting as many as two hundred a day," Lizzie said.

"We've even gotten letters suggesting Lizzie go on stage or take to the lecture platform," Emma added.

"Worst of all," Lizzie said, "are the multiple offers of marriage coming in the post. Do they stop for one moment to think that perhaps I am not married by choice?"

"Nearly everyone thinks marriage is the dream of every woman, but I have seen enough abusive homes to know the dream can turn into a nightmare. Have you ever thought of getting married, Lizzie?"

"When I was a child…but then I learned the reality of life for women. I've spent years being controlled by Father. Why would I want to choose another man to have dominion over me?"

Emma smiled. "Of course, you wouldn't. But I used to think a few years ago, when you immersed yourself in church and charitable work, that you might be grooming yourself to be a missionary's wife."

Lizzie was taken aback. It alarmed her that Emma realized that her Christian acts were a ruse—because they were, although her sister got the reason completely wrong. "I suppose it would make some sense that you would think that. A missionary wife's life is far more adventurous, fulfilling, and challenging. It would expand my horizons, though when you get down to the bottom of it, a missionary wife is still subservient to her husband."

"Very true," Mrs. Livermore said. "I have been very lucky in matrimony. Most men have little respect for a woman's intellect—but mine does and often defers to me. Also, he has erected no obstacles to keep me in my place, as many men do. Getting married is a big gamble—some men act as if they believe in equality while they are courting but turn into tyrants after the ceremony is done."

"You said that you've been receiving letters, too, Mrs. Livermore? Lizzie asked.

"Oh yes. Many, many letters. During your trial, most of them were regarding my support of your cause—mostly notes of encouragement, although some were quite ugly missives. Now that you are free, most of my mail is coming from men in Charlestown and Concord prisons, proclaiming their innocence and begging for my help. I suppose they think if I was inclined to believe in one person's blamelessness, I'd be more than likely to embrace their claims. I am sure that will all fade away soon. Do you girls have any plans in the near future?"

"Oh yes." A smile brightened Emma's face. "We are going to spend a week in Newport at the Covell's home, riding horses, relaxing, and forgetting about the rest of the world."

"I will do my best to keep my spirits in tune with my sister, but I do not believe I can ever be light-hearted again." Mrs. Livermore and Emma became a verbal tag team, each alternating encouragement comments and hope for the future. When Lizzie tired of it, she changed the subject. "There is one thing I'm excited about—our search for a home on the hill. Our offer on the first house we found was not successful, but we will keep looking until we find the right one at the right price."

"Honestly, I can't imagine how horrid it must be to live in this house—particularly for you, Emma. You've been under this sorrowful roof for more than a year. I think you both will be more cheerful in another home. Oh, and one piece of advice, Lizzie, before you leave for Newport, I think you should talk to that newspaper reporter you like and set the record straight about your plans. Rumors are flying everywhere—about Europe, Bridget Sullivan, and the future of this house. A definitive statement from you would squash some of the speculation."

"With all due respect, Mrs. Livermore, I am not certain anything I could say would stop the rumor mills and the gossipmongers. I will, however, take your advice and hope that at least some people will heed my statements."

The next morning, the sisters relaxed, reading and chatting for hours, and did not change into their wrappers until lunchtime. It would be a little late that day because they were waiting on the arrival of the train from Taunton carrying a special visitor. Mary Wright, the kindest jail matron Lizzie had known.

She was grinning from ear to ear as she pecked the cheeks of the two sisters before she was through the door. "Oh, Miss Lizzie, it is such a pleasure to see you in your own home instead of that miserable cell."

"Mrs. Wright, you made that cell more comfortable than I could have expected. And you were so kind. I did not appreciate you fully until I spent time in another jail. You are an angel of mercy in comparison to the others."

"Your incarceration was uncalled for, Miss Lizzie. It was the least I could do."

"You are modest, too, Mrs. Wright," Emma said. "Come lunch is ready, let us retire to the dining room."

When it was time to catch her train back home, Lizzie grasped both of the matron's hands. "I shall never forget you or your care for me as long as I live."

"Nor shall I, you. You were a godsend when I was ill. Please come and visit any time you wish."

* * *

At Lizzie's request, reporter Julius Ralph of the *Boston Herald* came to Fall River on the afternoon train. Emma ushered him into the parlor, and Lizzie thanked him again for his unbiased coverage of her trial. "Mr. Ralph," she added, I thought you might be amenable to my limitation of topic since you have been so fair-handed in the past."

"And what is that, Miss Borden?"

"I really do not want to rehash the trial or anything in the past. I would like you to ask about my future plans so that, with your help, we can put some of the wild rumors to rest."

"You want me to question you about the gossip being spread?"

"Yes, please."

"Okay," he said, pulling out his notebook. "When are you leaving for Europe, and is your sister going with you?"

"Emma and I have no plans to go to Europe. We do intend to take a few short excursions to visit friends and relax away from the hubbub of Fall River. But Europe is not a consideration at all at this time."

"There are those who say you plan on rehiring Bridget Sullivan to repay her for the role she played in your acquittal. Is that true?"

"Heavens, no. Bridget has her own life to do with as she pleases. She was a lovely servant while she worked here. On the witness stand, she merely spoke the truth and did not let Mr. Knowlton cow her into telling a lie."

"Some have said you plan to tear this home down—or even to burn it to the ground. Any truth in this story?"

"Goodness, gracious, no. You saw how close the neighbors are on this street. Can you imagine the conflagration that might ensue should I set this house ablaze? And I am far too rational to tear down a valuable real estate asset."

"It must be difficult, though, to remain in this house," Julius said.

"Yes, for both of us. Some of the blood stains will not wash away. But for now, Emma and I have no definite plans for the house and would very much appreciate a brief period of rest, which my health demands, and freedom from senseless and unfounded rumors."

"As you well deserve, Miss Borden. I hope my story in the paper will give you some comfort and respite from gossip."

Chapter Forty-Six

Emma and Lizzie were upstairs packing for their trip to Newport when the doorbell rang. "I'll get it," Emma said.

"Whoever it is, Emma, I am not at home." Lizzie hoped whoever it was, they did not linger long.

Less than half an hour later, Emma walked up to Lizzie's room carrying a framed photograph. "Our visitors were Augustus Smith, the foreman of your jury, and another member of the panel, Captain William Lewis."

Lizzie looked at the familiar faces of the men who acquitted her—six men standing and six sitting in front of them. "When did they have this done?"

"The same day as the trial. They went to a photographer and then had it framed. They were quite proud of it and honored to play a role in setting you free."

"How nice. Should we hang it?"

"Why not," Emma said, "but where?"

"Replace that photo of Abby hanging in the parlor with this one."

"Lizzie..." Emma said, shaking her head.

"Oh, come now, Emma. Don't tell me you want to be reminded of that mean old thing every time you step into that room."

Emma sighed. "I cannot say that I do, but it's so disrespectful to the dead."

"Give it to Abby's half-sisters. Tell them we thought they might cherish it."

"That should make it acceptable. I'll put it in the trunks of personal property that we will deliver on our return from our trip."

***

The moment the sisters and Annie crossed the water and landed on Newport Island, Lizzie felt untethered and unfettered, as if relaxation were a way of life. She felt cut off from the real world and its troubles, free to forget the past even existed. She did not understand why the impact felt as intense as it did since the Island was easy to reach, but her spirits lifted the moment she left the mainland.

The Covell's large home on Farewell Street had an elegant mansard roof adorned with lovely corbels, multiple dormers, and two broad chimneys. Emma, Annie, and Lizzie stepped into a welcoming foyer. They presented Mrs. Covell with a set of six pie forks as a bread-and-butter gift.

"Oh, you shouldn't have," their hostess said, but the sparkle in her eyes and the smile on her face reflected her delight.

"Auntie, we are all tired from travelling and would like to rest and freshen up before the evening meal," Annie said.

"Of course. Hiram will carry your luggage upstairs."

The three women followed him and were led to their respective rooms. As soon as Lizzie was left alone, she raised the window in her room to smell the fresh salt air—the water only blocks away from the house. Through the trees, she thought she got a small glimpse of the bay but was not sure if she really saw it or just imagined it. Either way, she enjoyed the idea of knowing it was nearby.

The first morning, Lizzie went downstairs for breakfast. Annie and Emma were already seated at the table, and Mr. and Mrs. Covell had gone for the morning. Annie leaned back in her chair, reading the newspaper. Suddenly, she bolted upright, her mouth agape.

"What is it, Annie?" Emma asked.

"I believe the *Newport Mercury* just welcomed you two to town."

"Whatever do you mean?" Lizzie asked.

"Have you heard of Lucy Stone?"

"Abolitionist, suffragist, and this first woman to earn a college degree in this country?" Emma responded.

"Exactly," Annie said. "She is quoted in the newspaper this morning. Listen to what she wrote:

The centuries-old assumption that is quietly made at New Bedford is, of course, that a jury of men is not only a jury of peers and equals but of superiors of any woman who may be arraigned for trial. But the nineteenth century would seem to be old enough now to concede that a woman on trial for her life or liberty has the right to have equal sex representation on the jury that is to pass judgment on her guilt or innocence.

Slowly, perhaps, but surely, the idea is growing that a jury ought to be composed of men and women and that a woman should have a jury of her peers, not her sovereigns, as in the case of Lizzie Borden.

"Is that wonderful?"

Lizzie laughed. "It is right, but I certainly would not want to go through that experience again, even for the cause of equality. And really, Annie, do you think that men would ever agree to cede some of their power over us?"

"But they must," Annie said.

"It truly is a matter of time," Emma added.

"I will not squash your hopes and dreams, but do not expect me to pin my view of the future on that possibility, for I do not believe it will ever come nigh."

Emma, Annie, and Lizzie went to the stables and rode out on the Covell horses. Another day, a friend of the family took them boating on the bay. They swarmed to shops, perusing the ware. Everywhere Lizzie went, she paused to breathe in the fresh sea air, finding it revitalizing and healing—an aid to softening the harsh memories of her confinement.

The interlude felt far too short and the Borden sisters' thoughts filled with excitement and dread at the thought of their return to their hometown. They both anticipated the delight of shopping for a new house but feared the reaction of one-time friends and neighbors. They hoped a new home would do a lot to quiet the noise and ghoulish interest in them.

On their return to Second Street, they were delighted to see the ruckus had died down somewhat. People still stopped in front of their home and stared. Occasional odd individuals walked into the yard and rang the doorbell. And some still wandered through the backyard like amateur detectives. At times, they still felt like circus animals on display, but the intensity had lessened—no more than a handful of people at any given time but no more noisy crowds intruding in their lives.

The morning after their return, Mr. Cook called on them. "I have good news and bad news, Misses Borden. The building you own at 100 South Main Street caught on fire. The principal damage was caused by water—an estimate of $500 in losses to the two of you, but your insurance will cover that."

"What about the businesses using the space?" Emma asked.

"Both of them had insurance on their stock so they will be okay, too. I've already started repairs on the building. The sooner we get them done, the quicker the businessmen can get back to earning their living."

"You said you had good news, too, Mr. Cook?" Lizzie asked.

"Ah, yes. I found a house that I think will be perfect for you. Again, just as I do for your business investments, I will make the purchase in my name and then transfer the property to the two of you soon after to keep the sale out of the public eye."

"Excellent," Lizzie said. "Where is it?"

"On French Street on the Hill."

"When can we see it?" Emma asked.

"We could go there this afternoon if you like. It is the Charles Marion Allan house—he's a distant cousin of your father."

Lizzie looked at Emma, who nodded. "Yes, we would like to do that. About three o'clock?"

"I'll bring my carriage around then. Is there anything else you ladies need today?"

"I believe we need to post our reward announcement in the newspaper for information securing the arrest and conviction of whoever murdered our father and his wife," Emma said.

CHAPTER FORTY-SIX

"Do you need any change in the wording from the previous postings?"

Emma raised one eyebrow as she looked at Lizzie. Lizzie nodded. "No, Mr. Cook. Please place an order for multiple runs over the next three or four months."

"Very well. Anything else?"

"It would be nice to have a non-trespassing sign on our property here," Lizzie said.

"It seems things have quieted down considerably from last month. A sign might just draw extra attention," Cook said.

"Look at the window across from me, sir," Lizzie replied.

Cook turned his head toward the glass, his jaw dropped, and his eyes bulged. He jumped from his seat and shook his fist at the man peeping in the window. The intruder ran off. "That is outrageous, Miss Lizzie. I will have a sign prepared that reads: 'Trespassing on these premises is strictly forbidden by the owners.' Or perhaps two signs—one for the door and one on the gate. What is wrong with these people? Have they no decency?"

"Most men do not, sir," Lizzie said.

Cook tucked his chin back to his throat and stepped backward. Emma glared at Lizzie and interjected, "Gentlemen like you excepted, of course."

When Cook had left the house, Emma turned on Lizzie. "I do not know what possesses you sometimes, Lizzie. Mr. Cook is helping us. Why would you insult him like that?"

"It was not an insult, Emma. It was an observation of what women must contend with every day of their lives. And you know it."

Chapter Forty-Seven

The excitement of going to see a new house had Emma and Lizzie bouncing on their toes like young girls as they peered out their window looking for Mr. Cook's carriage. When he pulled up, they shouted goodbye to the housekeeper and hurried down to the curb.

The carriage took them to the upper end of French Street, a lovely thoroughfare lined with pretty homes, neat lawns, vases of flowers, and plenty of shade trees. The house itself was on the summit of one of the loftiest hills and appeared to Lizzie as if it had escaped from her dream—Queen Anne style with a four-sided pyramidal turret and a gable with windows. The porch covering extended upward and finished in a little peak higher than the roof, with an ornamental weathervane perched on top. Clapboard and shingles clad the exterior, with the lower story painted a dull bronze green and the upper in a buff color—all set on a stone foundation. The surrounding grounds were well-tended and dotted with flowering shrubs.

"The house was built only a few years ago," Cook said. "It has spectacular views of the Taunton River and the green fields of Somerset."

When they stepped inside, Lizzie's heart quaked. She imagined living there with the first footstep. She grabbed Emma's arm and pulled her close. "In this house, we will assume our rightful place in the upper echelons of Fall River Society. Invitations to dances, parties, and dinners from the very best people. Imagine it, Emma."

Emma patted her sister's hand. "I hope all your dreams come true."

"Oh, Emma, look!" Lizzie hurried across the room to a magnificent, elaborately carved, richly grained oak mantle. She rubbed her fingers across the floral and curvilinear surface. "This is lovely. Read the inscription, Emma."

And Old-Time Friends, And Twilight Plays
And Starry Nights, And Sunny Days
Come Trooping Up The Misty Ways
When My Fire Burns Low."

"Quite lovely, Lizzie."

"Can you see yourself living here, Emma?"

"I believe I can. It is a comfortable place with elegant touches but without pretentiousness. I believe I'd like living here very much."

"Shall we go upstairs and see the bedrooms?"

"Of course," Emma replied. In one room, Emma gasped. "Look, look, it is as if the home was built for us. An inscription on another mantlepiece read:

AT-HAME

IN-MY-AIN

COUNTRIE

"And there are Scottish Thistle carved all around. With our Scottish heritage, this house is perfect for us," Lizzie said.

Back in the carriage, the sisters discussed their offer with Cook. "Please, Mr. Cook, go straight to your office to prepare the paperwork," Lizzie said.

"We will walk home from there," Emma added.

As the two women walked down South Main Street, Lizzie asked, "What shall we name our new home?"

"How about 'Refuge' or 'Soul's Rest'? Emma suggested.

"Oh no, those words sound like we are hiding from the world. I want to give it a dignified name that speaks of its surroundings."

"Green Hills?"

"Not bad, Emma. Not bad at all. But what about all the maple trees in the yard?"

"Perhaps Maple Hill would work."

"That's nice. But, oh, oh, I have it—a bow to our Scottish ancestors. We will call it Maplecroft."

Perfect," Emma said. "Maplecroft—our new home."

"Hopefully, Mr. Cook can finalize the sale quickly. It's like waiting for Christmas when I was small."

"I know, Lizzie. I cannot wait to see the last of our old house."

Two days later, on September 11, Cook called on the sisters. "The home on French Street is yours, ladies. There is, however, one condition. You will not be able to move in immediately. The Allens will need about three weeks to move out of the house and into their new home."

"Although I hate the wait," Emma said, it will give us time to organize our belongings and get prepared for the move."

"Oh, Emma, what a happy day! We will finally live where we belong."

"One more thing, ladies. Have you given any more thought to the disbursement of your father's estate?"

"Oh, let Abby's sisters take us to court. They have no right to any of the property," Lizzie said.

"Now, Miss Lizzie, you are right, but set your emotions aside," Cook said. "We need to talk about the situation rationally and practically. If we could get them to agree to settle with the portion of the estate that belonged to Mrs. Borden before her death, it would save you a lot of trouble and evaporate much ill will that challenging the women would generate in the community."

"What do I care?" Lizzie said.

Emma placed a hand on Lizzie's arm. "Sister, dear, why bring any aggravation upon yourself? Let's put it all to rest and not allow principle to stand in the way of our future peace."

"I don't know if that is a good bargain at all."

"But, Lizzie, it is a pittance compared to the rest of the estate."

"Still, it rightfully belongs to Father and, as a result, to the two of us. Not to Abby's sister and half-sister. What are they to us?"

"Miss Lizzie, Miss Emma, I will leave this to you to decide. Let me know what you want to do. The sooner, the better. I do want to forestall any legal action if I can."

Lizzie wanted to just forget about it and hope it would go away, but Emma pressed the issue day after day. "Why do you want to keep a share of the house that caused so much friction five years ago?"

"Because it belongs to me."

"Don't be foolish, Lizzie. It will just bring more conflict into our lives. It will just keep the memory of our father's death alive. You won't miss the money or property once it is gone. It is nothing compared to all else we have."

In the end, Lizzie succumbed to the pressure. She agreed to give the half-ownership of 45 Fourth Street, Abby's personal belongings, and a small nest egg to Sara Whitehead of Fall River and Priscilla Fish of Hartford, Connecticut. "It still galls me to be so generous to two undeserving women."

The next day, the sisters went room to room through the house, gathering up the smallest bit of Abby's belongings. "I think we've got it all, Lizzie," Emma said.

"If we missed anything, I'm sure those two vultures will blow it all out of proportion," Lizzie said.

"Please, dear sister, you must temper your bitterness over insignificant matters."

"After what I have been through, I have a right to be bitter for the rest of my days."

Late that morning, a messenger arrived from Mr. Cook, bringing the news that the real estate documents were delivered. After lunch, Lizzie and Emma sent the two trunks down the street to Mrs. Whitehead's home. Lizzie brushed her hands together. "Good riddance."

* * *

The Borden sisters visited their Uncle John at Bristol Neck on July 19th. After warm greetings, they settle down in the parlor with a pot of tea. Emma explained the settlement of the estate question with Abby's family.

"You are well rid of that potential source of antagonism, and you got peace of mind at a very low price. I am certain your father would approve," John said.

"That's not all we've accomplished this month. We also bought a new house."

"Is it in Fall River?"

"Of course," Lizzie said. "It is on the hill on the upper end of French Street. It is so delightful. You must see it. We will move in early September."

"What will you do with the Second Street home?"

"We have been talking that over with Mr. Cook. Lizzie and I thought it might be difficult to sell the house because of its history. What we will probably do is turn it into an income-producing property. Mr. Cook is getting the estimates together to see if it is worthwhile to return it to two apartments as it was when Father bought it."

"After making a major change like that, you should be able to find tenants with ease."

"You know what day it is, don't you, Uncle John?" Emma asked.

"I do indeed. It is Lizzie's birthday. My housekeeper has prepared a special dinner for us to celebrate. She is from Germany and told me about a birthday tradition over there. For dessert, Lizzie, she has prepared it as a surprise for you."

Lizzie blushed as she smiled. "Thank you, Uncle John. I'll be sure to express my appreciation to your servant as well. This birthday is so different from my last. Confined in that cell, there was really nothing to celebrate."

"That is all behind you now. You are thirty-three years old, and you can take pride in gaining your freedom."

"It is a lofty attainment, is it not? Emma and I are both free with financial independence. No man rules over us—that is a freedom that most women never achieve until they die."

Uncle John cast his eyes around the room—on the ceiling, on the floor, anywhere but into Lizzie's gaze.

"Don't be morbid, Lizzie. It's your birthday. You need to think only of good things," Emma said.

"Freedom is a good thing, Emma. The cost of obtaining it is never too high."

The tension in the room was palpable, rising like a miasma from the swamp. Fortunately, housekeeper Greta chose that moment to enter the room. "Dinner is served."

During the meal, the three diners spoke only of trivial things, Emma steering Lizzie away from anything that could raise a conflict. After clearing the table, Greta said, "Mr. John, It will only take me two minutes to get the surprise ready. Should I do it right now?"

"Yes, Greta, please."

"What is it, Uncle John?" Lizzie asked.

"You will see." John rose and flipped off the lights in the room.

"How will we see the surprise with the lights off, Uncle John?" Emma asked.

John chuckled. "You will definitely see it, Emma."

The kitchen door pushed open, and Greta entered, bearing a cake sparkling with lit candles. Lizzie and Emma gasped at the sight and said, "Oh, Uncle John," in unison.

"Set it down in front of Lizzie, Greta. And thank you."

Greta placed the platter and backed up a few steps with a big smile on her face. "Now, Miss Lizzie, what you must do is close your eyes and make a wish, then try to blow out all the candles."

"There are so many!" Lizzie exclaimed.

"Thirty-three, Lizzie," Uncle John said. "One for each year of your life."

Lizzie squeezed her eyes tight shut. *I wish, I wish, I wish that all my dreams will come true in my new home and that all my friends will return to me.* She inhaled deeply and exhaled in a rush, giving a last push of her breath to extinguish the one contrary candle.

John, Emma, and Greta applauded and shouted, "Happy Birthday, Lizzie!"

Greta sliced the cake and served it to the three at the table. As she turned to return to the kitchen, Lizzie said, "Greta, please, have a seat. You are part of my celebration, too. You made it happen. Have a piece of cake with us."

Greta looked at John, who nodded his approval.

Chapter Forty-Eight

Emma and Mrs. Bingham urged Lizzie to attend the evening service at the Central Congregational Church. Lizzie agreed, knowing that most of the attendees were supportive when she was arrested, some even visited her in jail.

The warm welcome Lizzie had hoped for did not materialize. She felt the chill in the air the moment she walked through the doors. People chatting in the narthex stopped talking and hurried to the sanctuary. She turned to her sister to see if she noticed what had happened. Emma, her eyes wide with surprise, nodded.

When they walked up the aisle, all those looking toward the back of the church jerked their heads around to face the front with reddened cheeks. Emma was shaking by the time they took their seats.

The minister began the sermon by reading a passage from Exodus. "He that smiteth a man so that he should die shall surely be put to death." A hymnal hit the floor with a shuddering thud. A few heads swiveled in Lizzie's direction, but when she returned their stares, they quickly faced front again.

The pastor continued through the next two verses without stirring the congregation but then continued to the next. "And he that smite his father or his mother shall surely be put to death."

Nearly every head in the sanctuary turned to Lizzie. A sound like the buzz of agitated insects ran through the pews and down the aisles. Lizzie started to rise, but Emma pressed her down into her seat, squeezing her hand and pleading with her eyes. Lizzie followed her sister's lead, but she seethed inside long after the commotion ended. Thoughts of revenge darted through her mind as she said silent prayers for God's wrath to fall on all their heads—for a bolt of lightning to strike the hypocritical preacher where he stood.

As everyone rose to leave at the end of the service, Lizzie hissed,Where is Jesus with his whip to run all these scoundrels and Pharisees out of the church?"

Emma grasped her hand and whispered in her ear. "Hush, Lizzie. Wait until we get home."

As they left, the minister reached out a hand to Lizzie. She looked at him as if he were handing her a poison serpent. All three women turned away and left him with an empty palm.

The carriage delivered the Borden Sisters to their home—but none of them, not even Mrs. Brigham, said a word. As they disembarked, Mrs. Brigham said, "I am so sorry. I expected expressions of Christian charity, but all I saw was hostility. I am ashamed of the pastor for choosing that passage and of the congregation for responding in such an unchristian manner."

"Do you think he chose that scripture intentionally?" Emma asked.

Mrs. Bingham sighed. "It is not possible that it was an accidental coincidence."

The sisters nodded and went into the house. Emma collapsed on the settee. "Please forgive me, Lizzie. I do not know how I could have been so blind. If there is any place on this earth that we should be welcomed, it should be our church. I was wrong. I'll never ask you to attend again."

"No need for an apology, Emma. I know that you do not look for snubs or ugly behavior unless you expect to find it. Somehow, you seem to stay above it all, and I can't judge you for that. I'm glad you realized that it was not my imagination twisting in my mind, but recognized their reactions for the spiteful acts they were. I may have been deemed not guilty in the courtroom, but out here in my community, I have not really been cleared of murder."

* * *

Later that week, Emma and Lizzie paid a visit to Jennings' office. Emma said, "We bought a new house at 7 French Street."

"Delightful," Jennings said. "That is near my home at French and June Streets. We shall be neighbors."

"We are glad of that, too, Mr. Jennings," Lizzie said. "We came to see you today about our desire to erect a proper monument for the graves of our father and his wife. However, one thing stands in our way, and we hope that you can help us with it. Our father's body is missing his head."

"Our stepmother, too," Emma added.

Lizzie opened her mouth to say we only cared about Father's skull, but Emma glared at her and briskly shook her head.

Repulsion and horror battled for control of Mr. Jennings' face. "They have not been returned to their graves yet?"

"No, sir," the sisters said in unison.

"That is an outrage. I will write a letter this very minute. You can read it when I finish. I'll get my secretary to bring you some tea while you wait."

Emma and Lizzie sipped as Jennings hunched over his desk before turning to face them. Miss Lizzie, Miss Emma, I think this is sufficiently strong to resolve the problem. Although I do think it is highly inappropriate of the authorities not to do so without being asked. If you approve, I will have it typewritten and sent to Dr. Dolan." Jennings cleared his throat.

Dear Sirs:

Mr. Jennings insists that the skulls of Andrew and Abby Borden be returned to his clients. As there is no pending case, and they were held for evidence only, I see no reason why they should not be returned.

"Are you comfortable with my wording?"

Again, they responded in unison: "Yes, sir. Thank you."

Knowlton agreed to the return but urged that the Borden sisters not view them. They were no longer recognizable because Dr. Dolan had removed all the flesh by boiling the heads in a pot of water in his kitchen.

The two denuded skulls were placed in separate boxes and buried two to three feet deep above their respective coffins. Mr. Jennings accompanied the women to the brief private ceremony at the graveside.

* * *

In early August, Lizzie received word that she had won second place in a contest she entered while still in jail. That sent her back to Mr. Jennings' office. "I have been awarded a trip to the World's Fair in Chicago from the *Boston Journal,* and I am not certain what I should do."

"Do you fear it may be too soon for you to travel there?"

"I don't want to be stared at like another exhibit and I would think that I need to get organized for our move and settle in our new home before I take a long trip."

"That is quite understandable, Miss Lizzie. I will write a letter to the newspaper asking them to give the prize to the next person on the list."

"They can do that?"

"Certainly. I will get it in the post by tomorrow at the latest."

"Thank you. That takes a worry off my mind. I can never repay you for all your kindness, Mr. Jennings."

* * *

By the end of that first week of the month, Lizzie had written a letter to each juror thanking them for the photograph and acknowledging her appreciation for the work they did on the New Bedford trial. She mailed all of them out on the same day.

The rest of August was a whirlwind behind the closed doors on Second Street. Lizzie and Emma decided which furniture pieces they wanted to take to their new home; sorted through their clothing, discarding what was worn or no longer wanted; disposing of worn-out kitchen utensils; and, most boring of all, separating the papers in Father's desk at home and the one at his office into three piles—one to discard, another to take to French Street and the third to go to Mr. Cook.

On September 6, the moving vans arrived. The first load included all they would need to spend the night at Maplecroft. The final load would arrive the next morning. As soon as the last item was removed from the Second Street house, Mr. Cook had a man remove the "Andrew J. Borden" nameplate from the front door and hired a crew to start the renovations, returning the house to its origin as a two-tenement dwelling once again. Lizzie hoped these changes would bring much-needed quiet to the old street since out-of-town gawkers could no longer easily identify the former Borden residence.

Emma and Lizzie experienced another intense week of activity, unpacking the boxes, arranging furniture, and putting everything in place. Nearly every room had a large patterned floral rug with wallpaper in a contrasting pattern that reflected the height of Victorian taste. There was an urgency to the work because they were committed to travel to Rockport, Maine, to be the guests of James and Emma Wight. They looked forward to evenings of musical entertainment since James had served as a musician in the Union Army during the Civil War.

Lizzie found the train trip very exciting, traveling from Massachusetts through New Hampshire and up past Portland, Maine. The big thrill awaited them at the Kennebec River. To cross the river, the train boarded a special steam ferry built with tracks to facilitate their transport across water.

Emma and Lizzie both put their hands over their ears as the sound of the locomotive moving into the tunnel on the ship echoed and reverberated, making an incredible, intense noise. Smoke filled the covered area, seeping through the passenger car windows and making both sisters cough. Just as they thought that part of the journey would never end, they reached the far bank of the river, and the train moved onto the tracks that would take them to Rockland. Emma and Lizzie looked at each other with wide eyes—it was uncomfortable and a bit frightening, but it was an experience of a lifetime.

The first thing they noticed as they approached Rockland were monuments to the city's prosperity—the tall smokestacks of the lime kilns, belching smoke that hung like a canopy over the city. Later that night, they would see the fires in those kilns brightening the night sky. In the harbor at Penobscot Bay, ships of all sizes and types lined the docks—sailboats, fishing boats, lobster boats, barges, and ferries. The abundance of granite mined in the area gave birth to great stone cathedrals, courthouses and federal buildings.

At the Wight home, Lizzie waxed eloquent about the cool air and the breeze from the bay. She was overwhelmed by the view of the coastline from her bedroom window. She saw a wildness out there that made her feel unfettered and free.

The main course for dinner the first night was a cheesy lobster dish. The sisters had never tasted the crustacean and embraced the new experience. Lizzie, in particular, was enamored with the sweet, succulent meat. Emma was more hesitant. "I will try it again, Lizzie, but I'm not quite sure about it."

"Just close your eyes when you take a bite. The flavor and the texture are unlike anything I've ever eaten. I can't wait to taste it again. We must return to Maine every year."

Emma Wight chuckled. "It is always a pleasure to introduce visitors to our state's lobster. We have never known what reaction to expect from them, but we have never had a guest who regretted the experience."

"Napoleon Bonaparte loved lobster," James added.

"Not surprised you know that since you are a veteran of war, Mr. Wight," Lizzie said.

"Well, my dear, no one has ever fought a war over lobster. Let's not start one over the dinner table."

"Seriously, sir, why do men have such a love of war?"

"I beg your pardon." James sat back in his chair and patted his mouth with a napkin.

"Men are always starting wars, so they must like it. We had our Civil War, and there are wars and rumors of wars all over the world. The Chinese and the Japanese are fighting each other right now. All these wars are started by men."

"Wars are often a matter of principles and honor. I know it is difficult for a woman to understand, but they are often necessary. Men, women, and children were held in bondage for nothing more than the color of their skin. That's why we fought the Civil War and it was a conflict worth wagering. At least now we can rest easy, President Grover Cleveland and most Republicans are not the type to start a war with anyone."

"I daresay he would like to start a war with women. He is ending the voting rights legislation, and if he would do that, he would never allow women to vote unless we could defeat him in a war."

Emma's scarlet face pushed toward Lizzie. "Sister, have you forgotten yourself?"

"Well, it won't happen. Women cannot defeat men on the battlefield, and they will never allow us to vote otherwise."

"Lizzie, please," Emma begged.

Emma Wight rose from her seat. "I think it is time for dessert. I'll go help cook."

* * *

After retiring, Emma went into Lizzie's bedroom. "What has come over you?"

"What do you mean?"

"That war and men nonsense. Were you trying to provoke our host?"

"While I was locked up, Emma, I had a lot of time to think. I thought about how Father, legally and with society's blessing, ruled over us and controlled our finances. I thought about most of the women I knew and how they were constrained and trapped by fathers and husbands and sometimes even younger brothers. I realized that the problem with this world is that men are in charge. They have forced us into subservience because of their violent and power-hungry natures."

Emma shook her head. "Lizzie, you need to accept the world you inherited. It does no good to tilt at windmills."

"Now, you are quoting Cervantes? Please! We did not inherit our world—men do that. What we gain is what we take from them."

"I am hoping you will learn again how to be accommodating. I pray your current attitude is merely a symptom of the harm done to you by imprisonment, and you will pass through this stage and return to who you were beforehand."

"Do not count on that, sister. My eyes have been opened, and now I see."

Emma sighed and left the room feeling defeated.

Chapter Forty-Nine

In their new property on the hill, the sisters relished the excitement of making it their own. They hung birdhouses and feeders in the trees. Lizzie kept them full of seeds and crumbs. She discovered with patience that she could coax the squirrels into feeding from her hand.

They both wanted to get around town and the surrounding area without having to hire a driver whenever they went anywhere, making their own horse and carriage a must. First, they needed to find a coachman to see to the upkeep. They travelled out to Swansea to find Alfred John, who their father employed at the farm.

He enjoyed the idea of being back in town and accepted the position with a smile on his face. In addition to driving the new carriage and caring for the horse, Mr. John kept the riding equipment washed, watered plants, mowed the lawn, brought in coal and wood for the kitchen range as well as the furnace, and shoveled paths through the snow in the winter.

Once the sisters were settled, their peace was disrupted by schoolchildren. They stopped on the way home from school to lob eggs, gravel, and other objects at the house. If Lizzie were outside when they arrived, they would taunt her and call her a murderer. Before long, an unknown person or persons disturbed Lizzie's and Emma's sleep by ringing their doorbell in the middle of the night. They called for police intervention. Assistant Marshall Fleet responded. "These disruptions are merely school children playing pranks. You do not need to fear for your safety."

"What kind of parents allow their children to roam the streets at night when all good people are asleep?" Lizzie asked.

Fleet shrugged. "I see stranger things every day, Miss Borden."

Lizzie was outraged at his cavalier attitude. Emma attempted to soothe her. "Lizzie, time will solve this problem. They will grow weary of provoking you and shift to a new object of interest."

"I suspect there are some who will hound me to the end of my life. Even if they think I am guilty, do they not see that I have suffered enough? I was confined in jail, insulted in the courtroom and shunned by former friends. Will they ever be satisfied? What more do they want from me?"

* * *

When the sisters' third cousin Caroline Borden and the Reverend Mr. Buck's daughter Alice paid a visit, they were a godsend. "Lizzie, Emma told us you needed a change of scenery. Why don't you come with us to the World's Columbia Exposition in Chicago?"

"That sounds like a wonderful escape for you, Lizzie," Emma added. And the timing is perfect. We're all settled in Maplecroft. I can manage everything while you are gone."

Lizzie purchased her tickets as Lisbeth Borden, hoping that a small change would keep curiosity seekers and the newspapers from knowing her destination. The train ride was quite long—nearly a day and a half. Despite the length of the journey, the on-board accommodations made the travel a delight: a comfortable cabin and better food than Lizzie had expected. The scenery was breathtaking. Lake Erie churned wild and rough, making Lizzie wonder how it all stayed within its banks. Lake Ontario was a different kind of surprise, its placid, dark blue surface reflected the light and shined like a beacon of serenity.

Past the two lakes, the fields of corn sprawled for miles. In some, the harvest was in progress. All three women stared with open mouths at the sight before them: huge steam-operated threshing machines grabbing the shocks of corn that men feed into its gullet, all pulled by a pair of horses. Scattered throughout the field, men, women, and children bound sheaves to prepare the shocks for the thresher.

As far as they could see, the fields stretched on, the labor intensified, then diminished, and then renewed as different levels of activity were required for each step of the process. "I will never toss out cracked corn for the chickens again without seeing these fields in my mind's eye," Caroline Borden exclaimed.

Lake Michigan came into view next, looking like nature's big disappointment in comparison to the two previous lakes. Surrounded by wasteland and scruffy sand, it looked old and neglected.

As they reached the Chicago area, they saw a building with a large dome and an unbelievably high Ferris Wheel dominating the skyline. They secured their rooms at a nearby hotel and hurried over to the exposition. Arriving at the Court of Honor, Lizzie, her face filled with awe, whispered, "The White City."

"What did you say?" Alice Buck asked.

Lizzie turned toward her with a smile. "The White City is the nickname for this fair. Haven't you heard of it? Just look." The view was blinding as the sun hit all the Beaux-Arts buildings covered in white stucco.

The women wandered around the area, stunned by its beauty. The transformation at sundown amazed them all. Everything turned magical with the lighted walkways and the supernatural glow from every structure. Exhausted from their travels and stunned by the sights, all four decided an early night was in order to have the energy to explore all day long tomorrow.

One of their first discoveries the next day was the moving walkway. They decided to try the slow one first that transported them forward at 3 miles per hour. The fast one went twice the speed. Lizzie was exhilarated and insisted on getting on again for the joy of it. Alice, however, was terrified and whimpered the whole length of the walk.

Exploring the exhibits was a global adventure. They were awed by the ostriches from the Cape Colony in Africa—enormous birds whose necks towered over the women's heads. "Look how stubby their wings are," Caroline said. "They seem totally useless."

"I imagine they can run fast, though. Look at the legs—just like those on a chicken—but much longer and far more sturdy," Alice added.

"Those huge feet could dig into the ground and propel them forward," Lizzie said. "Heaven help the creature or person who threatened them. Those sharp claws could rip any of us to shreds." Beside her, Alice shuddered.

Arriving at the map of the United States made entirely of pickles, they laughed at the absurdity of it. The next odd creations they encountered were Liberty Bells, one made of oats, wheat, and rye, the other composed entirely of oranges. Topping them all, though, was the statue of a medieval knight crafted entirely out of prunes. Arriving at the Canadian exhibition, they saw a mammoth 2,200-pound cloth-bound wheel of cheddar cheese.

Lizzie's breath was taken away at the sight of Bach's clavichord and Mozart's spinet. Tears rose to her eyes, and a lump formed in her throat when she gazed at the original manuscript of President Lincoln's inaugural address. She thought many things in the country would have been dramatically changed had he survived the attack in the theatre. Every president since had not measured up. If Lincoln could understand the plight of the slave, he surely would grasp the horror of the servitude of women.

They all noticed the striking difference in the architecture of the United States government building—all glass and flags. Inside a giant redwood tree soared over them all making the people around it look like insignificant insects. Lizzie's favorite exhibit there, by far, was the floor-to-ceiling aquaria filled with an innumerable variety of fresh and saltwater fish.

They wrapped up the day with a visit to the Women's Building. They oohed and aahed at exquisite dresses, cloaks, embroidery, and lacework, but when they exited the building, Lizzie said, "What a disappointment."

"A disappointment, Lizzie?" Alice said. "All those lovely things. How could you say that?"

"You do know the building was designed by a female architect, don't you, Lizzie? That certainly should give us all pride," Caroline added.

"I do know that Caroline, and for that I am glad. But what did we see in there? Lovely things to look at, as Alice said. But where were the exhibits that expanded a woman's world. That took us to the future. That gave us hope that men would not always rule us. I suspect that idea is nothing but a fantasy since it was not portrayed here. That is why I am disappointed."

On the second day, they travelled on the elevated electric railway to Buffalo Bill's Wild West Show and Congress of Rough Riders. Lizzie and Caroline were thrilled by the exciting ride, but Lizzie had to hold Alice's hand as she whimpered until it was over.

The show itself was overwhelming. Tremendous crowds gathered for the opening parade. The buffeting was constant as people craned for better views. The marksmanship of the men was remarkable, but Lizzie's attention was riveted when Annie Oakley skipped into view with a rifle held by her side. She reached the center of the stage, turned as she raised her rifle, aimed and shot at a lit candle, snuffing it out in a flash.

Dimes were thrown in the air, and at the apex of the toss, she shot each one down. When a playing card was thrown up in the air, she riddled it with bullets before it hit the ground. She shot a cigar and cigarettes from her husband's mouth. Alice gasped with each shot fired while Lizzie rejoiced.

When Annie's performance came to an end, Lizzie said, "We need more women like her. Women who can shoot a rifle as easily as they carry a baby. If we all knew how to fire weapons, we could protect ourselves from man's lasciviousness and avarice."

"If we had the fortitude to fire it at another living creature," Caroline said.

"Caroline, if women ever want to get the vote and get out from under the heel of man, we must be armed. Men listen to nothing less."

"I want the vote as much as anyone, Lizzie. But taking it by force, that seems a bit too extreme."

"And that's why we will never have the vote because most women do not have the willingness to battle men on their own terms to get what is rightfully theirs."

The show continued with one outlandish display after another: wild animals, battle reenactments, trick performers, and more. It lasted nearly four hours, and the noise of the crowds, the livestock odors, and the gunpowder-smoke-filled air gave all three women headaches and fatigue.

They chose to start the next day with more placid entertainment by viewing the actual Liberty Bell transported there from Philadelphia. Off to the art exhibit next, where works by John Singer Sergeant, Thomas Eakins, Winslow Homer, Pierre-Auguste Renoir, Mary Cassatt, and Camille Pissarro took their breaths away.

After that calm exploration, Lizzie and Caroline were ready for excitement, going to the Midway for a ride on the Ferris Wheel. Standing beside it, they craned their necks back to see its impossible height. Alice did not want to ride it. She did not even want to stand near it. The other two tried to talk her into taking the adventure with them, but she burst into tears. Lizzie thought she might swoon and led her to a bench to sit down.

Lizzie and Caroline tried to keep their eyes on Alice as they went higher and higher. "Where is she, Lizzie?"

"I don't know. I can't even tell the difference between men and women up here."

As they reached the top, both inhaled with surprise. "The whole world is at our feet, Lizzie."

"I know. We can see forever. Look at the huge, blue lake. It seems as big as the Atlantic."

"Over here, the whole of the White City, in fact, all of the fairgrounds seem like a miniature village."

"Look, we are nearly in the clouds."

"Is that a hawk?"

"Where?"

"Right at eye level, over there," Caroline pointed.

"The air! Have you noticed the air? It's fresh, it's cool, it's magnificent."

"Everything about this ride is more than I ever dreamed."

On the ground, they gave rapturous descriptions of the ride and the sights, offering to ride again if Alice had changed her mind. Alice would not budge. They walked around the Midway for a short while but found it too common with the bustling crowds, questionable entertainment, and endless cacophony of noise.

They escaped to the World's Congress building, where they explored the rotating roster of lectures on everything from architecture to moral and social reform, from history to temperance. Lizzie urged the others to go with her to some of them but found no interest from either woman.

As the sun set, they gathered with thousands of others to watch the water and music show. Glorious colored fountains turned the world into a kaleidoscope. More dramatic colors rose in the sky as fireworks were shot into the starry sky over Lake Michigan.

On the train ride home, they talked a lot about the new food they experienced at the fair. "My favorite was the Aunt Jemima pancake syrup," Alice said.

"I want to have nothing but cream of wheat and shredded wheat for breakfast as long as I live," Caroline said."

"But, the hamburger," Lizzie said. "I'd never heard of anything like it. Ground up pieces of beef between two slices of bread. I love it."

"I did, too," Caroline said, "but it's German. I can't imagine it would ever be popular here."

"I brought some Juicy Fruit gum with me. Do you two want a piece?" Alice offered.

They all chewed in quiet bliss for a few minutes, and Lizzie broke the silence. "Cracker Jack. I don't think I'll ever get enough of that. I wonder when the Fall River shops will start carrying it."

"What about that Pabst Beer?" Alice asked. "Did you like that, Caroline?"

"I told you I didn't drink any."

"You tried hard to convince us to join you, Caroline," Lizzie said.

"So what?"

"Well, tell us then, Caroline, what made your cheeks so rosy."

Lizzie and Alice laughed. Caroline stammered. "You embarrassed me, that's all."

Chapter Fifty

Lizzie was delighted that no one on the whole trip seemed to even wonder at her real identity. She thought a permanent change would serve her well. When she returned she had her name changed to Lisbeth Borden in the City Directory.

"Lizzie—Lisbeth—I do not think it will do much good, but I do understand your desire to change your identity in some small way. It would probably be more effective if you changed your last name," Emma said.

"Never. The Borden name still retains a lot of influence in this town, and I will not strip myself of that advantage."

* * *

When the transformation of the Second Street house back into a two-tenement dwelling was complete, Cook told the sisters he believed it would be rented soon. Emma and Lizzie walked over to their old home to see the work before it was occupied.

Reaching the fence, Emma said, "It looks a lot better than it did when Father first bought the house."

"I am too young to remember anything about the house before we lived in it," Lizzie said. "I do think it does not appear much different than it did when we moved out."

Inside, though, the changes were dramatic. Entering the front door, going up the front stairs was the only option out of the foyer. A small but adequate kitchen was installed on the second floor. "That is exactly where the upstairs kitchen was before Father removed it and converted the house," Emma explained.

The back staircase was closed off so that the second-floor residents could not access the first floor but could still get into the attic. To enter the lower-level apartment, you had to enter the house by the side door that opened into the kitchen. Inside, neither one of them could find the entrance to the stairway to the upstairs—it was covered over to the point of being invisible. The dining room remained where it had been, and the lounge had been turned into a parlor. The former public rooms were now bedrooms. "Emma, I often felt cramped in this house when we occupied both floors. How could a family live on this one level and not burst out of the seams?"

"Someone will want to live here. It would be an improvement for many to have this much space," Emma said.

"The house may never rent to anyone because of the tragedy," Lizzie responded.

"Well, then, we shall sell it."

"If anyone will buy it."

Cook met them at the house as they prepared to leave. Much to Lizzie's surprise he informed the women that he found new tenants the same day he advertised the apartments. "A grocer and his family and a horse trader and wife and children are moving in tomorrow."

"I certainly hope the out-of-town curiosity seekers leave them in peace," Emma said.

Returning to Maplecroft, a breathless Annie Holmes awaited their arrival. "I just had to tell you. I'm not sure you care but still, you might."

"What is it, Annie," Lizzie asked.

"The foreman of the grand jury committed suicide."

"The same grand jury that indicted my sister?" Emma asked.

Annie nodded vigorously, and she and Emma turned to see Lizzie's reaction. Lizzie repressed the glee that bubbled up in her throat. "I suppose the guilt of indicting me was too much for him to bear." She turned abruptly and retreated to her bedroom.

As she left, she heard Annie gasp. Emma came to the rescue, "Do not pay her any mind, Annie. We just visited our former home, and I believe it disrupted her peace of mind. You must forgive her."

The bitterness in Lizzie's heart curdled and strengthened, knowing that many begrudged her of harsh feelings. She doubted that most would cease doubting the verdict until the finger of blame was pointed at another culprit. She thought about pushing them all toward her Uncle Hiram. His words and actions to her and her sister were unforgivable. She believed with a little effort, she could twist them into the responses of a guilty man and paint a scarlet M for murder on his forehead.

She was also disturbed by the friends who protested her innocence yet still were judgmental of her. No one would fault a man for speaking his mind in a forthright manner. Why are women held to a different, unfair standard? It would be more understandable if only the men did this, but it was women, too, and that was far more exasperating.

Chapter Fifty-One

The Holmes family invited the Borden sisters to Thanksgiving dinner at their house. Lizzie gave their housekeeper a day off with her family. "There is so much she could be doing here while we're gone," Emma objected.

"We are spending the day with friends. Why should she not be allowed to celebrate and feel genuine gratitude on today of all days?"

The Holmes' table was laden with a glorious feast. A golden, fragrant turkey bigger than any Lizzie had ever seen, served with mashed potatoes, stuffing, squash, corn, green beans, and cranberries. All of that plenty was followed by coffee and pumpkin pie.

Lizzie felt at ease for most of the day, but her discomfort grew when Mr. Holmes asked each of them to speak about their gratitude. Mr. Holmes started the round table. "I am grateful for my family, the food, and our home. And we are most blessed to have our beloved Lizzie Borden with us today with all her suffering and confinement behind her."

Lizzie did not feel grateful at all—she simply felt resentful for all she endured. She regretted the reality that made her father's death a necessity—gratitude felt like a sacrilege. Nonetheless, she knew that she was obligated to express a similar sentiment whether she felt it or not. "I am grateful for the magnanimous judges who sat on my trial, the twelve worthy men who found me not guilty, and the courage and fortitude of my team of lawyers."

Lizzie ended with a weak smile. She wanted to forget about her many days in jail, the dreadful trial, and the long-lasting consequences of being accused. She realized, though, that no one would allow her to do that. If ever her memory grew dim, someone else would bring it all up to her for the rest of her life.

Lizzie brooded through the remainder of the holiday season while Emma attempted to prod her into a better mood. The day after Christmas, Emma asked,"Have you made any resolutions for the new year, Lizzie?

Her sister glared at her.

"Well," Emma continued. I have resolved to walk every day and be cheerful to all I meet, regardless of their attitude. How about you?"

"I will have no more concern for decorum. I shall do what I want, say what I want, be who I want. And I shan't waste any more time doing church charity work. It did not earn me the respect of the congregation when I faced my biggest adversity."

"Then what will you do with your time, Lizzie?"

I will buy beautiful dresses, travel to Boston and Providence as often as I like to visit museums and go to the theater."

"But, Lizzie, you cannot do nothing for anyone but yourself."

"Animals. That is the answer. Poor dumb animals never judge or disapprove. I will support rescue societies for horses and other animals. And I will help deserving female students advance their education at college. The next generation needs to be prepared to wrench power from the hands of men."

Emma had grown weary of Lizzie's constant litany against men and changed the subject. "I have an idea. Why don't we go shopping in Providence, that always cheers you up."

"Providence is an excellent idea. The local shops here are always full of people who whisper and stare. We should find some peace to enjoy the outing."

The next day, they left on the morning train and returned late in the afternoon. They visited every shop that caught their interest, including their favorite, Tilden-Thurber.

* * *

On December 29, a disheveled Mr. Cook called on the sisters. "I wish I did not have to see you about this matter, but it does concern you, and I am certain it will be in the newspapers."

Lizzie and Emma looked at each other alarmed at what he said and at how he looked. "Whatever is the matter, Mr. Cook?"

"In your old home on Ferry Street—in the place where both you and Emma were born—in that house—in the attic space—an old man died of starvation and neglect."

"My heavens, Mr. Cook, why would you rent that space to anyone," Emma said.

"It was unheated and unfit for habitation," Lizzie added.

"I did not. I did not know anyone was living up there."

"Someone must have known," Emma said.

"His wife did. He became ill, and she did not call a doctor."

"Two people were living up there?" Lizzie asked.

"I am afraid so, Miss Lizzie."

"That's dreadful," Emma said. "Are they pointing the finger of blame at my sister again?"

"They might—gossip is a vicious thing. Do not respond to any questions from newspapermen. If any police show up, do not discuss it with them either."

Emma crossed her arms in front of her chest. "I thought we had to answer their questions."

"Tell them you know nothing, and do not let them force you into saying anything else at all. Miss Lizzie, I am aware that it is a dreadful way for the year of your freedom to end, and I am sorry."

* * *

Caroline Borden visited Fall River in the first week of the new year. "I have some exciting news. Your Mr. Jennings is running to replace Mr. Knowlton as District Attorney."

"That explains why he wrote to me and said I needed to find another lawyer to represent me in legal matters. Obviously, since he is seeking office, he does not want to be stained by associating with me," Lizzie said.

Caroline waved a dismissive hand. "Really, Lizzie? He spoke very passionately of your innocence in court and out. I imagine he knows he will be too busy with the campaign and with his new job if he wins the election.'

"A politician is a different creature, Caroline. They use the accused to vault into prominence and then avoid us to stave off contamination. He must have been considering this run for quite some time. He has never has invited Emma and I to his home since the trial."

"That is surprising since he lives nearby. I wish people were more concerned with substance than image. The world would be a far better place."

"Yes, but politicians and men, in general, are far too judgmental and shallow for that. Emma and I admire your loyalty and courage in maintaining a connection with us in spite of your father's disapproval."

* * *

The sisters paid one last visit to the office of Andrew Jennings for Emma to sign the final executrix document. "You'll see, Miss Emma, that I left out as many details as possible to preserve your privacy. There is no inventory of goods or property and no accounting for cash."

"Thank you, Mr. Jennings."

Lizzie pursed her lips. "I hear you are running for District Attorney, Mr. Jennings."

"Yes, Miss Lizzie, I thought that would please you. I know how much disdain you have for Mr. Knowlton."

"That is true, sir. However, I am surprised that you would want to have anyone see us in your office."

"I have to complete the business I have started before I can focus on my campaign."

"I suppose it would be more harmful to your image if you actually brought the papers to our home."

"Miss Lizzie, I say this with all sincerity. I have always believed in your innocence, and I am proud to have played a part in your acquittal. And I will tell that to anyone who asks."

Lizzie raised her chin and looked away.

Emma cleared her throat. "Mr. Jennings, we are very grateful for all you have done for us. Come, Lizzie, let us leave Mr. Jennings to go about his business."

* * *

Early that spring, Mr. Cook approached the sisters about requested changes and repairs for a space rented by the Young Women's Temperance Union. Lizzie bridled at their demands. "Tell them they can pay for that out of their own pocket. Their members snub me in the street, ignore me when I call at their homes, and pretend that I don't exist. Still, they have the audacity to ask me to provide improvements to suit them."

"I agree with you completely, Miss Lizzie. When I went to their offices, I spoke to them about defacing the space with tobacco juice and other substances. I can't say that they have been the best tenants."

"Are you sure, Lizzie?" Emma asked. "Should you not turn the other cheek? I think some of them genuinely fear guilt by association, however ludicrous that may seem. Pity them for the narrow views."

"I will not tolerate disdain from my tenants, sister. If they don't like it, they can vacate the premises."

Cook took care of the matter, and the group moved out of the Borden property and into the Friends Meeting House. At his insistence, they issued a statement saying that they had no quarrel with Lizzie or Emma Borden and simply preferred the new offices. Learning of that, Lizzie said, "They were worried that any negative comments would put our annual donations to the organizations in jeopardy—not because they thought they did anything wrong."

Chapter Fifty-Two

Overnight on June 5, burglars launched an assault on the house of the sisters' next-door neighbors. Only a few window screens were damaged, but it sent a ripple of fear throughout the community. Like everyone else, Lizzie and Emma made a complete search of the exterior of their home, looking for any signs of an attempt on their residence. None were found, but uneasiness hung in the air.

To make matters worse, the heat and humidity were ghastly that summer. Emma and Lizzie took the first opportunity possible to visit their country home in Swansea. While there, they paid a visit to a much older friend, Mary Gardner. Exploring her grounds, they noticed that much of the view of the bay was spoiled by an old woodshed standing in the way.

"Mary," Emma said, "I cannot believe you have not gotten rid of that dilapidated thing. Your view would be stunning if it were gone."

"You are very right. I have been thinking about that for quite some time. The very next time Mike comes, we must remember to have him knock it down for firewood."

Lizzie rose to her feet. "Why wait for Mike? Give me the axe."

The silence roared in Lizzie's head. No one spoke or moved a muscle as if fearing lightning would strike them where they stood. She felt the heat rise in her face. She turned and walked away from them all. *I will never be completely trusted by anyone—not even my own sister.*

Returning to Maplecroft, Lizzie had no desire to see a single soul. She turned away visitors and took meals in her room. It took an invitation from the Morse family to pull her out of her despond. She agreed to travel with them to Jolly Island on Lake Winnipesaukee, at the foot of the White Mountains of New Hampshire.

She reveled in the fresh, clean, crisp air—a remarkable change from Fall River, where factory stacks filled their air with smoke and the humidity pushed it down around their heads. The lake was a beautiful shade of blue dotted with lush emerald islands. All surrounded by the backdrop of the soaring mountains.

Lizzie jumped into all the activities: fishing, rowing in canoes, walking in the woods or simply sitting in the shade reading a book or conversing with her friends. She rejoiced that no one mentioned her ordeal or treated her as if she were soiled. She did not want to return to the critical glances, heat, and humidity, but she knew that she must.

In October, Emma and Lizzie traveled up to Westerly, Rhode Island, to hire the Smith Granite Company to build and install a monument for Father. They had a simple design in mind—tall, substantial, and elegant with no frills or ostentatiousness, just like Father.

"$2250?" Lizzie exclaimed.

"It will be a grand stone that will show what a grand man your father was in life," Mr. Smith said.

Emma pulled her aside. "Don't be penurious, Lizzie. You remind me more and more of Father every day—always haggling for a better price. You cannot afford to appear miserly."

"I am tamping down my ire, sister, and I will not say another word. Just remember, we came by our funds the hard way, and our future depends on holding on to what we have."

* * *

Mary Livermore invited Lizzie to join her in Boston for the Artists' Festival in December. Lizzie readily accepted—It was her kind of event with a kaleidoscope of activities. In addition to students displaying their work and performing in plays, there were lectures on art and singing from prominent and established entertainers.

Before going to see the play *The Fair Persian* in Copley Hall, Lizzie talked frankly to Mary, telling her about the axe incident in the country, her sister's comments at the monument maker, as well as the behavior of many erstwhile supporters.

Mary sighed, "Suspicion is a cloying thing, my dear. Even when it has proven to be totally unjustified. Once you have entertained it—even only for a moment—it is like stepping in horse dung. Even after you dispose of it, the aroma remains."

"What can I do, Mrs. Livermore?"

"Nothing, really, Lizzie. It will take time, and you must be patient. Soon, your tribulations will be forgotten by everyone living but you. Then, you will have peace."

At the theatre, Mary and Lizzie left the cold of Boston behind and entered the courtyard before the palace of the caliph and breathed in the intoxicating scent of a Persian summer filled with the beauty and fragrance of roses. Through a huge gateway hung with artistic scenery, they found the caliph's throne on their left, flanked by two gilded lions. Opposite was the stage, an interior scene of the palace with a view of a moonlit outdoor garden brimming with lotus flowers and an elaborate fountain.

Inside, Lizzie looked back at the gateway. "Mrs. Livermore, turn around." She pointed to the masonry wall with domes and minarets of an Eastern city interspersed with towering, regal palm trees. Flowering vines flowed up the walls and cascaded over the capstones.

"Breathtaking, Lizzie. If only we could be surrounded by this much beauty every day."

Lizzie found the Persian princess to be the most captivating of all. She presented a striking image on stage, dressed in Nile green silk and embroidered chiffon, adorned with magnificent jewels. Lizzie daydreamed about walking in her footsteps and receiving admiring glances from the audience seated at her feet.

Chapter Fifty-Three

The sisters expected the delivery of the monument in early March 1894. However, it arrived early in mid-January. Once it was placed and washed in Oak Grove Cemetery, the sisters took a carriage over to inspect it. To their dismay, a small crowd had gathered around the graves. Lizzie hesitated to disembark.

"Come on, now, Lizzie, we must examine the stone," Emma urged.

"Look at them." Lizzie pointed at the cluster of people around the stone. "All they want is to stare at me and gossip about how I behaved and how I dressed. I am so sick of them all."

"The gossip will be worse if you just ride off without paying respects to our father."

Lizzie sighed and stepped down. The sisters agreed that the monument was perfect. A substantial chunk of white Westerly granite rose ten feet from its four-foot-square base. The sides tapered in before spreading out at the top to accommodate a cap of Grecian ornamentation. At the base of the south side, A.J. BORDEN was carved in bold letters that could be seen from a distance. On the panel above the inscription read:

ANDREW JACKSON BORDEN

1822-1892

His Wife,

SARAH ANTHONY BORDEN

1823-1863

ABBY DURFREE BORDEN

1828-1892
On the west side, it read:
Children of
ANDREW J. AND SARAH A. BORDEN
ALICE ESTHER
1856-1858

"One day, Lizzie, our names will be added there with Alice's."

"Let us hope it is a long time coming, Emma."

After making sure all the names were spelled correctly, Lizzie returned to the carriage to get away from the gawkers. She pressed her body into the corner and waited for Emma. She grew impatient as her sister spoke to the workmen, exclaiming over the job that had been done.

* * *

Lizzie and Emma sat in the parlor after breakfast—Lizzie reading the newspaper, Emma preparing a menu for the housekeeper. Emma looked up at the angry rustling of newspaper and saw disgust on Lizzie's face. "What is it? What has happened?"

"It is too disgusting. He was supposed to lose. After losing my case, I did not think he would ever be elected to anything again. What fools voted for him?"

"Are you talking about Mr. Knowlton?

"Who else? He just won the election for the Massachusetts Attorney General. I thought he had no chance since all his supporters wanted me in prison or hanging from the scaffold," Lizzie said.

Emma stood behind her and looked over her shoulder at the newspaper. "Well, he is a Republican, and that did give an advantage."

"God save the poor women of Massachusetts."

"Just because he was dreadful to you, Lizzie, does not mean he will behave terribly toward all women," Emma said.

"It is another insult to me. They voted for him to put me in my place."

"But look, Lizzie." Emma leaned forward and pointed to a spot lower on the page. There will be a special election soon for his replacement. Our Mr. Jennings is running to take his place as District Attorney for Southern Massachusetts. He surely will win, and that will provide you a cushion of protection if there anyone had thought of prosecuting you for any real or imagined crime in the future."

"But Knowlton is now his superior. I fear that does not bode well for me at all." Lizzie rose from her chair, haphazardly folded the newspaper, and tossed it on the floor. She marched outside to the garden. She deadheaded her roses, pulled weeds, and talked to the squirrels. Her anger subsided as she accepted that it was all out of her control.

She acted as if she didn't care, but she'd paid close attention to Jennings' race. If he loses, she believed, it would be because of her, but if he wins, it would be because the majority thought she was innocent and his cause righteous. When he won, she thought her social circle would expand, but it never did.

* * *

Annie Holmes called at Maplecroft in February 1895, totally breathless from the heavy load of gossip she pulled in her wake. "Oh dear, Emma, what now—she is as bad as Mrs. Churchill, always wanting to be first to announce any news."

Emma scowled at her sister. "No more of that while she's here, Lizzie."

As soon as they were all seated, Annie said, "Did you hear about the Baldwins' performance at the Academy of Music last night?"

Lizzie stifled a grin. "No, but it must be sensational if you are here to tell us."

Emma leaned over to Lizzie's ear, "Shush."

Annie, however, did not notice the sarcasm. "The evening started with musical performances, and then Mr. Baldwin did tricks with a cabinet, but the most exciting part was Mrs. Baldwin. She came on stage blindfolded, and her husband led her to a seat in the middle of the stage.

269

"And despite not being able to see, Mrs. Baldwin called out the names of people in the audience, describing the clothing and jewelry they wore and answered questions that the audience members had written down on slips of paper and held up in the air."

Lizzie raised an eyebrow. "Did you personally know any of the people who posed these questions?"

Annie furrowed her brow. "I don't think so, but Fall River has gotten so big, it is impossible to know everyone. Anyway, people's questions concerned money, marriage, things that they lost, absent relatives, and even a few political queries. And she answered every single one of them. And here is the most important part—the reason why I had to tell you about it—she described a man in the upper gallery. She said that his question reminded her of a crime—a fearful crime."

"Oh, no," Lizzie sighed. Emma patted the back of her hand.

Annie nodded her head. "Oh, yes! She saw someone in a bedroom sneaking up on an older woman, and at that point, she rose from her seat, paced around the stage, gesticulating wildly, and in an emotion-filled voice said, 'It is murder. It is murder.' Her husband led her back to her chair and placed a flag over her to prevent her magnetism from escaping."

Lizzie twisted her head to the side. "Her magnetism?"

"Yes, yes. He said she was laboring under such excitement; it was a big risk to her health and well-being. The audience was full of questions about the murders, and Mrs. Baldwin said, 'Lizzie Borden did not kill her parents.' Just like that. You can imagine the buzz going through the hall. But she didn't stop there. She said, "A dark, swarthy man entered the house intent on burglary. When Mrs. Borden discovered him, he killed her to cover his tracks.' Then she said, 'He killed Mr. Borden to hide his first murder.' She said his name was Tony. She started to say his last name, but Mr. Baldwin interrupted her. Do you know anyone named Tony?" Annie looked from Lizzie to Emma, then back to Lizzie again.

Both women shook their heads.

"Well, then she described your house, said the time of the murders, and talked about the axe, but all the while, her voice was getting weaker and weaker. Mr. Baldwin removed the cloth on her body and the handkerchief from her eyes. He waved his hands in front of her several times, then led her off the stage. Isn't that remarkable, Lizzie? She knows you are not guilty. She's seen the man who is."

Lizzie looked at her friend with pity-filled eyes. "Annie, as interesting as it might be in a theatre, police officers don't place much faith in the word of spiritualists."

"Oh, but they should. They had so many facts about other things right that night. It was amazing."

As they watched Annie leave, Emma sighed. "What is amazing to me is how so many people can be taken in by smoke, mirrors, and a spouting of random gossip."

"If Annie is a true believer, as she seems to be, there is no talking sense to her. Reason is no match for blind belief."

* * *

The next month, Lizzie received a letter from Will Hamilton, the colored man who had worked for the family for eight years. He had written to her previously for some financial assistance and Lizzie assumed that was his purpose this time.

She was horrified when she read the contents. Will, who could not read or write, stopped in a business to get a shopkeeper to write a letter to her. The man did as requested, but then jumped to a terrible conclusion. He believed that Will was the murderer of the Bordens and contacted the police. Will was locked up in jail. No one who knew Will could think that it was possible that he committed such a gruesome crime.

Since Will had worked for Governor Robinson before coming to her house, Lizzie sent an urgent letter to her former defense lawyer. She got a quick reply. She read it out loud to Emma: "The matter has been taken care of, Miss Borden. Mr. Adams and I heard of his arrest and hurried to Allston jail, where we vouched for him. He has been released but is quite shaken by the ordeal. He missed work because of it and was worried he

271

would lose his position at Wilton House. The poor man is getting up in his years—I believe he said he was 54—but he still works as hard as ever. I'm sure he would be delighted to hear from you."

"Poor Will," Emma said. "We need to send some funds his way and apologize for the problems his connection with our family caused."

Lizzie agreed with her but did not want to allow her sister to know it. "That seems a bit excessive, Emma. After all, we did not turn him into the authorities."

"Lizzie, you can't mean that. It is not just you who suffered from your incarceration. I did, too. And Will? It's like a delayed response. He never would have been locked up if he had not worked for our family. Compensating him for his travails is the Christian thing to do."

"Well, if you think so, Emma." Lizzie turned away before her sister could see her smile.

* * *

In May, fresh news from events of the past came knocking on the Bordens' door by way of Annie Holmes. "Did you know Bridget Sullivan sailed for Ireland on the Luciana?"

Lizzie shrugged. "Who is she?"

Emma scowled. "You don't remember our loyal servant?"

"Oh, Maggie. Our Maggie."

"Yes. Sometimes you shame me, sister."

Lizzie rolled her eyes. "We called her Maggie the entire time she worked in our home. Bridget Sullivan is nothing but a remnant of my horrible inquest and trial and a product of the sensational newspapers. It was an ugly time that I have tried hard to forget."

* * *

Lizzie realized she did not want to remain in town on the anniversary of her acquittal. The local newspapers would rehash the events endlessly. She decided to stay in the Berkshires at the Stockbridge House, the town where Herman Melville wrote *Moby Dick*. Since Lizzie had turned down multiple invitations from Alice Buck because of prior commitments and her boring personality, Lizzie invited her to accompany her there. She had few loyal friends and did not want to risk losing even the dull ones.

At a stop along the way in Pittsfield, a large crowd gathered around the tracks, many shouting out Lizzie's name. "Alice, did you tell anyone where we were going?"

"Only my mother and father, Lizzie, and they told me not to mention the destination to anyone else."

"Oh, bother. I must have been seen boarding the train in Fall River." Fortunately, the stop was short, and when they reached Stockbridge, no one noticed Lizzie's presence, and the check-in at the hotel caused no unwanted commotion.

The lush landscape and lovely gardens soothed Lizzie's soul. She dared not read a newspaper in the time she was there, fearing what she would find. She read books from the library and took long walks around the grounds.

* * *

"Do you see Annie coming our way?" Emma said.

Lizzie looked out the window. "I certainly do, and she has quite the bounce in her step. I wonder what gossip she has to share today?"

After greetings and the serving of tea and cookies, Annie cleared her throat. "I went to see Mrs. Pennell at the G.A.R. Hall last night."

Emma cocked her head to the side. "Are you a believer in spiritualism, Annie?"

"I am undecided. Mediums know amazing things—I imagine some of it is trickery, but I am not convinced that it is all nonsense. I do believe some people can see things that the rest of us cannot. Anyway, before delivering any exhibitions of her prowess she said that someone had spoken to her of Lizzie Borden's innocence, but she'd been out west when it happened and saw no news of it at the time. She also said she did not know you, Lizzie. Is that correct?"

"I do not recall meeting her."

"She added that if you came up on stage, she would not recognize you. I am surprised that she would admit that. Shouldn't mediums be able to recognize strangers? Anyway, she was all alone in her room the previous night at three o'clock when she woke to three sharp, distinct raps. In response, she read the Lord's Prayer aloud from her Bible, and the table beneath lifted as high as her head.

"She asked and was told that it was the spirit of Mrs. Borden."

"Oh, my heavens," Lizzie muttered.

"She asked the spirit if you were guilty, and the spirit told her, 'In the eyes of many people, she was condemned and called guilty, but the time will come when she will stand before the people entirely innocent.' And then, she said that she thought you were as innocent of those murders as she was."

Lizzie tried to scrape the sarcastic edge from her voice as she spoke. "I'm glad to hear that." She certainly appreciated the woman's support and her willingness to spread her story around town, but she did not believe that Mrs. Pennell had spoken with someone beyond the grave. It did not, however, hurt her standing in the community when her believers accepted her word as truth.

Annie furrowed her brow. "Who do you suspect committed the murders, Lizzie?"

"My Uncle Hiram. His behavior after Father's death was churlish and indicative of bad blood between him and Father."

Emma sat upright. "Really? I didn't care for his questioning of you or his interview with the reporter, but guilty of the killing?"

"Emma, the first thing guilty people do is point the finger of blame at others. As you know, I never did that before my trial, but Uncle Hiram certainly did."

"But Lizzie, he is family," Emma said as she rose and paced the room.

Noting Annie's discomfort, Lizzie came to the rescue. "Annie, let's talk of pleasant things."

Annie's eyes flitted around the room, seeking inspiration before landing on Lizzie. "Have you met Phoebe Davenport?"

"We've exchanged a few words," Lizzie said.

"You know she is a widow, don't you?"

"Yes, I believe her husband died eleven years ago."

"Yes, yes, very sad. You should get to know her niece, Harriet Henry. She lives with Phoebe now and is a teacher at the high school. She's very close to your age, lives nearby, and I think you would enjoy her company."

"I'll speak to Mrs. Davenport about her next time our paths cross." Lizzie kept to herself the fact that she had already met the woman, and Mrs. Henry made it abundantly clear that she did not wish to further the relationship. Phoebe was shocked by her niece's rudeness, but Lizzie was not. She'd grown used to being shunned by her neighbors.

Chapter Fifty-Four

Emma was eager to visit the old Second Street home to see the new no-trespassing tablet Mr. Cook had erected for the peace of mind of the tenants. Lizzie was reluctant but agreed to go with her. "But not in the carriage, Emma. If I am going on this senseless trip with you, I might as well get the benefit of a walk in the fresh air at the same time."

Walking was quite pleasant that day, the air was brisk and smelled like snow, yet here and there the sun peaked through the gathering clouds. All the children were in school, sparing the sisters from the usual taunting. They still got a lot of stares, but the venom, once a constant presence, seemed to have drained away.

The wooden sign was painted white with black molding and attached to the outside of the building. The bold black letters read: "Trespassing on these premises is STRICTLY FORBIDDEN (By the owners) C.C. Cook, Agent."

"Sad that the sign was necessary," Emma said.

Lizzie huffed. "Sad that so many think our lives and every detail of it belongs to them." An image of her father, stretched out on the sitting room sofa, his face, slashed and bleeding, took hold of Lizzie's thoughts. *It was such a shame that he had to die.*

Emma noticed the troubled expression on her sister's face. "Lizzie, Lizzie, are you okay?"

Lizzie shook her head and focused her eyes on her sister. "Memories, Emma, memories. Sometimes, they haunt me."

"Let's go then. We want to be home before the schoolchildren are back out in the street."

* * *

Christmas and New Year's Day went by, and still, in 1896, many continued to hold Lizzie at a distance. No one she had known before the trial would call her anything but Lizzie. She could only get servants and new acquaintances to call her Miss Lisbeth. With the changing seasons, Lizzie hoped for a change in society's heart—prayed to be welcomed back into the fold. She focused on her beautiful home and lovely garden and kept busy tending flowers and feeding the birds in a wide assortment of feeders she had spread through the yard.

Toward the end of February, Lizzie was sitting in a comfortable chair by the fire, reading a book. Emma was on the other side of the hearth, flipping through the newspaper. Without warning, Emma rose with a strangled gasp.

Lizzie looked up from her book. "Whatever is the problem, sister?"

Emma swallowed hard and spoke in a wavering voice. "Listen to this article: 'Last Tuesday, Governor Robinson was walking to his office from superior court with his son. He became confused and was feeling ill. His son summoned a carriage to take him to his house and called for doctors to examine him.' It was an attack of apoplexy, Lizzie. He had an apoplectic stroke."

"He's an old man, Emma."

"He's dead, Lizzie!" Emma shook the newspaper. "He died three days after the attack."

"As I said, Emma, he was an old man. Old men die. You should have learned that when we lost Father."

Emma sputtered. "Lizzie, sometimes I do not know you. I do not recognize my sister behind your words." She stalked out of the room, tossing the newspaper in Lizzie's lap.

Lizzie pushed it to the floor and returned to her book, grateful for the quiet Emma's absence provided.

* * *

In the spring, Orrin Gardner of Swansea visited the Borden sisters for a few days. He was from one of the oldest families in New England, and his actions betrayed his heritage. He was always solicitous of Emma and Lizzie, making sure the servants were behaving properly and that the neighbors were not causing any problems. He acted as if the lack of a man in our house, gave him an obligation to ensure their comfort and safety.

Emma appreciated everything about him. Lizzie, on the other hand, was often irritated by his attitude. She had been handling all the problems she and Emma faced quite well and resented his belief that she was not capable of doing that because she was a woman. Yet, at times, his behavior made her feel protected, like she did when her father was alive.

As they watched him ride away, Emma sighed. "He will make someone a good husband."

Lizzie laughed. "Do you have designs on Mr. Gardner, sister?"

"Oh, my, no." A blush spread across Emma's cheekbones. "I am far too old for a young man like him. He would be more appropriate for you."

"Emma, you know my feelings on that subject. No man, no marriage, no loss of freedom."

"I venture to say that the right man would make you change your mind."

"The right man does not exist. I would not want to live with a man under the same roof again. They have one set of rules for themselves and another for us."

"Every woman, if she succeeds at anything, does so by gaining some man's attention."

"Really, Emma. Look at me. Look at yourself. And look what men brought down on our heads."

* * *

The second anniversary of Lizzie's acquittal left her in a muddle. Her mind felt like cotton wool, and the few friends that dropped by to congratulate her could not penetrate her haze and distance. For weeks, Lizzie was lost in that numb state until suddenly she realized July had arrived.

Lizzie returned from a shopping trip and hurried to find her sister. "The Reverend Mr. Jubb has resigned."

"Why? Is he ill?"

"I don't think so. After five years here with us, he is sailing away back to his home in Mosely, England."

"He was such a good friend; how much we shall miss him."

Lizzie sighed. "My most stalwart defender, never to raise the banner in my defense again. I cannot believe he is abandoning me."

"He is not abandoning you, Lizzie. He is returning home, and home means as much to him as it does to you."

"In all likelihood, we will never see him again in our lifetimes."

On the day he left, as if a sign from the heavens, armyworms attacked the Borden's field of oats on the other side of the river. Thoughts of biblical locusts and raining frogs filled Lizzie's head with dread. The crop was a total loss.

Lizzie's urge to escape city life to relax in the country was gratified when Mrs. Gardner, Orrin's mother, sent a message welcoming her to visit them at their home in Coles Station near Swansea. "Leave the smokestacks behind and come enjoy nature in all its glory." Lizzie spent a month there and left with warm feelings for the entire family and with a promise that Orrin would visit again in the fall.

He arrived just in time for the Sound Money Parade celebrating the Republican victory of William McKinley. He defeated William Jennings Bryan, who was the nominee of the Democratic party as well as the Populist party. In addition to the two front runners, there was a third candidate, Senator John Palmer, who was nominated by the New Democratic Party, an entity formed by conservatives who did not support Bryan.

The powers-that-be in Fall River were determined to make their celebration the best one in Massachusetts. Emma and Lizzie jumped into the spirit of the excitement—spreading bunting across their porch railings and windows and hoisting American flags on poles. Throughout the yard, they hung lanterns from trees and fence posts and put torches by the gate. Everyone on their block joined in, creating a festive street scene and a strong sense of community. When Orrin arrived, he brought fireworks to set off in the yard when the parade wound its way up to their street.

At 7:30 that evening, they sat on the porch sipping iced tea. They all jumped when a large blast from the fire alarm roared in their ears. Orrin rose to his feet. "Is there a fire?"

Lizzie and Emma laughed. Lizzie said, "No, no, no, Orrin. That's the first signal that the parade is about to begin."

"I would think that would terrify some people who have lived through a fire."

"We all knew, Orrin." Lizzie smiled at their guest. "We simply forgot to tell you."

The second blast fired off. "They are on their way now," Lizzie said.

They heard the parade before they could see because of the loud noise produced by fourteen bands, five drum corps, and ten thousand parade marchers heading toward the hill.

"I can already smell the gunpowder from the fireworks," Emma said.

"Yes, I wish they would hurry—the anticipation is building like a fire in my chest."

When the show began, they were overwhelmed by the display. The Quequehan Club marched up the street in stovepipes, dark hats, canes, and mammoth yellow chrysanthemums sprouting from their chests. A delegation of 300 from the Fall River hat factory, accompanied by the Fall River Brass Band, marched by wearing beaver hats covered with pure gold leaf, carrying flags, and wearing red, white, and blue neckties.

Forty men on bicycles and sixty men on foot—one hundred in white caps and gloves—represented the Sanford Spinning Company. They were followed by the company float featuring two women dressed in puritanical garb spinning and winding yarn.

The Globe Street Railway made their presence known with horses caparisoned with lights and their extension ladder covered with illumination, creating a spellbinding brightness. Lizzie and Emma blinked their eyes after they passed. Orrin said, "Those lights were blinding, I can hardly see the next group."

The trolley repair wagon was decorated with bunting and flags, and Charley Tolman led a band of 75 conductors and motormen from the company. Twenty-four coal teamsters armed with regulation scoop shovels followed in their wake. The Butchers and Grocers Association members were all clad in white duck and were followed by two men with giant gold bugs on their backs.

At that point, Orrin lost sight of proper decorum. He jumped up and down and cheered as the Swansea band came into view. "Look, look, that's J.J. O'Brien leading them. That music is enough to make me want to go down and march with them. And Kilburn and Lincoln company's division are following them wearing stovepipe hats. If I only had one with me, I could slip in unnoticed."

"I do not think you could go anywhere unnoticed, Mr. Gardner," Emma simpered.

Lizzie stared at her—*flirting at her age. I was right, she does have designs on him. I wonder if the feeling is mutual.*

Lizzie's favorite part of the parade came into view—the Golden Rain Makers. Eighty men led by Chief Lots of Noise, George Hoar. Each man was canopied by an umbrella and carrying implements for making a racket— clanking pans, scraping graters, whistles, and more. Lizzie laughed at the cacophony and the comic moves of the marchers. Emma put her hands over her ears and thought about retreating inside the house.

The sisters cherished that night on the hill and felt embraced by the gayety and the strong sense of community. Emma believed the camaraderie and acceptance would remain long after the night was over. Lizzie, though, was certain it would fade away with the last firework. Lizzie was right.

Chapter Fifty-Five

The visit with Orrin Gardner was quite pleasant, and viewing the parade with him made it twice as exciting. Lizzie was certain that their enjoyment would come at a price. And it did. The newspapers launched new gossip.

Lizzie choked on the headlines: "WEDDING BELLS May Soon Ring Out for Lizzie A. Borden;" "TO MARRY A SCHOOL TEACHER: Reported Engagement of Miss Lizzie A. Borden and Orrin T. Gardiner of Swansea, a Fall River Suburb." The article talked about the new wardrobe being made for her as if she did not have new clothing created every year. They pointed out a white satin gown in her garment order as proof that the lies were the truth.

Lizzie paced the living room. "Why can they not forget I exist? Why do they feed on the remnants of my soul."

"You cannot stop the rumormongers, but one would think the newspapers would have gotten as much attention for mocking the gossip as they are for promulgating it."

"Why will they not leave me alone?"

"If you did get married, Lizzie, that would stop all the rumors of your suitors."

Lizzie banged her fist on the back of the sofa. "No! Never! I will not put my life under the thumb of a man ever again. You can if you want. Perhaps you should marry Orrin. You seem much closer to him than I."

"Do not be ridiculous, Lizzie. He is only 30 years old—I am more than a decade older. I would look foolish, and he would look greedy."

Reporters came in droves, but each one was sent away with minimal courtesy. Orrin Gardner set the story straight, confronting the newspapermen with the truth.

* * *

Just before Christmas, Emma and Lizzie went to Providence to do some shopping. At Tilden and Thurber, a shop where they had made many purchases over the years, Lizzie saw two paintings on porcelain, *Love's Dream* and *Love's Awakening*. "Emma, aren't they beautiful? I must have them."

Lizzie brought them home and hung them in the parlor at Maplecroft. Mary Gardner paid a visit and was as smitten by their beauty as Lizzie. In the holiday spirit, Lizzie told her to pick the one she liked best and take it home with her.

Early the next February, Lizzie, and Emma were reading when their new "Maggie," Helen Smith, interrupted her. "Miss Lisbeth, there is a detective here to see you."

"Tell him I am not receiving visitors today."

A few minutes later, Helen returned. "Miss Lisbeth, he is very insistent. He said that he is not paying a social visit. He is here on official business, and he has a uniformed policeman with him."

Emma raised her head on the other side of the room. "Lizzie, it is best if you see him. As you and I well know, the police do not give up until they get what they want."

Lizzie exhaled her displeasure and straightened her posture. "Very well, Maggie, show him in."

With bushy eyebrows and beady eyes that bore down on Lizzie, the detective introduced himself. "Miss Borden, I am Inspector Frank Parker from the Providence Police Department. I believe you have already met Officer Allen."

Lizzie turned to Allen. "Officer, I wish you no disrespect, but I have been trying to forget the day we met."

As his face pinkened, Lizzie was pleased. "I regret we met under such horrid circumstances, Miss Borden. I am not here in any capacity except as an escort for an out-of-town detective."

"I imagine you will gladly arrest me if the gentleman requests that you do so."

Allen's face brightened to red. "I doubt that will be the case, Miss Borden. There is no warrant."

"All of you lied about the warrant before, Officer Allen. I am certain you recall that."

Allen cast his gaze on the floor, inhaling deeply, but he did not utter a word.

Lizzie turned back to the detective. "You've neglected to introduce the third person who arrived here today."

"He is the art manager at Tilden & Thurber. Having said that, you probably know why we are here."

Lizzie was miffed that the man's name was not mentioned, but she let that disrespect pass without comment. "I cannot say that I do, sir."

Detective Frank pinned her with his eyes. "There has been a theft of porcelain paintings from the store, Miss Borden, as I am sure you are aware."

"Why should I be aware of that, and what does it have to do with me?"

"We believe you stole both of them."

"Oh. And did I murder someone to keep from being caught in the act?"

Emma hissed at her, but Lizzie shrugged her off. Officer Allen shifted on his feet, clearly not at ease.

The third man raised his arm and pointed at the far wall. "There it is. That is the missing painting."

The detective asked, "How did you come into possession of that porcelain art, Miss Borden?"

"I purchased it."

"Where, Miss Borden?"

"At Tilden & Thurber, if I am not mistaken."

"How much did you pay?"

CHAPTER FIFTY-FIVE

"As I recall, $16."

The art manager exploded. "Ridiculous! One of them was priced at $75, the other at $50. Sixteen dollars? Unheard of."

"Excuse me if my memory is faulty," Lizzie said.

"Is that the only thing you purchased at Tilden & Thurber that day?" the inspector asked.

"I believe it is."

"How do you explain, then, the porcelain painting you gave to Mrs. Gardner?"

"What are you talking about, sir?"

The art manager smirked. "She brought it into our store for a small repair and framing. She told us you gave it to her. Is she lying?"

Lizzie swallowed hard and forced a smile and a giggle. "Oh, yes. I'd completely forgotten about giving that to her. I give so many gifts to friends during the holidays. Yes, I purchased them both from Tilden & Thurber."

"There is no record of the sale of those artworks, Miss Borden," the detective said.

"The faulty bookkeeping at the store is not my fault."

The art manager took a step towards her and glared. "We know you stole them, Miss Borden."

"How dare you, sir? I have been a loyal customer of your business for years. I have spent quite a bit of money in your shop. And you call me a thief? I am outraged."

"We want the painting returned, Miss Borden. If you refuse to return it to me today, the company will have no recourse but to request a warrant for your arrest."

Lizzie jerked to her feet and pointed at the door. "Out! Out! Get out of my house, and do not darken my door again. And you, Officer Allen, tell your Marshall Hilliard if you continue to assist these charlatans, I will complain to the governor."

Once Helen had seen the men out, Lizzie collapsed on the sofa. Emma sat beside her and patted her arm. "Lizzie, is there any possibility that you might have walked out of the store and forgotten to pay for them."

Lizzie pushed her away and stood, looking down at her sister. "You, Emma? You, too? You think I am a thief?"

"No, Lizzie, no. Just sometimes you are a bit absent-minded, that is all."

"And furthermore, sister dear, if that was the case, why did they not come straight to me or ask me about it the next time I was in the store? But, no, they go to the police. Why? Because they want to terrify me and threaten me with another arrest. The employee is lying or confused. Otherwise, he would have done what others have done in the past when they came to Father about something I picked up and forgot to pay for before leaving the store. Father always paid. I would have done so as well if that were the case. I am sick of being mistreated by everyone."

At dinner time, Lizzie still seethed. "I am going to go to Newport in the morning to avoid the reporters who will surely show up at our door. Helen, you know how to handle them, don't you?"

"Yes, Miss Lisbeth. No problem."

It took the journalists a week to grab the story and run with it. Lizzie's timing could not have been worse. She arrived home just as the articles hit the newspapers. The articles confirmed Lizzie's suspicion that a warrant was issued for her arrest but had never been served. In hopes of stopping the deluge of bad stories, Lizzie returned the artwork in her possession and swore to never darken the shop's doors again. And just like that the incident dissipated like fog in the sunshine.

Despite the continued negative press, Lizzie and Emma were making a substantial sum of money on their rental properties. "Emma, we have not had a vacancy in our rental properties for quite some time."

"Surprisingly, tenants—many of whom would not associate us socially—do not feel a social obligation to avoid business arrangements with us."

"I was thinking about buying a new property, but then I talked to Mr. Cook. He thinks that we could pay off our investment far more quickly if we built a brick addition to one of our buildings."

"Did he suggest which one?"

"I suggested our building at South Main and Anawan, and he agreed. He thought we could construct it to add a store and more offices. I told him to seek a permit from the authorities."

"Without checking with me?" Emma raised her chin in defiance.

"Please, Emma, I am not going behind your back. Even if he gets the permit, we will not start building without your approval."

"I should hope not. Still, you should discuss these plans with me first."

"It was a spontaneous moment that arose between Mr. Cook and me. Do not make this any more significant than that." Lizzie wondered how her sister would react if she knew that she had visited Mr. Cook for the sole purpose of discussing an expansion of their rental properties.

One evening after dinner, Emma and Lizzie sat in the parlor reading. Lizzie was immersed in an odd book, *Dracula* by Bram Stoker, that Mary Holmes brought back for Lizzie when she last visited London. She had read only a few pages and was not certain she would be able to finish it.

Emma was perusing a copy of Pearson's, a British magazine of literature, politics, and the arts—another gift from Mary—which contained a new episode of H.G. Wells' *War of the Worlds*. The pages fluttered, and the periodical hit the floor with a thunk as Emma screamed.

Lizzie thought her sister had been frightened by H.G. Wells until she followed her sister's pointing finger. In the window, she saw a frightening sight: the face of a man pressed against the glass of the window, peering in at them. He disappeared, and the doorbell rang one sharp note, then another, and the bell was held down for a protracted time. Emma and Lizzie clung to each other.

Helen went to the front door and yelled, "Get out of here, you old sod, or I'll call the police!"

"I just want to meet Miss Lizzie Borden," he slurred.

"Well, you cannot. You are trespassing. Go away."

Everything grew quiet. "Is he gone, Helen?" Lizzie whispered.

The man's face popped up in another window loudly babbling unintelligible noises.

Helen drew close to the sisters. "Miss Emma. Miss Lisbeth. Into the kitchen, please." When they were all in the other room, she added, "I am going out the back and fetching the police. You can either stay here or go up to your rooms. Whatever you do, do not go into the parlor before I return."

"No, Helen," Emma protested. "He could attack you."

"If he does, I'll scream my head off, the neighbors will hear, and the police will come. Either way, the job will be done."

Lizzie and Emma stood in the kitchen, too unnerved to sit down and too frightened to risk being seen if they attempted to go up the hallway stairs. For the first moments, they held their breath, listening as hard as they could for Helen's screams. All they heard was the man's muffled voice ranting nonsense and his fists pounding on the walls of the house.

Without any sound to give him away, the man's voice grew louder and closer. He taunted in a sing-song voice. "Miss Borden, Miss Borden, please come to the door." The sisters realized that he now stood by the kitchen wall. His ranting fell out of rhythm, and his words were indistinct.

Emma's breathing grew ragged. "Should we go up the back stairs and shelter in Helen's room?"

"No. We'd be trapped there if he got inside. We are safer here than anywhere else right now." Lizzie hardly heard the man now because the beating of her heart echoed in her ears.

At last, they heard a policeman's whistle. They felt the tension melting and their internal shaking growing still.

Outside, the shouting continued as the police chased and restrained the man. Both sisters jumped and gasped when they heard a knock on the kitchen door. "Miss Lisbeth. Miss Emma. It's Helen, please let me in."

Once inside, she said, "The police want me to come to the station and answer a few questions. I shan't be long. I will take the keys so that you do not need to stay up, but if you do, I will tell you what I find out."

The sisters sat down at the dining room table to wait. "Should we get a painting for that wall?" Lizzie asked.

"I don't know. Do you still like the paint color in here?"

"I suppose." Lizzie's eyes roamed around the room and back to Emma, but she could think of nothing to say.

Emma stared at the floor and slumped in her seat. They sat in silence, lost in their own thoughts. Sighing as they relived the evening in their heads.

Both women startled and jumped when the key slid into the front door. They hurried to the hallway to greet Helen.

"He was drunk—horribly drunk—so drunk he could barely walk without the assistance of the officers."

"Who is he?" both sisters asked.

"A journeyman hatter from Boston by the name of John Bleyle. He kept repeating that he was fascinated with you, Miss Lisbeth, and just wanted to meet you. They put him in a cell to sleep it off."

"Thank you, Helen. Your courageous willingness to help us in our time of distress will never be forgotten," Lizzie said. "please let us know if you need anything."

"No need for gratitude, Miss Lizzie. You have paid me back tenfold since you hired me. No one has treated me with more kindness since I left my home in Scotland eight years ago."

None of the three women rested well that night. Every small sound reverberated from the street, waking them from slumber. When the sun rose, the bright sunshine wiped away their cobwebs of worry. Lizzie hummed as she stepped outside to fill the bird feeders. Emma and Lizzie both smiled at each other during breakfast but dared not speak for fear it would disrupt the new day's blissful peace.

It shattered that evening. The ugly, debauched face peered in the window again. No one screamed, but Helen sighed. "I'll go out the back door. If I went out the front, he might slip inside."

"Helen, are you sure you want to do this again?"

"He is harmless, Miss Emma. I'll be fine. Just ignore him." In a short time, Helen returned with two police officers who escorted him back to jail with the housekeeper by their side.

An hour later, Helen was back. "The officers told me when he left the jail this morning, he had no memory of what happened last night. You won't have to worry about him coming back tomorrow, though. This time, he was fined thirty dollars, which he could not pay. They committed him to the jail."

"Will this ever end?" Lizzie wailed. "Why won't they leave me alone? It's been five years since Father died, and they still hound me. All I want is to be forgotten, by everyone, forever."

Chapter Fifty-Six

Lizzie and Emma purchased the property adjoining their home on French Street. They planned to hire a team of men to build a barn in order that their carriage horse would have decent shelter. "Emma, It needs to be big enough to accommodate two horses," Lizzie said.

"Why? We do not need two horses, Lizzie."

"No, Emma, not now. But think ahead. When our horse is too old to pull the carriage, we want to have space for him to die in peace. Then, we will need room for a horse to replace him in the harness. After years of hard work, I will not sell him to a glue factory or to anyone who would mistreat, neglect, or abuse him." While she spoke, she thought of her father and wished that someway, somehow, she could have her independence while he still lived. She saw him sitting in a rocking chair on the porch, growing older and grayer with a carriage blanket wrapped around his legs while he slowly faded into eternal night.

"You are right. They do much for our ease and comfort. We need to do all we can to support them as long as they live."

The next year and a half remained peaceful for the sisters. Lizzie hired Ida Carlson, a Swedish immigrant, as her personal maid. Ida washed and brushed her hair and took care of her clothes. Emma and Lizzie spent a lot of time out of town on shopping trips and visiting friends. Newspaper reporters left them alone. Lizzie thought the world had finally forgotten her.

In January 1899, the spotlight returned to their lives. Emma and Lizzie sat down for a meal in the dining room when a loud sound echoed in the distance. Emma clutched her arms around her stomach. "That sounded like an explosion."

"Really, Emma? Most likely, a large tree toppled over nearby."

"I am going out on the porch to see if I can find anything amiss."

Lizzie followed her through the doors and sniffed smoke in the air. "It looks like another street fire Emma."

"I wonder if it is one of our properties."

"They are all insured. You don't need to worry about that."

Emma wrung a handkerchief in her hands. "But what about the tenants?"

"It's after six. The shops must be closed by now."

"Still. I need to know. I'll send the coachman for the carriage and bundle up for a drive downstreet. Are you coming?"

Lizzie could not imagine any good they could do, but if it kept Emma from fretting all night, it would be worth it. As soon as they got near, navigating the carriage grew difficult because of all the gathered crowds. The air filled with enormous clouds of dense, gray, smelly smoke that billowed out of C.E. MacComber company's clothing store in the A.J. Borden building.

The new coachman, Joseph Tetrault, jumped out into the crowd and reported to the sisters. "What sounded like an explosion was the glass blowing out into the street from the MacComber windows on the first floor. If you look where the light hits, you can see big and small chunks of glass lying all over the sidewalk and street. Lucky no one was injured by the flying glass."

"Thank you, Joseph," Lizzie said.

Emma did not want to leave, but she was terrified. She clutched her sister's hand to the point of causing pain. Her eyes were wide and darting like a cornered animal. She moaned and whimpered every few minutes.

Police officers arrived with rope to push the crowd back from the fire. Joseph did not have to move the carriage back very far, but it did make a difference—the horse's agitation settled down considerably, and the sisters could breathe easier. They doubted, though, that they would ever get the smell of smoke out of the dresses they wore.

At first, the firefighters were all focused on that one building. A few broke loose and moved over to the 5- and 10-cent store when they saw smoke billowing up into that space as well. A fire raged in the basement of both structures.

The store had still been open for business and police officers had to rescue the clerks inside. They emerged bedraggled and coughing. A fireman opened the windows on the building's first floor to allow the smoke to escape up to the skies.

"Look, Emma," Lizzie pointed at the Borden building. "That is Mr. Cook, is it not?"

Emma followed the direction of the finger and saw a man stumbling out with an armload of paper and books.

"Joseph," Lizzie said, "please go speak to Mr. Cook and find out if we can be of assistance."

Joseph helped the business manager carry the burden to his carriage and then returned to the sisters. "Mr. Cook stuffed everything that was irreplaceable into his large safe and was trusting that it was as secure from fire as it was advertised. He said just to be sure, he brought all the Borden records with him."

"Thank you, Joseph," Lizzie said.

"That was the third time," Emma spluttered. "Now I know I heard you correctly the earlier. You called our coachman by his given name."

"Of course, I did. He is a good man and always available when we need him. Why wouldn't I?"

"That is not the proper salutation to a servant."

"Oh, please, Emma. You think you do better by calling our housekeeper Maggie? I've been trying to correct that bad habit myself, but I cannot always remember to call her Helen. Who cares about artificial niceties any longer? You know a lot of coachmen would not consider working for us because of the past. Why should I not demonstrate an appreciation by being less formal with him?"

Emma gasped. "And does he call you Lizzie?"

"Of course not. He calls me Miss Lisbeth and you Miss Emma. Don't say that is improper. If he called us both Miss Borden, we would never know who he was talking to."

A large blaze spewed out of the air shaft on top of the building, putting a quick end to their argument. "It's been more than an hour, and the firemen still do not have it under control," Lizzie said.

Emma's hand went to her throat. "My eyes are burning, and my throat aches. We will not learn anything more tonight. Let us go home."

Lizzie was about to argue but then she noticed their horse shaking his head and acting distressed. She ordered the carriage to head home. The sisters coughed all the way inside and late into the night.

A couple of mornings later, they walked downstreet to meet with Mr. Cook for a tour and summary of the fire damage and its cause. Long before reaching Main Street, the unpleasant odor of burnt fabric clung to the damp air. Carriages travelling the road in front of the damaged building slowed as occupants gaped at the ruins. Voices were hushed as if at a funeral, but the birds sang melodies in the trees, their cheerful voices striking a discordant note amidst the destruction.

Mr. Cook took them first to the A.J. Borden building. "I heard glass exploding. I thought at first someone had thrown a rock through the window. I went out into the hall and saw it was full of smoke. I rushed to each upper tenant and warned them before returning to my office and shoving files into my safe. I grabbed my typewriter and as many papers as I could and groped my way down the stairs and out into the street where you saw me.

"The basement was flooded from the efforts to put out the fire. The fire department spent hours pumping it out to uncover the cause of the conflagration. It is still a bit damp down there, but it is drying out."

Lizzie peered down the basement door. "Can we see it?"

"You can, but I do not recommend it. You would soil your dresses on the floor. In a couple of days, though, you won't be able to tell it had been full of water. You had $40,000 worth of insurance on this structure, but the damage estimates are in the range of $30,000. You'll have no trouble recouping your losses.

They stopped next at the clothing store where they met up with the manager, Mr. Chilson. "We did all right. We were covered for up to $17,000 but the destroyed stock only had a value of $8000. We'll be able to start right up once the building is repaired."

"We are committed to completing that project as soon as possible," Cook assured him.

Charlton's Five and Ten Cent shops did not fare as well. "Looks as if we had $15,000 in merchandise loss but only $12,000 in insurance. The steams of water played havoc with the crockery and chinaware, causing extensive breakage to many items that would have survived the fire itself."

At the fire department, Cook asked Fire Marshall Whitcomb, "Have you been able to isolate a cause for the fire?"

The Marshall sighed. "Arson. We think it was arson. A fireman found a tin pail of oil-soaked waste and several bunches of matches in the basement of the A.J. Borden building. Can you think of any good reason for those materials to be there, Mr. Cook?"

Cook shook his head. "No, I cannot. Do you know who is responsible? Do you have any suspects?"

"No, not yet. If we find out, you'll be the first to know. I'm sorry, Misses Borden. We will keep investigating and hope for the best."

On the walk back home, Emma wrung her hands, mumbling about why anyone would want to destroy their property. Once they reached Maplecroft, Emma paced in the parlor before stopping in front of her sister. "Was this personal, Lizzie? Do you think the building was set on fire because we—you and I—own it?"

"I do not know, Emma. I am pleasantly surprised that no one has yet accused me of striking the match. Will you ever learn to call me Lisbeth?"

"Oh, Lizz—Lisbeth, at a time like this, you squabble about the name I call you? No one would think that you started the fire."

"At a time like this, Emma? At a time when the past is about to be dragged out of its grave again? It's been years, Emma, and still you refuse my request. As for no one accusing me, why not? There are many who still snub me. There are those who think I am guilty of murdering Father. Why would they not think I would be an arsonist, too?"

Emma stared at her in silence before sitting down on her favorite chair and picking up a magazine.

The next morning, Mr. Cook dropped by bringing bad news. "The insurance rates for the building and the businesses are taking a dramatic turn upwards—nearly a twenty percent increase."

"Did you check out rates with other companies?" Lizzie asked.

"Finding another insurance business that would be willing to take us on will be impossible because of our recent history."

Lizzie huffed. "Arson is not the fault of the building owner or the businesses unless they find proof to connect one of those people to the blaze."

"That is the other bad news, ladies. They found no direct evidence of the perpetrator. In fact, what they found in the basement puts a lot of the blame for the extensive damages on our company."

Emma furrowed her brows. "Why is that, Mr. Cook?"

"The fire spread as rapidly as it did because all that separated the two basements was a wooden picket gate—a barrier that the flames passed through as if it were paper. Chief Langford pointed out another problem in the building itself. The superior construction of the building made it difficult for the firefighters."

"Superior building standards are now a problem for the insurance company?" Lizzie said.

"In this case, Miss Lizzie, it caused problems for the firefighters. The structure was supported by the kind of great beams usually used in mills. That was topped by two inches of cement with two inches of hard pine on top of that. When the firemen tried to cut through the floor to get to the fire below ground in the notion store, it was nearly impossible. The government is planning to require regular fire inspections and insisting that all public buildings submit detailed floor plans in case of another fire."

Lizzie snorted. "So, our fire will help prevent further fires and the insurance companies are rewarding us by raising our rates? Ridiculous."

"There is a bit of good news. Mr. Charlton's losses are not as bad as he feared they might be and his insurance covered it all. He is having a fire sale of salvageable goods, and once his stock is gone, we can tear up the floor and replace the beams. The workmen have estimated a month to return that building to its original condition. We do not know the extent of damages to the music store yet because we need an expert to assess water and smoke damage to the pianos and other instruments."

Lizzie sighed. "Any more news?"

"A sad note to add. The oldest member of the fire department has died because of the conditions he faced in our fire. The two of you should send some monies to the widow. Don't look at me like that, Miss Lizzie. If you do not compensate her, you will be criticized for a lack of concern."

Chapter Fifty-Seven

Because of the intimate nature of the services provided by a personal maid, Lizzie and Ida enjoyed a close relationship. Lizzie felt free to talk to her openly about her tribulations of her legal problems and her disappointments with life on the hill. When Ida planned to marry, Lizzie offered to host the wedding at Maplecroft. Lizzie hired her own dressmaker to make Ida's wedding finery.

The marriage on September 23, 1899, was the bright point of the year for Lizzie. She threw herself into the preparations and decorations and provided a harvest table full of food and drink. The dancing went on into the wee hours of the night.

Less than a month later, Lizzie's bad luck returned. A runaway horse pulling a wagon threw two passengers on Third Street. The crazed horse rounded a corner onto Pleasant Street and headed straight for a carriage holding Lizzie and her coachman, Joseph. They saw him coming and feared he would collide and knock them to the ground—perhaps to their death.

Joseph yelled at the horse and waved his arms, causing the horse to veer away at the last minute. Joseph leapt to the ground and to Lizzie's side. He made sure she was unharmed. They turned around and headed for home.

Lizzie repaid Joseph's kindness and devotion with a gift of a heavy gold watch chain and fob set with an onyx intaglio intricately cut with a horse's head. When Emma heard what she had done, she exploded. "How could you give a servant such an expensive gift?"

"He saved my life, sister. Do you think that has no value?"

"Yes, it does. It is bad enough that you call him Joseph in front of others but now, this gift, what were you thinking?"

"I was thinking that I was grateful to him, and he deserved to have that acknowledged."

Emma stood, placed her hands on her hips, and glared down at Lizzie. "Well, you know what you have done now? Gossip is spreading all over the hill."

"What is new?"

"They are saying you are having an affair with Joseph."

"The people of Fall River lie about me all the time."

Emma shook her head. "Do you not see the gravity of this rumor? First, they are accusing you of the sin of fornication, a violation of the rules of God and the church. Secondly, you are involved with a servant—a servant—that is an abomination to everyone in society. It is just not done."

Lizzie smiled. "Emma, please. It is not being done. There is nothing more to my relationship with Joseph than a grateful employer and a loyal coachman who saved my life."

"I live here, too, Lizzie. The appearance is unseemly. Many may doubt the rumor, but they will clearly see that you have behaved in a manner to bring opprobrium on us all."

"Emma, after what I have been through and how I have been shunned despite my acquittal. I cannot afford to care about what others think of me. If I did, I would not sleep at night, and I would never leave this house."

"I do not believe you, Lizzie. You care every bit as much as I do. You are simply more reckless than I. Please think of me before you make any further rash decisions. What you do impacts me as well." Emma swirled her skirts as she turned and went up the stairs to her room.

As 1899 approached its end, newspapers were filled with reflections of the last century and predictions for the next. Pulitzer's World published special supplements to the newspapers including fold-out illustrations of bridges and airship vessels soaring over the New York City skyline. Henry Siegal, a retail magnate, predicted that the addition of moving staircases would revolutionize department stores.

Everywhere, predictions of cataclysmic disaster and visions of idealistic utopias crowded the pages of periodicals. Newspapers ran full-page ads heralding the arrival of the twentieth century as the impetus for the Second Coming of Jesus Christ.

The *New York Times* quoted scientists saying, "The sun would become solid and go out, leaving the solar system in darkness. The earth will become a lifeless, uninhabited ball of ice." A *Baltimore Sun* editorial called for social improvement before technology: "The twentieth century will do an excellent work if it shall make no more discoveries or inventions of any kind but shall utilize for the good of all men the discoveries and inventions of the nineteenth and more especially if it shall develop the moral and intellectual forces to keep pace with those material forces that the past century has set to work."

To Lizzie Borden, the coming of the new century was a ray of hope. The last decade destroyed her peace. She hoped the arrival of a new age brought with it a generous dose of good luck, good fortune and calm.

Chapter Fifty-Eight

In the new year, Lizzie determined to make 1900 a better year than the last. In January, she attended Boston Theatre's performance of "Mary Stuart: A Tragedy in Five Acts." Lizzie was moved by the luxurious life and untimely death of the flamboyant queen. She saw Mary as someone who was as misunderstood and judged as much as she had been.

Lizzie was back in Boston in February at the Bowdoin Square Theatre to see "The Bowery." Although not impressed with the performance, she still rejoiced at the experience—sitting in the audience with hubbub all around, people talking, chairs creaking, papers rattling, all leading to the magic moment when the curtains begin to part and a hush spread like a magic spell over the theatre.

She was optimistic about the year until the death of Justice Dewey in March thrust her into the public eye again. His obituary and remembrance pieces all mentioned his role in the Lizzie Borden trial. She stayed at home to let the renewed interest in her die down. She felt Maplecroft was her sanctuary, and she curled into its comfort for a couple of weeks.

Ida kept her company during the day. Ida's new marital home was on North Main Street, but every day, she travelled up the hill to care for Lizzie's needs. Early that summer, Lizzie noticed something had changed. "Ida, are you well?"

"Oh, yes, ma'am. My stomach is giving me fits in the morning but the rest of the time I have never felt better."

Lizzie drew close to her, put a finger under her chin, and tilted it up. "There is something very different about you." Lizzie gasped and put her fingers over her lips. She whispered in Ida's ear, "Are you with child?"

Ida stepped back, grinned, and nodded.

Lizzie kept a close watch over her from then on. When the intense heat rolled in, she saw that Ida's fingers grew puffy and stiff, making her drop hair pins and brushes while she tended to her employer.

"Ida, you need to take a leave of absence. Your fingers must be causing you intense pain when you fix my hair," Lizzie said.

"I appreciate the thought, Miss Lisbeth, but we really do need the money I bring home. We are saving all we can to open our own business."

"Don't be silly. I will send money to your home, and I will hold your job for you until you can return. It causes me pain to see you suffering."

Ida's baby, Alice, was born on August 2, 1900. In a couple of weeks, Ida returned to her job at Maplecroft with her infant. Lizzie adored her. "She is the most precious, precocious thing I have ever seen."

Soon after the new year, Alice learned to crawl. She picked up speed and an independent attitude quickly and needed more active attention. Ida retired from service to Lizzie's great disappointment. "I will miss seeing both of you every day. Please, please, visit me as often as possible."

* * *

In early 1901, Lizzie returned from a theatre trip to Boston and noticed that all the pictures on the parlor wall were cockeyed. "Helen, Helen, please come into the parlor."

"Yes, Miss Lisbeth. I am on my way."

"Helen, what happened to all these pictures."

"Sorry, Miss Lisbeth. I put a cloth on the broom to wipe all the dust off them. No matter how hard I tried, I couldn't straighten them out."

Lizzie sighed. "Get the stepladder, please. I will show you the only way to do it correctly.

Helen retrieved the stepladder, set it up and checked to make sure it was sturdy. Lizzie climbed up the rungs to the top and straightened the picture directly in front of her and then reached to the right and straightened that one as well. "See Helen. It is so easy when you use the ladder."

Lizzie leaned to the left to adjust one more picture before descending and moving the ladder to another spot. As she reached, the ladder teetered. Helen rushed up to steady it, but she was too late. Lizzie lost her balance and fell to the floor, stretching out an arm to break her fall.

Helen ran to her side. Lizzie's face turned ash white, and the pain raced up past her elbow to her shoulder and exploded in her head. Helen tried to get her into a more comfortable position, but every little movement made Lizzie groan in agony. Helen yelled for Emma, who rushed into the parlor. With one woman on each side, they eased Lizzie off the floor and into a chair.

"Lizzie, your wrist is swollen," Emma said.

"Don't touch it, don't touch it, or please don't touch it." Lizzie moaned and gnashed her teeth.

"Helen, go get the doctor." Emma hurried to the kitchen and returned with a wooden spoon. She slipped it into Lizzie's mouth. "Bite down on it when the pain intensifies."

With the next surge of pain, Lizzie bit down hard on the wood. It helped manage the pain, but Lizzie feared she would break it in two and end up with a mouthful of splinters.

Dr. Gordon arrived and kneeled in front of Lizzie with one raised knee. He carefully laid the injured arm across his leg. Lizzie struggled to keep from screaming straight into his face, biting down even harder on the spoon.

"You've broken your wrist, Miss Borden. We will have to make a plaster of Paris cast to immobilize it until it heals." He filled a syringe with morphine, and as the drug surged through her veins, Lizzie drifted farther and farther away from her pain and the room itself. Her only awareness of the casting procedure was that it seemed to last for an eternity.

Lizzie turned grumpy as she chaffed at her limitations. Emma was always by her side when needed but avoided her company, her complaints, and her rude comments as much as she could. When Dr. Gordon finally removed the splint and the cast, Lizzie was appalled. "Look at my arm. The wrist is puny and as white and disgusting as the worm in an apple. Is something wrong with it?"

The doctor chuckled. "The only thing wrong with it is that it had to be covered up to heal. In no time, it will look like your other arm. Try to be gentle with it until its strength returns. You will soon forget that it ever looked that strange."

In May, Joseph opened the back door and asked Helen to have Miss Lisbeth join him outside. "There is something she needs to see."

Lisbeth joined him in the yard, and he led her to the bed of imported tulips she had planted last fall when the popularity of the flower swept through society. The ground was torn up, and all the flower bulbs were gone. "Oh, Joseph, who could have done this to me?"

"I don't know, Miss Lisbeth. Should I go get the police?"

"Yes, Joseph, thank you."

Tears slid from Lizzie's eyes as she stared at the desecrated ground. *Will it ever end? Will my persecution continue until the day I die?* By the time an officer arrived, she'd agitated herself from sorrow to anger. "You must find the culprit who violated my property."

"We are looking for the guilty party, Miss Borden. You are not the only one in the neighborhood to lose your bulbs."

"Are you sure? I thought it must be one of my enemies."

"Not unless Mr. Kerr and Mr. Skiff have also antagonized the same people. Adding your bulbs to the list of stolen ones, there are more than $100 worth that have been taken in this area."

Two days later, Marshall Hilliard knocked on the door with news that the perpetrators had been apprehended. "There were four young thieves involved, Miss Borden, ages 11 to 14. They no longer had the bulbs because they had sold every one of them to the highest bidder."

"Are you charging their parents with theft?"

"No, Miss Borden. The parents had no idea of what their boys had done."

"I doubt that," Lizzie snipped. "I will have to sue them for damages."

"You might want to check with an attorney, but the families have nothing of value. I would guess you would win the case, but still be left with empty hands."

Chapter Fifty-Nine

For a year and a half, Lizzie and Emma had a time of peace together. The newspapers ignored them, and no one made their lives any more uncomfortable. The world outside their doors, however, caused a major uproar.

Much to the sisters' delight, President William McKinley was reelected in 1900. He went on a two-day trip to the Pan-American Exposition in Buffalo, New York, early the next September. While attending a reception, a twenty-eight-year-old former steelworker and anarchist, Leon Czolgosz, approached McKinley at 4:07 pm on September 6, 1901. The president smiled and held out his hand. Czolgosz pulled out a gun wrapped in a white handkerchief and fired two shots at point-blank range.

McKinley fell to the ground. James "Big Jim" Parker punched Czolgosz, averting a third shot. Soldiers and detectives then piled on the assailant, punching and kicking. They only stopped when ordered to do so by the wounded president. McKinley was rushed to emergency surgery. The first bullet ricocheted off a button and did no real harm. The second shot went completely through his stomach.

The surgeon sutured the wounds but could not find the bullet. Doctors were enthusiastic about his recovery. He was sitting up, reading the newspaper and on his way to hale and hearty. Vice President Theodore Roosevelt was so confident of the president's health, he went off on a trip to the Adirondack Mountains.

Sadly, everyone was wrong. Gangrene developed on the walls in McKinley's stomach, causing a severe case of blood poisoning. At 2:15

am on September 14, the president died. Teddy Roosevelt, hero of the Spanish American War, was now the 26th president of the United States.

Across Europe, monarchs proclaimed periods of mourning in their empires. This country was devastated. Three presidents now assassinated: Abraham Lincoln in 1865, James A. Garfield in 1881, and now William McKinley in 1901. Three presidents murdered in less than forty years. The public worried that the killing of their presidents was becoming commonplace and feared no one would want to run for office again.

Attention was once again back on Lizzie Borden when another man met his death. In December 1902, Hosea Knowlton, her nemesis and chief prosecutor, died. Lizzie still loathed the man and would have celebrated his demise except for the journalists. A herd of them knocked on the door of Maplecroft. The newspapers resurrected a surfeit of stories about the trial and the death of Andrew and Abby. The stares and jeers in the streets haunted them once again.

Ida brought Alice for a visit in the Spring of 2003. Lizzie fussed over the little girl and then instructed Helen to bring tea. "And bring a piece of chocolate for Alice."

Alice's eyes shone bright as she waited for the treat. She loved coming to Maplecroft, where she always received something special, and she loved spending time there with its pretty flowers and birds flitting around feeders.

Ida picked up her cup and took a sip. "Miss Lisbeth, I come bearing great news. Mr. Soderman and I have saved up sufficiently to start our own business. We have opened a new Meat and Grocery store on North Main Street."

"Good for you. I shall have to visit to see it for myself. And I will send my housekeeper to you for our shopping. I know this new venture will keep you busier than you have ever been before, but I pray you will still find the time to visit me with your lovely daughter."

"Of course, I will, Miss Lisbeth. Even if I were not inclined, Alice would make me come here." Ida chuckled. "Seriously, you have always been so generous to us. I think of you as part of the family."

Lizzie glowed. It was not the acceptance of society that she had long sought, but it was something she appreciated more than she would have thought possible a decade ago.

* * *

To escape the oppressive heat and humidity of Fall River's summer, Lizzie took an extended leave north of Boston to a seaside resort in Lynn, Massachusetts. The second day after her arrival, she noticed a well-dressed, exuberant woman at a table on the other side of the room. Everyone approached the lady, exuding warmth and bonhomie. Lizzie thought she looked quite familiar, but she puzzled over her identity.

Lizzie ate her meal while keeping her eyes on the mysterious woman. She dawdled at the table, hoping for a clue. Then, she got it. The lady rose from the table, revealing her amazing height. She towered over many of the men with her. Could that be actress Nance O'Neil? She walked past Lizzie's table while speaking to a companion. Her deep, distinctive voice gave her identity away. Lizzie was thrilled. She cast her eyes around the members of Nance's party but saw no one she could approach to arrange an introduction.

That evening, she thought about ways she could engineer a casual encounter—something that would not violate social norms but at the same time give her an opportunity to speak to Nance without a formal introduction. As luck would have it, the opportunity arrived the next morning at breakfast.

A young woman came into the dining room at the same time as Lizzie. "Are you here alone?"

Lizzie nodded.

"So am I. Let's have breakfast together."

A fearful shadow of being recognized and condemned caused Lizzie to hesitate.

"I know this is very forward of me, but the whole company sleeps in so late, and I always end up alone in the morning."

Was she a member of Nance O'Neil's theatre company? Maybe. Maybe she could introduce me. Lizzie smiled. "I would be delighted, Miss—?"

"Allen, Ricca Allen. And you are?"

"Lisbeth Borden. Pleased to meet your acquaintance."

They settled at their table, placed their orders, and chatted about the pleasantness of the hotel while waiting to be served. Lizzie took her first bite before gaining the courage to ask the pressing question. "You said that your company sleeps late. What group is that?"

"I am a member of the Nance O'Neill theatrical company. Have you ever seen one of our productions?"

"I certainly have. I have seen performances of your troupe in Providence and in Boston—in the Touraine Theatre as I recall. I enjoyed both productions very much."

Lizzie was star-struck to the point of being speechless. They ate quietly. When Ricca rose from the table after a last sip of coffee. "I must be off. I need to be prepared for the rising of the others."

"A pleasure, Miss Allen."

"No, no." Ricca waved off the formal address. "Ricca, please."

Lizzie grinned and lowered her chin. "Certainly, Ricca. I do have one question before you go. Would it be possible to meet Miss O'Neil?" Lizzie's stomach tensed into a tight knot as she waited for a possible rejection.

"Why not? I'll introduce you. Pleasure to meet you, Lisbeth."

Lizzie watched Ricca walk away. Her heart swelled with excitement, but her head filled with doubt that it would ever actually come to be.

That evening at dinner, Lizzie's wish came true. As the maître d'hôtel led her toward her solo table, Ricca approached and placed a hand on his forearm. "One moment, sir. Lisbeth, would you like to join us? I saved a seat right across from Nance just for you."

Lizzie swallowed hard. "Really?"

Ricca tinkled a laugh. "I told you I would introduce you, and what better time than dinner." She looped an arm in Lizzie's elbow and led the way.

Lizzie has often felt awkward in life, but this was the crowning jewel of feeling inept. The color rose in her cheeks as she took her seat. Standing at her shoulder, Ricca said, "Nance, this is Lisbeth Borden. Lisbeth, Nance

O'Neil. I think you will both enjoy each other's company."

"Thank you, Ricca. Pleased to meet you, Lisbeth."

Lizzie fought the urge to slide under the table. "The pleasure is all mine, Miss O'Neill."

"Nance, please. That Miss O'Neil nomenclature is for journalists and the blur of theatregoers, not for someone recommended by a friend."

Lizzie dipped her head as the blush rose higher and turned deeper on her face. The sound of Nance's voice was captivating. Lizzie could have listened to her all day. Up close, it seemed even deeper and rather seductive.

"Do not be shy, Lisbeth. We are all just friends here. Stage make-up gone, director shouting over, we are on vacation. Where are you from?"

"Fall River."

"We are performing at the Academy Music Theatre there in October or November. How delightful! We'll have to make sure we meet up again."

Another evening in the dining room, between the serving of the entrée and dessert, Nance embraced the stares and covert looks she received by rising to her feet. One fork clattered off a plate and onto the floor; the rest of the room grew as silent as in the darkness before first light. When all eyes were on her, she began, *"Why should I be worse than you, that I must prolong my existence by a lie!"* Lizzie recognized the line immediately from Herman Sudemann's Magda.

She continued in her commanding voice,

"Why should this gold upon my body and the luster which surrounds my name only increase my infamy? Have I not worked early and late for ten long years? Have I not woven this dress with sleepless nights? Have I not built up my career step by step, like thousands of my kind? Why should I blush before anyone? I am myself, and through myself I have become what I am.

"See how much the family, with its morality, demands from us! It throws us on our own resources, it gives us neither shelter nor happiness and yet, in our loneliness, we must live according to the laws which it had planned for itself alone. We must still crouch in the corner, and

there wait patiently until a respectable wooer happens to come. And meanwhile the war for existence of body and soul is consuming us. Ahead, we see nothing but sorrow and despair, and yet shall we not once dare to give what we have of youth and strength to the man for whom our whole body cries? Gag us, stupefy us, shut us up in harems or in cloisters—and that perhaps would be best. But if you give us our freedom, do not wonder if we take advantage of it."

Applause erupted, and everyone stood. Lizzie was breathless. No passage in a play moved her more than that one. She felt it in her heart—her personal declaration if she ever had the courage to pronounce it to the world. "Thank you," Lizzie said to Nance when she returned to her seat.

Nance beamed. "It touches you, too? It is the most autobiographical play I have ever encountered. When I am on stage, I am Magda."

"It resonates deep in my soul. I never left home, but the yearning always was there."

"You know, in the original German play, Magda's father shoots and kills her in the final scene. But my Rankin rewrote the ending for me. When Magda's father draws a gun on her, he suffers a stroke before he can pull the trigger. Because of that, my Magda comes out victorious at the end."

"As I recall, that revision engendered some harsh criticism when you first performed it."

"It certainly did, Lisbeth. Society does not like a strong woman to win. Ever."

The evening flew past Lizzie's starstruck eyes. She and Nance talked about theatre, books, and travel. Lizzie could not wait to spend more time with her. *But did Nance enjoy my company as much as I did hers?*

Chapter Sixty

Before long, Lizzie had her answer. Nance invited her for a visit to the O'Neill Mansion, her two hundred and fifty-acre country estate near Lowell, Massachusetts in Tyngsboro on the Merrimack River.

Nance welcomed her warmly and introduced her to the scores of dogs, cats, monkeys, and parrots that she had brought home from her overseas tours. "Here is Chico," Nance said. "He is the most affectionate of all the monkeys."

Chico scampered across the floor and threw himself into Lizzie's lap. Lizzie gasped and then relaxed, giggling as he ran across her shoulders, fiddled with her hair, and peered around into her face.

After Chico ran off in search of new amusements, Nance left the room and returned with the most glorious bird Lizzie had ever seen—a flamboyant burst of red and blue and gold. "This is Bernie, a Macaw from Argentina. Isn't he gorgeous?"

"Oh my, he certainly is."

Nance moved closer. "Here, hold out your arm."

Lizzie did so, and the bird transferred smoothly from one human perch to the other. Although the claws did not dig into her arm, she could feel the sharp points of each nail poking her skin. Lizzie bit her lower lip.

The macaw craned his head forward, tilted it to one side, and focused an eye on Lizzie's face. That eye looked more and more sinister with every passing moment. Tightness clenched Lizzie's chest, making it difficult to breathe. "Nance, please, take him."

"Oh, he is just getting to know you, Lisbeth. He will not harm you. Stroke the feathers on his back."

"I can't. I can't. Please."

"Oh, all right. I thought you liked animals." Nance offered her arm to Bernie and moved a few steps away.

"I do, I really do. He just makes me a bit unsettled—his claws, his eyes—I know I shouldn't be, but he frightens me. It seems as if he can look right into my soul."

"Oh, twaddle, Lisbeth. But I shall forgive your rudeness to Bernie. Come, let's go horseback riding before lunch."

Lizzie was surprised to find both the horses wearing western saddles. "I have always ridden sidesaddle, Nance, I do not know how to do this."

"If you can sidesaddle, then you surely can do this. It requires less skill, and it's far more comfortable."

"But this kind of riding is for men."

"Have you ever wondered why, Lisbeth? Men always keep the best for themselves. Try it this one time. If you don't care for it, you can go back to the other way. But you must try it. It is so liberating."

With the help of the groom, Lizzie managed to mount and get comfortable. The position, however, embarrassed her and she prayed they would encounter no one on the ridge. At one point, Nance pushed her mount into a gallop. Lizzie followed suit but was fearful she would tumble off. After a few yards, she relaxed and enjoyed the wind blowing across her face and the sense of security of having one leg on either side of the speeding beast.

A few of Nance's friends were waiting for them at the stable when they rode up. The blush rode up Lizzie's face at high speed. She was embarrassed to be seen throwing her leg over to dismount—it was so improper. She knew her sister would be appalled if she could see her. Although thrilled with the ride, Lizzie decided to avoid the temptation and rode sidesaddle for the rest of her visit.

In the evenings, Lizzie and Nance often talked about books they had read. Nance's new favorite was *Deliverance* by Ellen Glasgow. "You cannot help being pleased when slave owners descend from their aristocratic perch to end up as laborers. It is a well-earned turnabout."

Lizzie nodded. "I also noticed that the author did not have a very positive attitude about marriage—it greatly resembled mine."

"Not to mention her attacks on the barriers caused by class. I imagine you have noticed that yourself in life all around you."

"Definitely," Lizzie said, "I have been criticized for treating servants like human beings and being overly familiar with them. They know me much better than most do, and yet I am to hold them at arm's length? Makes no sense to me."

"Lisbeth, have you read *Little Shepherd of Kingdom Come* by John Fox."

"I loved that book. At times, it was horridly bleak, but to watch Chad evolve into an admirable adult was inspiring."

"I did find some of the passages a bit too explicit for my tastes."

Lizzie twisted her face as if she had sucked a lemon. "War is an ugly thing. You cannot pretty it up for your comfort. I do not understand why men are so enamored with it."

"Nor can I, but you still must admire the courage it took for a young Kentucky mountain man to fight for the Union."

"No, I cannot deny his courage, and I do understand that the uncivilized slave culture needed to be destroyed," Lizzie said. "Nonetheless, it is still troubling that men glorify war so."

"And that sums up my fervent wish that one day our world will embrace strong women and give them the power we have long been denied."

"Please, Nance, please recite those lines from Magda again like you did at the resort."

"Happily." Nance stood to her feet and delivered a performance worthy of the stage.

After an enjoyable evening with Nance, her friends, and a handful of theatre reviewers, Lizzie rented a nearby house and threw a weeklong party to show her appreciation of all of them. She decorated every room with potted palms and streamers. Caterers provided a cascading cornucopia of food on long, elegant tables. The bar was kept stocked with spirits, and the music rolled into the wee hours of the night. Lizzie felt, for the first time that she could remember, that she belonged—that she was among her people.

The night rocked with good cheer and dancing. In the morning, she woke to the sound of laughter as the earliest revelers to recover from the night before got started up again before noon.

Early one evening, Lizzie asked Nance to deliver the lines from Medea's famous speech. Nance rose and looked over the crowd. When silence descended, she began.

Often the night of thunder I have a message from the gods on high.
They ask me why I have not slept. Why in the morning I will touch no
food.
Then, I'd tell them of my sleepless night and why I did not sleep.
Because, I tell them, this house smells of blood.

Her enchanted audience applauded and cheered. Lizzie rejoiced that Nance O'Neill was a woman who would understand her even if she knew the secrets from the bottom depths of her soul.

Chapter Sixty-One

October 1904 was a pleasant month for Lizzie. When she opened the Boston Globe, she found her name, and for the first time, it brought a smile to her face. The article highlighted her charitable gifts to help horses who labored on the streets, delivering everyone and their goods where they were wanted. Lizzie was aware that many were worked to death without sufficient food or rest. She was disappointed by the small number of people who displayed the gratitude the loyal animals deserved. She gave freely to organizations that helped these noble beasts retire in peace.

The next pleasant event was the arrival of Nance O'Neill's theatrical company in Fall River. They were performing the play "Elizabeth, Queen of England." Lizzie invited the whole group over for dinner and sent Joseph with the carriage to wait by the stage door and drive Nance to Maplecroft.

Nance swept into the home like a queen. "What a lovely home, Lisbeth. I cannot wait until morning to see the outside in all its glory. It is everything you said it would be and more."

Lizzie beamed. "Thank you, Nance. I am delighted that it pleases you. Would you like some tea while we wait for the rest of the company to sit down for dinner?"

"Tea, no. But…" Nance reached into her valise and pulled out a bottle. "I did bring champagne. Will you join me in a glass?"

For a moment, Lizzie was speechless while her mind raced. *Champagne? I have never had a taste of it, and so many forbid the consumption of alcohol. But if I don't accept her offer, she may think I am a bumpkin not worthy of her time.*

Lizzie forced her tongue to operate. "But of course. I am afraid, though, that I do not have any champagne glasses."

"Any old glasses will do."

Helen brought two from the kitchen and popped the cork on the bottle while giving disapproving glances to her employer. At least, that is how Lizzie interpreted them. *Or was it just my imagination, my guilt at tasting the forbidden fruit?*

Nance lifted her glass. "Raise yours with me, Lisbeth. "To strong women everywhere. May they prosper. May they thrive." She clinked the edge of her hostess' glass while Lizzie mimicked her every move.

Lizzie first felt hundreds of tiny explosions flying from her nostrils into her cheeks and head. Then, the warmth struck, gliding down her throat and making her feel a deep glow inside. She could not comprehend how a cold liquid made her feel so warm. She feared the effects of the next sip but could not wait for another taste. When Nance raised her glass again, Lizzie, too, took another sip.

Much to Lizzie's surprise, Nance drained her glass completely. Lizzie quickly took another taste from hers and did the same. Her head spun for a moment and then stopped. Nance laughed—a big, bold, unrestrained laugh—as she poured them both a second glass. Lizzie never felt better in her whole life.

At dinner, Maplecroft never felt more alive. Conversation and laughter filled the air. Lizzie had never had a more boisterous meal in her life and loved every second. Emma, however, sat rigidly in her chair, her lips pursed, her disapproval obvious. Lizzie wished her sister could understand that after all she had been through, throwing decorum out the window was the best thing in the world.

As they rose from the table, Emma caught Lizzie's eye. "I am going to my room. It is quite late, and I have had enough excitement for one evening."

Nance rose from her chair. "Wait. Oh, please, Emma, stay and have an after-dinner sherry with us. Ricca brought enough for everyone."

Emma glared at Nance, who burst into laughter at the rigid expression on Emma's face. Emma's chest heaved in response. "Lisbeth, goodnight.

We will talk in the morning." She turned on her heels, exiting the room to a chorus of snickers.

The champagne had felt like a burbling stream going down Lizzie's throat, but the first sip of sherry was more like a mighty river surging inside her. The initial warmth was intense, and she had to struggle not to choke or cough. Once it had settled down, Lizzie took a second sip, it felt like the soft touch of an old friend.

The noise level in the room rose with every glass refilled. Joseph took a member of the crew back to the hotel, and they returned with Nance's Victrola and a box of shellac records. Once the music started playing, the dancing never stopped. Lizzie had never danced before but could not help tapping her foot to the rhythm. A young actor led her out of the parlor and into the dining room to show her how to move her feet. After practicing, they returned to the party, and Lizzie was thrilled to move around the room with some semblance of grace.

The night wore on, and one by one, the company departed to the hotel. Some left on foot; others had carriages they had hired for the night. Many of the latter had to wake their drivers before they could depart. At last, only two were left in the parlor—Lizzie and Nance.

"A lovely evening, Lisbeth. We will have to do this again."

"It was a pleasure to have your company, Nance."

"You are so sweet." Nance placed her palm on Lizzie's cheek. "We shall meet again." She stepped into the carriage and leaned out the window. "I'll send someone over tomorrow to help Joseph move the Victrola and bring it back to the hotel. Feel free to use it in the meantime.

Lizzie waved goodbye until the carriage was out of sight. Inside, she roamed around the rooms, touching chairs, mantles, and walls, hoping to hold on to the enchanted feeling that now inhabited her home. Her eyes swept over the clutter of abandoned glasses, empty bottles, plates of half-eaten cakes, and overturned chairs. She reached for a couple of glasses but set them back down with the realization that her head was spinning too much to return them to the kitchen without risking breakage. She left it all where it was with gratitude that Helen would clean it up in the morning.

She glided up the stairs, barely noticing the treads beneath her feet.

In the morning, Lizzie woke with a throbbing headache that intensified each time a bang or slam from downstairs echoed against the walls. *Helen usually cleans quietly when she knows we are sleeping. What had gotten into her this morning?*

She threw her legs out of the bed and stomped hard on the floor. Her pounding was answered by a sharp rap from the floor below. *What impertinence!* She threw on a wrap and ran a quick brush through her hair. *That kind of behavior from a servant was intolerable.*

As Lizzie reached the top of the stairs, she quickly reassessed the situation and dropped her assumption. Emma screeched at Helen, and she responded with whispered "yes-ma'ams" over and again.

Emma swept the floor at the foot of the stairs, pausing only to kick a chair out of the way. Lizzie never knew her sister was even capable of such fury. She considered retreating back to her bedroom when Emma stomped into the kitchen, but then reconsidered when she heard another screech and a loud noise coming from there. She feared Helen would not be safe from her sister's wrath.

Lizzie went downstairs and stood in the doorway to the kitchen. "Really, Emma, I am certain the neighbors can hear your caterwauling up and down the block."

Emma spun around to face her sister. "Do not dare criticize me. You should have cleaned up last night before you went to bed. Or you should have risen early to set everything right. I am appalled that you just left your bawdy companions litter all over the house."

"It was just a party, Emma. I have never had a party before. I had a wonderful time."

"Of course, you did. You were drinking. I thought you vowed to never let a drop of spirits cross your lips."

Lizzie put her hands on her hips and squeezed to quiet her rising anger. "I am sorry, dear sister. But I never knew the unfettered joy I was missing."

"You disgust me, Lizzie. I will make one thing perfectly clear: you will not bring those immoral barbarians into my home again."

"Emma, you are making a mountain out of a molehill. It was only one night! There are 365 of them every year. And you begrudge me after all these years of hardship, one simple night of uninhibited pleasure?"

"You need to stop spending time with theatre people. They will be the ruin of you. They have no sense of right and wrong. They do not have enough sense to act like decent human beings when in a proper home."

"Yes, Emma, that is why they please me. They are dismissed and shunned just as I am. No one understands their years of hard work and struggle. We just come to take pleasure with them on stage and then want to hide them in a closet until we want another performance. Those theatre people understand me and the calamities that have befallen me. They would understand why I did what I did—that it was for you as well as for me."

Emma opened her mouth and shut it again. She stared at her sister for a moment. "What are you saying, Lizzie? What do you mean by that?"

"Nothing, Emma. I mean nothing." Lizzie spun around and walked to the kitchen, choking on her unspoken words.

Emma followed her. "Explain yourself. What did you do? What do you mean you did it for me? Stop, Lizzie, and talk to me."

Lizzie turned to face her. "No, thank you. You are overwrought. We will talk sometime after you gain your composure." She mounted the stairs as Emma continued to shout questions at her. She went to her room, closed, and locked the door.

Chapter Sixty-Two

Emma and Lizzie did not talk about their argument and avoided each other when they could. They went to separate friends' houses for holiday celebrations and managed to maintain an uneasy peace. The week after Christmas, Emma answered a knock on the door. A young man handed over an envelope addressed to her with "PRIVATE" written beneath her name.

"Please come to 92 Second Street as quickly as possible. Do not inform your sister of your destination. Do not bring her with you."

Charles Cook

"Wait a moment." Emma retrieved a handful of coins from inside.

The young man smiled as the coins fell into his palm. "Do you want to send an answer?"

"No. Yes. Tell him I'll be there as soon as I can." Emma furrowed her brow, thinking about the hidden message in Mr. Cook's words before going upstairs to retrieve her hat, gloves, and winter cape.

For a moment, she considered calling Joseph to bring round the carriage, but remembering the servant's loyalty to Lizzie, she set off on foot. Throughout the walk, her mind raced from one possibility to another. Did he find the murder weapon? No, if he had, he would have called the police. Did Father or Abby leave a diary behind with scandalous news? Hard to believe, but maybe. Did the last tenant do some damage to the home? Wouldn't he just have repaired it?

Emma stepped at the gate looking at the front of the house that looked so familiar, yet so alien. Mr. Cook met her on the porch and grasped both of her hands in his own. "Miss Emma, my housekeeper, was cleaning out the property in preparation for a new tenant. She discovered a loose board in what used to be Miss Lizzie's bedroom. She thought better of investigating it and instead called me without lifting it up. After I lifted it, I closed it immediately, told the housekeeper to go back to my home and sent for you."

"What was in there?"

"You need to see for yourself." Mr. Cook led Emma upstairs into Lizzie's old room and pointed. "There. See it. The loose board."

"Yes, Mr. Cook. But what is in there?"

Cook crouched down and lifted the piece of flooring. A hatchet was laid on top.

Emma gasped. "It doesn't necessarily mean…"

"No. But—"

"The previous tenant could have left it. In fact, he could have created that hidey-hole."

"True if that were all that was inside." Cook pulled out a ladies' gold watch and chain. Emma swayed in place. Then, he pulled out a red leather pocketbook. "Do they look familiar?"

Emma staggered back until her back ran into the wall behind her. "No. No. No. It can't be."

Cook pulled out a few other pieces of jewelry and placed them at Emma's feet. "Did you ever suspect that Lizzie was behind the robbery the year before your father met his death?"

Emma shook her head. "Never."

"I don't think we should leave the hatchet here."

"No. Not the hatchet—not anything at all. You must never speak of this to anyone, Mr. Cook."

"Of course not, Miss Emma. I have never betrayed the confidence and privacy of the Borden family, and I won't start now. What shall we do with it all?"

"I don't know. My first thought was to throw it all in the river. But I worry it would wash up on the bank."

"I could lock it in my safe."

Emma looked him in the eye as she considered his offer. It was tempting, but she feared allowing anyone else, even a trusted man like Mr. Cook, to hold on to those incriminatory items was a prelude to disaster. "No. I will take them with me and think about what to do with them."

* * *

On the last Saturday of January 1905, fire struck the Borden block again. This time, it ignited in the rear of the five- and ten-cent store, blowing out the plate glass windows. The damage was less severe than before, and the fire department contained the blaze with efficiency.

Their tenants involved E.P. Charlton, Higgins and Frazes, Boston Painless Dentist, Ellis Manufacturing, Fall River Medical Society, the shoemaker, and Clark's colleges suffered losses ranging from $346 to $15,000—all covered by insurance. Emma and Lizzie put Mr. Cook to work managing the repairs to the building. They also sent a check for $100 to the new fire chief for a job well done.

In May, Lizzie was struck by another loss: Mary Livermore, her fervent supporter, died. Lizzie loved her as one would love an adoring, doting aunt. She wished she had visited her over the holidays. Mary could have helped her sort out her disagreements with Emma. When she received an invitation to the funeral, she took the train to Boston wearing the deepest black she could find. Lizzie cried more for her than she ever had for anyone else.

Lizzie arranged to visit Nance after the funeral. She was shocked by her appearance—she was like a shadow of her formal self. "Are you ill, Nance?"

"Just exhausted, mentally and physically, Lisbeth. I desperately need a rest."

"Come with me and recover in the peace of Maplecroft. I would be delighted to nurse you back to your normal, robust physique."

When Nance and Lizzie stepped through the front door at Maplecroft, Emma rose from her chair and walked upstairs without greeting either of them. Lizzie knew she had to confront her sister's rude behavior, but first, she wanted to get Nance settled.

Joseph carried her luggage upstairs to the guest bedroom. Lizzie escorted the actress upstairs and showed her the location of the amenities before going down to the kitchen to get the tea and toast Helen had prepared for Nance. Lizzie carried the tray up to the room and made sure Nance needed nothing further.

Back in the hall, Lizzie's knocked on Emma's door. "Meet me in the kitchen."

"Not now, Lizzie."

"Now, Emma. We need to talk." Lizzie went downstairs, and Emma followed.

"Helen, you can take the rest of the evening off," Lizzie said.

The sisters waited for the housekeeper to depart. Lizzie twisted her hands together. Emma held her head high, a stern, granite expression carved into her face.

Lizzie faced Emma the moment the back door closed on Helen. "You were rude to my friend. I am never rude to yours."

Emma refused to meet Lizzie's eyes. "I told you. I will not have those barbarians under my roof again."

"I did not bring the whole company here. Just Nance. She is ill with fatigue. She needed a quiet place to rest and recover."

"And when she recovers, they will all descend here and engage in another bacchanalia, stirring up an additional round of gossip in the neighborhood."

"Nonsense, Emma. She is here to rest. No late nights. No dancing. And she did not bring the Victrola you hate so much."

Make sure that she does not. I have never trusted theatre people, and now, I have come not to trust you." Emma rushed out of the kitchen and back up the stairs to her room. Lizzie hoped she was not as rigid as her sister when she reached her age.

In less than a week, Nance was her old self again—telling stories and bellowing her engaging laugh that caused Emma to wince every time she heard it. To Lizzie's relief though, Emma was being polite. She ate meals with them and even engaged Nance in conversation about the most recent book she read, *Troll Garden*, a collection of short stories by Willa Cather. Nance promised to read it after she finished with *The Scarlet Pimpernel*.

On Nance's last evening before her departure, she and Lizzie stayed up late talking and sipping sherry. Nance cleared her throat. "Lisbeth, did you know my real name is Gertrude Lamson?"

Lizzie's jaw dropped. "No! That absolutely does not suit you."

"McKee thought that, too. Because of that, I have never told anyone else."

Lizzie took a moment to decide that Nance's revelation merited one on her own part. "My name at birth was Lizzie Andrew Borden."

Nance leaned towards her. "Are you saying you are *the* Lizzie Borden?"

Lizzie hung her head and whispered, "Yes."

The actress nodded her head in response. "I suspected as much, but all that matters to me is who you are today." She slid her index finger under Lizzie's chin and raised her head to look into her eyes. Nance fixed Lizzie with a steady gaze. Lizzie blushed at the intensity she saw in the other face.

Nance placed a palm on each of Lizzie's cheeks and brought her face close. "I am very fond of you, Lisbeth." She pulled her closer, and her lips met Lizzie's—softly at first, and then she applied more pressure.

Lizzie's head started to spin. *I do not know where this will lead, but I do not care.* The unusual sensation of passion built in her chest.

A gasp sounded from a few feet away. Emma looked on in shock. "How dare you?"

"Oh, please, Emma," Nance said. "It was just a little kiss."

"Not so little if I judge by the heightened color in my sister's face. I knew you were up to no good. You are bent upon corrupting Lizzie. And I will not have it Not under my roof. I promised my mother on her deathbed that I would look after my baby sister and be her little mother. Lizzie, go to your room."

Lizzie's spine straightened, and her eyes sparkled. "How dare you?"

"I dare because I once mothered you as our mother requested when you were young. Now, you are showing the need for maternal attention once again."

Nance laughed. "Oh, please. This is much ado about nothing. I shall retire now and tomorrow I will leave your home, Emma. For heaven's sake, get control of yourself."

As Nance mounted the stairs, Lizzie spun toward her sister. "How could you?"

"How could I not?"

"Don't expect me to speak to you anytime soon." Lizzie raced upstairs and knocked on Nance's door.

"Not now, Lisbeth. I need my rest for travel tomorrow."

"I'm sorry, Nance."

"I know you are. Get some sleep, and I'll see you in the morning."

Chapter Sixty-Three

Lizzie walked Nance out to the carriage and waved goodbye until she was out of sight. Emma greeted her in the hall, holding a battered suitcase tied together with a stout rope. "I gave Helen the rest of the day off. I have something to show you, Lizzie, that I do not want anyone else to see."

Lizzie pointed at the case. "In there?"

"Yes."

"What is it?"

"It is what you were hoping no one would find."

Lizzie's face blanched white. "Whatever do you mean?"

"Let's go into the library."

Lizzie followed her sister down into the room, and Emma closed the double doors behind her. She set the suitcase atop the writing desk and untied the rope, letting the ends hang down to the floor.

Emma flipped the latches. "You are not going to want to see this, Lizzie."

Lizzie's breath grew ragged as her heart beat an angry tattoo. "Show it to me, Emma."

Emma flipped open the lid, and they stood side by side, looking down at the contents. No one spoke, but the ticking clock roared like a raging fire in Lizzie's ears. Lizzie turned toward her sister. "What does that have to do with me?"

"It was found under a loose board beneath where your bed used to be."

"I haven't been in that house for years. Who knows who left that behind."

Emma pulled out the gold watch and chain. "Abby's, is it not?"

"How should I know? I paid as little attention to that woman as possible."

Emma shrieked. "You are impossible. I show you the evidence of your transgressions and still you deny the truth before your eyes."

"Emma, you are making no sense to me at all. I think you are becoming hysterical. Perhaps you should lie down and rest for a while."

Emma bellowed an inarticulate response and fled from the room, throwing open the double doors so hard they bounced on the wall.

Lizzie, shaking inside, struggled to stabilize her emotions. Breathing deeply, she closed up the suitcase and stuffed it up the chimney until she could determine how to get rid of it for good. She went into the front room, picking up a magazine on the way. She sat down to read while she waited for her sister to come back downstairs.

She'd flipped through all the pages not seeing much of anything. She realized Emma might not be coming back down. She went up the stairs and knocked on Emma's door.

"What?" Emma's tone of voice left no doubt she was still angry.

"May I come in, sister?"

"Of course. It's your house."

Lizzie pushed open the door. Open suitcases were sprawled across the bed, half-filled with clothing. "Are you going on a trip?"

Emma did not look in her sister's direction. "In a manner of speaking. I am moving out."

"Emma…"

"Don't Emma me. I told you I would not tolerate theatre people in my house again, and I will not. Since you will not honor my request, I shall find other accommodations."

"We're back to that now? I thought you were disturbed by the mysterious items you found. Did Mr. Cook tell you I left them there?"

"No. He did not. It just seemed obvious to both of us. Even if I believed you had nothing to do with those items in your old room, I still could not live under the same roof as you any longer after your behavior with those theatre hooligans."

"You are overreacting, Emma."

"Oh, really?" Emma spun from the bed and faced Lizzie, her arms akimbo. "It was bad enough watching those people corrupt you with drink and dancing. Now, I am supposed to stand idly by and allow them to beguile you with more perverse, sinful pleasures?"

"Emma, please calm down."

"Calm down? I saw you, Lizzie. She was kissing you. And you, God save your soul, you were enjoying it. That image will haunt me until the day I die."

"Emma, give it a day or two. We'll talk and work things out."

"No. You will not listen to me, and I cannot stand by and watch your soul deteriorate in front of me. I need to be gone to have a few moments of peace before I die."

Lizzie planted her hands on her hips, too. "My soul has had me on the racks for nearly twelve years. I have had it, Emma. I am tired of trying to live my life to please others. The only moments of peace I have had since Father died were in the theatre, getting lost in a play, or in my home, being caught up in the joy and frivolity of the theatre people you condemn. Do I not deserve some happiness after all I have been through?

"I still wake in the night with images of Father's battered, dead face floating before me. I do not think my nightmares will ever end, but still, Emma, I cannot understand why you will not tolerate me having some joy in my waking hours."

"I am haunted by Father, too, Lizzie. And, by Abby. And by my promise to our mother to care for you. But you will not let me do the latter. And I cannot be here and do nothing."

"Abby? You think about Abby? You should not give her a moment's pity. She is the reason it all happened. If it had not been for her, Father might still be alive."

"She did not kill him, Lizzie."

"No, I did. Because of her." Lizzie squeezed her eyes shut. She could not believe she said those words out loud.

Emma stared at her sister, stunned into silence, fighting acceptance of Lizzie's forthright revelation. She wanted to deny that discovery in the hidey-hole but with those words, Lizzie had made it impossible. She slumped to the floor, her skirt ballooning around her like an aura.

Lizzie pushed the fabric aside and knelt down next to her. "Speak to me, Emma."

Emma gave no response.

"Please, Emma."

"You're lying. That's the only thing that makes sense. You are lying in a deliberate attempt to hurt me."

"Hurt you, Emma? Never! I did it as much for you as I did it for me."

Emma shook her head, again and again, as if she could shake away her thoughts. "I do not understand. I do not think I want to understand."

"You need to understand, Emma. I was protecting us."

"Protecting us from what?"

"I heard Uncle John and Abby talking in the back yard. They were plotting to put Swansea Farm in Abby's name in the next few days. They were urging Father to rewrite his will. They wanted Father to leave everything to Abby."

"Everything?"

"Except for $25,000 for each of us."

"That wasn't enough for you? You killed them because you were greedy for more?"

"No, Emma, I killed them for our survival."

"Surely $25,000 is enough for us."

"Think about it, Emma, think. Would we now be in a lovely home like this one? Would we be able to afford a housekeeper, a groom, and these lovely gardens?"

"We would not need them. The Second Street house would not be filled with tragic memories, and we could have stayed there and lived as we always did."

"Really? In Abby's house. Do you think she would give us a $200 allowance every year as Father did? No. Do you think she would buy us a new wardrobe in the spring and in the fall as Father did? No. All those expenses would need to come out of our inheritance. How long would that $25,000 last? Abby would not cover our medical bills, or our shopping accounts, or our train tickets. And how long would we have been able to live under her roof, follow her rules, tolerate her lording it over us and treating us like poor dependents?"

"But we could manage with a little discipline."

"Could we, Emma? Could we? What about when Abby died? Would she give us the house to spend our last years in reasonable comfort? No. She would give it to her family—not to us. We have no way to earn a living. Our clothing—our very lives—would be threadbare because of that woman."

Emma pushed herself up from the floor. "I refuse to believe you. You are simply trying to make me feel a debt of gratitude to you."

"You saw that hatchet—the murder weapon. You saw what I stole from Abby and hid away beneath my bed."

"But, Lizzie, it is perverse. Perverse that you would even think this story would stop me from moving out."

Lizzie rose and pushed her sister with both hands, pinning her against the wall. "Let me tell you what I did for you and our future. I grabbed that axe and snuck up behind Abby, and drove the blade deep into her back. When she fell, I struck her again and again and kept at it even after she stopped moving. I could not stop myself until my arms were too weary to lift the axe. All the rage I felt for that woman and her grasping hands had exploded into fury. She never cared for Father. She never cared for us. She only married Father for his money, and we were the nuisances she had to tolerate."

Emma pushed Lizzie away and moved to the other side of the room. "You are wrong. Father and Abby had a good marriage."

"Abby was good at pretending. You complained of her avarice when Father gave her the property where her sister lived. One time, you said that you wished she would drop dead."

"That was just an expression borne of my frustration."

"But it showed the true tenor of your heart. You hated her. You know you did. Do you understand that she was plotting with Uncle John to steal our inheritance? We are Father's blood relatives. She is not. All she cares about is herself and her family."

CHAPTER SIXTY-THREE

"Enough, Lizzie!" Emma turned her back on her sister.

Lizzie strode over to her, grabbed her shoulders, and spun her around. "I have not finished, sister dear. After I released the outrage I felt towards her, I leaned back on the wall to rest. I was exhausted. I went to my room and took off the dress I was wearing—you know the one. You saw me burn it in the stove. I wadded it up in a ball, concealing the blood stains in the folds of clean fabric. I crawled under my bed to my hidey-hole."

Emma's eyes widened, and her jaw dropped.

"Ah, even though you saw the hidey-hole with your own eyes, you refuse to believe. I can tell by your face you did not know I had one. I did not create it. It was already there. Someone else, obviously, had something to hide."

"Stop it, Lizzie. Stop it. I cannot accept this." Emma turned her face away, refusing to look her sister in the eye.

Lizzie's jaw tightened, and her eyes closed to narrow slits. "After I finished putting away the dress and the axe, I washed the blood spatters off my hands and face and out of my hair with the water in my basin. I poured that into the slop bucket and put on another dress. I dumped the bucket in the basement and went back to my room.

"While I waited for Father to come home, I realized that our future was still in danger. I knew Father too well. I realized I may have killed Abby for nothing. Father cannot live without a woman taking care of him. He would find another wife, and we would be back in the same situation again. The only answer was to get rid of Father, too. I didn't want to—I had to—for me, for you. Else we would be two old spinster women with no places to live unless some rich relatives took us in out of charity. I would not have that for me. I would not have that for you.

Emma shook her head back and forth. "No, Lizzie, no. I do not want to hear anymore."

Lizzie pushed her back into the wall. "But you must, Emma. You must know it all. You must know what I sacrificed for you—being forced to kill my own father, being held captive behind bars, being humiliated in the courtroom and on the street. I paid the price for you, and you must carry that burden, too."

"Lizzie, you are mad."

"If I am, then more women need to be mad. We need to tear down the walls that keep us from freedom, that control our behavior, our lives. We are no more than slaves when there is a man standing above us. Pampered, spoiled slaves, perhaps, but slaves nonetheless."

"Lizzie, let me go." Emma squirmed.

"Not until I finish." Lizzie's eyes were large and round. A sneer filled her face. "I waited for Father to come home. I was so anxious I would be discovered upstairs with the body. It seemed like he would never get here. When he arrived, he had trouble unlocking the front door. Maggie let him inside, and I sent her back outside to finish the windows. He looked very tired, very old. I settled him down on the sofa. He looked so peaceful.

"Then, I retrieved the axe from my bedroom to perform my duty to you and myself. I slipped into the parlor and put his coat on backwards over my dress to protect me from the blood. And I bashed in his head, too. It hurt me to do that, Emma, but I knew it needed to be done. I could not let him live the last couple of years of his life just to destroy the rest of our lives. We had many years to live—he only had a few. When I was done, I removed his coat, folded it, slid it under his head, and said goodbye."

Emma's face grew long. She held her hands in front of her chest. "No. If you did kill him, you did it because he would have known you killed Abby. He would have disinherited you and thrown you out in the street."

Lizzie pressed her sister harder against the wall. "No, Emma. I was always his favorite, and that is why you resent me even though I have done so much for you."

Emma strained against Lizzie's arms. "Let. Me. Go."

Lizzie dropped her hands. "Do you understand now? Do you realize the value of the gift I have given you?"

"I do not know whether to believe you or not and that to me is proof that I do not trust you. And if I do not, how could I possibly have a single moment's peace under the same roof with you? I would rather wipe all memories of you from my mind than continue to live in this purgatory of your making. If you are telling the truth, your hands are as bloody as Lady Macbeth's. If you are lying, you are totally mad. Either way, it is time for me to wash my hands of you. No, please, in the name of all that is decent, leave me in peace to finish my packing."

Lizzie backed up and folded her arms across her chest. "Our mother would have understood. She believed in equality for women. She wanted us to stand up for ourselves. She would have applauded my actions."

"Oh, of course, Lizzie. She is looking down from heaven, counting her blessings that her baby daughter has committed not one, but two brutal murders. I am sure she is pleased with you and your bloody, bloody hands. But then, up there, she probably knows the whole truth and realizes that your incarceration has driven you completely mad. Now. Leave my room."

Lizzie's shoulders slumped, and a tear trickled from one eye. "If you ever speak of this, ever admit that you knew anything, they will arrest you as my accomplice. They can no longer touch me, but you? They can torment you for decades." She had hoped her sister could understand, that she would accept her for who she was and appreciate the freedom she gained. Instead, Emma was rejecting her, fearing her, leaving her. Lizzie dropped her head and shuffled out of the room.

In a fog, Lizzie went downstairs and out to her flower beds, feeling hollow and numb. She dead-headed roses and pulled up weeds among the tulips. She did not look up until she heard Joseph drive away with the carriage, taking Emma to points unknown.

Chapter Sixty-Four

That evening, Lizzie paced through the house, dropping down to a chair in sorrow, then rising up again in anger. In the latter state, she stomped through rooms, picking up fragile items, hefting them in her hand, fighting the urge to throw them against the wall. She set each item down gently as she was flooded with sadness too painful to last long.

The next morning, she cleaned up at her basin and dressed is if for a special occasion. She walked down the hall, certain her sister must have returned in the night. She knocked gently on the door and whispered, "Emma, Emma, Are you awake?" When she got no response, she smiled as she imagined Emma was sleeping late. She eased open the door one inch at a time and peered at the bed, convinced she would find Emma wrapped in blankets lost in her dreams.

Seeing no one there, she was stunned. She could not believe her eyes. Her sister was not in the bed—not in the room—not anywhere. She had not returned in the wee hours. She was gone—truly gone.

A wave of rage rose in her chest as hot as a coal fire. She strode across the carpet, ripped the bedcovers off, and threw them to the floor. She pulled off the sheets and sent pillows careening across the room. She choked back a sob and fled down the stairs and into the kitchen. She grabbed a potato, placed it on a breadboard. With a wooden mallet, she hammered on the potato, breaking it into bits, scattering smashed pieces on the table and the floor, and sending potato juice flying through the air. She growled and muttered as stray strands of her hair worked out of their confinement and hung limply by her face.

The back door opened. Helen looked at her disheveled employer. She rushed to her and wrapped her in her arms as if she were a distressed child. "There, there, Miss Lisbeth." She wrested the mallet from Lizzie's hand and set it down in the sink. "Come now, you need some rest. Let's go up to your bedroom and get you back under the covers. I will make you a pot of tea and sit with you until you fall asleep."

Helen helped her out of her dress and undergarments and slid her nightgown over her head. She gently wiped the potato starch spatters off her face and her hands. Back in the kitchen, she started cleaning up while she waited for the kettle to boil.

She carried the tray with the teapot, two cups, and the sugar and cream upstairs. Helen sat by Lizzie's side until she set down her cup and fell into a fitful sleep.

* * *

For weeks, Lizzie waited for Emma's return. She looked for a letter from her in every day's mail. When she heard the news about John Hill, the proprietor of a bird store near their old home who claimed to have found a broken-handled, rusted hatchet in the Borden's yard on Second Street, she knew that would be just the story to get a response from Emma. She wrote to her about how he hung it in a shop with a sign that read: Is It It? Police, Lizzie wrote, confiscated it to add to their evidence. "They have never lost hope in the dream that one day they will be able to hang me."

Lizzie waited for Emma to send back a letter of reassurance, to try to calm her fears. But it never came, day after day, one disappointment after another. No response from Emma.

Mary Bingham, Louisa Stillwell, the cousin of Anna Holmes, Anne Sheen, Lizzie's confidante who held her hand throughout the trial—many of the sisters' mutual friends now tossed Lizzie aside and only socialized with Emma. Some friends still called on her in her Queen Anne refuge. For the ones with children, Lizzie kept a dish of chocolate-covered peppermints wrapped in foil in the front hall.

335

To fill the void of those who deserted her, Lizzie sought companionship from her housekeeper, Helen, whom she believed was a good woman with a full heart. Her devotion stemmed from her gratitude. Never before the Borden home had she ever lived such a comfortable life—never aching from hunger, never beaten, rarely scolded. She was now the one to console and comfort Lizzie.

Nance continued to write to Lisbeth from different locations across the country and overseas as she travelled on her new theatre tour. She often expressed her desire to see Lizzie again. The two women made tentative plans to spend time together at Nance's Tyngsboro estate in the summer of 1906.

Then, in May, that dream was crushed, too, in a heart-rending letter from Nance. Lizzie learned that McKee Rankin and his poor business management had driven her into bankruptcy, and a creditor won a judgment against her property, and the farm no longer belonged to Nance.

Lizzie wrote to Nance offering financial assistance, but the actress never wrote back. After the court proceedings were finished, Nance was to appear as Lady Macbeth in Savoy Theatre on North Main Street in Fall River. Lizzie contacted her again, but there was no reply at all. Nor did she hear directly from her sister—despite all the letters Lizzie had written—the only communication was through her lawyer regarding business matters.

* * *

Another of Lizzie's dreams turned to dust in January 1907. She visited her cousin Grace Howe and learned that her Uncle Hiram had died. She collapsed on the sofa upon hearing the news.

Grace was confused. "But, Lisbeth, you did not care for that man, and he was cruel to you. Why should you despair at the news of his death?"

"Because now, cousin, my one last chance of being cleared is now gone."

"How could Mr. Harrington clear you, dear?"

"By confessing, Grace."

"You believe he was—you believed he murdered your parents?"

"I always have." The lie oft told slid with ease off her tongue. She wondered how long she could continue to use it. She had hoped enough people would be convinced that he would be arrested and thrown in jail.

The next year, Lizzie's closest friend and housekeeper, Helen, travelled to visit her brother in Rhode Island. While there, she succumbed to dysentery. It was a terrible addition to Lizzie's recent litany of loss.

Lizzie withdrew even more into her private world. She hired men to build an 8-foot-tall fence along the edge of my lot to protect her from the stares of tradesmen and delivery men at neighboring houses. It gave her the peace she needed to walk out and check the squirrels living in the little houses she had built for them in the trees. She drew great pleasure from going out at dusk and feeding her furry friends as their tiny feet and pointed claws scampered on her arms and shoulders. With them, she felt a sense of belonging she had not known since the party in Tyngsboro.

Epilogue

Lizzie never saw Emma or Nance for the rest of her life. Lizzie took much solace from her Boston Bull Terriers: Donald Stuart, Royal Wilson, and her favorite, Laddie Miller.

When her neighbors all bought automobiles, Lizzie felt the need to buy one for herself and allow her horses to have a well-earned life of leisure. She chose an elegant black limousine that she felt perfectly matched her actual, though not often acknowledged, social position.

She engaged the services of James Allardice, a Scottish immigrant, and friend of her Father, who was the most highly regarded builder in the area, to design and build a garage twenty-eight feet wide and thirty-seven feet long. It had two large, glazed doors bound on either side by reeded columns set on granite bases. A bay window on one side brought in an abundance of light and endowed the garage with a touch of glamour. Inside, there was running water, steam heat, and an ingenious rotating device on the floor. When the chauffeur drove the car into the garage, the platform revolved, allowing the front of the car to face the doors. The driver would never have to back the vehicle out.

Additionally, Mr. Allardice's structure was large enough that if Lizzie ever wanted to procure a second vehicle, there was more than enough space to accommodate it. She loved her limousine. Every afternoon, unless it was raining, she went for a drive across the river. Those were the times she thought most about Father. She imagined him sitting next to her, prattling on about the modern-day miracle of the automobile.

Lizzie wanted to get involved in something worthwhile. Mrs. Livermore had strongly encouraged her to be active in the suffragist movement. Although she agreed in principle, the whole idea sounded too much like tilting at windmills—she had enjoyed reading Don Quixote, but that did not mean she wanted to accompany him on his journey. *It was just as preposterous to believe that Quixote would find adventure and true love as to think that men would ever allow women to vote—they would lose some measure of control over our lives, and what then? No, they grip the reins of their power too tightly to ever let them go.*

Nothing ever breached the skeptical walls of Lizzie's heart until December 1913. She attended a Women's Club meeting for a presentation by Mrs. Huntington Smith, who advocated for a horse fund to rescue old and abused workhorses. She gladly contributed to the cause.

The following February, Helen Leighton opened the Animal Rescue League. The fund bought a cottage at the corner of Maple and Durfee Streets and drew up plans to fit with the latest appliances for the comfort of animals as well as the equipment needed to end the suffering of those who were too far gone to enjoy any aspect of life.

Much to Lizzie's surprise, Emma contributed heavily to the organization as well. At the opening ceremony, Lizzie met Helen Leighton, the president of the organization and a suffragette.

Helen Leighton talked about her arrest in Boston, where she had demonstrated for women's right to vote. "We all had to spend the night in the Charles Street Jail. One woman in the group was from a very old, wealthy Boston Brahmin family. She obviously had no comprehension of the difference between prison and home. She rose in the morning and said to the female jail guard, 'Matron, you may draw my bath now.'" Helen inhaled on her ivory cigarette holder, tossed her head back, and laughed loud and long. At that moment, she reminded Lizzie of Nance, and her heart felt a stab of longing.

Soon, the organization began buying old, lame, half-starved horses on the street to prevent and relieve their torment. Some were purchased for $4—others were free. Then, the World War commenced, and the demand for horses unfit for work went up to $75. Still, they brought all of them they could to their stable to enjoy good food and rest before the end. Lizzie loved walking through the stalls, stroking their noses, and giving them apples, carrots, and other treats. Most of them looked so much better after a week's stay.

Caring for the horses made her think of her father and how she wished he could be with her now. If he were alive, he would have never abandoned her. For decades, she'd been telling herself his death was necessary, but now she thought her father would have understood the need for Abby's death if only she explained it to him. And there was no one there to tell her otherwise.

Another loss diminished Lizzie's life in 1917 when she lost her faithful companion, Laddie Miller—an adorable and affectionate Boston Terrier who was always by her side. In his name, she purchased a lifetime membership in the Animal Rescue League. She laid him to rest at the Pine Ridge Pet Cemetery in Dedham with a tombstone that read: "Sleeping Awhile." She believed If there was a heaven, she would see him there. She often wandered through the meandering walkways of the cemetery and contemplated how the faithfulness of Laddie put human beings to shame.

* * *

In January 1918, Lizzie was surprised to learn that Jeanne Rankin, the first woman ever elected to the House of Representatives, had introduced an amendment to the Constitution guaranteeing women the right to vote. She admired the woman's courage but did not think anything would come of it. She was shocked when it passed the House. However, she was certain it would never get the two-thirds majority needed to clear the Senate.

Lizzie was even more amazed when, on June 4, 1919, the Senate approved the Susan B. Anthony amendment. Still she believed it was highly unlikely that 36 states needed to ratify would sign on. By June of 1920, 35 states had accepted the amendment. Only two states remained as possibilities to cast the vote that would make it federal law—all the others had cast their lot against or for it or had voted not to consider it at all. Tennessee and

North Carolina were the bastions of hope that stood between death knell and fruition.

When on August 17, North Carolina voted no, gloom descended on many women's hearts. Lizzie, though, had her belief confirmed that men would not willingly drop the reins of their power over to women. Tennessee, however, proved Lizzie wrong. The 19th Amendment became law.

Lizzie boarded a train visit to Mary Livermore's graveside and lay flowers by her stone. She told her that her valiant struggles had reaped success and that she was ashamed for not having faith in her cause. Lizzie vowed to vote in November.

* * *

Emma sat for an interview with the Boston Herald in April 2013. "The Tragedy seems but yesterday and many times I catch myself wondering whether or not it is some frightful dream after all."

The reporter said: "Some people have said that they considered Lizzie's actions decidedly queer."

"But what if she did act queerly? Don't we all do something peculiar at some time or another? Queer? Yes, Lizzie is queer. But as for her being guilty, I say 'no' and 'decidedly no.'"

Reading these statements, Lizzie could not decipher their meaning. Was Emma asking her forgiveness indirectly? Or was she including her confession in the list of her queer actions? Unless Emma wrote or came to visit, Lizzie would never know, and with every passing year, that possibility grew dimmer.

* * *

Lizzie never lost interest in Ida's child. After Alice graduated from high school, Lizzie made it possible for her to go to school and study to become a draftsman. She worked in that capacity while continuing her education with Lizzie's help, eventually becoming an architect. Lizzie remembered

Alice in her will bequeathing her $2000 and her American Waltham watch in a hand-engraved 14k gold case and its slide chain.

****

In 1925, Lizzie lost a considerable amount of weight, her hair turned gray, and her energy faded away with the shortest walk around the grounds. She had no desire to leave Maplecroft for any reason.

The only place she went was to the Truesdale Clinic on Rock Street to see Dr. Annie McRae. She had no desire to see anyone else. After a few visits, Dr. Annie recommended gallbladder surgery. Lizzie made sure everything was in order before she underwent the procedure. With Mr. Cook, she made her will, leaving generous bequests to servants, friends, acquaintances, and charities, with her largest one—$30,000—to the Animal Rescue League of Fall River.

"What about your sister Emma, Miss Borden?"

"Emma? Oh, heavens, no. Write this down word for word, Mr. Cook. Nothing is left to my sister Emma: she received her share of Father's estate and is supposed to have enough to make her comfortable. I want that statement in my will."

"Are you certain, Miss Borden? She is your flesh and blood."

"Really, Mr. Cook. You know as well as I the turmoil she has put me through the last two decades. I don't care what she thinks. I don't care what anyone thinks. She has separated herself from me in life, and I shall separate my wealth from her in death."

Toward the end of January, Lizzie entered the Truesdale Hospital under the name "Mary Smith Borden." For the rest of the year, she remained bedridden. When she felt her end was near, she summoned Mr. Cook to make the arrangements for her funeral.

She laid out the details for the privacy of the service, the songs to be sung, and many other details and then added: "I wish my body to be laid at my father's feet with a small headstone to match the others in the family. And this is important, Mr. Cook, I want Lisbeth to be cut in stone—Lisbeth

Andrew with the birthdate July 1860. I would like the minister of the Church of Ascension to conduct the services and my grave to be bricked so that it will not sink after internment."

Despite her fears that her death was imminent, she was able to take walks in her garden again in February 1927. By March, she was strolling around the neighborhood and calling on friends. Soon, she was strong enough to plan a trip to the theatre. She thoroughly enjoyed the performance, but when the curtains closed, an ominous feeling filled her with foreboding, as if the end of the play portended her own end.

Upon her return to Maplecroft, her fatigue reasserted itself making it impossible to walk around the grounds without stopping and resting on a bench every few minutes. She was bedridden in short order.

On May 26, her pain and distress intensified, and Dr. Annie McRae came every day to monitor her decline. Lizzie grew aware she only had a few days to live—maybe only hours.

When she woke on June 2, her first thought was of her chauffeur, Mr. Terry. She had made him a promise to him that she had not kept. She asked to see him, and he greeted her, standing by the door. Lizzie beckoned him closer to her bedside and handed him a blank check. "Here, Mr. Terry. I promised to cover the cost of repairs to your home some time ago. Make it out for whatever amount you need to fix your house and add a bit more for the unexpected."

"I can't accept this, Miss Borden. I don't know how much it will cost."

"Just take it, Mr. Terry. I made a promise, and I want to keep it before I die. If I wait another day, it may be too late. Please take it for me to put my soul at peace."

"Thank you, Miss Borden."

"Now, go straight to the bank. Fill it out for the amount you think you'll need. If they give you any trouble about it, tell them to check with Mr. Cook. He'll approve it."

"Thank you again, Miss Borden. You are a good and generous woman."

Lizzie slipped in and out of awareness for an unknown amount of time, but when she rose to the surface, Dr. Annie was by her side. They talked about Maplecroft's gardens, and Lizzie spoke of her longing to see the sea once more. And then, she was gone.

***

Emma outlived Lizzie by only nine days. She died of chronic nephritis when she was seventy-six years old. She was buried in Fall River by her sister's side.

About the Author

Diane Fanning is the Edgar-nominated, best-selling author of fifteen true crime books and 11 mysteries and a recipient of the Defender of Innocence award from the Innocence Project.She has served as a consultant to *48 Hours,* was a regular presence on 14 seasons of *Deadly Women,* and appeared on the *Today Show, 20/20, Forensic Files, Snapped,* the Biography Channel, Investigation Discovery, E! and the BBC as well as numerous podcasts. Raised in Baltimore County, she moved to Virginia, then south Texas, and she now lives in the shadow of the Blue Ridge Mountains in Bedford, Virginia.

AUTHOR WEBSITE:

http://dianefanning.com

SOCIAL MEDIA HANDLES:

Twittter(X) : @dianefanning

Instagram: @dianefanning

Facebook: dianefanning, Lucindapierce, Truecrimebooks, Libbyclark

Linkedin: Diane Fanning

Also by Diane Fanning

True Crime
Through the Window
Into the Water
Written in Blood
Baby Be Mine
Gone Forever
Under the Knife
The Pastor's Wife
Out There
Her Deadly Web
Sleep My Darlings
Poisoned Passion
Mommy's Little Girl
Under Cover of the Knife
Bitter Remains
Death on the River

Fiction standalone:
Bite the Moon

Lt. Lucinda Pierce Series
Trophy Exchange
Punish the Deed
Mistaken Identity
Twisted Reason
False Front
Wrong Turn
Chain Reaction

Secret City Series